LIFE ∞ LINE:
ORIGINS

Ben + Larry –
Welcome to my universe!

Grant Miller

By Grant Edward Miller

 FriesenPress

One Printers Way
Altona, MB R0G 0B0
Canada

www.friesenpress.com

ISBN
978-1-03-914699-0 (Hardcover)
978-1-03-914698-3 (Paperback)
978-1-03-914700-3 (eBook)

1. FICTION, SCIENCE FICTION

Distributed to the trade by The Ingram Book Company

For Seann Alderking: your unwavering patience and guidance pointed me in the right direction during the countless drafts and rereads.

For Masoud Razfar: your belief in my writing pushed me forward as you read my first draft.

For Berend McKenzie: you are my brother in arms when it comes to writing. You got me started on this project and stood by me to the end.

For Gary Hayashi: you always "get me!" You have been my guide through the battlefield of doubt turning to belief in myself.

You are all my heroes!

Table of Contents

Acknowledgements · 1

Prologue · 2

Part 1
Change May Come and Change Must Go

Chapter 1
Trash Is What Trash Does · 6

Chapter 2
Hated Hearth · 10

Chapter 3
Learnèd No Longer · 14

Chapter 4
Passages · 20

Chapter 5
Revelations · 30

Chapter 6
Sirens · 32

Chapter 7
Ponderings · 39

Chapter 8
Unified · 42

Chapter 9
The Road Leads Upward · 47

Chapter 10
A New Path · 54

Chapter 11
The Point of No Return · 61

Part 2

Stowaways

Chapter 12

Looking Through the Lens · **68**

Chapter 13

Flight to the Prison World · **70**

Chapter 14

Origins · **75**

Chapter 15

Diversions · **80**

Chapter 16

Bennett's Reckoning · **83**

Chapter 17

Stowaway's Reckoning · **85**

Part 3

Pirates and Potentials

Chapter 18

Detour · **94**

Chapter 19

Parlance · **97**

Chapter 20

No Prey, No Pay! · **101**

Chapter 21

The Order's Awakening · **114**

Chapter 22

Tyranny, Trysts, and Tight Spots · **118**

Part 4

Senate Infiltration

Chapter 23

Crossroads · **126**

Chapter 24
The Magistrate's Power: How It Came to Be · **132**

Chapter 25
Infiltration Begins, Histories Unfold, Truths Be Told · **137**

Chapter 26
A Page's Day of Work is Not Always an Honest One · **142**

Chapter 27
A Page's Quest and a Pirate's Query · **145**

Chapter 28
Gaining Trust, Finding Insight · **148**

Part 5
Fates Entwined, Voyages Divined

Chapter 29
Curved Space for Bennett · **154**

Chapter 30
Thievery, Justified · **157**

Chapter 31
Twists of Fate · **160**

Chapter 32
The Challenging Life of a Level Ten Conduit · **171**

Chapter 33
Allies Come in the Strangest Forms · **174**

Chapter 34
Tam's Dilemma · **180**

Part 6
Voyagers

Chapter 35
Cocoon · **188**

Chapter 36
Wormholes and Wandering Waifs · **191**

Chapter 37
The Floodgates Open · 195

Chapter 38
Stratagem · 200

Chapter 39
Dragon's Den · 206

Chapter 40
Betrayal · 212

Chapter 41
Fight or Flight? · 216

Chapter 42
Blurp! · 225

Chapter 43
Slipping Through the Lines · 229

Chapter 44
Kruger's Master Plan · 233

Chapter 45
Next Level · 236

Chapter 46
Waves · 241

Part 7
Battles

Chapter 47
Back Door Planning · 248

Chapter 48
Engaging Enemies · 251

Chapter 49
Contact · 256

Chapter 50
Parallel · 260

Chapter 51
Facing Demons · 265

Chapter 52
My Path Laid Out to You · **269**

Part 8
Meeting of the Minds

Chapter 53
The Meek Shall Fight · **274**

Chapter 54
All for the Sake of One Man · **279**

Chapter 55
Tit for Tat · **283**

Chapter 56
The Gathering Storm · **291**

Chapter 57
He Who Fights... · **297**

Chapter 58
Come What May! · **306**

Chapter 59
Crossroads · **313**

Chapter 60
Whose Revenge is it Anyway? · **321**

Chapter 61
The Apex · **327**

Chapter 62
Take the Back Door, Please! · **343**

Chapter 63
Through the Looking Glass · **352**

Chapter 64
New Beginnings · **356**

Epilogue · **364**

Acknowledgements

I'd like to acknowledge Gary Siegel for guiding me on my voyage to find my own "Hero's Journey." You gave me the courage to find my way.

Thank you to the crew at FriesenPress for supporting me through my first publishing jitters. You are an amazing group of people who made the whole process easy!

There is also a long list of people who helped me reach my goal of self-publishing my book: K. Abramovich, Bryan Acevedo Reyes, Seann Alderking, Lawrence Arundel, David Bellamy, Felix Blanco, Scott Boutilier, Gerald Box, Zach Bulls, Hal Carty, Tim Coates, Adam Cohen, Brian Curry, Charles Delano, William Denis, Tarek El Bizri, Douglas Feltis, Wesley Frost, Gary Hayashi, Celeste Hayne, Jon Hemingway, Marty Kreil, Jennifer Lawless, Peter Leek, Berend McKenzie, Ron Maddox, Bonnie Maxilom, Tim Marshall, Victor Martel, Terry McHale, Glenn Miles, Faith Miller, Kaylee Miller, Lisa Miller, Omar Moh, Masoud Razfar, Brendan Rideout, Jonathon Rivera, Raymond Rodgers, Daren Sage, Theodore Salger-Smith, Lisa Gail Schwarz, William Selender, James Southerland, Max Spragovsky, Richard Stilwell, Fernando Vélez, Chris Wardale and Brian Wotton.

I celebrate all of you. You are the stars in my eyes!

Prologue

In a minor spiral of the Milky Way, on the third planet of a small solar system, lay the cradle of humanity. The tiny planet, known as Earth, rested alone in a sea of stars. For centuries, humankind sent out signals and sought proof of life's existence elsewhere. It was to no avail, however; they remained alone.

As humanity grew and the planet became overcrowded and rather dilapidated, they reached outward and began exploring space. First, they conquered their own solar system and founded small settlements on Mars and various moons of the gaseous giants. However, this settling was relatively short-lived and though the colonies remained, the restless search continued.

The desire to seek and to explore never subsided, and the human race began looking further outward as new technology allowed for interstellar travel. These humans spread out, first through their tiny spiral arm of the galaxy, then into the major areas of the Milky Way. Each time the area the humans settled grew, their sense of emptiness did, too. Why were they all alone? Where were the other spacefaring species that humanity had predicted would live there? There should have been other sentient species in the Orion Spiral, where Earth was located. But there was nothing anywhere.

Some life was found in other solar systems close to home. But what they found were species of plants and animals that were similar to common species on Earth. Sadly, there was no sentient life. How had life evolved the same in a repeated manner, over and over, across the galaxy? How did evolution explain this commonality?

Certain humans insisted that this was, indeed, proof of something grander than humanity itself. Only a deity could be powerful enough to cause species to spread across the galaxy! The search for this deity became an obsession for many eons of human existence. More and more ships were built that could travel from star to star at speeds almost to that of light itself. Later, folding space became a more practical method of covering these vast distances.

Ultimately, there came a time when humanity seemed to have conquered the whole of the Milky Way. Many felt that this was the end of humankind's voyages. Exploration slowed, becoming almost archaic and stagnant. The network of the human race stalled at the edges of its galaxy. They called it their galaxy, since there was no one else there but themselves.

Humanity almost began to take on a sense of itself as a deity—they were the only sentient species in all of the far reaches of the galaxy, after all. If they were indeed deities, they were convinced they should look beyond it. They turned their eyes to the nearest galaxy, Andromeda, and, suddenly, humanity again felt the thirst for travel.

Large transport ships were built, designed to take large chunks of the populace with them through a fold in space they could now create across the distances between galaxies, thanks to the improved technology. That was the plan: jump to Andromeda and Messier 100 to see what was there.

With all this planning to conquer new galaxies, humanity missed a vital point in their history. It never occurred to humans that their evolution had not progressed. Historical records indicated that humankind should have continued to evolve into something quite unrecognizable in the future. In fact, in the time it took to populate the Milky Way, there should have been substantial evolution. But there had been none. It was as if humanity was stalled. "Experts" in evolution explained it away as humans being at the peak of their evolution—there was no reason, they argued, that evolution should insist change to continue.

But if evolution wouldn't change humankind, perhaps humanity could do it themselves. They began to play with the DNA structure of their species and those around them. A few changes here and there in a certain demographic of the population could carry that change into the future. This would provide the ability to trace the human race back to its origins in case something ever went wrong. It was a good thing that they did so—because something did go very wrong.

By the time the myriad of large ships had left the Milky Way and traveled to the Andromeda and Messier 100 galaxies, a darkness had fallen across it. In the beginning, it wasn't anything that was tangible. The darkness started on Earth and made its way outward, in the exact path humanity had taken to colonize the galaxy eons before. However, it spread much faster than the human race did. A sudden feeling of dread spread, quickly, from system to system. A fear of the unknown suddenly caused humanity to stop and take stock. It was a fear that became so deep that a desire to hide themselves instead became their main drive. Was humanity being watched and judged for what they had done? By whom?

So, the great purges began. The populace began covering up its tracks, as it were. In a few short eons, humanity had done such a thorough job that few remembered or could find records of humanity's origins. It was though humankind had become tethered to their galaxy.

Those who went to the Andromeda Galaxy lost contact with their brethren in the Milky Way. No news ever came back to them. Humans quickly spread out through the core of the Andromeda Galaxy, but stopped short of colonizing its outermost edges, because the darkness had slipped through the fold they had made in space along with them. It quickly darkened the Andromeda Galaxy as well. The purge happened there, too, and eons passed, until humanity had forgotten its origins.

The Messier Galaxy fared better than Andromeda. The humans there managed to colonize many arms of the large galaxy before the darkness hit. However, when it did, they were cut off from each other, and the human populace there, too, forgot from where it had come. Humanity was trapped in three relatively small galaxies in a large universe that seemed to remain empty and out of reach.

Then, the signals from Earth began. They beamed out in a repeating pattern, but there was no one to hear them. Humanity had become oblivious to their own messages.

The genetic changes that the human species had made to certain demographics were poised to provide an answer to the prayer for contact being sent from that distant planet in that obscure, small arm of the Milky Way. The message pulsed outward and onward forever, never knowing if anyone would ever hear the call.

Humanity eventually forgot the darkness and went on living in their systems across the three galaxies. But, being ignorant of each other, they came to believe they were the only humans in any galaxy. The spread of the human population, like that of a virus, had been stopped in its tracks by an invisible force.

The message beaming across space was eventually heard, but not in the manner its designers had developed it for. This is where this story starts: in a far corner of the Messier 100 Galaxy, in a small system of humans who are heedless to what is out there. A search begins with its sole purpose of finding other humans somewhere out there. From where had humanity come?

Part 1
Change May Come and Change Must Go

Chapter 1
Trash Is What Trash Does

Tam wiped his forehead with his arm, looking across the garbage piles lying in the ditches between the rows of ramshackle huts that lined the streets of the internment camp. He placed his chin on top of his arms, which were crossed overtop the handle of his shovel, and with a sigh, surveyed his surroundings. Two similarly-clothed workers further down the alleyway were picking up trash and tossing it into almost-full carts. His cart was still half-empty.

Back to work, I suppose. He sighed again and bent over, continuing to shovel his trash pile into his cart. The sodbent he sensed earlier would have to wait. Right now would not be a good play time—he could not be caught doing something so degenerate. *Focus on the job. No point losing your life over something so basic.* Sex would have to wait, even though his loins told him otherwise. He curled the shovel a little to the left, deftly lifting a layer of garbage off the ground and into the cart.

The garbage stank. Tam's sense of smell was nearly as powerful as his sense of sodbent-searching. Balancing his shovel against one arm, he reached into his satchel with the other and pulled out a small, round container. The oil was used to dampen out the smell. He applied a generous amount to his large concave nostrils and wrinkled his nose. It stung a bit—sometimes, to the point that his brown skin would lighten at the edge of his nose.

Majoris poked its light through the clouds above. As they cleared some more, Minoris added its weaker, reddish light to the mix. The binary stars never really competed much for his attention but when he felt the light streaming down, his mood changed somewhat. He paused again. Tam noticed his willpower start to waver and began searching anew for the man who had appeared in his mind earlier. He looked up and to the left. But he wasn't really looking at anything; he was searching beyond his sight. *He must be somewhere nearby; I can sense his thoughts and can see that his sodbent is strong.* It was the same sodbent as before! The man's actual desire was to be pushed over a bench and be penetrated from behind—anonymously, so as to not attract the police. *Goddesses, if anyone were ever to discover this degenerate event, the police would haul both of us to prison.* Death penalty, obviously. Was it worth it?

A stirring in Tam's trousers distracted him from his worry about being discovered. He tossed his hesitation aside as instinct took over. *Garbage can wait. There is always more to pick up.* Tam looked up and down the row of huts and saw no supervisor in sight. He dropped his shovel mindlessly and it clattered noisily against a random piece of metal. He walked to his cart and reached for his clothes satchel, from which he pulled a bar of soap, a towel, and a change of clothing. Feeling a little nervous but rather aroused, Tam headed for the public baths to clean up. *One can't have sodbent with dirty hands or smelly privates!* It was almost the end of his shift anyway; no one would notice his absence. He walked down the alley, turned the corner onto the dusty main street, and approached the baths.

Thankfully, they were mostly empty. As he entered the main door for males, which was open, he saw three collectors like himself casually pouring water over themselves and lathering themselves with soap. Tam understood the constant battle against the grime and horrid stench that enveloped each worker. The goal was to be almost free from the smell of trash when done.

Tam gathered two buckets of lukewarm water from the dispensing troughs by the door and approached an empty basin two down from the three men who were bathing. There was a silence that was only broken by the sound of water being poured by one of the men or an occasional cough. He stripped off his satchel and then his uniform, which he tossed on the floor, then untied his braided hair. Tam clambered into the basin and reached for the first bucket. He raised it over his head and allowed some of the water to trickle off it. The water streamed across his broad shoulders, down the front of his chest, through the clumps of coarse curly chest hairs.

Tam picked up the soap and began applying it to his arms. Reaching downward, he lathered up his genitals, then reached around to clean his ass and down his legs. He then stood up and applied the soap to his long, black hair, which trailed down over his shoulders. With his body fully lathered up, he reached for the first bucket and poured the remaining water over his head, allowing it to rinse the soap away down the drain of the basin. He watched the soap circle the drain, around and around, until it disappeared to Goddesses know where. Life seemed to go down the drain the same way sometimes. He sighed, picked up the second bucket, and completed the job at hand as the rest of the soap drained away.

Suddenly, a sodbent image spun into his head. The thought took shape and he rotated it to see it from several sides to best understand what the man's intentions were. He wanted to receive sodbent! The signs were unmistakable. One of three men was definitely sodbent. The man must also have known that Tam was there.

Tam searched the minds of the two men closest to him. The one beside him, in the basin two spaces over, was empty. He was not sodbent. The one next to him, though, was the one. Tam felt a rush of adrenaline. The man knew that Tam desired sodbent, too. Tam gave him a quick glance and he flashed his interest—not only in his mind, but in a very discreet, physical look.

[There is a cleaning closet at the row's end. No one goes there during the day. I will meet you there,] the man projected as he toweled his pale skin and rubbed his genitals and backside with a sense of urgency. He then stepped out of his basin. He moved toward the closet, casting a quick look at Tam as he went.

Tam sniffled as he dried himself off and began to step out of his basin when, suddenly, noises came from the entrance of the bathhouse. He started, feeling the hair on his arms stand up and a knot develop in his stomach as he turned and looked through the humid, misty air. Two police in red tunics and yellow sashes appeared and began approaching Tam, who started and then stopped himself from foolishly fleeing. He urgently tried to access their minds to see what their intentions were. One thought popped into his mind, spinning furiously with intent: *A degenerate is here. Arrest him!*

Tam swallowed nervously as he closed his eyes, praying. He began to pull on his clean pale blue tunic and brown sash. Surely, just *thinking* about sodbent couldn't get him caught. He gathered his things and waited for the inevitable as he heard the men approach from behind him. Tam's knees felt weak, and he shivered despite the warm temperature of the room.

The men pushed into him, almost knocking Tam into the basin, as they carried on. He wasn't the target! It was the man who had sent the message. The police continued down the aisle to the cleaning room and opened the door.

Tam didn't wait to hear or see what transpired. His dirty uniform and socks would have to stay near the basin where he had forgotten them. He dashed out the door and headed back to his waiting cart, uncharacteristically out of breath. Adrenalin pumped in his veins and his flight response was almost impossible to ignore. He had escaped a situation that was becoming all too common in the mining communities and internment camps on Zemitis. In fact, it now felt more like a prison than Corustloth did. The world had become a dangerous place for men like Tam.

He felt perspiration dripping down his armpits and the middle of his back. His escape was a close one. He would have to be careful, or he would end up in a Senate prison, like the man being dragged out of the bathhouse at that very moment probably would. Worse, he could be shipped to Corustloth, the dreaded prison world. Was it all worth it for a few moments of sexual pleasure with another man?

Tam let out a breath to try to calm his nerves. With a bit of resolve, he decided to proceed to the processing plant on the other side of the internment camp. Once his cart was delivered, he would receive his meagre pay and be free to go home. Mother would be waiting by the door, tapping her foot and rolling her eyes.

Chapter 2
Hated Hearth

"What in Goddesses' names have you been up to, Thamara Amergan?" Mother demanded as Tam entered the hut. She had been waiting at the door, as Tam had predicted. "Getting up to no good as usual, I'll wager! Not doing the job that you get paid for, I'd guess!" She closed the door and crossed her arms, waiting expectantly. With no instant reply, she turned away and went back to the pot cooking on the stove.

"Mother, I did my job and received my pay. I'll leave it in the jar as usual." He sighed and went to the hearth, as he did every day that he worked. Mother expected the money would be placed there without fail.

Cassie burst into the room singing, as she usually did. Seeing Tam, she smiled. "Tam, I can smell you all the way from over here! Did you forget to bathe, stink bug?" She giggled and ran to hug him. "I'm glad you're home!" Then she whispered: "Mother's been angry all day."

"That really isn't a surprise," Tam whispered back to her. "What is she upset about now?"

"Father came home drunk and stomped around like a furious Banderbeast! Mother almost threw a pot at him. He tooked some of the money from the hearth and went out for more beer."

"It's *took*, sweet pea, not *tooked*!"

"I knows it!" she replied. She giggled at her little joke and darted behind the curtain separating the room from the sleeping area. She turned and peeked around it, sticking her tongue out and winking as she disappeared.

Tam wondered if Mother would bring up the need for Cassie's education with Father. That's assuming he was sober, which he often wasn't. Poor Cassie needed to go to school to get an education, but the Senate seemed to be changing their minds about that, too. Life had changed so much since Kruger II had become the Magistrate. Was school now a thing of the past? He sat down in one of the rough chairs in the seating area, looking at his nails. They still had dirt under them. It made him angry to know that so much had changed in the past ten years.

He still remembered the day when their old home had been taken from them by the Senate police. The family had been told that they would be moved to the new town created especially for their kind. Upon arriving and discovering that this was to be where they now lived, both Mother and Father had been indignant and had raised a fuss. But it went unheard until, one day, the police took it upon themselves to show their intent. Mother's screams still rang through Tam's ears five years later as he remembered the police kicking Father to the dirt floor of their hut.

They took the family's last piece of old technology—the land vehicle that Father used to use to drive to work. Father lost his right to work for the University of the Learnèd as a computer attendant for the Kashtiloth system's history department. Old information was now forbidden and new information, all pertaining to the "glorious life" the Magistrate claimed would be coming their way, was promoted. Kruger crowed about the renaissance that would make the system great again. Five years later, though, nothing had changed. In fact, it had gotten worse.

Father's spirit was broken, and he became depressed. That's when the drinking started. Mother became increasingly shrill, as angry as Father. Even the arrival of new technology didn't change things. Each person received a holopad, which worked based on the person's job and stature. Tam's family had access to food, heating, electricity, and tax-paying information. The Senate also supplied every person with all they ever needed to know about the "Wonderful Senate" and its plans for the future.

Tam had lucked out—he received more information as a garbage attendant. His holopad was able to search for information pertaining to the identification of garbage that might turn up. This gave him access to a lot of the new technology, as the Senate was on the lookout for old technology—even in the garbage. Tam was no fool; he knew the Senate was dumbing down the masses. But there was little he could do about it. In his spare time, he would search for information about animals, farms, and other technologies that seemed to exist on Alorion, the next planet in the system. Dreaming became a daily activity.

He read about sail gliders and how farming was becoming a major industry on Alorion. He learned about life on the three other worlds and dreamt of a time when he could escape this horrid place and make his way to Alorion. Start a new life. Yes, that would be it! *It might even be safe to pursue sodbent!*

Tam's daydreaming was interrupted by his father's entrance into the hut. It didn't take a mind sifter to know he was drunk. In fact, the odor of the alcohol wafted into Tam's nostrils almost immediately. Father grunted and headed for the curtain and his bed.

Cassie's immediate reappearance didn't surprise Tam. She tried to avoid Father as much as possible, in case a foot might be directed at her. She scampered back into the room and sat down on Tam's lap. She leaned her head onto Tam's chest and sighed.

"I know, sweet pea. I'm here for you." He set his holopad down and hugged her as he rocked her gently. Life for an eight-year-old girl on Zemitis wasn't any better than for a twenty-five-year-old man. He caressed her black locks, tightly woven and short. Mother's latest haircut on Cassie didn't really show much skill, and it saddened him to think that the family couldn't afford a haircut for his beautiful little sister. In the old life, she would have been in a different situation—probably as talented as Tam in whatever she put her mind to. Here, the little girl's spirit was broken. It didn't seem right that she might never get a chance to get out of the internment camp.

Mother's call interrupted his thoughts. "The food is ready! Wash your hands and come to the table."

She turned back to the pot and gave it a final couple of stirs. As the two arrived, she handed them each a bowl and went to the table to eat her share. Tam scooped a portion for Cassie and one for himself. They each went to the table and began to eat silently.

Father appeared several minutes later, rubbing his eyes and scratching his head. He served himself and sat at the other end of the rough-edged table, as far away as possible from the others. He grunted and began spooning the stew into his mouth immersing his face as deep as he could in the bowl. His eyes were red, and it looked like he was in discomfort. He tossed his spoon loudly onto the table.

"Thamara, what in the Goddesses' names were you up to today?! The police came to me as I was walking home. There was another arrest at the bathhouse. They dragged some disgusting degen out of the place and threw him in prison. It could have been you!" he spat as he wiped his mouth on his sleeve. "You will be the death of us all. I know you were somehow involved. You always are! I didn't raise my son to be a degen—to be thrown into prison at a moment's notice!"

He picked up his spoon and continued to eat, ignoring the others.

"Mother, why do they call people like that *degens*? Why is Tam a degen? What did he do wrong to be punished?" asked Cassie, her brow furrowed. She stopped eating to wait for a response. With nothing coming, she continued to eat in silence. She glanced over at Tam, who had placed his elbows on the table and lowered his head into his hands. The spoon was still in one hand and dripped broth onto the tablecloth. "*Psst!* Tam, your spoon!"

Tam started and looked at the drips. He took his ragged napkin and wiped it up. He really had nothing to say that he hadn't already said. There was no point in arguing about his orientation. There was no sense in trying to explain how strong his urges were. He could never figure them out either. It was as if they had total control over his decisions. He grimaced, pushed back his chair, and left the house.

"Run away as always, Tam! Don't think about us or our safety!" Mother screeched as he closed the door.

He paused and closed his eyes for a few seconds as he held his breath.

He turned and thought about leaving the camp and escaping. *What about Cassie? What about Mother or even Father? Who would care for them?* He felt trapped, which almost destroyed his will to fight for himself. I have to take care of everyone else and what I want is of no importance!

He wandered down the main road of the settlement and then out into the Senate-owned mining lands. Even at this hour, people still toiled to complete their tasks. The Senate said that everyone had a duty to the rest of the community, whether it was mining minerals, crushing gravel, or delivering materials to build new settlements. Then there was his job... Was his future picking up the trash of those around him? *There has to be a better way! Life shouldn't be like this!* Tam's thoughts went to that usual better place: a world where he wasn't degen and could live in peace.

Tam had sometimes wondered if he could be with a woman. What bothered him the most was that he wouldn't want to hurt her. She deserved something more than a degen for a husband. *I guess I would be better off alone, living my life in some hut on the edge of the farmlands.* A tear slid down his left cheek and he wiped it away angrily. *What choice do I have?*

His walk continued for several hours, until he returned home to a dark house with no lights. He washed up and brushed his teeth in the dark. Then, he slid into his narrow bed like he did every night.

He hated himself for it.

Chapter 3
Learnèd No Longer

Tam wandered to the community gathering area on his one afternoon off from work. This was the only place where Tam felt comfortable, because he could chat with others. It broke the isolation for many and in the years since the community had been built, the gathering place had become almost a haven for the tired and dissuaded.

As Tam approached a series of benches gathered around an empty fire pit, he heard his name called. "Thamara Amergan! How wonderful to see you again!" a man said as he turned.

"Professor Hartman, this is a surprise! How have you been doing?" Tam asked as he approached and motioned to the empty spot on the bench beside the man. Tam sat and turned to the professor.

"I've been working with the Chemical Verification Taskforce," said Professor Hartman. "It is my job to analyze the core samples from the mine drillings. I'm blessed to have the work. It's so much better than sitting at home or doing menial tasks, as some poor souls have to do. But I digress. What have you been up to since graduation?"

Tam's smile dropped and was replaced by a slight grimace. He turned his eyes away. "I was finally assigned work."

"That's wonderful! What do you do?" Professor Hartman inquired.

"I am on the Sanitation Task Force," Tam responded, still looking away.

Professor Hartman put his hand on Tam's shoulder. "With your technological knowledge from the university, you must have landed a great job analyzing the refuse to be reused or recycled into usable products. What an honorable way to use your qualifications from the University of the Learnèd!" He paused and looked at Tam, who turned, nodded and then changed the subject.

"Professor, are you happy with your new job? I mean, you used to be an esteemed Professor of the Learnèd. That was one of the highest honors back in the time before—" he paused and looked around, "—the Senate took over and changed everything."

Professor Hartman laughed. "Tam, I'm getting too old to worry about what'll happen. It's been quiet since Cara passed on." He paused, then smiled. "I miss her, but she's no longer suffering. It was her time."

"Professor, I'm so sorry about your wife. When did this happen?" asked Tam.

"Two years ago. She had been sick and there were no longer any potential medical treatments. If I'd had enough money, I would have flown her to Alorion, as I've heard that there is a convent of women there who care for the sick. However, the Goddesses took her, for whatever the reasons may be, and I am not one to judge them."

Tam swallowed and bit his lip. "Professor, I don't know what to say." He looked down at the ground and pushed his boot around in the dust.

"That's OK, my young man! I've come to peace with the Goddesses and with life itself. I'm seventy-five years old—and I probably have a good ten more to contribute to society. I can be happy with that!" He placed his arm across the back of the bench and patted Tam's shoulder with the other. "What have you been up to? Have you been keeping yourself safe?"

"I... I have been doing my best. Why do you ask?" Tam responded, looking at the professor out of the corner of his eye.

Now it was the professor who looked around warily. "Tam, I know about your sodbent! It doesn't take a mind sifter to know these things."

"By the Goddesses! How did you know?"

"I saw the looks that you gave some of the other young men in your courses. I am a Professor of the Learnèd, after all! We're an inquiring bunch!" He paused and patted Tam on the shoulder. "Rest easy, Tam. You secret is safe with me."

Tam nodded and looked down at his dusty boots. "It's been hard, Professor Hartman. Sometimes my urges take over and I find myself giving in to them. It's been a very trying few years."

"Tam, I have no doubt. You are a mentalist and you are sodbent. Those two are not exclusive. They go hand in hand. I'm fairly certain that you are unique, as there are no mentalists who live with women. Only sodbent possess these mental capabilities. That is why I am worried for you!" He rubbed his greying beard and placed his hand on the back of the bench. He looked straight forward. "Tam, you need to get off Zemitis as soon as possible. Your life depends on it."

"Professor, that's not possible. I've not earned nearly enough to get passage to Alorion. It will take me another ten years or more to earn enough. I don't think that I will make it that long, though, because my urges often win out and, one of these days, I'll be caught and thrown into prison." Tam gripped his thighs with his hands and gently leaned forward. "I can't go on living like this. I want to make for Alorion, but I have to think about Cassie and my parents."

"Son, you don't have to. You must survive. You're a mentalist, and that makes you very valuable. The Senate seeks you out for that very reason."

"What? I thought they wanted to imprison me for being sodbent!" exclaimed Tam.

"That is one of their reasons, but it is nothing more than camouflage for their real intent. They want to locate all the mind sifters and mentalists. What they want them for is not within my understanding at the moment, but I'd wager it is not for any good. You must get out of here as soon as possible."

"How, Professor? Stealing is just as bad as sodbent, even if I stole from my family! I could never do that—not to save my own life. I've got Cassie to think about. I know that Mother and Father have given in to the harassment. They are no longer the parents I knew before the camps." Tam scuffed his foot across the ground in anger. "I can't even trust them. They might turn me in for money! I have no way of knowing what they think now! All they do is scream and yell at me! Poor Cassie doesn't stand a chance either. I have to take care of her." He paused again, then said, "There is no way. I can't leave without her."

"There is another way," said the professor. He smiled.

"How? I can't see any other way. I am bound to take care of Cassie! I can't trust Mother or Father anymore. It's up to me."

Professor Hartman's hand returned to Tam's shoulder. "Let me help you. I've got enough money to keep me happy for the rest of my life. I've saved a lot these past couple of years. I'll give you the money to get to Alorion—and more to get you settled into something that interests you for work!"

Tam shook his head in wonderment. "Professor! I can't accept that!"

"Of course you can! I want to do this because you have so much value. Even if you weren't sodbent, I'd still offer you the money, because your life is important to me. You studied under me and showed me you are capable of learning—of being so much more!" He paused and looked around again to make sure all was safe. "My son, there is a calling for you as a mind sifter and a mentalist. That's all I can say for now. It's imperative you leave as soon as possible."

"And what about Cassie?"

The professor paused for a moment. "Look, I'll make a deal with you. Take the money to get to Alorion, at least. I'll use the rest of the money to have Cassie moved. I can have her taken in with my daughter. I'll speak to the authorities. I may no longer be a Professor of the Learnèd, but I still have a little pull." He looked at Tam expectantly. "Think about it, son! It might be for the best for both of you. I can even keep an eye on your parents. Maybe get your Father some help with his drinking."

"You know about that, too?" asked Tam with surprise.

Professor Hartman nodded. "The Learnèd were the most powerful in the system because of our wisdom, derived from the use of the old technology. The Magistrate destroyed all of that out of fear for what we could do. With the Learnèd put down and almost powerless, he has no fear. But though he may have defeated us, he expects us to remain useless, and blunders in this. It is my goal to get you to Alorion—and your sister into a safe environment. So, yes, I know about your Father. Let me help you, please!"

Tam placed his hand over his mouth, feeling a great sadness, tinged with hope. He smiled and dropped his hand. "Surely we won't get arrested for having a friendly hug between friends, Professor?"

"I think that would be fine!" Professor Hartman stood up as Tam did the same. They embraced, and he continued, "Meet me here tomorrow after your shift and I'll have the credits to get you to Alorion. Your parents will be distracted by your departure and not focused on Cassie. She will be taken care of, as I promised. Can you leave tomorrow?"

Tam stepped back and nodded. The tears were running down his cheeks with abandon. "Thank you, Professor! I guess the Goddesses meant for me to meet you today! Blessed be the Goddesses!"

"Quite right," Professor Hartman responded. "Quite right!"

∞

"But why?" pleaded Cassie. "Why must you leave me here?" Cassie began to whimper, pulling her doll closer to her chest. "It's not fair! I want to go with you!"

"Sweet pea, you can't come with me. I know that you don't understand, but one day you will. I'll come back for you, somehow!"

"I don't care. I want you here with me!" she continued. Cassie started to wail. The doll went sailing across the room. "Mother and Father don't want me anymore and now, neither do you!"

"Cassie, Professor Hartman has offered to help us. You will go to stay with his daughter. Just think: you can get some schooling and learn new things!"

She thought about this for a minute, then continued to cry. "But I want to be with you!" Cassie ran to Tam and hugged him, her head butting up against his chest. "I'm not going to let you go. You have to stay with me!"

"Professor Hartman has promised that Mother and Father will get some help. When they're feeling better, you can rejoin them if you want!" A tear slid down his cheek. "I'll miss you too, you little stink bug!"

"You're the stink bug!" she sniffed.

Tam knelt down in front of Cassie and grasped her by her shoulders. "I need you to be brave. Can you do that for me?" he asked.

She sniffled and wiped her eyes on her sleeve. She didn't say anything, just nodded, as more tears slid down her face.

∞

Tam completed his shift, spent extra time washing up, and then headed to the community gathering place to meet Professor Hartman. He was there, as promised, sitting on his bench. The professor smiled as Tam approached. He motioned for Tam to sit.

"I'm glad to see you here. Are you ready to leave?"

"Yes, Professor Hartman, I am. I just have to go home and pick up my satchel and say goodbye to my family. Not much happened when I told them I would be leaving last night! The only unhappy one was Cassie. The poor thing really thinks I'm abandoning her. It's for the best, though—she needs to go to school and now, because of you, she can!"

"I'm sure that she will understand soon enough. You are making the right decision. I'll make sure she gets a proper education. I promise, Tam."

"That was what helped me make my decision. I am in your debt. How can I ever repay you?" he asked.

"You already have. I get to see a promising young man, beaming with hope, not just for himself, but his sister as well. Oh, and one more thing—give me your holopad."

Tam stopped, looking at the professor inquiringly as he handed over the holopad.

He spent a few minutes inputting something into the device. "Aside from the credits, I have another parting gift for you. Here is some helpful information for you on your trip, grace of the Professors of the Learnèd. I'm glad that we can still be of service, limited though it may be." He sighed, then smiled, handing back the holopad, before looking deeply into Tam's green eyes. "Tam, be well. May the Goddesses grant you safe passage and allow you to go forward and do whatever you are meant for!" He stood up and motioned to Tam to do the same. He hugged him. "Find your calling, young man!"

Tam swallowed hard. "I'll do my best, Professor."

"That's all I ask! Now go!"

∞

His ticket to Alorion cost him most of the credits he had been given by Professor Hartman. Luckily, he still had some of the credits from the jar on the hearth. Mother and Father at least allowed him that much.

His parents might even have been glad to see him go. It was clear they felt his sodbent would get the whole family into trouble. The ever-growing power of the Senate government was insidious, slowly ingraining its propaganda into society and peoples' minds. He realized he was not sorry to see the last of that dump of a settlement. There was really nothing left for him there.

When he said goodbye, Tam's mother looked at Cassie instead of Tam. She obviously didn't feel comfortable meeting his eyes. *Probably guilt*, he thought. Father, in his usual manner, had disappeared inside without a word. Cassie had looked glum, digging her worn-out shoe into the dirt at the entrance of the lean-to. She was trying very hard to not cry.

"Don't forget to took a picture of me, Tam," she sniffled, wiping her nose on her sleeve.

There had been no waving hands and tearful eyes as he shouldered his satchel and left the decrepit home he had known for five years. Maybe they didn't give a flying leap off the falls of the blue moons about his wellbeing. Mother turned, went in, and closed the door. Cassie stood there, watching, until he was almost out of view.

"Take a bath more often, stink bug!" she shouted.

As he left the internment camp, he began to feel relieved by his freedom from his parent's disapproval and the life they had forced upon him. *"Help yourself first, Tam, and you'll be better prepared to help your family."* That's what Professor Hartman had said. *I think I understand that now.*

One day, he would be back for Cassie.

Chapter 4

Passages

Though the attendants had obviously done this many times, Tam felt a sense of dread as he listened to the preflight instructions. After all, no one in his family had ever left Zemitis. Not even his father had taken a trip into outer space before the old technology had been banned. He listened intently to everything they said about takeoff, landing, what to do in case of emergency, and how to use the panels on his seat. He had some food in his satchel, a drink he had purchased before boarding, and his holopad. He was ready, both nervous and excited.

The attendant assigned to his section approached, checking in with everyone as he walked the aisle. When he reached Tam, he stopped and asked the same questions he had asked the others. He looked at Tam's hands clenching the seat arms, smiled, and looked back at Tam. "Is this your first flight off planet?"

Tam nodded and smiled as best he could. His hands still clenched the seat arms.

The attendant scanned his holopad and looked up Tam's name. "Mr. Amergan, it will be helpful if you relax your hands and breathe normally." Seeing that Tam still wasn't relaxing, he made a suggestion: "Here, have some of this." He handed Tam a small bottle. "It will help you relax. You'll stay awake and experience the flight all the same."

Tam took the bottle and nodded. "Thank you. I guess I'm a little nervous." He opened the bottle and drank the contents.

The attendant retrieved the empty bottle and said, "You should feel less nervous momentarily. If there's anything else you need, let me know via your holopad."

"Thank you again," Tam replied as the attendant carried on. To distract himself, he allowed his mind to travel around the compartment. *No point looking for sodbent here.* Realizing this, he began to research Alorion on his holopad. He had heard, through whispers at the government camps, of a place on Alorion where men could meet other men, if they were discreet. It was called the Tigress Eye Café. He requested information on the café and how to get there from the spaceport on Alorion. The holopad even gave points of interest between the spaceport and the café, should he wish to see the sights.

The attendant completed his trip around the compartment and returned to the front of his section, where he pressed the intercom on his holopad. "Attention, everyone! We are ready for departure. Please stow all your belongings in the compartments under your seat or above your head while we take off. Ensure that your restraint is clicked in, as I showed you earlier. Please be aware that Alorion has a twenty-seven-hour day compared to our twenty-six on Zemitis. Also, note that your holopad will reset itself upon arrival—just a helpful tip for those of you new to traveling. Wonderful! I see by my panel that you are all buckled in, so relax as we begin our pre-takeoff procedures. We will be leaving shortly. Have a nice flight to Alorion!"

Tam looked out the window to his right and could see the entrance compartment retracting from the side of the spaceship. As it did, the sun reflected off the side of the spaceport building, which extended down two hundred floors. His eyes traveled across the drab colors of the planet, longing for something more vibrant. Tam wanted to see the green and blue of Alorion, as he had seen on his holopad.

The ship floated next to the pylon that tethered it to the building. A soft vibration became noticeable as he saw the pylon let go of its grip on of the Alorion-Class spacecraft. The ship started to lift away from the building, rising upward. The vibration was now accompanied by the sound of engines revving up as the spacecraft gathered its upward momentum. Tam found this new feeling a little unnerving. His discomfort was short-lived, though, as the blue sky quickly turned to black as the spacecraft gained speed and altitude.

Tam gasped when he saw the stars above—as he'd never seen them before—and again when he looked at the diminishing planet below. Even though it was primarily dry deserts and high, rocky plateaus, Zemitis had a distinct beauty that was hard to ignore. Maybe it was the feeling that he was escaping that made him feel a little nostalgic. But he was certainly relieved to be leaving, too. It was all so confusing.

"Preparing for drive engagement," the head attendant announced. "All passengers are required to stay in their seats. We will arrive at Alorion Spaceport in four Zemitisian hours. Thank you, and enjoy your voyage!"

Tam willed himself to let go of the seat armrests and breathe inward, and the stress began to fade away. He turned his eyes to the viewing screen and watched as a rainbow of colors shone in front of the ship. It was hard to know what to expect next. The ship was then enveloped inside the rainbow, which flowed around the ship as though it were traveling through water. The sight was mesmerizing. Tam felt as though he were traveling down a long tube that was slowly rotating around him. He found himself going beyond the ship in his vision, only focusing on the view screen, so that it felt like he was flying alone through the rainbow. He continued to stare until he heard the announcement that it was safe to leave his seat.

He shook his head, took a sip of his drink, and pulled out his holopad to continue his study of Alorion and its wonders. The farming was highly evolved, and many crops upon which the entire system depended were grown there. Since there was an abundance of resources, Alorion also had fantastic entertainment, including the Tigress Eye Café. It was located in the "darker side of the port city, Ali-Alorion," as reviewers described it. There were night markets and brothels in what was called the "Town of Transgressions." All sorts of spicy entertainment could be had. Though it was described as "spicy," there was no mention of sodbent or degen activities. But why would there be, since it was illegal? He would have to depend on his own intuition and figure out what to do when he got there.

"First time to Alorion?" the woman beside him asked.

"Yes, my first time off-world," Tam replied. "It's all very exciting."

"Are you planning your activities in Ali-Alorion when you arrive?" the woman inquired. "I hear it is a wonderful place for a handsome young man like yourself to meet a woman."

Tam smiled. "Thank you. I'm sure that I will have time to see the sights, as I am moving to Alorion."

"Really? What do you plan on doing?"

"I'm not sure yet. I'll travel around and get a sense of things first. How about you?"

She smiled and placed her hands in her lap. "I'm joining my husband for a well-deserved vacation. It has been such a long time since we have had time to travel together. I haven't seen him in a few weeks, and can't wait to get to the resting places, where I can be pampered. It's quite exciting!"

"I'm sure," replied Tam politely. He continued to study his holopad and the woman, thankfully, turned to the person on her other side, leaving him to his research.

Breathing a light sigh, he continued searching for more information about nightlife on Alorion. He silently thanked Professor Hartman for his gift, as he found that he could search for just about anything and not leave any trace. Still, he found it hard to get the nerve to search for the word *sodbent*, for fear of someone discovering him. Instead, he stared at the view screen for a while longer, until he became totally mesmerized. He slept, and didn't realize time had passed, until he was suddenly jarred to attention by a very unpleasant sensation.

Tam awoke to his stomach reeling and realized he was going to vomit. He quickly reached for the illness container and put it to his mouth just in time as his stomach vacated itself in a forceful lurch. He hadn't heard the announcement for the curved space exit so he hadn't been prepared.

Now, Tam was afraid and confused. Sweat beaded on his forehead and he felt like he might faint. Then an urge to escape hit him with so much weight, he almost screamed. Tam searched the compartment for a way out. The woman who had talked to him earlier was staring at him.

[Focus on my thoughts and let me help you, young sodbent. You are experiencing what all true mentalists feel,] she commanded. *[I can ease your distress and keep you from being discovered. Stay in your seat, young man. I am here to ease the pain.]*

[Who are you?] Tam projected, not being used to communicating with a woman mentally. His surprise distracted him from his panic. *Women weren't mentalists...?* He retched one more time into the container, wiped his mouth with a napkin, and lost consciousness.

∞

"Passengers, prepare for descent to Alorion Spaceport," the captain announced as Tam awoke with a start. Looking quickly at the view screen, he realized he had been unconscious for over an hour.

[You are safe, young man. I am glad to be of service to you. Please say nothing of this. Discretion is necessary for both you and for me. You will recover from any ill effects shortly. I bid you Goddesses' speed to where you are going.]

[Forgive me, but I did not realize that a woman can be a mentalist! Who are you? How can I thank you?] Tam projected back.

[There is no need to give thanks for the services I am required, by code, to do. When the time is right, you will know of us. Be well, Thamara Amergan.]

Tam's eyes widened in surprise as he heard his name in the woman's thoughts. He nodded to her, and she smiled as she turned away to chat with the person on her other side.

The ship began its descent and the view ports showed blue light beginning to pour in as the spacecraft descended into the Alorion atmosphere. As he watched, the spaceport came into view. Tam saw the landscape unfold two hundred floors below and felt his breath catch as he saw the blues and greens of the world beneath him, so foreign to him, being used to the drab browns, blacks, and silvers of his home world. It distracted him from his waning discomfort. As the woman had promised, the symptoms were disappearing. He had arrived.

∞

After discreetly discarding the illness container, Tam proceeded to disembark. He slung his satchel over his shoulder and exited the travel tube that had extended to the Alorion class spaceship. How exciting! He was actually in the main spaceport building on Alorion!

He was amazed by the light that streamed into the station windows and how clean and airy the hallways felt. He followed the masses as they mostly went to the elevators. Tam had an incredible view through the glass as the elevator car closed its doors and descended, at a rather disconcerting speed, to the ground below.

Cassie, I wish you were here to see this! He felt the descent in the pit of his stomach. It almost tickled. He breathed in and out, bringing his excitement level down a bit, as the elevator arrived in a sort of bobbing motion and the doors opened to the lobby with a gentle *whoosh*.

As the people emptied out, Tam looked around, seeing merchants selling their wares and people milling about. There was music in the air, and the smell of food wafted up to his nostrils. Tam smiled and breathed in. The music was kind to his ears, and he felt his heart soar in an emotion he had never before experienced. There was joy here! The people seemed truly at ease. It felt strange to him. Why was life so hard on one planet and so easy on another?

The crowd was flowing toward the large exits at the end of the lobby. Tam followed, reached the open doors, and was again amazed. The air had a sweet, earthen smell—humid and almost salty to the nose. His eyes turned to his right and, in the distance, saw a massive blue area he couldn't at first identify. It was darker than the sky, but echoed the colors above as it glistened and moved. It was the Mengal Sea he had read about.

So much water, he thought. As he pondered the sea, he saw flying creatures gathering in small groups as they glided overhead. *Birds,* he recalled from his holopad.

Amazing to see things fly! He stood there, feeling like he was drinking his fill to quench a massive thirst.

People began to bump into him, and he realized he was blocking an exit. He stepped aside, against a rail, and he looked downward to the green lands not far below. There were people lounging on the vegetation—some of them sitting, others lying on chairs. Children laughed and sang as parents kept watch. It was all so overwhelming! But he was exhilarated—and restless. He found himself almost dancing as he proceeded along the rail until he reached a set of stone stairs that descended to the green areas below. He allowed himself to flow downward with the crowd.

[Thamara Amergan, may joy and happiness be with you!]

It was the woman from the spacecraft.

[May the Goddesses send you blessings and good tidings!] he responded.

[Make your way to Tigress Eye Café, as planned. This is the path you are to take. I am blessed in helping guide you on it. Safe travels, Thamara Amergan!]

Tam smiled, though he couldn't see her, and projected back to her, *[I shall do as planned. It is a mystery to me why you are here to help me, but I thank you all the same.]*

[You will understand soon enough, young man! Goodbye!]

[Goodbye!] he responded, and her mind was gone, though it echoed inside his. *Onward,* he thought, pulling his holopad out of his satchel to plan his route to the Tigress Eye Café.

∞

The late afternoon progressed into early evening as he made his way. He stopped to get a drink and eat the last of the food he had brought with him. Doing so made him feel like he was ending his life on Zemitis and starting fresh here.

At first, the streets were pleasant and clean. But gradually, the scenery changed, and he felt a familiar sense of grittiness as he realized he had made his way to the darker side of the port city, Ali-Alorion. As he progressed deeper into the seedier side of the port, a sense of mystery enveloped him.

He arrived at his destination over an hour later, sweaty and nervous. He pulled his satchel off his back, rolled up his holopad and placed it inside, and sat down on a soft fabric chair by a window in the Tigress Eye Café. Tam felt the fresh air coming off the nearby Mengal Sea wash over him, helping him relax a little, hopefully making it seem like he was less nervous.

The café was bathed in sapphire light, which shone into the half-full house through windows and skylights. Music from a mysterious source filled the room, enveloping the crowd, making the atmosphere almost electric. This was definitely a place to hook up. He wondered what his chances of meeting a man were. He was there after a long trip, so he might as well stay and give it a shot, should an opportunity arise. At the very least, he would eat something.

Tam watched the other patrons come and go and listened to the bustle of the crowds. He traced his finger across the antique woodgrain table nervously. He wasn't really there for the food or the old-style décor. He was watching for a signal that would let him know someone was like him—a secret cue of sodbent.

He watched women in long, glittering, nearly see-through gowns glide from table to table, seeking a man. They didn't have to worry about being caught! Some sent their eyes over Tam's way—perhaps noting his good looks, or maybe picking up on his sensitive nature. He averted his eyes, pretending to be interested in the menu holocard.

Men also came in, clearly seeking a woman. Their brusque nature and open tunics, which exposed their hairy chests, seemed ill-mannered to Tam. But he'd learn to imitate them, for survival's sake.

The light of the moons continued to travel across the sky, casting glimmering shadows on the table in front of him. His empty glass and nearly-finished meal made him wonder if he would be able to remain much longer without raising doubts about his reason for being there. The last thing he wanted to do was make an accidental connection with a woman.

He stared out the window as he toyed with his food, pushing it around with his fork, dreaming of an ideal encounter. *What kind of man would I like? Let's see... a man that has blue eyes and is very muscular. Someone who is sure of himself and clear about what he wants. Maybe short hair?* He imagined the instant connection they would feel. Maybe this time it would be more than just casual sex. Most of his past hookups had been in some back alley or behind a market stall. Mental communication had helped him find sodbent, but nothing more. *What would it feel like to be in love?*

Tam opened his eyes and returned to reality. Surely nothing like that would come to pass! After all, he did not have the luck of an Alorion sapphire ring, though he could have bought the superstitious trinket at the market. He stared out the open window at the cobbled streets and sighed.

Suddenly sensing something very different in his mind, he looked away from the window and back to the room. Oh, Goddesses! There, to his rising excitement, was an enchanting man at the table across from him. He was dressed in a light blue tunic and a dark blue sash, with a multicolored scarf tied loosely around his neck. His light skin was very different from Tam's darker brown skin. His tawny hair was cut short and swept to the side, with a short tail of hair on the back of his neck. Tam was taken aback by his bright blue eyes, which he had somehow predicted only a few minutes earlier. Blue eyes were rare on Zemitis, as brown eyes were most desired by parents, and other colors were being slowly weeded out of the gene pool—including green ones, like his. The man's blue eyes glowed like the turquoise-speckled light from the shadow-laden moons outside. The stranger was fending off women nonchalantly, declining all invitations to join them at their tables.

He felt a thrill as he realized his fantasy was perhaps becoming real. His head was coursing with energy as he felt the possibility. But was this man interested?

Tam closed his eyes, sought the stranger out, and found him almost immediately, seeing his face in his mind. He was smiling! The stranger was indeed interested in him, and he was able to mentally link with an ease Tam had never felt before. He peeked through his half-open eyelids at the man and could see his blue eyes doing the same.

[Meet me under the wooden bridge, near the shore of the warm sea that laps at its boards.]

Seeing the image of the place, Tam reasoned he could leave, so he called up the holobill. He paid for his meal, slapping his holocard against the silently rotating holobill. He only had a hundred hard-earned credits left. That was not much good for finding a decent place for the night. But he had more important things to do than worry about sleep!

He stood up, quickly closed his eyes, and pictured the stranger's face. The signal was still there—and an unmistakable message.

[We'll meet soon. Make Goddesses' speed to the wooden bridge on the sandy beach.]

He left the Tigress Eye Café without turning his eyes towards the stranger. Tam knew, however, that he was nearby, making his way to the bridge as well. He pulled out his holopad and proceeded to find the best route.

Tam wandered the streets, weaving in and out of booths bathed in the inky light of the city. The pungent smells and brash sounds of the night market wafted around him. He was so excited about what might happen that he failed to notice the smell of salts, exotic spices, and vegetables side by side with illicit drugs in many stalls. The sounds of marketers hawking their wares rang through the night air, enveloping Tam as he tried to vanish into the crowd.

"Hey, stranger, do you want some gear spice to make you feel good?"

Tam shook his head, looking down at the cobbles, and hurried away from the shady-looking man. He switched from one side of the street to the other to prevent others noticing him heading to the beach beneath the bridge. *Why must I feel guilty for what I am about to do?*

His sandaled feet made a loud, worrisome slapping sound on the smooth brown cobblestones. It seemed to draw unnecessary attention. If the streets were cleaner, he would have considered going barefoot, but that was out of the question. The dirt of the parade of marketgoers would stick to his feet and follow him for the next two months, betraying his foray into the darker and more dangerous sections of Ali-Alorion. Why risk drawing yet more attention to himself by showing he had been wandering around these parts?

Down the street and through more stalls, he continued. He would sometimes catch a glimpse of the stranger through the thick smoke of fires as he passed along another row. Despite the danger of what he was doing, his mind was full of anticipation. He felt a rush in his groin and pushed onward to his goal, his heart pounding. He was nervous and excited at once.

He turned a corner suddenly and came face-to-face with patrolling police dressed in tunics of red, with yellow sashes across their waists. They stood out against the dark clothes of the people around them, who were trying to fade into the background. The policemen were roughing up some poor soul. Tam held his breath and carried on his way, sweat running down his brow and across his broad nose as he prayed to the Goddesses that he not be discovered committing a crime against the Senate.

He convinced himself to relax. They were not Life-Line police searching for mind-reading sexual deviants, but ordinary officers reacting to something involving the man they were now beating. The poor unfortunate's pleading voice made Tam shiver and falter in his quest. Was he risking too much? Would they also notice him and beat him, too? One eyed him as the other continued clobbering the poor sap, now lying on the cobblestones. The victim's begging became shriller, distracting the policeman from Tam. He didn't wait for the opportunity to be noticed again. He left the scene with his heart pounding, his emotions stirring inside him.

More switching of side streets allowed him to calm down and return to his plan of finding the beach near the bridge. Tam continued to weave his way slowly to his destination on the sandy beach below. Soon, there were fewer and fewer stands with people calling for him to come and see their wares. He kept going until there was just the empty and silent cobblestone street winding down the hill toward the wooden bridge.

The three blue moons were lower in the sky now, and the light was more diffuse and mysterious. As he reached the bridge, Tam cautiously glanced around to see if there were any people present. There were none. He closed his eyes and sensed the stranger nearby. His heart leaped and he swallowed, feeling both the panic and the rush of the sexual hunt.

Tam stepped off the street, over the barriers of the walkway and allowed his sandaled feet to dip into the soft, cool sand that glowed in the moons' light. The sound of nearby waves gently breaking on the shore wafted up the beach along with their salty smell.

He slipped silently under the bridge and sat down, waiting breathlessly. As he closed his eyes in anticipation, Tam sensed the stranger's presence. Then, there was the unmistakable, glorious smell of a man's musky scent beside him. He opened his eyes to find the stranger with blue eyes sitting with his face close to his. Tam swallowed nervously and smiled.

Chapter 5
Revelations

Daylight streamed through the curtains above him. As Tam's head cleared, he remembered the night before, when he and the blue-eyed stranger had talked for hours on the beach. Brogan was his name. Like Tam, he was also a refugee. He was from Kashtiloth, the Senate's governing planet for the binary system. Brogan had left home and spent many years searching for his lost parents without success. Maybe they were still alive, he said.

Tam had found himself sinking into the many stories Brogan had told. He was enraptured and even a little frightened by those blue eyes. There was something very comforting about the nature of his conversation, though, which made him an easy companion.

His thoughts returned to his position in bed, behind Brogan's turned back. He was still sleeping. Their clothes were strewn across the flagstone floor of his rental unit, which was at the northern end of Port City. Tam could hear birds in the courtyard below and boat horns floating up from the port to the south. The fragrant breeze coming in through the window was warm, indicating that it must have been early afternoon. It was quite a difference from the cool breezes they had felt as they had run up the hill with giddy abandon before dawn.

Tam's gaze turned to Brogan, still softly snoring, his tattooed back showing through the sheets. The tattoo fascinated Tam. He touched it and marveled at the snarling creature that Brogan had claimed was a mythical animal from eons before, in humanity's past. He had never heard of a *tiger* before. From what he could gather from their conversations, it was an ancient feline species similar to the smaller, domesticated felines living in Port City and on Zemitis. There were no tigers on any of the planets of the system, though. It made Tam wonder about its origins. Brogan had told him about how the tigers had followed humanity to the stars in the ancient past, but there were no existing records of when and where.

Tam reached out his hand and ran his fingers across the tiger's striped body, down its etched thigh, onto the small of Brogan's back. He stopped at his firm buttocks. Tam remembered the morning's frantic tangle, bringing back the wonderful sensation of intimacy with this mysterious man. He felt a stirring in his groin and reached around Brogan's chest, pulling him toward him. His hard member rubbed up against Brogan's firm buttocks. The memory of the fierce lovemaking came back in a flood, and he found it difficult to not start all over again.

Instead, there was a gentle sigh and he felt Brogan's hand meet his. Even though his back was turned, he could sense Brogan was smiling. Sex was forgotten for the moment, as the feeling of closeness made him relax. He felt content. Tam had never felt intimacy like this before, and he relished it.

Brogan's voice broke the silence. "Good tidings to you, Tam. Sleep well?"

"Wonderful! I was exhausted after the hours of sodbent with you."

"Glad to hear you slept about as well as you enjoyed yourself!" He paused for a moment. "I know it must be difficult to sleep in a strange place." He turned his head as far as he could and looked at Tam expectantly.

"There is no feeling of strangeness, Brogan. I am very much at home here. I've never felt this comfortable, actually." Tam pulled him closer.

"You feel a connection with me, too? I know I can almost always read your thoughts, but I can't as clearly as I would like. At least I know, right now, you are very happy to be with me."

"I am."

Brogan rolled over looking with his startling blue eyes into Tam's green ones. He smiled and tousled his unbraided hair, then tucked his palm under the back of his head. His lips parted and met Tam's.

[I sense your emotions, Tam. There is no need to fear sharing your mind with me. Let your mind sink into mine. Make love to me one more time before you go.]

[Leave? Do I have to go?]

[No! I would like it very much if you stayed a few days… if that is what you want… I cannot be sure what your mind says. But if it says to stay, stay.]

The next hour was another whirlwind of explosive emotions and cries of pleasure that left both of them ready for another nap. Later, they rose and slipped into the bathing pool together, washing one another in silence, always communicating so much more than what words could.

Chapter 6
Sirens

"Come on Tam, hurry up! The Convent is just ahead. I don't want us to be late!"

Brogan urged him on as they walked the quiet, treed side streets of Port City toward their destination. Tam focused on the street ahead, feeling Brogan's loving gaze. *[The Sirens await our visit. We've made quite the rumble with the priestesses. They're anxious to meet you!]*

[Why am I so important? You've only told me about them just today. Before I arrived, I had no clue they existed! I'm also amazed that one of them contacted me on the spacecraft! Do you think she knew you and I were to meet? Can they truly foresee things as you claim? Or was she directing me here?]

Brogan laughed. *[So many questions! First of all, stop doubting yourself, my handsome man! It is quite clear you have a strong mental ability. They want to test your abilities. You may even be a stronger mentalist than me!]*

[All of this linking and these tests about which you're so positive scare me. Are you telling me they can be trusted? There are too many out there who would do much to receive the reward for turning both of us over to the authorities.] Tam peered around nervously. He felt as though there might be someone lurking around any corner ready to grab them.

Brogan frowned, and Tam felt his frustration. He wanted to make him understand. *[What do I have to do to get you to let your guard down a little? You need to understand that the Sirens exist to create Life-Lines! That is their sole purpose in life. They actively seek out pairs like us.]*

Tam turned his head toward Brogan and grinned. This time he spoke out loud. "Perhaps I'm a bit of a cynic sometimes. But I'm just a realist, mostly, Brogan. You're telling me they may have helped us meet somehow? So I'm not in control of what I do or who I do it with?"

Brogan grinned and replied, "Maybe, maybe not! Ask the Siren Mother and then we won't have to quibble about it. She's the one with the answers. Though, I must warn you that what she means doesn't always match what we think she means. She can be quite cryptic." He waved his hands in the air, conveying the helplessness of communicating with cryptic priestesses with hidden agendas. They continued their walk toward the Convent. "These women may be bizarre to your unrefined sensibilities. But they can be trusted with your life, Tam."

"It's a little unfair to say I'm unrefined. It's not my fault I grew up on a mining colony, and time in a refugee camp. I think I've done an exceptional job just by surviving!"

Brogan's eyes softened. "I understand. Look, I'm sorry that I'm pressing you to do this. Are you sure you're OK?" Brogan's deep blue eyes quizzed Tam.

[I am OK with you, Brogan. I know you wouldn't lead me into something dangerous. You act like that creature on your back sometimes, but I know you care about my well-being.]

Brogan smiled and discreetly squeezed Tam's arm with his large, strong hand. He had found comfort in his response.

The two men turned the corner of the cobblestone street and came into view of the compound, surrounded by lush trees draping their fronds to the ground as though they were bowing to the Convent. The whole place appeared to be *grown together*, with dark trees strategically forming what appeared to be solid walls and a roof. Even the doors seemed to have been grown somehow to fit their frames. Tailored lawns of grass flowed beneath the structure. There were nasty, serrated thorn hedges to keep unwanted things out of the grounds. It was a peaceful oasis amid the noisy and sometimes dangerous city.

Both men stopped in their tracks as they felt the familiar sensation of their minds being probed from somewhere ahead.

[Greetings, my young friends! We welcome you to the Convent. The Mother anxiously awaits your arrival.]

Brogan looked at Tam and smiled an *OK* signal. This was all normal, it said. "Don't get yourself worked up. They are acknowledging our presence."

"Nothing like free will, right?" Tam chided. "I get the feeling all of this is going to happen whether I want it to or not. So, let's do this, then." He strode forward without hesitation.

They opened the gate and walked through into the solitude of the Convent's gardens, immediately feeling a sense of happiness. The surprise sensation sent a shiver down Tam's back.

[You feel that, Tam! We are safe here. The priestesses shield us from unwanted, dangerous eyes and probing, suspicious minds. This is how they've remained a secret society for so long! We can be at peace for a short while. Enjoy the freedom and for Goddesses' sake, let your guard down, just once! You may be pleasantly surprised!]

Tam sent nothing back. He smirked at Brogan and let out a laugh to show he was, indeed, letting his guard down for once.

They reached the broad, dark brown door of the Convent. The even darker wood of the Convent's building framed it. Tam couldn't help but run his fingers across the wood. It demanded his attention. How did it grow to form such a structure?

Tam knocked and stepped back, forgetting his question as the door creaked open.

They entered a dark, cave-like corridor. It took their eyes a while to adjust from the strong sunlight to the flame-lit corridors of the Convent. The smell of burning incense filled the air, and there was marvelously delirious singing echoing down the corridor. Tam felt the urge to run towards the sound. Standing in the dim light was a priestess in white, flowing robes, with a red sash tied around the middle. It was hard to know she was, indeed, a woman under that frock. But asking questions about why they wore these outfits would have to wait.

"Welcome, Master Thamara Amergan, and welcome back, Master Brogan Faolin, to our holy abode. We are honored by your presence, and sense your questions. All will be answered once our inquiries are satisfied. Come with me."

Her white robe shimmered and rustled softly as she led them down the hallway to the Mother Priestess's chamber. Tam's eyes wandered from side to side, taking in the paintings of the Sisterhood that hung on the wooden-paneled walls. These were holy faces, with minds that seemed to reach out and touch him from the past. He shivered.

Brogan took his hand. "Tam, it's alright here. We have nothing to fear."

"Sorry!" he whispered. "I'm so used to hiding from everyone."

Brogan's hand squeezed his. Tam smiled and squeezed back. They continued to walk through a multitude of dark corridors and large wooden doors until they arrived at the Mother's chamber.

Two priestesses sat in broad chairs at each side of the doorway. They seemed to be meditating but rose when they approached. Their white robes rustled like whispers in a breeze.

"Are they ready to meet Mother?" one of them asked their guide.

"They are, Sisters," she replied. "Is Mother ready to receive them?"

The second replied, "She is. Enter."

The heavy wooden door creaked open to reveal pitch-black darkness inside. Tam and Brogan entered, and the door swung shut behind them. They waited for a few moments before light began to stream down from above.

"What's going on?" whispered Tam.

Brogan said nothing, but pulled him closer, laying his head on Tam's shoulder.

Mother Siren spoke from the darkness: "Welcome, Masters Faolin and Amergan." She leaned forward from the darkness into the fog-like light. Her wise and piercing eyes peered through the hood of her white robe, which shimmered with rainbow colors in the light beaming down from the unknown source above. Her hand reached out to Tam and her sleeve gently slid down her arm, revealing her aged but strong arms. She was wizened and matronly, he thought. *I like her already.*

"Very kind of you, Master Amergan. I am pleased that my aging face piques your desire for motherly advice. I can fulfill that need. Come forward, and let me have a closer look at you."

Tam and Brogan stepped into the light. The room's darkness made it seem infinite.

"Master Faolin, you have landed yourself a handsome one! I can see your mind has honed itself. I was beginning to wonder if you would ever bring me a good-looking one, let alone a mentalist—and a strong one, at that!"

"My pleasure, Mother. But you make it sound like there has been a parade of men coming up the hill with me for a while! I wouldn't want Tam to think that I have loose morals!"

Tam felt a little miffed, but remained silent. He decided he would not enter the conversation until one of them addressed him directly. Better to wait for more clarity so as not to sound like a fool.

Mother turned to him. "Master Amergan, come closer."

Tam swallowed and approached hesitantly.

"No need to be frightened. There is nothing in the mind I haven't experienced."

[Lean forward and give me permission to access your mind.]

[Why, Mother? What do I have that you need to know?]

[You may be a Life-Line being, like Brogan. I need to know your abilities. To do that, I must dig deeper. Do you give me permission?]

[Once you answer a question.]

[35]

Mother laughed softly. *[I sense it already, Tam. Brogan would make a fine soul-mate—perhaps a Life-Line—for you.]*

[I understand "soulmate," Mother, but not "Life-Line." We can send messages to each other. Is that a Life-Line?]

"Hardly, young man." Mother frowned, then softened her gaze. The boy was so unsure of himself. "A Life-Line, once formed between you and another man with your capabilities, will mean more than sending each other love notes. Your minds will be linked, your souls entwined —never to be undone, except in death. What he feels, you will feel."

"Tam, Mother told me to bring you to her," Brogan gently admitted.

"We've just met!" Tam didn't understand.

"Lean forward, Master Tam, and let me touch your head. I'll tell you immediately if there is a need to worry about Life-Lines. You may not be a true mentalist—just a mind sifter. Brogan is more than that, though. He is a true Life-Line being, lacking his twin. If you are a match, you'll experience something the average human could not even comprehend. Hold the questions and let me inside. I can tell you all if you do."

Tam glanced at Brogan and pursed his lips. Did he really want this old woman probing his mind? It was one thing to send messages back and forth, but to have someone else's mind in his, rooting around, seemed a little much.

"Go on, let her in, Tam," urged Brogan. "She is honorable, and very gentle. I think you'll find the process quite enjoyable."

Though Tam still wasn't quite sure, he gave in.

[I give you permission, Mother. Will it hurt?]

[Not at all!]

Mother leaned forward in her chair and Tam crept in front of her. She motioned for him to kneel. Her wrinkled hands trembled as they crept onto his temples. She closed her eyes, sighed, and began to enter Tam's mind.

Tam shivered, felt his eyes roll back, and began to experience a whirling sensation of what felt like random thoughts jumping into his head—the sadness of leaving a home from parents who didn't care, their angry faces, the herds of destitute people in the refugee camps he had left behind, the memory his first flight through curved space, here, to Alorion. This was where Mother paused. A whining sound ground in his head, like metal on metal—one long annoying screech, three shorter ones, then silence. It repeated several times before stopping. *[Why are you showing me this memory? I was spacesick.]*

Mother ignored his question and turned the spacesickness memory around as if it were a real, three-dimensional object. She searched the sickness, again and again. It was unmistakable.

"Master Faolin, he has the capability," she finally said. "He gets sick from curved space exits!"

"He is a true Life-Liner, then? Blessed be the Goddesses!" cried Brogan.

Mother's joy was apparent in her eyes and voice. "That he is!"

"What does me getting sick in space have to do with anything?" inquired Tam, confused. "Don't other people experience that?"

"It is only Life-Liners who get ill after curved space exits," answered Brogan. "It is not known why. I get violently ill for almost two hours. How about you?"

Tam was stunned. "I got sick for about an hour."

"Impressive, right, Mother?" crowed Brogan.

"Indeed, young Master. We have a match, if you so wish."

"Wait a minute!" Tam interrupted. "Do I have a say in this?"

"Of course you do!" Brogan replied. "The process may begin now, but you can still back out any time—at least until about one Alorion year later. More than enough time for the two us to get to know each other—maybe fall in love!" Brogan was on the verge of jumping for joy.

"This is a lot to think about!" Tam chided, watching Brogan with a curious eye.

[Take as much time as you need,] he felt Mother say. *[Go back to Brogan's apartment and discuss this. You will be better equipped to make a decision in a few days.]*

[And if we become linked, what happens then?]

[You will remain linked for life, until you both die. If one of you dies, the other dies, too. However, the joy of linking is so much more than the risk of early death. Discuss it with Brogan.]

Brogan knelt down and took his hand. "There's a lot of time to think, Tam. Let's go home and get to know each other. It'll be fun." He leaned closer and whispered, "We can play all night long."

Tam's cheeks flushed.

Brogan ignored him and continued. "Tam, I love the feeling of you inside me." He grabbed Tam's arms and almost shook him. "Can you imagine what it would feel like when we are Life-Liners? Double orgasms!"

"Something is telling me to say yes—and no, it's not just the double orgasms! I'll consider it. Can we discuss this in private?" He cast a guilty look at Mother, then turned back to Brogan. Tam's eyes softened as he looked at him. It was hard to be annoyed with him. Still held in Mother's grasp, he became more solemn. Clearing his throat, he asked her, "Mother, when do you want us back here to give you my—I mean, *our* decision?"

"I'll know when the decision is made, young Master Tam," she laughed.

Brogan bent down and hugged Tam before turning back to her. "Good evening, Mother. Blessings to the Sirens. We'll see you very soon." He stood and bowed.

"Certainly," she answered as she sat back in her chair, finally letting go of Tam's temples. Tam let out a breath, rose, and bowed.

As she faded back into the darkness, the light from above fading to nothing, Mother sent a message to the other Sisters without their knowing. *[We may soon have another connection to help us toward our goal!]*

The two men stood for a moment in complete blackness, until the heavy door creaked open, allowing the light of the corridor to spill over the threshold and guide them out.

"Time to go, Tam," said Brogan.

Time, indeed. Tam blocked the thought from being shared with Brogan, though he could probably sense the truth by the look on his face.

They walked out of the room, past the sentry priestesses beside the door, past the mesmerizing chorus of voices, and out through the massive door, which clunked closed behind them and was followed by the sound of latches being bolted.

"Home, Tam." Brogan pulled his hand.

They left the grounds of the Convent, letting go of each other at the exit, though they still longed for each other's touch. But Brogan didn't let it bother him. He was almost skipping down the street. Tam found himself wishing he were more like Brogan. But his practicality would always win out in the end. Still, the thought of double orgasms lingered in his mind. But they had no choice but to hide from the eyes and ears of the Senate. The walk was a lot more subdued than the thoughts that flew back and forth between them on their way home.

Chapter 7
Ponderings

"You are pushing for something aren't you, Brogan? This is the spot where we met."

"It was quite romantic, wasn't it?" Brogan whispered in his ear.

As they were hungry, they had stopped at the Tigress Eye Café, where, a little more than three weeks ago to the day, they had met. The sunlight was low in the sky. Tam noticed Brogan had chosen the table at which they had first laid eyes and minds on each other.

"Well, yes. But also mysterious, and a little scary for me," Tam whispered back.

"Tam, you can't hide your thoughts from me. I can sense your feelings. Why are you afraid of linking?"

Tam squirmed in his seat and looked at the floor, but remained silent.

"Come on, honest now. Are you afraid of commitment?"

Tam crossed his arms and stretched his legs out under the table, looking the other way.

Brogan's eyes softened. "Maybe a little too much to absorb in such a short time, I suppose."

"That is an understatement, Brogan. Look at it from my point of view." Tam paused for a moment and frowned. "I met you in this bar several weeks ago. We've had passionate sex, and I've spent a few weeks living with you. But I've only just arrived in Port City, and now I'm expected to move to a farm in the mountains, link with you to make us a so-called Life-Line pair, and become some sort of ward for the Siren Mother and her Convent. To top it off, I don't understand why the Mother Priestess thinks I'm important. Why is she in such a rush to have us linked anyway? Couldn't we spend some time getting to know each other?"

[*Do you feel any kind of emotion for me, Thamara Amergan?*]

Tam refused to send a message back, sensing the more formal use of his name as something serious. "It's hard for me to understand, Brogan. I feel so many emotions—when we have sex, spend time together, and just be." He wiggled a bit in his seat.

"Is that so bad?"

"Of course not. I might even venture to say..." Tam paused and felt himself blushing. [I think I have feelings for you—something I've never felt before.] "I find it all so unnerving. I don't understand it." He placed his head in his hands and turned away from Brogan so he wouldn't see the tears brimming in the corner of his eyes. But Brogan wasn't fooled.

"I think it's wonderful you feel something for me, Tam. You don't need to hide your feelings anymore. The Mother Priestess will see that we are safe. She told me the farm is quite productive. There's room for chickens and other animals if you want, Tam. I bet we could get a couple of horses to ride." Brogan placed a gentle hand on Tam's shoulder.

Tam thought about the horses. He had always loved the animals on his home world. Having his own would be wonderful. And then there was the beautiful, sexy, carefree Brogan. Was it really possible to fall in love with someone in less than a month? He frowned.

"Look, I'm just overwhelmed. If I told you I was becoming very fond of you, would that be enough?" He looked around with fear in his eyes, in case someone might be eavesdropping. He whispered: "I'm afraid of the Senate."

[Tam, all the more reason to send me messages. We can be more private and safe that way. Take a risk and share with me, please!]

Tam smiled as his eyes wrinkled up. A tear ran down the right side of his face. [I guess I can't hide from you, can I? I feel very strong emotions for you.]

Brogan felt on the verge of tears, too. [Can you sense that I'm falling in love with you, too, Tam? I've known gentle love before, but nothing this deep. I was drawn to you that night as I wandered the streets alone. I couldn't help myself. I had to walk into this café and find you.]

[How would someone like me know what it feels like to be in love?]

[Well, describe it to me. Come on—don't hold back.]

[I feel sick to my stomach. I can't seem to focus on anything. I have difficulty making decisions. I didn't sleep well, either, last night.]

[Sounds like love to me!] Brogan laughed. [I've been feeling the same way.]

Tam laughed, too. [What will it feel like to be linked with a Life-Line, Brogan? Will we have private thoughts, as well as shared ones?]

[*You mean, will I know when you're lying?*] He smiled and discreetly squeezed Tam's leg under the table.

Brogan paused as the waitress sailed up to their table in her glowing, almost see-through dress. "Want anything, boys? The holomenu has new items on it today. You might like the Siren soup." She winked at them before projecting to them: [*The Mother is everywhere. I will keep prying eyes and minds off you while you are here. Priestess Anghelloise at your service, boys!*]

Without missing a beat, Brogan responded. [*You can't hide from the priestesses, can you? It is nice to know you are here, Anghelloise. Maybe you could explain a Life-Line to Tam better than I.*]

[*Serve soup and explain Life-Lines? I had better get a decent tip!*] She grinned and responded, "Boys, take all the time you need to order. I still suggest the soup." She moved onto the next table, her dress shimmering, and sent a parting message to Tam: [*You have a lot to learn, young mentalist. You have power that is almost unheard of on this planet. To link with Brogan would bring you such completeness. Do not doubt your feelings for him. You love him, and I can assure you he is the one for you. There are no permanent Life-Lines meant for you other than this.*] She was speaking to the women at the next table. "And what would you like tonight, ladies?" She was talented, sharing this mental conversation and speaking aloud at once.

Tam couldn't hear the response from the women ordering their food but heard one more thing from Anghelloise: [*Your love is preordained. Trust in the Siren Mother, Master Amergan.*]

[*Trust them, Tam,*] Brogan echoed.

"The soup it is, then!" he said to Brogan, grinning.

Chapter 8
Unified

A week later, he stood in front of the Holy Siren Mother, his decision made. There was no doubt in his mind that it was the right one. After so much mental linking and such intimacy, Tam had no doubt he knew who Brogan was.

He was back in the room. Mother was leaning into the light from her seat. *[I now know what I want, Mother. I wish to be linked with Brogan.]* He shuffled his feet nervously.

[Bless you, young man! It is about time!]

Brogan stood beside him, a tear running down his cheek. His hand was in Tam's, noticeably shaking with excitement. His usual joviality was held in check, as though he knew what was about to happen.

[What must we now do, Mother? How do Brogan and I join together?]

[You need to do little. The Sisterhood will take care of the final steps. They will guide you to the choir room. I'll join you there. First, I must ready myself for the ritual.] At this, the room went dark, like last time, and they stood waiting for the door to open.

[Bless you, Mother!] Brogan's exclamation echoed in Tam's mind as he turned to Brogan and embraced him in the darkness.

[I should be frightened, Brog, but I'm not.]

Brogan squeezed him harder. *[Mother said it is our path to take. We belong together. Are you ready to be mine forever?]*

A bright stream of light and the sound of Siren song entered the room as a Sister opened the door to Mother's chamber. She guided them out into the incense-filled hallways, the light wavering through the smoke, the ever-present singing echoing down the hall. It grew stronger as they approached. Both men began to feel a little unsteady, but they were soon supported on both sides by Sisters, dressed in their rustling white robes and red sashes.

Dazed, they felt as though they were slowing down in time. The sound of the Sirens' singing was a crescendo of angelic voices vibrating in their ears. They entered through the archway of song, which seemed carved. The carvings were alive, vibrating to the sound. They seemed to be echoing the same message: *[You are home. You belong. You are to be Life-Lines.]*

"Prepare to take your place with other Life-Lines," the disembodied voice rang from above as they entered the choir room, which seemed to be without end. "Take the pews in the middle of the room and be at ease."

They both did as instructed, and Tam gazed upward to try and see the source of the song. But it remained veiled from their sight. Despite the request to relax, he could not. He felt his heart might leap from his chest. His hand clenched Brogan's harder. Brogan caressed it back in a relaxing manner from the pew beside him.

The singing grew stronger and more vibrant. Both men began to feel the music coursing through their bodies until they vibrated in unison with the chorus. Tam began to feel his teeth chatter and his mind melt into what felt like unconsciousness. They could no longer see in the natural sense. Real light was absent, but they could see the singing—a coursing stream of energy enveloping them. They felt their minds leave their bodies and rise to a realm that was new to them both.

In this incredible state, Tam found Brogan and smiled broadly at him. He could see him as energy with his mind, though his physical body's eyes were closed somewhere below him. *[Where are we?]* Tam pondered.

[We are in our Life-Line, Tam. Doesn't it feel glorious?] The Life-Line pulsed and glowed. *[I can feel your heart beating in tandem with mine. I sense your breath coming and going from your lungs.]* The energy between them flowed like a tide—forward, before drawing backward across their souls—pushing, then pulling, flowing like waves. *[I can hear the rushing of your blood through your eardrums.]* Their spirits curled together in a blaze of energy. *[You feel all I do, Tam. Mother told me of this. But to experience it is more incredible.]*

Tam's spirit body flowed and merged with Brogan's. *[I feel it all, Brogan. It is incredible. It's more than just mind-linking. I feel what you hear, see, and touch.]* His spirit stopped at what seemed to be a chasm. *[Your leg hurts. Why?]*

[The song is causing my leg to ache. It is a bone I broke in the past.] The image of a broken line appeared across the chasm and mended itself, glowing on the edges.

[We can feel each other's pain. Will I feel your sadness as profoundly as you?]

[Yes. It is part of being in a Life-Line. I feel all you are, all you experience, Tam. Only love this deep allows me to be part of your physical, mental, and spiritual being for all time. May there be little pain in our future.] Their spirits entwined and rolled across this new space, knotted together, never to let go.

[Brogan, love is such an intense emotion.] The love became hot streaks of lightning coursing like static across two conductors: themselves. *[It feels like the song of the Sirens. Are they singing pure love?]* Their spirit bodies vibrated.

[They're pure love. They do all of this for us—for our Life-Line, and for Mother's purposes.] Their hearts raced.

[What will she want from us?]

[Don't concern yourself with that. Her goals are above us and therefore divine.]

[I'm sleepy, Brog.] Their spirit bodies were now woven together, supporting each other.

[Sleep, Tam. When we awake, we will be integrated into our Life-Line.]

Tam rose through the clouds of song as he drifted off. *[I now know what love is.]*

∞

Hours later, in their chamber, the men drew strength in rest. For Tam, the experience had been so new that he had to keep telling himself he was still alive, still linked, still vibrating with Brogan. Confused, he sat up and spoke to the Sister tending to them. "Blessed Sister, I must talk to Mother. My heart feels like it is rending itself out of my body."

"Do you feel pain?" she inquired.

Tam rubbed his hand across his chest and thought for a moment. "No, I don't think so. My heart begs questions of the Mother. Once they're answered, I'll be able to rest."

The Sister conferred with Mother across the expanse of the Convent and nodded to him. "She agrees to see you. Let me get another Sister, so that we may support you. Walking will be difficult on your own."

Brogan was in a deep sleep, a smile across his face showing his total contentment. He would be fine for a time without him.

Tam smiled and gently touched his forehead, caressing it, experiencing the sensation from two points—his and Brogan's. It unnerved him, but he was starting to like it.

The second Sister entered through the door, soft singing coming with her momentarily as the door hung open and then closed. They gently lifted Tam from his bed and helped him stand. They walked across what seemed to be glowing embers spreading to the door, opening it to reveal the singing again. They seemed to flow down the hallway instead of walking. In his state, perhaps he then realized they *were* floating.

When they reached Mother's chamber, the light streaming from the ceiling looked different to Tam. There were themes and ideas in it, though they did not reveal themselves to him. He may even have seen the link between himself and Brogan in that stream of light.

"Mother?"

She leaned into the light and smiled.

"Yes Thamara-Afil. I shall hear your queries."

"What is our purpose?" Tam asked.

"You are part of a long line of men. You are no longer just sodbent, but *Mentis sapiens*— the Life-Liners."

"What does it mean for me?" He paused, still confused. "I mean, for us? I feel Brogan's mind linked to mine. I can experience what he feels. Is it possible that others may tap into this connection and betray us? Could we not be imprisoned for this?"

"Do not concern yourself with the mental capacities of others. It is the Siren Sisters that concern themselves with that. Your Life-Line is known only to the Motherhood, and we exist to protect it."

"Will you protect us from being hunted by the Senate, Mother? Will we have to hide our love?" Tam frowned as he looked at her for an answer.

She paused, then threw her hands above her head. "That is not within our control. Your physical actions are your own, Tam. We can only govern your Life-Line, not your body. However, the Sisterhood has a place to hide your Life-Line and your love for one another. You are already registered with the Senate Farming Department as residents of the Gorbander farming commune in the Montooth Mountains. You will find it has a pleasant and temperate climate and easy access to the natural gifts the Goddesses grant from the soil. The Senate does not often send officials to the commune. We have seen to that. You will find safety there."

He relaxed momentarily before tensing with a new thought. "What will you require from us, Mother? What are our obligations to the Sisterhood?"

"Nothing, my son. We will contact you when we are ready. Leave me now, and take the rest you need to recover. Your Life-Line is like a wound: it needs time to heal. Quizzing me will not help that." She smiled, despite her stern words. "Go sleep and heal, Thamara-Afil."

"I like the sound of the 'Afil' part. I am more than just affiliated with Brogan, now! Bless you, Mother."

The room darkened and the Sisters opened the door, supporting him across the flaming bed of coals that had drawn him there. Brogan's breath coursed gently in his mind. He was at ease. As he lay back down, he smiled, curling up against Brogan before falling into a deep well of sleep.

Chapter 9
The Road Leads Upward

The sail glider lifted off the tarmac of the Ali-Alorion flight centre. Tam and Brogan looked out the window and saw Anghelloise waving to them. *[Safe flight to your new home, my two amazing men! I know that you will love your new home at the farming commune! It's beautiful. We will contact you when it's your time to assist the Sisterhood with our search. Goddesses be with you, Tam and Brogan! I love you dearly!]*

[Goddesses be with you too, Anghelloise!] Brogan projected as he squeezed Tam's leg discreetly. The sail glider gained elevation, their view of Ali-Alorion expanding as it turned toward the Montooth Mountains.

Tam looked around at the other passengers. They were mostly farmers returning to their homes, along with a few employees of the Senate who worked the perimeter fences around the compounds. There were two other Life-Line couples onboard. He could sense them in the cabin. He didn't intrude on their presence, as discretion was key in keeping everyone as covert as possible. It was nice, though, to realize there were other Life-Liners and sodbent in the Montooth Mountains.

[Isn't this incredible, Tam? I can't believe we actually have our own farm to tend! What an amazing adventure we're going on! I am so blessed to be with you and experience this new life with you.]

[It will be amazing,] Tam replied. *[It's a shame that the Senate owns the farm and we're only leasing it. Wouldn't it be wonderful to own it outright?]*

[A minor issue, Tam! We have a farm to work, crops to grow, and animals to tend!] Brogan responded. *[The best part is that I get to do all of that with you, my love.]*

[Indeed, my beautiful man!] Tam looked out the window and saw the low mountains looming above them. They were shrouded in a slight mist, showing they were

moisture laden—a perfect location to farm. *[Brog, can you imagine the horses? I have always wished to have my own—and never thought it possible until now!]*

[That will be wonderful, my love,] he replied. *[I have a surprise for you!]*

[You're skilled at blocking your partner's mind, aren't you, Brogan? What is it?]

[You'll just have to wait. The block stays up until we arrive. You realize it takes a lot of energy to block out your mind from this thought,] Brogan replied. *[I dare you to try and bypass my block! If you do, you'll spoil your surprise, but I'll also promise a little something special in our sodbent tonight if you can!]*

Tam took up the challenge. He took up the thought Brogan was blocking and rotated it around in many different directions. Tam laughed quietly. *[I stand to get the prize tonight! I can peel your defenses off with ease, my mate! Sorry to disappoint you!]* He peeled aside what seemed the outer layer of the thought and revealed what was inside: another blocked thought. Tam opened his mouth in mock disbelief.

[You are crafty, aren't you, Brogan?] He began trying to access the inner thought.

It was Brogan's turn to laugh. *[You should find the many layers challenging. It'll keep you busy for the remainder of the trip!]* He grinned as Tam narrowed his eyes at him.

About thirty Alorion minutes later, Tam was still working on it. It continued to elude him when they disembarked. They caught the transport to the town centre, and he managed to finally peel off enough to reveal what was inside just as they arrived at the secret destination.

[You're kidding me! Really?! Oh, Brogan what an amazing idea! I love you!]

No message came from Brogan. He simply smiled as they went into the kennels and amidst the barking dogs inside. After inquiring at the office, they were introduced to a litter of eight puppies, all of whom were all adorable.

[Let your mind sink over them, and tell me which jumps out at you,] Brogan instructed. *[You may not know it, but dogs can sense a lot of our thoughts. Which one would you like?]*

Tam, not feeling his usual, practical self, felt giddy as he surveyed the litter. He began picking them up one by one, staring into each of their eyes. After looking at the eighth one, he paused and projected a thought to the mother, who looked him in the eye, lifted her paw, and gently prodded a little black and white male, the third puppy Tam had picked up. Tam knew in his heart this was the one that wanted them as much as they did him. He leaned down and picked him up, and sent a message to the mother. *[Blessed be the Goddesses for allowing us to take your offspring, my good canine mother. We will take great care of him for you! I have a name for him already. It will be Finn!]*

The mother barked and panted. She approved. Brogan smiled and nodded as he approved of the choice and the name. *[Come on, Finn! Let's go home!]* he projected. It made him glow to see Tam so happy.

[Brogan, you sly one! You know I love animals. Finn, say goodbye to your mother! She'll miss you!]

Finn yapped once, then licked Tam's face. "I guess that means it's time to go home, Finn! Come on, Brogan! Let's check out at the office and be on our way!"

They signed the papers, received a bag of food and a leash, and off they went. Tam held Finn, petting him as he squirmed and yipped happily in his arms. "Come on, you little stink bug! I can't wait for you to see our new home!" Tam smiled. "Oh—and you too, Brogan!"

Brogan laughed.

Off they went to the compound, the transport quietly proceeding on its way, leaving the three of them to ponder what it was going to be like. Tam held Finn close to Brogan, who received a wet kiss. Brogan laughed out loud and slapped Tam's knee. There was no need to worry about anyone noticing in the driverless transport.

∞

The transport continued onward down a sweet-smelling path, which was lined with fruit trees. They arrived.

When he saw the place, Tam clapped his hands, then placed them on his mouth. "My Goddesses! Is this really our place?!" he exclaimed. A tear ran down his cheek.

Brogan wiped it off and kissed him. "It is, my love. It's our home!"

Tam stood there and gaped. "Brogan, this home is *massive* compared to where I lived with my family. The Sirens honor us with such a beautiful home!" He headed for the door as Brogan released the transport. It turned around and went up the lane to its home destination, somewhere in town. Turning back, Brogan glowed at Tam. Tam put Finn down and squeezed Brogan so hard he grunted.

"I'm as happy as you are. You can sense that, of course, my love!" Brogan said. "I am so glad to be here with you and Finn. Let's go inside and see how the Sirens prepared things! I'd love to change out of these clothes I've been wearing all day."

Brogan followed Tam into the house. They both stopped in the doorway, taking it in with awe. Brogan put his arm on Tam's shoulder and squeezed it. "We're home!"

Tam laughed and turned to hug him again. "Let's explore!"

And explore they did. They scanned the ample kitchen, complete with cooking surface, oven, and chilling cabinet. There were plenty of dishes and cups to use, and a wonderful seating area around which they could eat. There was also a sitting area with two padded benches that looked comfortable enough to sleep on. Brogan tried them out and declared them as such, pulling Tam down onto one.

Tam picked up Finn and put his other arm around Brogan. They surveyed the space and felt at peace. "Let's check outside before we look at our bedroom!" Tam suggested.

"Good idea!" Brogan said. "Who knows what might happen when we do!" He winked.

Tam elbowed him, got up, and led him outside by the hand. Finn followed, and promptly did his business in a grassy area.

[Guess who gets to pick that up?] Brogan joked. Tam laughed.

[I'll find a shovel or something later, I promise. In the meantime, let's explore! I want to see the horses!]

They sauntered down the lane where the transport had let them out and turned to the left, toward what appeared to be the barn where the animals were kept. As they approached the barn door, it opened. A young woman stepped out. She had brown hair and the same skin tone as Brogan.

"Well, hello! I am Lucinda. I've been tending to your animals. Welcome!"

"Very nice to meet you, Lucinda! I am Brogan, and this is my associate, Tam."

[You can drop the 'associate' with me! I live here in the commune for half the year and spend the other half at the Convent.] She turned her mind elsewhere, away from them. *[Rita, come out here to meet the two Life-Liners. They've arrived!]*

Another woman exited the barn. She had amazing red hair and her pale skin was covered in wonderful little spots Tam had never before seen in his life. *[Welcome, my two Life-Liners, Tam and Brogan. The Goddesses are pleased that you are here. It has been a blessing to support the farm in your absence.]* She turned her mind back to Lucinda: *[Don't forget the gift!]*

[Yes, of course. I'll be right back!] Lucinda went into the barn and returned with a basket. In it squirmed four little kittens. "They've been weaned from their mother and are destined to guard your farm from the rodents that sometimes visit the barn." She handed the basket to Brogan, who took it and glanced down at the tiny little beasts.

Tam was taken aback by the sight of big, masculine Brogan looking down at the kittens all glassy-eyed, cooing to them like a bird. Brogan pulled one out and looked at it. Its little blue eyes reflected his own. The little critter proceeded to walk up his arm and perch on his shoulder. He was shocked by the sound that emanated from the little creature.

"Cats purr when they are happy and content," Tam explained. "She obviously likes to be on your shoulder." Soon, there was a kitten on each of their shoulders. They listened to the purring in both ears, standing there, almost in a trance.

"Cats have an almost mystical insight. They know how to tame the most wounded heart," Rita said. "They let you know you are loved. It's obviously a pairing made by the Goddesses!"

"Come on, kittens," said Lucinda, gently lifting the four little purring balls of fluff off the two men and placing them back in the basket. "Time to go back into the barn while these two continue their tour. They'll be back later!" She turned and re-entered the barn.

"Come," Rita beckoned, "let me show you the horses!" Tam and Brogan followed her.

Tam found the smell of the farm comforting. He could smell the horses and most of the other animals. To an untrained nose, it might not have been such a pleasant scent, but to Tam, it was glorious. It reminded him of the horse farm at the mining community where he had worked. He probed Brogan's mind and saw it would take him a bit of getting used to. But Brogan was willing and open to anything. Tam admired Brogan as he walked one pace ahead of him. He stepped forward and jammed his thumbs into his sides, giggling in his ear. *[I love it here as much as you do, my big stink bug!]*

Brogan tickled Tam back. *[As long as I'm with you, I'm happy, my beautiful Tam!]*

Rita was getting ahead of them, so Brogan grabbed Tam's hand and hurried them around the corner to the field. It contained four horses. Rita whistled and they ran up to her, sticking their heads over the fence to nuzzle her.

"Meet your new companions!" she said to them. "You have wonderful men to share your life with now!" She turned to Tam. "You have two males and two females. I sense that one of the females is pregnant, so you'll be getting a foal sometime soon!"

Tam leaned against the fence as the horses gathered in front of him. One rubbed its head gently against his arm. They snorted and pawed the ground. Tam reached over the fence and stroked each one of them individually, looking them straight in the eyes. Each looked back, then lifted its head and squealed a pleasant welcome sound.

He called out: "Brogan, come meet our friends!"

Brogan approached slowly. "I've never touched a horse before, Tam. Are they gentle?"

"Trust me, big man," Rita responded, "they are gentle souls. They have wonderful personalities. They'll also love to carry you on little outings!"

"How about I try just touching one first?" he ventured.

Tam laughed and held his hand out to Brogan. "Come here and meet them! I can sense they want to meet you, too."

Brogan approached slowly and stroked the closest horse's head. His blank face turned into a smile as he sensed the good will of the horses and the way they enjoyed the attention he was giving them.

"You'll be riding them in no time, you big Banderbeast!" Tam roared.

"You think?" Brogan replied. He was coming around.

Lucinda rejoined them. "You also have sheep in the next field and some pigs inside the barn." She looked down at Finn, who was happily trotting behind Tam. "Hello, little man! Your kind is wonderful for guiding the sheep into the barn. With a little training, you'll be a master herder!" She reached down and patted him. "Rita, let's get some pictures of these two with their animal friends."

"Of course!" she replied, pulling out her holopad. Brogan and Tam turned around. Finn sat patiently as the horses stuck their heads in between the men. "Wonderful," Rita said. "Some memories of your first day on your farm! With that, Lucinda and I will let you settle in. I've sent the pictures and instructions about the farm to your holopads. Everything you need to know should be there."

"We wish you wonderful tidings, our beautiful Life-Liners," Lucinda added. "The Sirens will watch over you as best as possible." She paused. "But do be careful around others!"

The men nodded, holding each other's hands. They approached the two women and gave them both a hug, which seemed important to do.

[Thank you!] Brogan projected. [Both of you are wonderful. Safe travels home, Sisters!]

[Be well, Tam and Brogan!] Rita responded. Then, she took Lucinda's hand and pulled her close. [Come along, my love! Let's let these two have their privacy!] She turned her thoughts back to them. [We'll return in a week to check in on you—and to say hello to our friends here. We've become very attached to them all!]

Both Tam and Brogan bowed, projecting at the same time: [Blessed be the Goddesses! May your paths cross ours again!]

The two women returned the bow and turned to the lane, where a transport had arrived. Rita went into the house, coming back out with two satchels. She gave one to Lucinda.

"Off we go! Enjoy your farm and your new friends! Keep an eye on old man Becker at the farm next door. He can be a little rough around the edges! Nice enough man, though!" She waved. "Goodbye!"

They got into the transport and closed the door. The two women waved as it took off.

Tam and Brogan stood there for a moment watching them leave. When they were out of sight, they looked at each other. *[What shall we do first?]* The same thought popped into their minds instantly. *[Right—Finn's gift on the grass!]*

Chapter 10
A New Path

The rustic smell of seed crops being harvested moved with the warm breeze flowing gracefully through the window, stirring the loose clothing that hung around Tam's strong frame. Brogan sat at the kitchen table.

"Tam, I want to ride a transport sail glider to the city today." He pointed at the sky out the window. "The weather is perfect for a trip. The winds will help the glider reach the port a lot faster than usual."

"Not a good idea! We have to finish the harvest, Brog. Think about it." Tam was cleaning the breakfast utensils. Finn sat beside him on the floor, tail wagging, in hopes a treat might be left from their meal. Tam ignored him so Finn went back to his bowl.

Having used the short form of his name, Brogan knew Tam was on the verge of relenting. "It's about time we took a break from work—and besides, playing is more fun." He grinned his usual flirtatious smile from behind the table.

Tam was less playful. "The Senate will be demanding their monthly tariff soon." He gave Brogan a severe look. "We don't have time for useless trips—especially since the taxes went up another four percent this past month! Forget the sail gliders for now. Maybe after the harvest." He turned back to the dishes.

"Always so practical, Tam." Brogan got up to approach him from behind. He put his arms around his lover and whispered in his ear: "If we sneak aboard, there's no need to worry about a tariff." Brogan reached down and pulled Tam's hand from the water as a dish fell back into the water with a gentle clatter. "You can tell what I am thinking, my Life-Line mate!"

Tam sighed and smiled, relenting. He shook his hands almost dry, reaching for a cloth before wiggling from Brogan's grasp to turn and face him. He pursed his lips and narrowed his eyes in mock protest as he gave into the game. *[Brogan, you are as transparent as Alorion quartz! I know what you want!]*

[So, what am I thinking, then?]

"That we can have sex and then shower together in the waterfall."

"That's my man!" Brogan reached down and squeezed Tam's crotch. "But first, I want to explore your body." He slid his hands under Tam's tunic and ran his fingers over his chest. He breathed into his ear. "Then we can bathe together." His hands went down his chest to Tam's stomach, then continued downward. "Afterward, we can hitch a ride on the gliders returning to the port."

Brogan's strong hands came out from under Tam's tunic. He held him squarely by the shoulders as he looked straight into his olive-green eyes. "There will be at least another four automated flights from the communion fields going to the port with harvest produce. There will be enough room to play stowaway—and do it on the sly." Brogan's grin widened as he pulled a lock of Tam's braided black hair from his face.

Tam's resolve began to weaken as he reflected on this. Cocking his eyebrows, he remarked, "Well, it would be good to bathe in the warm salt waters of the Mengal Sea." He looked down at some of the farm-induced injuries on his arms, which could benefit from a saline soak in the famed sea's soothing waters. Then, he looked directly into Brogan's bright blue eyes. Tam pulled him even closer, trying again to look severe. "I'm not sure about the stowaway part. What we don't need is harassment from the Senate police or, worse, an automated bot with no sense of human rights questioning us." He looked away from Brogan and out the window as he continued to ponder. "The blasted Senate, they've stolen so much from us." He paused, stopping himself from going off on one of his usual tangents. He smiled and nuzzled Brogan's neck. "OK. How do we explain ourselves if we are caught?"

"Play innocent—what else? If it's a bot, I have a few tricks." He pulled back against Tam's arms and raised an eyebrow. "Just think, after bathing in the saltwater, we could go to the Tigress Eye Café just before nightfall. We could drink fruit nectar cocktails and watch the sky fires as they sail across the equator. Did you know they're reaching perihelion tonight?" He smiled. "It would be fun to go back to where we first met. Please?"

Tam knew he was losing the game. He tried to keep it going with a mock stern look as he projected: *[And the crops? When will we harvest them? Who's going to look after the animals?]* He looked down at Finn, who wagged his tail and panted happily.

Brogan grabbed Tam's hand. *[The commune members will help out with the farm animals. Finn can almost take care of himself! Come on! Let's make love and worry about getting caught later.]* Brogan's tanned hands came up to Tam's face, cupping his dark brown cheeks.

Tam caved in, breathing out slowly. He reached for Brogan's other hand, brought his lover's strong fingers to his lips, and gently bit the palm of his hand. Making love might be a distraction from hopping a sail glider—or maybe not...

"At last!" Brogan sighed, closing his eyes at the sensation of Tam's bite.

Tam drew Brogan closer, feeling the pleasure of their minds meshing together, each experiencing the sensations of the other. Brogan's loose clothing slid off his body effortlessly as Tam's hand ran down his back and grabbed his buttocks.

∞

Having just helped Tam pull on his pale blue tunic, Brogan tied a black leather sash around his waist. "You are a handsome one, you know that?"

"Brogan, I love you to the ends of time. So, we'll go. I hope we won't regret this."

"Stop all the needless worrying, my man! We are just Gorbander commune farmers from the Montooth Mountains on a little trip to Port City, right? We're getting supplies, nothing more. Relax, Tam, and let's have some fun for a change! We deserve it."

"Well, it *is* our anniversary. It's been a whole year! We are now bonded." He paused and smiled slyly. He actually liked the thought of a trip to the city. "The time we've had together is something to celebrate." He paused again, then cracked a laugh. "OK, Brogan, let's go before we miss the next sail glider. One should be along in an hour."

Tam and Brogan jogged through their fields of maize and soy beans, their hands entwined. The sun was rising, and the air was warm and moist.

Passing through the last field of sugar cane, they arrived at the barrier, where they dropped each other's hands, on guard. The metal barrier was three times the height of either of them and was considered impassable for humans and land animals alike. The top five metal panels were electrified and would jolt the life out of anything stupid enough to try to climb them. The Senate, for some reason, felt it necessary to create this type of barrier to keep poachers out and unregulated farmers, trying to travel off to do Goddesses know what, in. They had to be regulated. Doorways at regular intervals accomplished this. Either bots or humans guarded the entrances in and exits out of the communion farmlands. A bot manned the one at the bottom of their cane field. Brogan had named the bot *Mechanic*—"Nick" for short.

"Open the barrier door, Nick! It is Brogan-Afil Faolin-Amergan and Thamara-Afil Amergan-Faolin. We would like to travel to Port City."

A sliding window in the barrier opened, and Nick popped into view as he separated from his resting cradle inside the fence. He floated in front of the two men standing at the edge of the field.

"Produce visual credentials and prepare for a body scan for verification of identity," droned Nick. Tam felt uncomfortable talking to a robot that used the same voice as every other bot in the barrier doorways. His language always seemed a little contrived, and Tam often felt like he was talking to a child. Both Tam and Brogan extended their hands and allowed Nick to take their identity passes from them.

"Come on, Nick, you recognize us!" Brogan assured the bot.

Nick's metallic body was a round sphere, with a human-like face on his side that could rotate around his body at will. He had two arms for grasping documents and some sort of mechanism that allowed him to fly free of the doorway. Brogan had once told Tam it had to do with magnetic fields pushing against the metal plates that surrounded Nick's doorway. As long as he was over or beside one of these plates, he would "fly." A pale green light streamed out from what would have been his navel if he had one, scanning Brogan, then Tam, from head to foot. "Officially identified as Brogan-Afil Faolin-Amergan and Thamara-Afil Amergan-Faolin, farmers of the Gorbander farming commune. Purpose, destination, and estimated time of arrival back to communal farm required."

"We're going to Ali-Alorion to visit friends and pick up supplies for the harvest. We'll return tomorrow morning after spending the night," Tam replied. "Is that sufficient?"

Nick paused for a fraction of a second before answering: "Passes have been approved for your identity holocards. Entrance allowed. Deadline for return: tomorrow, before both suns set. Have a safe trip." Nick gave them a mechanical "smile" that looked more mocking than friendly.

"Thank you, Nick," Brogan replied as he took back the holocards. The door slid open for the two men to pass through. The bot retreated to his cradle and the window panel shut with a soft click.

As they stepped through the doorway, they could hear the sail glider powering up across the airfield.

"Run, Tam! We can make it."

They ran alongside each other, running their hands down the silver metal sides and the helium balloon attached to the main section of the glider as they sped to their intended destination: a cargo port door about ten body-lengths in front of them. Computers and bots controlled the unmanned glider. Evading the bots' sensors was a lot easier than trying to fool a doorway bot like Nick.

Spraying a little sugar cane dissolved in water created a sticky substance that gummed up the sensors long enough to get into the cargo hold. Brogan was proud of having come up with this brilliant plan. Tam worried the Senate might end up programming the bots to solve the little issue of fogged-up sensors. He also hoped this wouldn't be the time the bots would question why there was extra weight in the glider hold. Their bodies added enough weight to be noticed, should someone or something check.

As they ran along the helium balloon of the sail glider, Brogan reached into the pocket of his blue tunic and pulled out the bottle of sugar water. They reached the main metal structure, where they encountered the sensor, which was pointing toward the exhaust jets of the main drive. The sensors were busy monitoring the takeoff protocols, not searching for stowaways. Brogan sprayed the sensor eye and picked up speed past the unit, Tam jogging alongside. They reached the cargo hold and used a maintenance code Brogan had won in a game of cards over six moon phases ago. He had used it three times now.

As they reached the port door, Brogan keyed the code into the panel beside the door, causing the sensor to open the cargo pod door in order to clean the rim and reseal it. They had exactly three breaths to get inside before it closed. Diving in after his beloved, Tam rolled into Brogan's arms and felt his adrenaline pumping, sensing the same in Brogan.

The door sealed shut. Brogan was laughing. Tam found his sense of adventure fun and very appealing, but he sometimes worried about how it might get them into trouble. But his attention was soon turned toward other matters.

With the success of their little adventure secured, Brogan promptly removed Tam's tunic and pushed him into the soy beans the glider stored. He leaped in beside Tam, grabbed him, and ran his tongue down Tam's chest and over his penis. Tam play-acted the shock of having sex in such a place, then smiled with a sigh and gave into pleasure. Brogan's wandering hands explored Tam's nipples. He slid upward and ran his tongue up Tam's stomach, his chest, and his throat, to his awaiting mouth.

As they kissed, their emotions began to heighten. Tam's hands went around Brogan's head, pulling him closer to him. Brogan kissed back even harder, moaning as their tongues entwined and their bodies ground into each other, feeling an intense intimacy. With his eyes closed, Tam felt the familiar blue aura appear in his mind's eye. He saw the image of Brogan and himself entwined, floating in the ether.

Brogan lifted up off Tam and stood above him. Looking down at him, he grinned a devilish grin and pulled his tunic over his head, revealing his muscular body and his member, standing erect with expectation. He removed a bottle of lubricant from his tunic pocket and tossed the tunic aside. He lowered himself, prepping Tam's penis with a generous amount of lubricant, pulsing Tam's member gently but firmly with his hand.

"Take me, Tam," Brogan breathed in Tam's ear as his body slid on top of his.

Tam moaned and closed his eyes, feeling the pleasure of penetrating from his body and being penetrated via Brogan's.

Their bodies soon fell into a rhythmic pushing and rolling, Brogan straddling Tam, his knees bent, riding him. Brogan leaned forward and began kissing him passionately. Their aura began to shine brighter in their minds' eye, their mental bodies entwining into one entity of pulsing light that sent shockwaves through their physical bodies. Gradually, they rolled across the soft pile of soy beans being sent to Port City for processing, arms and legs flailing, until they climaxed at the same time, their bodies hitting the far side of the cargo hold. Brogan leaned upward and forward on Tam's member, turning his head upward, crying out in a way that caused their aura to twist and tighten into a wave that was breaking in multiple directions.

Tam opened his eyes as Brogan collapsed onto his body, both still vibrating from the dual sensations of their intertwined Life-Line. As the wave receded, they both gasped and breathed in—first quickly, then slowly, returning to normal. Tam opened his eyes to find Brogan's blue eyes staring into his, a smile on his face showing that he, too, was satiated. Tam's body quivered from the dual orgasms.

[I love you, Thamara-Afil.]

[I love you, too, Brogan-Afil.]

Brogan pulled himself off Tam and gently ran his hand down the side of his face. He lay down beside him and placed his head on his chest, wrapping his body around Tam's. They continued gently running their hands across each other's bodies, both still tingling from their lovemaking. Brogan sighed and closed his eyes. Tam gazed down at Brogan's form lying close to his. He smiled and closed his eyes, seeing Brogan's image smiling back at him in his mind's eye. Their images embraced as the aura faded from bright blue to pale indigo to black as they fell asleep in each other's arms.

They awoke an hour later to the sound of the jets of the sail glider firing to steady the glider's landing on Ali-Alorion's airstrip. Quickly dressing and heading for the glider door, they made their escape the same way they had entered. They faded into the tall grasses on the side of the strip without being caught, giggling like young boys that had successfully raided the neighbor's garden.

Chapter 11
The Point of No Return

Brogan and Tam were in the Tigress Eye Café having nectar cocktails as they had planned. That night, the roof had been opened and the night sky was a flaming blur, alight by the equator sky fires. They were very drunk from the cocktails—apparently, they'd picked a night when everything was two for one. Tam hadn't drunk so much in eons.

With the night deepening, fluorescent insects descended from the trees and swooped into the restaurant, attracted by the treats supplied by the owners of the café, who knew the genetically altered fireflies were a big draw on the nights they were active.

Through Tam's drunken eyes, it appeared that heaven's stars were descending, bathing him in sparkling fireballs, which glittered and flitted all around them. It was all quite magical to him. He felt satisfied and ready to take on the world, no matter what. Issues of sexuality and farm inventories were forgotten in his drunken bliss. All he knew was that his lover was there, experiencing everything in minute detail from both their points of view, just as he was. Life-Line connections still amazed him. They were double drunk, too!

Brogan and Tam stumbled down the cobblestone streets of the market and made their way to their lodging for the night. They talked only in their minds, for safety, as usual. To passersby, they would seem like two men in deep, silent thought. Nothing suspicious to report to anyone.

Suddenly, Brogan stopped in his tracks and turned to Tam.

[Let's go to the spaceport and watch the ships take off and land! I love watching the way they shimmer and float in their anti-gravity fields.]

[You're kidding right?] Tam asked. *[We are very drunk!]*

[It would be a great way to end the night before we get some sleep, Tam. We can pick up the rest of the inventory early in the morning and be back to the farm by curfew. Nick won't be upset with us for being a little late!]

[How are we going to get to the spaceport?]

[We can hitch a ride on any of the transports going to and from the water port to the spaceport.] Brogan smiled. *[It's only a few credits! Come on!]*

Tam, still in a drunken stupor, agreed to go. They arrived at the spaceport thirty minutes later, feeling a little more sober, but still quite under the influence. Brogan was parading around, as usual, with a bit too much bravado.

[Brogan, you should really nix the silly behavior!] Tam warned. *[The spaceport authorities will wonder what two drunken men are doing here. They may suspect us to be thieves—or worse!]* Despite these thoughts, he giggled, shuffling his feet a bit.

[Relax, Tam. You worry too much. Let's go to the viewing station at the top of the spaceport terminal. The biggest and fastest ships leave from the tethers there. It'll be fun to see!] He gently elbowed Tam toward the terminal.

Into the elevator they went. Up two hundred floors, they sailed to the top. As the doors opened, though, Tam shivered, his senses as alert as they could be in his state.

[Brogan, I sense something very wrong here. Watch your step. I think we should have a look quickly, then get back to our lodging. Something does not feel right.]

[Always the doubter, aren't you, my love?] Brogan rolled his eyes, smiling. *[Tam, relax.]*

[I am going to get a cocktail inhibitor. I don't want to be drunk anymore, Brogan. You should have one, too.]

[Fine! Let me experience the drunken part—you can feel that anyway. At least we'll both be half-sober, through you!]

Tam, still in doubt, headed back down the elevator to the food and drink kiosks at the main entrance. They were open at all hours, every day of every week of the Alorion year. With so many passengers coming and going and so many cargo ships loading and unloading, profits were high for the Senate-run food and drink kiosks.

[Blasted Senate's grabs for profit!] Tam thought to himself, receiving a grunt of agreement from Brogan, two hundred floors up. *[May as well get an inhibitor and be the sensible one in this union!]* Another grunt from Brogan made it clear he wasn't in agreement about the sensible part. Instead, the image of "stuffy and uptight" popped up.

[Brogan, if I didn't love you so much—no, I am not treating you like a child! Maybe you need an inhibitor more than I do! I'm bringing you one, too!]

"That will be thirty credits for two inhibitors, sir!" the woman said from the kiosk. "Been partying a little too much with your girlfriend? Better sober up before you take a flight out! The authorities don't appreciate drunkenness!"

"Madam, thank you very much for your insight into spaceport procedures— and kindly give me my change!" *[Beastly, bottom-dredging worm!]*

Brogan grunted his appreciation of Tam's consternation with the woman.

[Brogan, I am going to get this inhibitor into you as soon as I can, before I hear any more gibes from you! Something is making me very scared right now, and I don't know what it is. I know that you can feel what I am feeling. Please, I beg you, wait for me, and take the inhibitor.] Tam opened the seal of the inhibitor and swallowed the concoction in several gulps. It didn't have a very good taste. *[Oh well, a bad taste is better than getting sick to your stomach. Brogan, you'd better not get sick. I don't want to have to experience that through you!]*

Another grunt came back to Tam, then, suddenly, a flash of pain like a blow to the head, which immediately sobered him up and knocked him to his knees.

Then nothing.

[Brogan, what's happening? I can't sense you. Where is this pain coming from?]

No response.

Tam picked himself up off the floor and made his way unsteadily to the elevator. The trip upward seemed to take forever as fear welled up inside him. A fog of uncertainty filled his mind. Brogan was no doubt dazed and in pain.

As the door opened, Tam broke into a run, panicking, sobering up with each passing second as he raced down the terminal floor. When he reached the end of the hallway, he stopped and stared in horror, seeing Brogan being slapped into whip-irons by the spaceport police. After knocking him to the floor plating, one of the policemen pulled him to his feet. Now he knew why Brogan hadn't responded.

[Brogan, what's going on?!]

Brogan didn't turn to face him. *[Tam! Stay back! Do you understand?! Don't come any closer!]* He faltered, so that his fear felt like a tangible stab in Tam's heart. *[Don't, please! The spaceport police asked me what I was doing here, and they didn't believe me! My Goddesses, they didn't believe me!]* His message felt like a sputter to Tam. *[They body scanned me. They found your sodbent in me. Tam, help! Help me, somehow! What have I done? I'm a degenerate!]*

[Brogan! No!] Tam stood there in shock, his body numb, unable to move. *[This can't be happening! No, Goddesses, no!]* His disbelief felt like an electric shock coursing through his body.

In his mind's eye, he felt Brogan's eyes looking deeply into his, pleading. It was eternally etched into his mind. He would always recall how he reeled and clutched his chest in horror as Brogan was pulled through the airlock by the police. It slammed shut with a loud clang that resonated down the hall and through Tam's body.

Tam was frozen in fear at the other end of the airlock. His body told him he couldn't respond. The whole situation played over and over again, short-circuiting Tam's brain.

[We shouldn't have taken this trip! I told you, Brogan! Goddesses, what are we going to do? Goddesses, help us both!]

[Help me, my love!] projected Brogan. *[I'm scared, Tam! Stay with me, please! Find me! I—]* He was cut off suddenly.

Tam reeled and fell against the wall. Lights sprung in front of his eyes as he felt a blow to the head. He tumbled to the floor, losing consciousness.

Something horrifying and inexplicable had happened. Tam no longer felt any connection whatsoever to Brogan. He felt as though he had had a weight placed on him that was so heavy, he could not breathe. His lungs heaved and his tears flowed without pause. He felt utterly alone for the first time in over a year. His shock was gut-wrenching—too hard to bear. He curled into the fetal position and bawled at the top of his lungs. His body had truly given up, too shocked by having lost contact with its Life-Line in Brogan.

It was there that Anghelloise found Tam, lying on the floor, whimpering. Mother had sensed something wrong and dispatched her to the scene. She looked down at Tam's poor soul, lying there in shock, and felt his pain and suffering. With much effort, she projected thoughts to him about getting up and being taken back to his room, where he could be safe from prying eyes.

∞

The trip back to the farm the next day was desolate and lonely. Even Anghelloise's presence didn't lift his spirits. He felt like a lifeless shell and prepared himself for the worst, expecting his own death as well as Brogan's.

The scene played again and again in his head, whether he was awake or asleep. Each time, it felt like a wound being reopened.

Part 2
Stowaways

Chapter 12
Looking Through the Lens

[Picture, if you would, a series of planets in an arm of our galaxy opposite our part of space. I wave my hand across the holomap of our galaxy, which the Ancients named Messier 100. How it came to be so named has long been forgotten. Our galaxy is a spiral, with many blue stars that are relatively young and hot. Our arm of the galaxy is also filled with another kind of blue—the blue of mental powers, and a gathering of strength.

If you look closely at that far arm of our galaxy and focus your mind, you will see sentient life living on a series of planets. These beings are unaware we are watching. In that system, there is a binary star system, with four planets with humans like us.

Join me as we meditate on the holomap of our galaxy. Our minds are now traveling these vast distances. We follow a path that swirls around the brilliant star-clustered centre of our galaxy. We then feel the pulse of the stars and sense the two major nebular arms of myriad colors exploding across the sky. We watch the light of stars speeding by us, faster, in a swirl of whirling balls of light, until we arrive at our destination—the binary system with the four planets inhabited by beings who are unmistakably human.

They are our distant relatives, who must have arrived there, somehow, in our distant and long-forgotten past. Recently, the Order discovered these humans amidst the chaotic emissions of the galaxy.

Do you notice something out of place? Yes, there is a ripple moving through the fabric of space. Yet at once, it is seemingly not there. As our minds pause to consider this paradox, we realize it is a sort of bubble, traveling between two worlds. With a little effort, it can be penetrated so that we may look. There in the bubble is a spaceship moving through curved space. A cargo ship is voyaging between the planets Alorion and Corustloth, carrying goods and passengers.

Amazingly, there are mentalists in that arm of the galaxy, too, who can be probed—though only to some extent. We have garnered certain information thus far: names of planets, the operations of the government system known as the Senate, and how each of the four planets are governed.

But I digress. This ship in the curved space bubble is what is important to you, my young trainee! On that spaceship is a human being whose mind is battling some sort of life-threatening circumstance. Let's allow our minds to flow across the curved, slender bow of the ship until we sense the humans inside. There is a crew situated in most of the front section, scurrying back and forth on the captain's orders. Let us not dwell, looking for the captain's mind—he is not the one we're seeking. His mind is almost blank, like most humans. He is no mentalist.

—Yes, that's right! There is a mentalist onboard! He has capabilities similar to those of the members of the Order. This is the reason I have taken you away from your training.

Let us slide our minds toward the box-shaped stern of the ship, just ahead of the propulsion systems, where there are cargo pods and holds containing goods to be delivered to Corustloth. There is the unmistakable rhythm of a mentalist's mind here. It is he who is in need. Do you not feel the kinship of such a mind? He may be one of those for whom we have long searched.

Ah, my young trainee, his mind is within your grasp now. It will signal like a distant mirror to you. I believe you have the ability to link with him and experience what he experiences. He may allow us to finally find the truth of the eons past.

Accompany him, as I must turn my mind elsewhere, to learn more of someone else's fate and struggle. I shall share more with you as soon as his story is revealed to me.

I sense your fear, friend. Do not be alarmed; your training has led you to this. You are ready. Sink through the fabric of space into his mind. Be witness to his experience. He will not know you are there, as he is untrained, possessing far less than our abilities.

There is hesitation in your thoughts. I shall assist you to your destination. Allow your mind to traverse across the cargo pods. Yes, I see you sense his mind now. Sink into him, friend, experience his life story, and prepare yourself to report back to me. I wish you mind-speed, my friend.]

Chapter 13
Flight to the Prison World

The vibrating continued, never stopping or changing frequency. The sound was like a gigantic insect clattering incessantly against the confines of a ventilator shaft. It was without end. The noise even seeped into his dreams, where his visions vibrated, shooting bright colors across the tapestry of his subconscious. When awake, his eyes would throb in their sockets and he would rub them until they began to hurt, sending flashes of light onto the back of his eyelids.

Tam's little hiding place was lit by a small red light next to his foot. It signaled a sequence of one long flash followed by three short ones. It would pause for a few moments, then restart. It was unclear to him what the light communicated, but the flashing sequence was now seared in his brain. Without the light, it was pitch black. Tam had a light stick, but seldom used it. He would be in darkness for the rest of the trip once the battery ran out.

Sometimes, he turned it on so that he could trace the lines of the metal plates and their rivets. He knew the total number, starting from his head, all the way to his feet. There were fifty-four. He counted them again to make sure when the light was on. He could still locate them with his touch in the darkness.

Occupying his mind prevented the onset of deadly boredom, which might lead to sadness, which would probably lead to hopelessness. Counting the rivets helped.

Tam was hidden in a storage tube that had a stale taste to it. There was little airflow among the crates containing supplies being shipped to Corustloth. All he could smell was himself. The suit's recycling kit still worked, but he felt constricted. He'd rather relieve himself like everyone else. But if he didn't use the suit, he'd be discovered by the smell of his own shit.

He adjusted his position with a small grunt and reached into his satchel to feel the contents: four water packs and seven foil-covered rations. The supplies should get him there—unless he was discovered first. And discovery would mean death.

He went over his memories, beginning with his mad flight to the station airlocks in search of his love on that fateful day. He recalled Brogan's pleading eyes looking deeply into his as he was pulled through the airlock by the police and slapped into electronic whip-irons that shone in the dim light of the corridor.

Now look where he is. Now look what I must do.

Tam remembered the blazing, yellow-white color of the whip-irons wrapped around Brogan's arms, sapping his will to escape. The image still reverberated through his mind as he fell in and out of what might have been sleep. He felt constant guilt, always wondering if he could have done something to save him.

He drifted off to experience his memories of Alorion, his beautiful world. They paraded slowly through his mind like a holovideo on a loop.

∞

Tam was jolted out of his dream. His arms and legs kicked out instinctively. His long, braided black hair draped across his face in response to his movement.

The vibrating ship had taken on a new whine. The ship was dropping out of curved space and slowing down to a stop at the latest curved space pylon. This would be one of nine times that he would have to experience the madness. Corustloth had a very long, elliptical orbit in relation to the other planets in the system, hence the need to have nine pitstops on the way the prison world. Curved space made the voyage easier than regular space, but it was maddening to experience each time the ship dropped out of it. Too bad it couldn't be done in one quick jump...

The ship shuddered and Tam's whole body vibrated in tandem, shaking pleasant memories of Brogan out of his head, insisting he wake up. Again, he had to experience this awful feeling like a slap across the face. It must have been something to do with the ship's mechanics, the reason he almost went insane each time they dropped into normal space. One of the negative aspects of being a Life-Liner.

He swallowed and fought the urge to be sick. Dreams forgotten, his dubious plan was at the forefront of his mind. How could he somehow succeed in rescuing Brogan from the prison on Corustloth? He quickly turned on his side, bringing his knees closer to his chest so that if he were to be sick, he would have enough time to pull an emergency bag from his satchel.

At that moment, he neither sensed the minds of the others on the ship nor Brogan's, which had dimmed even more substantially during the past week. There were no shared feelings, sensations, or thoughts; just a sense of presence that didn't echo much back to him. In effect, he was blind to what Brogan was experiencing. All he felt was his own potential madness—skittering images and flashes of color, like blue stars in a nebula.

He'd be caught and killed, too. He was sure of it. *It might be a bitter fact, but it's better to do something*, he thought. There was no turning back.

Tam shifted, allowing a numb leg to be free from the weight of his body. Sanity seemed to return as he settled into being in normal space. However, he hadn't had a full bladder before coming out of curved space and now, he had to urinate like one of his horses back on the farm. He did, into his suit reserve. The transition from curved to real space was always difficult. Hard on the head, stomach, and the psyche. As usual, over an hour had passed.

Tam felt for Brogan's mind, feeling its faint glow. Brog would have been in a brig on Corustloth since the beginning cycle of the blue moons of Alorion, which rose and set every three days. If he were Brogan, he would ponder the existence of those three moons that encircle Alorion, racing around in orbit. He would wonder how they aligned, creating a series of wonderful night skies filled with blue light and sky fires of perihelion. Tam, however, was much more practical. Instead, he dwelt on the doom ahead.

What would Brogan be experiencing in prison after four months that I haven't already sensed or felt through his soul? Have they been torturing him more than usual or even worse, has he been scheduled for conversion? If not, he will languish in the brig for several years, until his spirit is broken and he repents to the warden for his deviant "lifestyle." Although their lives would still be linked, Brogan's mind and his experiences would not be open to him as his lover—only the pain would remain shared.

Tam always wondered why all the worlds of the system had subscribed to the new rules coming from the government world of Kashtiloth. A man was free to love another man before the Senate took power. Now, those like Brogan and himself were hunted down and arrested without question. The police had started searching the hills where they lived, seeking others among those who eked out a living on government farms. That said, they were safer there than they had been in Ali-Alorion.

Tears appeared in the corners of Tam's eyes, and he reached up to wipe them. *Losing precious water*, he thought. Practical as always.

Tam's emotions were interrupted by the horrifying sound of an airlock being opened at the end of the tube where he was hidden. He quickly extinguished his light stick and crammed his body as close to the wall of the tube as possible, holding his breath. With the grace of the Goddesses, the crates Tam had hidden behind would prevent him from being discovered. He could not make a single sound.

Thank the Goddesses there were no sensor drones on these prison ships. The makers didn't think them necessary, as the ship was filled with prisoners who had been drugged into a state of harmlessness—near-hibernation, really. They were wrapped in "living cloth"—a material that injected their bodies with drugs to drain both their wills and their mental abilities. The living cloth mimicked their life signs, copied them, and then rearranged their bodily functions to suit the captors. The men were, in effect, powerless. All the prisoners of the ship would be invalids when they arrived at Corustloth.

Sweat beaded on Tam's forehead, his arm hairs trying to stand on end inside his suit. So far, no one had looked behind the crates to see the makeshift hole where Tam rested. It amazed him he had not yet been discovered.

The airlock door creaked open further still and torchlight swept across the crates, grazing the small hole where Tam was lying, frozen in fear.

"Gods! These holds stink!" the unseen steward said to his workmate. "Smells like the horrid agri-world stench of Alorion. Give me the clean smell of Kashtiloth—even sterile Corustloth in a pinch."

Tam heard a muffled response from behind the first man, and though he couldn't make it out, he suspected it was nothing positive about Alorion.

"There are no loose materials shifting around in this hold," the first steward said. "Don't want to allow any moving crates to make the ship go off-kilter in curved space. Gods be begged! We don't want to prevent the captain the joy of discharging this load of degenerates. He'll take a good ransom, then head back for the next load. Wish I could get his ransom, given how little we're paid." Tam heard the man scuffing his boot against the bulkhead.

Tam knew that the captain did not care about the destroyed lives of those in the brigs. He saw only profit in shipping the "filthy" prisoners to Corustloth.

The airlock creaked shut, the light was extinguished, and Tam found himself again in the relentless darkness. One long flash, then three short ones and a pause—the light continued its incessant flashing. The adrenaline in his body began to subside and he stopped shaking. As he lay in wait, he knew the vibration would pick up again, the whine would turn into a shriek, then the ever-familiar vibration of curved space would resonate again as the ship continued on its way.

Tam fell into a trance, free from reality; he remembered nothing for at least a day or more. He didn't even care. Reality could be days away. Time dragged on as faint images washed over his brain.

He felt nothing but regret.

Chapter 14
Origins

Bennett Davis opened his eyes and detached from Tam's distant mind. He felt drained. It took all his mental strength to remind himself that these experiences were not his own and to separate his own feelings from Tam's. Remarkable. He had seen life through another man's body on the far side of the galaxy. He sensed a kinship with Tam, almost as though they were the same person. He now knew what it meant to be linked to another being.

What bothered him most was the question as to why the Order had chosen *him* to link with Tam. He was a novice. If this Tam was so important, why didn't the Father of the Order do it himself?

On cue, the intercom screen beeped and Father's face appeared. Bennett sat up to look more appropriate.

"Are you rested from your trip? Shall we discuss what you have seen?" he asked. "I'll expect you in one hour. We may as well dine as we discuss."

The screen went blank, not giving him the chance to respond. Bennett continued to stare at it thoughtfully.

"Will Father ever respect me enough to call me by my name?" he murmured to the empty screen. "I hope Tam's story is of value—that I'm not just on some sort of random search for the 'right mentalist' Father talks about. Maybe, I'll actually serve a purpose."

Bennett sighed and stood up. He pulled on his brown robe, straightened some stray hairs, and left his room, still feeling hazy. He slowly walked down the broad hallway, which was lined with silver windows that faced out toward the flower-filled courtyards. Here he was, in a high-tech facility, working on the mentalist business of the Order, in the midst of the jungle of genetically-created flora and fauna of the Order's world.

Bennett paused for a moment, then reached for a window. He placed his palm on the glass and silently sent the command, *[Open]*. The holographic window disappeared and a cool breeze proceeded to rustle his brown robe and brush across his face. He inhaled deeply. Despite all the mentalist training, he could still stop to enjoy the fragrant breeze of his world. He looked down at the blue bell-shaped flowers bowing to one another in the breeze and smiled. There were benefits to the tangible world, Bennett reminded himself. He allowed himself a few more minutes to enjoy the vista before reluctantly voyaging down the hallway to Father's chamber.

Bennett approached the priest's door and paused, taking a deep breath, bringing himself back to the task at hand: the intensive interview he was about to face. *Well, no point in delaying the inevitable.* Bennett's holosymbol was flashing on Father's awaiting door. He was expected. He placed his palm on it and sent the command, *[Allow me to enter]*. This would issue Bennett's holosymbol on the other side of the door, for Father. He would know Bennett was here anyway, though, with all his mental strength. But he may as well be polite.

The holographic door vanished in an instant.

"Please, come in, my dear friend. Dinner is on its way—and we have so much to talk about!"

"Of course, Father. It would be my pleasure to serve, as always." The door phased back into a solid behind him after he had walked through.

"Sit down." Father signaled Bennett to take a large lounge chair across from his. "Bring up the holomap of our galaxy, if you would. I'd like to show you something."

Bennett waved his hand across the table and issued the mental command, *[Summon holomap]*. His luck with mentalist commands was at an end, however, as the holomap failed to appear.

Father's eyes didn't waver from Bennett's. He smiled gently as he lifted his hand from his lap and effortlessly summoned the holomap of the Messier Galaxy, which began to slowly rotate between them.

Bennett's face reddened at his failure. He made a mental note to practice his commands when he had more time. He didn't want to be an embarrassment to the leader of the Order. As he brooded, some of the stars on the holomap began to sparkle.

"Do you see all these blue points of light?"

"I do, Father. Those markers indicate the presence of mentalists."

"Do you notice anything else?"

"Well, our system is here." Bennett, still embarrassed about his failure, tried to rotate the holomap to point to what he was looking at. It continued its unaided spinning despite his command.

Bennett sighed. Father looked out of the corner of his eye, effortlessly placed his index finger on the holomap, and oriented it to the point Bennett had been trying for: their arm of the galaxy, shining with solid blue light.

Bennett stuttered and continued, "Father, we are located here in the middle of the mass of blue light." His finger glanced off the holomap and it finally started to move—which he hadn't intended. He managed to stop it and prevent losing face in front of Father entirely by repositioning his finger and issuing the mental command, [Stop]. Thankfully, it did. He continued, "Father, our arm of the galaxy has the highest concentration of known mentalists, because we, the Order, gather here for the sole purpose of focusing our abilities on the search for the truth of our origins."

"Well said, friend. You are better represented by your fact-learning abilities than your telepathic ones!" Father chided. "What you do not yet know for sure is that our new discovery on the far side of the galaxy may be a vital new lead in our quest."

"Yes, Father," Bennett sighed.

Father's gaze was, thankfully, averted from Bennett. "Dinner has arrived, I believe."

Bennett turned to the door, where the holosymbol for dinner had appeared. Dinner had arrived without his knowing it. He had missed another mental point. Father missed nothing.

"Friend, don't make the effort. I'll get it." He waved his hand, the door phased out, and the dinner cart floated through toward them. The door reappeared behind the cart. "Ah, splendid! You are no doubt famished after your first foray into that distant mind. Eat, and tell me what you know."

Bennett was indeed hungry after his mental ordeal. However, it was proper to wait for Father to begin to eat first, so his hunger had to wait. Father was probably toying with him.

"Father, the mentalist is a young human male in his mid-twenties. His name is Tam. He's currently stowed away on a spaceship traveling between the planets Alorion and Corustloth. He's pursuing his male lover, who has been imprisoned on Corustloth. He's been labeled a deviant for his sexual orientation and is destined to either be killed or to rot in a prison cell."

"Are they in contact with each other?"

"Barely. But he knows there is a what he calls a Life-Line connection between them, however faint. He is running out of supplies and has no plan other than to arrive and somehow rescue his lover." Bennett paused. "Father, why would he be considered deviant because of his sexual orientation?"

"Not all worlds are as diverse as ours," Father replied wistfully.

"We are free to make our own connections and find our own mates. Why is their society so backward? What makes them different? How did they arrive on those worlds?"

Father frowned and held up a hand. "Hold on, young man! So many questions! Your youthfulness shows in your brashness. You lack the experience and the vision to know there are offshoots of humanity scattered across our galaxy—and possibly those adjacent to it. Your last question is the one for which I have no answer, though. I do not know from where we came! It is the Order's highest priority to find the truth. As for the rest, that is for you to discover yourself."

"Why are these humans any different from the rest of us? Why do they pique your interest, sir?" Bennett leaned forward in his chair, placing his hands on his knees.

Father rubbed his chin and reached for a plate from the cart. "The aromas rising from the dinner cart are absolutely captivating this evening. The chef has outdone himself once again. Have some of this salad! It looks wonderful!"

"Thank you, Father, I shall." Bennett finally got his chance to reach for a plate.

He served himself and waited to see if Father would answer his question. When he did not respond, Bennett pursued other dishes of savory soups, baked fowl, and steamed vegetables from the cart. Father sat, continuing to eat, seemingly ignoring him.

Father reached for a napkin, neatly wiped the corners his mouth, and placed his plate on the cart. "Friend, Bennett, it is up to *you* to find out what is different about them. Like you, I was also famished from my voyage. I've been attempting to make contact with this partner of Tam's, without success! It's quite annoying for someone of my stature." He shook his head.

"You know about Brogan, Father?"

"Ah, you know his name, then."

"Yes, Tam's mind is constantly meandering back to Brogan," replied Bennett. "Just before I left his body, Tam was reliving the period in his life when they first met."

"You will need to take an exercise break and sleep period before you attempt another connection, Bennett. I cannot spare any more mental energy to help you, though. I have four connections in three other arms of the galaxy to coordinate, and they seem equally important to me. So, I have called you from your training to become a full mentalist in this time of need. All other trained mentalists are busy. The leads are coming in, but I know of none of major consequence at the moment, other than the four I'm looking after and the one you are undertaking. My gut feeling is that it is one of these five who hold the key to help us in our task."

"Why me, then, Father? Why choose an inexperienced mentalist such as me to aid you in your tasks?"

Father sighed. "That, Bennett, is something that I cannot answer with surety, but I suspect I may know. I am reticent to say anything until we explore more. Again, it's quite disarming for the headmaster of the Order to be so helpless. There is something that you and those two distant men hold that makes it important for you to pursue this. It is something even I cannot do."

"I am honored to serve, Father," Bennett said. "I will begin my task soon, after I get some exercise and a sleep period. When will you want me to contact you?"

"You will know when it is time, Bennett." Father's eyes narrowed, then he waved the door open.

"Thank you, Father." Bennett got up from his chair, bowed, and left the room without a sound.

He passed down the hallway, deep in thought. Father had finally acknowledged his name. Bennett figured Father had felt compelled to do so because he needed something from him. *But maybe he has more respect for me than I thought. I hope I can do what he thinks I need to do. I don't have as much faith in my abilities.* He sighed and walked up the corridor, ignoring the flowers this time.

"My work is cut out for me!" he said aloud, with no one to hear.

Chapter 15
Diversions

Four days later, exiting curved space, reality rushed painfully back. Once Tam regained his senses, he reached into his satchel and realized some time had passed—along with most of his rations and half the water. He sipped the remaining water and ate a protein ration. He reached around and squeezed the bags on the back of his suit; once the water was gone, there would be the recycled water from his suit to drink. The bags also functioned as padding, cushioning him from the hard metal of the ship's skeleton.

Tam's stomach let him know how hungry he was. He had two food bars left. He cautiously nibbled on one, trying to satiate his hunger with what would have been considered a mere snack back home on Alorion. He missed the taste, smell, and texture of the fresh plantains, apples, broccoli, and the other vegetables from their farm—all staple foods for the star system. The dehydrated rations had a stale and artificial taste he couldn't shake.

He drank the last of the water from his last pack. Now, any water that he drank would come from his suit. Fighting his revulsion, he had to remind himself it was recycled. The idea of drinking his own waste didn't sit well with him. Tam recalled when he had purchased the suit in the spaceport on Alorion after losing Brogan to the police. He had used two months' worth of credits from their farm to get it.

"It could save your life, young sir," the man had said in the technical department of the spaceport purchasing store. "What you intend to do with it is beyond me, but it is not my business, I guess. You'll be traveling a distance by space, I'll warrant. It's one of our best suits. It is guaranteed to give virtually 100 percent purity of recycled water for drinking, and has small storage units for solid waste. The cubes click out the side of this panel." He had pointed to the energy pack on the side of the suit, neatly tucked away in the hip pockets.

There were now fifteen waste cubes in the plastic crate at the other end of the storage pod. The man selling the suit had said that the cubes would remain inert for months on end. At least the smell of his own shit wouldn't give him away. The name "stink bug" came to mind and he smiled as he remembered Cassie. He reached into his satchel, pulled out his holopad, and looked at the pictures he had of her. Then, he looked at the pictures of him and Brogan on that first day at their farm. He traced his finger over the one with Brogan, Finn, and the horses. *We were all so happy.*

Looking at pictures wasn't enough of a distraction, though. He began to sense a feeling of panic rising in his gut. He might starve to death or die of thirst! The instinct to run and save himself was very strong at that moment, and it was all Tam could do to keep himself from screaming or pushing the crates away from himself. Sanity somehow prevailed, though, and he calmed himself down by thinking of other things.

Goddesses! I'm bored of just lying here for hours on end. My body is so stiff and sore. I need to walk about. I'm like a caged animal.

He was used to constant physical labour on the farm—lifting bales, forking animal dung, harnessing the horses, building fences. The nearly two weeks of inactivity in this little claustrophobic prison had been debilitating. He wanted so much to get up and walk down the corridors of the ship, or better yet, to be on Alorion again, tending their farm. *[I miss all of that so much. Brogan, do you hear me]?*

There was no response from Brogan—just a faint glimmer of a feeling that indicated he was alive and awake. Nothing more. Tam felt like screaming.

He tried to divert his attention away from his longing and his fear. He allowed his mind to reach out across the ship and see if there were any "receptive minds" that would allow him in to scan through their experiences. Maybe it'd do some good to keep himself occupied with a few pirated thoughts.

There was so little else open to him at that moment that he risked probing the one person that scared him the most on the ship. He cautiously felt the edge of the captain's mind for the first time.

He recoiled as his mind approached the edge of the strange man's world of star charts, pod inventories, and crew management. The man scared Tam. This was the man who transported deviants—either to their prisons or their deaths. He may very well have been the one who had delivered Brogan to his prison months before.

The captain was like a blank slate, almost mechanical in nature. Most of the crew were the same. There were no Life-Lines like Tam or Brogan on the ship—only untrained minds susceptible to being partially probed. There was the man who paced back and forth in his room in the crew quarters, worried about his wife cheating on him while he was in space. There was the female doctor who enjoyed toying with the crew's health, dreaming up strange diagnoses to keep herself entertained. There was even a man who dreamt of being a lover of men but was too afraid to do so. His mind was not open to receiving thoughts from anyone.

Finally, there was a shadow of a person who he couldn't really locate. He seemed to be there, but also not. He had been struggling to figure out why there were occasional flashes of blue bell-shaped flowers and silver glass windows that disappeared with the touch of a hand. He even saw people dressed in strange clothing he did not recognize. The images quickly disappeared and then reappeared at random intervals. It almost felt like some of his first attempts as a child to make mind connections on Zemitis—those ghostlike connections that showed nothing but shadows of reality. The ghost image he saw then was particularly strong. Tam addressed the image with a call: *[Make contact if you can]*. Nothing happened, of course, but Tam felt he should continue to try—even if it was to just relieve his boredom.

What confused him was where these images came from. They were neither from Brogan, nor even from the people on the ship. With the images fading, his mind wandered. The red light continued to flash one long flash followed by three short ones, then a pause. Tam sighed and shifted his position. Sleep could no longer drown out his boredom. Time dragged on, deepening his desperation.

Chapter 16

Bennett's Reckoning

Bennett opened his eyes with a start, blurred images still washing across his mind—flashes of his connection with Tam. The intercom screen was beeping insistently, like Father was pushing the buzzer. It must be important for him to have been pulled out of his task.

"Yes, Father?" he replied, sitting up and waving acceptance to the incoming signal. His mind was clearing, coming into focus.

"My young friend! How was your latest foray into Tam's mind? What have you learned?"

He yawned as he sat up straight to address his elder.

"Forgive me. I've just returned," said Bennett. "Father, I've managed to learn how he met his Life-Line, as well as of his meeting with a commune of women known as the Siren Sisters. He has very powerful mental abilities for an untrained mentalist. He seems, from time to time, to know I'm there. He actually tried to initiate contact with me."

Father's right eyebrow rose, his face otherwise expressionless. "Really?! How extraordinary! What do you make of this?!"

Bennett fumbled with his robe ties as he felt Father's gaze bearing into him, even through the video panel. "I... I... I..."

"Spit it out, young man!"

"He has the ability to search other people's minds, without the training we've been through. It makes him quite high on the mental ability scale—for an untrained, that is."

Father's image seemed to grow, becoming more menacing. "Fires of Messier!! What is so different about him, though?! Yes, he has powerful mental abilities—much more than I had thought—but what prevents me from being able to penetrate his mind? What is it about you—a mere rookie just out of training—that allows you to do what I cannot?"

Bennett looked downward, acknowledging their difference in training. He didn't have anything to say, so just shrugged and smiled sheepishly.

In the projection, Father, calmer, seemed to recede back to his normal, electronic self. He tapped his finger against the table: one tap, shortened thrice, then a pause. "Well then, we don't have any answers as of yet. We have no choice but to have you go back. It is time you found what is so different about these two men. Please take your necessary rest periods and food breaks, and get back there as soon as possible." Father continued to tap his finger as he spoke.

Bennett paused to consider something on his mind. "Father?"

"Yes, my boy?"

"I discovered a memory of the Convent of the Siren Sisters, but all of the images began to waver and blur. I was almost cut off from his mind. I suspect that if he were to enter the Convent while awake and not dreaming, I would not be able to mind link with him. After seeing fleeting images of the interior and a discussion about the Mother of the Convent between Tam and Brogan, I awoke on my couch, just as you contacted me. It is all so confusing."

"All the more reason to get back into his mind as soon as possible. You need to find out more—clarify the issue and get to the truth!"

"Yes, Father. I serve to find the truth." Bennett got up to prepare himself as the screen went blank.

Father had a lot of expectations of him. Bennett just wasn't that sure he was up for the task. But he had a job to do, regardless of his fear. Father dictated what was to happen, and he would follow through. It seemed his reckoning had come.

Chapter 17

Stowaway's Reckoning

Tam returned to consciousness abruptly and, as usual, had problems remembering where he was. He opened his eyes, hearing the insistent whine of the curve drive and seeing the regular flashing red light nearby. Without warning, the ship shuddered, and the light went dark. Tam felt the hair on the back of his neck stand up. There was something very wrong happening.

Tam found himself totally disoriented, having become accustomed to the red flashing light. He felt like he was totally blind as he fumbled about. He located his light stick and lit it, then sighed, feeling better. It was a lot easier to deal with fear when you could at least see.

The whine of the curve drive changed pitch again. What on Alorion was going on? It was too soon—the ship couldn't be at Corustloth yet.

He cast his mind outward and found the crew in chaos. Their minds were jumbled, rambling and urgent. Their combined brains created a din in Tam's head of screams, questions, orders, and even prayers for salvation. He was right. There was something going terribly wrong.

Without warning, the ship dropped out of curved space. He knew because he could feel the usual panic of reality welling up inside him. There would be no avoiding it. It hit him hard. So hard that he vomited semi-digested ration bars and bile across his chest, onto the wall beside him. He wiped his chin with his hand and shook it clean as best he could. *Blast. If I had been ready, this wouldn't have happened.* Waves of reality hit him, causing him to shudder, again and again. He felt the smothering heaviness of real space. He had enough time to lament his fate—and Brogan's, too. He cried with abandon until he lost consciousness.

∞

Tam awoke some time later. There was no whine of curved space, no sickness. His fit had passed. But there was nothing else, either—no light, no sound—and very little air. The compartment was painfully short on oxygen. He had no choice. His friend, panic, was returning. His friend, the flashing light, had not.

He felt around for his fallen light stick, which was extinguished, but thankfully still partially charged. Its light revealed the all-too-familiar riveted walls and plastic and foam crates stacked and fastened to the walls. Nothing seemed out of place. Why was there so little air in the compartment? Tam felt more bile welling up in his stomach, his hands and arms shaking.

As he gained a bit more composure, he sipped some water from his suit and reached out with his mind to see if he could determine what was wrong. He couldn't make contact with anyone, except... except the man Tam had perceived earlier in the trip—a fearful man who lusted after other men. *What on Alorion?* The others' minds were absent. Why this particular man? Why only another sodbent?

The stranger was in a state of panic. His mind was full of nonsense. Tam caught snippets of images of food, sounds of cries, and a mind that could not accept what had happened—a mind that was operating instinctively, not rationally. Tam didn't bother to make mental contact to figure out what was going on, but grabbed on occasionally to images spinning in the man's mind like a book being fanned. He decided he had no choice—the man was hysterical and afraid for his life. He had to open the door of the cargo bay, betray his presence, and find oxygen, or else he would die, along with Brogan.

Tam pocketed his holopad and pushed the crate in front of him so that it tumbled to the floor below, making him cringe as the sound echoed inside the chamber. He climbed down and nearly stumbled to the floor, gasping for breath. The cargo pod door was just eight body-lengths from his position, but he doubted he could reach it, as he was starting to feel light-headed. Nausea rose in him again as he stumbled toward the door, reached for the handle, and turned it. The door opened with a gentle hiss. Tam had found more oxygen, but it still seemed in short supply. He breathed in as best he could and continued to stumble down the corridor, dragging his booted feet as he went.

Most of the lights were dimmed or off—just a flashing red warning light glowed, casting eerie shadows on the walls and deck plating. There were no people to be found anywhere. Where was the crew? He faltered along the dimly-lit corridors until he came to the compartment that divided the living quarters from the cargo space.

Tam panicked, breathing in and out several times. He had no choice but to open the door. Tam took one last shaky breath, turned the handle, and pulled the door toward himself forcefully. A loud hiss issued from the door as the pressure equalized. His ears popped. Breathing became a lot easier.

Stepping through the door, he was startled to see a woman unconscious on the floor, her face blank and eyes wide open in fear. What had happened here? Tam was shocked to see more people crumpled on the deck plating at odd angles. Some might be in need of medical help if they had broken limbs, but he didn't know enough to be able to help them. He soon gave in, rearranging some poor soul's head so that he wasn't facing down against the deck. The man seemed to have a pulse, so he moved on.

Tam wandered the corridors, looking for evidence of what had happened to the ship, but found nothing but more of the crew lying unconscious. As he pushed through the half-open door of the bridge, he found the captain slumped in his chair. The viewscreen was blank and the room was silent. A few lights blinked randomly on the panels beside the captain.

What about the other man who had been conscious earlier? Where was he? Tam closed his eyes and felt for his mind. He sensed him hiding in a wardrobe closet used for crew uniforms.

He reached out his mind to the man. *[What's happened?]* The man refused to respond. Tam bit his lip and resolved to go find him. He opened the door to wardrobe compartment just off the bridge.

"Are you there? Can you please help me?"

No response. There was flotsam and jetsam strewn across the deck. Dress uniforms were everywhere, thrown out of their resting places when the ship had come out of curved space. It must have been an accident when it did. The ship must be damaged, unable to make use of the gravitational forces that dampened the entering and exiting of curved space. But everyone would have been dashed against the walls and floors, exploded into bits everywhere. There had to have been something more than just a sudden exit out of curved space.

Tam finally found the man in the wardrobe compartment as he had envisioned him. Fear emanated from his psyche—and from his pleading eyes, which stared blankly at Tam.

"Why don't you answer me? What has happened? Why is everyone unconscious but you?" demanded Tam.

The man stuttered and shook his head, scratching the back of it nervously.

"I don't know," the man whimpered. "Who are you?"

Tam ignored his question and asked him another: "Do you know how to operate any of the machinery on the bridge?"

The man looked ready to cry. "Some of it, but I've only got level two clearance—pretty minimal training in bridge operations. For Gods' sake, I'm only the cook! I can't operate a Minorian-class spaceship! We're going to die!"

Without thinking, Tam yanked the man, protesting and blubbering, to his feet. "Come on, pull yourself together! Tell me what happened." He just continued his insistent, hysterical crying.

Tam slapped him across the face, leaving a nasty red mark that would probably become a bruise. He winced, guilty for having hit him.

The man seemed shocked at being struck and became quiet and almost calm. He fumbled with his words, rubbing his face, and whimpered. "I, uh, was in the kitchen, uh, preparing for the second run of lunch when there was a loud, horrid whine that issued over the communication systems. I watched as people fell unconscious all over the place. I still have a blasted headache from that sound."

"I didn't hear the sound where I was. What did you feel when we came out of curved space? Did you become sick?"

The man was clearly confused. "What do you mean? What is with these meaningless questions right now?" His voice began to rise to a higher pitch, signaling that he might need another slap across the face. Anticipating this, he ducked behind his arms and stated calmly, "Curved space jumps are easy to navigate. First, there is a blur around me. Then, when I look out the windows, I can see space bending around the ship. When we come out, I see the stars become points of light again. I get a nasty headache afterward, but the doctor cleared me weeks ago for space travel." He paused. "And please, don't hit me again. I've had a horrible time with all this. I should have stayed in my restaurant on Kashtiloth."

Tam softened his face. "I'm sorry. I have a very different reaction to curved space than you do. When we exit into real space, it feels like the world is crushing me. It feels like my head might explode. There's a sickness in the pit of my stomach, and I feel totally hopeless. It takes me more than an hour to regain my senses. You don't you feel any of that?"

The man looked shocked, clearly not understanding what Tam was talking about. "No. Not at all." He paused to survey the room—presumably for an escape route—then continued: "Look, I'm calmer now. Can you tell me who you are? You're wearing a government issue level three survival suit. What are you doing here?"

His eyes narrowed as he realized something foreign in Tam's nature. "Are you responsible for the ship stopping? How did you even get aboard?!" He began to grow shrill again.

"I am not responsible for what happened. You must believe me. What's more important, though, is to figure out where we are. We also need to find out why that noise from the speakers caused everyone but you and I to go unconscious. We must discover what happened to the ship. We're obviously not at Corustloth... it's still too early in the trip. Since we can't do anything here, we must get to the bridge."

Perspiration beaded on the man's forehead. He straightened his yellow cook's tunic and began to move reluctantly toward the door with Tam. His face was still red from the hard slap from Tam. "Yes, this is strange! Why are you and I the only ones awake?"

Tam lied: "I don't know." He pondered his hypothesis about sodbent being impervious to whatever sound from the speakers had caused the crew to faint. There must be a mental reason for this. Life-Lines or mentalists were impervious, but why? How?

With no answer forthcoming from Tam, the man squared his shoulders and headed off to the bridge, sniffling and wiping his nose on his uniformed sleeve.

They got to the bridge to find the captain still slumped in his chair and various crew members lying where they had fallen.

"I'll check the computer sensors," the man said. As he moved to do so, he paused and turned to Tam. "I don't even know your name. I'm Artagan."

Tam stuttered for a moment, shaking off the fear of being discovered, and gave in to the question. "Tam," he muttered, looking at the many arrays of buttons, displays, and digital readout panels Artagan was trying to survey.

Calmer now, Artagan looked at him and replied, "Well, Tam, we have a problem. From my limited knowledge, I can tell the ship is dead in space. We are not in orbit around Corustloth and are nowhere near a curved space checkpoint. The computers are functional, but not engaged to the curved space drive—wait, there's something else—by Gods, there is another ship at our port side!" Artagan punched a few buttons and brought the image up onto the main display screen. "It's a large cargo loading ship of some sort. It must be Alorion pirates, here to steal our cargo supplies!"

"Maybe they're here to rescue the men in the prison cargo section?" Tam queried.

Artagan looked horrified at the thought. "You mean the degenerates?! Why would someone do that?!"

Tam remembered Artagan's visions of lusting after men on the crew. If this man lusted after men, and was as conscious as Tam was, there had to be a connection. He then was struck by the thought of all the men imprisoned in the cargo hold suddenly awaking in their living cloth bindings. They would need help to escape the cloth if the monitoring computers weren't functioning. He pictured them trapped in the cloth as they screamed and begged for escape. He would not want to be in that state; he must help them, just as he must try to save Brogan. *[Brog, help me! I need your strength right now].* A feeling of empathy washed over him, and he smiled. Brogan, despite his desperate situation, was somehow alert to his need right now.

[I love you! I am with you.]

Tam felt himself tearing up. Brogan had never yet mustered the strength to respond like that. A shake of the head and the sound of Artagan's sniffles pulled him out of his thoughts. He decided to take action.

"We should get down to the cargo hold and check on the prisoners."

"Why would we want to do that?!" Artagan was astounded. "Do we want to be raped and killed by those degens, should they be awake?! They're dangerous!!"

"Nonsense. They are like you and me."

The man glared back at Tam.

"Don't look at me like that. I know your mind, Artagan. I can sense you lust after men!"

"You lie!!"

"For Goddesses' sake, I don't care whether you want to admit to your sodbent inclinations or not," replied Tam. "We can't just leave them down there!! Help me get to the cargo hold."

"Fine," said Artagan, "you want to put both of us in danger. Has it occurred to you that the ship that rests off our port might be more important than saving degenerates? Maybe you came from that ship and are preparing for an attack!! You obviously don't belong here—you use the Goddesses as a prayer! Only Alorion farmers and low life would do that. Do you not worship the true male Gods?!"

"Enough of the stall tactics, Artagan," said Tam. "I may be an Alorion farmer, but I'm not a low life. I'm also not from that ship. I realize you don't have a reason to believe me, but you must. I don't know anything about that vessel. In fact, it scares the Alorion blue sun out of me! There's little we can do about that right now, though. We're going to check on the prisoners first. Move it."

Artagan hesitated, then agreed, as his face still tingled in pain from Tam's hand. He needed no more convincing. "This way, then," he sighed, rubbing his face for sympathy.

He led Tam off the bridge and headed to the cargo bay through the same dimly-lit airlocks through which Tam had come. As they passed Tam's cargo pod, Artagan paused and turned to him. "You still haven't told me what you're doing here. I don't remember you on the manifest for the dinner menu. You obviously don't belong here, with the suit and all."

"As I told you earlier, we'll discuss who I am later. I'm begging you! It's more important to find out the state of the prisoners." As Tam headed past his cargo prison pod, he felt for the minds of the prisoners. *Goddesses, they're waking up.* "We'd better get in there and free them from the living cloth. Now."

"Are you out of your hell-forsaken mind?! We can't let them loose on the ship!!"

Tam had had enough of Artagan and his denials. "Forget it. I'll go by myself. Do something useful—get back to the bridge and keep an eye on that ship. I'll find my way from here."

"Blessed are the Gods. May they be with you when you are killed or raped by those men." With that, Artagan left, racing down the hall without turning back to look.

There's no redemption for that one. He's too fearful of his calling.

He continued to the end of the cargo pod section and arrived at the airlock door between the cargo pods and the rear prisoner hold. As the door opened without resistance, Tam realized the irony of having no locks on a prison transport. But why would they be needed when the prisoners were supposed to be unconscious and imprisoned for the entire trip?

Tam crossed through the second threshold and closed the door. At the very moment he spun the mechanism, he sensed something horrific about to happen.

He grabbed for the door to steady himself. The ship jolted violently, knocking Tam to his knees. There was another massive shudder and the sound of rending metal. It was the unmistakable sound of the cargo hold between the second cargo airlock and the prisoner hold being crushed by some unknown force. Suddenly, Tam was thrown against a wall as the cargo hold was seemingly ripped from the main ship. His head connected with the bulkhead, and he crumpled to the floor, senseless.

Part 3

Pirates and Potentials

Chapter 18
Detour

There was nothing but pain and darkness. Tam couldn't tell where he was or what was happening. It was only when he sensed the telltale feelings of exiting curved space that he realized he was somehow traveling. He lost consciousness again, a mysterious singing filling his ears.

> *"The soul of a man will sense the destination*
> *On the eve of belated arrival to salvation.*
> *A man with such sorrow and loneliness*
> *Has no need for sadness, strain, or duress.*
> *Sleep now, sweet man!"*

Bennett, in his distant room on the other side of the galaxy, shuddered as he awoke from the link, and began weeping.

∞

Tam groaned as he felt life coming back into his limbs. He tried to open his eyes but couldn't. Dripping water echoed in his ears as he realized he was lying in tepid water. He ventured a look by cracking his eyes open slightly and saw his survival suit draped over the chair beside the bath he was in. He felt his forehead and winced, feeling an egg-sized bump.

His eyes were now wide open. "What happened to the ship?" he wondered aloud. "Where am I?"

Tam eased himself up into a sitting position. He heard movement behind him. He turned to see an immense man sitting there, watching him. Tam had never seen such a big man before, nor someone who was darker skinned than himself.

"You are lucky to be alive, boy! We were surprised to find a Life-Liner in the holding area when we took it and ripped it from that Minorian-class freighter," he laughed. "Aye, quite a haul, mate." The man grinned widely, showing a set of very white teeth.

"The men in the hold—are they OK? What have you done with them? Why?"

"Funny for a naked, injured man sitting in a bathtub to be so adamant about finding the truth. He should just accept what he sees and knows!" The man laughed. "You are aboard the pirate ship *Starfinder*. I am Captain Farthing, at your service." He waved and half-bowed from his seated position.

Tam covered himself, realizing he was in an awkward position in front of this very large, rather intimidating man. "You didn't answer my question about the men in the hold," he stuttered.

"Goddesses, the nerve of some people!" Farthing exclaimed. "If you must know, they're squared away. We've released them from their cloth prisons, and fed and clothed them. They now pledge allegiance to the pirate confederacy of Kashtiloth."

"They're your prisoners, like me?" Tam asked.

"No, on both accounts!" Farthing stood up, lumbered over, and placed his massive hand on Tam's shoulder. "You're among friends here—we are all Life-Line supporters. The big question I have is: who are you and why were you neither imprisoned in cloth nor on the crew manifest? You are obviously sodbent—I can sense the energy bubbling inside that injured skull of yours."

"I was a stowaway," Tam confessed. "I needed to get to Corustloth without them knowing."

"Why in Goddesses' worlds would you want to do that, you pretty, young thing? Something very important, I gather. Let me guess—you are in search of your Life-Line partner who is imprisoned on Corustloth."

"Yes," Tam acknowledged. "He was taken at the Alorion space port over four months ago. I was hoping to be able to get to him and free him."

Farthing laughed again and placed his massive hand on his large forehead, feigning surprise. "A brave but foolhardy wish. These things are best left to experts like me. But wait. I notice you are weary. You must sleep now."

Farthing reached into the bath and scooped Tam out. Tam didn't even try to fight him—he must have outweighed him two to one. He patted Tam down and wrapped him in a towel.

"It seems I have no choice," he responded, still embarrassed by his nudity.

"Trust me. You're among friends. Give me your name and I'll let you rest. Then I'll tell you more."

Farthing hadn't reached the bed yet, but slowed, holding Tam in his arms as if he weighed the same as a newborn.

"My name is Thamara Amergan..."

"Aye, but try again. I know your name is longer than that—you are a Life-Liner. Those in the know understand the naming the Siren Sisters have blessed you with. There must be an "Afil" in there somewhere to show you are affiliated with someone. Come now, Master Thamara Amergan. Spill it."

"Thamara-Afil Amergan-Faolin."

Farthing stopped walking. "Gracious the Goddesses be! Faolin?! Is it Brogan?" His grip tightened around Tam, who winced, and Farthing realizing that he was a little overexcited. He eased up. "Sorry, my little blo'!"

"It is Brogan." Tam was taken aback. "How do you know him?"

"We mates go way back. But, as I said before, I'll let you rest, young man—then answer all your questions." He placed his hand gently on Tam's forehead, looking into his eyes as he continued carrying him. "Mother will be pleased."

Farthing reached the bed and gently placed Tam on the mattress. He pulled a single shimmering cloth up to his chin. "There you be, young Amergan-Faolin. Rest, worry-free. Be at peace." Farthing leaned down and, surprisingly, planted a strong kiss on Tam's forehead.

[Aye-aye! We are at your service, pretty man!]

Tam's eyes widened as he received the message, but as he felt the cooling kiss of the massive man's lips on his head, he realized he had no choice but to let himself be bewitched by this very large pirate.

His eyes shut slowly, but he could not find sleep. He tried to send a final message into the ether: *[Brogan, I am still coming for you. I love you.]* He could still feel the spark glowing, but nothing more.

Sleep was not possible for a long while, so his mind wandered back to happier times. Seeing his holopad, he reached for it. *That's a good sign! I still have it! Maybe I'm not a prisoner after all!* He fell asleep looking at a picture of Brogan.

Chapter 19
Parlance

"Wake up, Master Amergan-Faolin. Do you plan on sleeping for another two intervals? It's time you met my crew, my little blo'!" Captain Farthing stood at the foot of the bed where Tam had slept for the past day and a half. He smiled his wide-toothed grin and laughed.

"How about some clothing? The survival suit doesn't make much sense at this point," Tam remarked, not knowing what else to say. The whole situation still confused him. He might be in danger, but he didn't have enough information to make any judgements. Was there reason to run? He looked at the massive man and wondered.

"Young man, there is a uniform at the base of your bed. You should cut a very handsome figure in it. Call me when you are squared away."

Farthing turned, ambled out of the room, and closed the door behind him. Tam didn't hear a lock of any sort. *Maybe I'm really not a prisoner. May as well do as I am told and get up.*

He climbed out of bed and checked out his frame in the mirror. There were a number of bruises running down his left side and a large, bluish-purple one on his forehead where he had hit the wall in the cargo hold. *Despite those weeks in the pod, I still look pretty good.*

Tam walked to the bathing room to find something to tie his hair with so that he could comfortably braid it back into its usual form. The room was well stocked with odor inhibitors for his armpits, lotions for his bruises, and even a sonic brush for his teeth. A piece of natural cord lay on the counter. Farthing must have left it for him. The cord would secure his hair and keep it from unraveling. Tam found it a bit sad, though. It was often Brogan who would braid his hair, tying it up and then kissing the nape of his neck.

Tam sponged himself off quickly with a damp towel, applied the odor inhibitor to his underarms, braided his hair, and turned to look at himself. He felt a little like the old Tam, so he smiled. Life would be complete if Brogan were here right now. Grimly, he realized that Brogan was currently awake, and in pain. Tam could feel sympathetic responses in his leg to what Brogan must have been feeling at that moment in his distant prison cell.

[Brogan, I'll get to you somehow.]

No mental message came back, as usual—just a sense of helplessness.

He walked back to the bed and picked up the sapphire-colored pantaloons, black sash, and white, long-sleeved collared shirt, which buttoned up at the front. As he looked in the mirror, he noticed there was an insignia on the left breast:

$$\lambda \infty \, \Omega$$

Must be Farthing's pirate insignia. Am I a pirate now, too? It reminded him of the sail glider flight from their farm to Ali-Alorion before his stowaway run to Corustloth. The glider had had an infinity emblem on its side, too.

Tam returned to the present and realized he had been staring at the insignia for some time, still holding the shirt in his hands. Peeking around the corner, Tam saw Captain Farthing standing at the door, smiling, as usual.

"Squared away yet, young man?"

Seeing Tam's naked body slink out of the bathroom, it was clear he hadn't dressed.

"Not yet, I see. Young man, you are obviously ready to be dressed. Come on, then! Hasten, my mate!"

Tam reached for his uniform, pulled on the tunic, and placed the sash around his waist.

"Satisfied?" he retorted.

"Aye-aye. You are now a Farthing pirate, handsome boy. Come with me." He walked through the door and motioned for Tam to follow. "I'll fill you in on our plans as we walk."

Tam looked up at the imposing man. "What's all this about? Why have you hijacked a Senate spaceship, taking a hundred male prisoners?"

Tam contemplated the man's massive body as he waited for a response.

"The Lambda Infinity Omega League is a resistance unit formed between the Pirate Confederacy and the Sirens. We fight the Senate's plans of kidnapping sodbent and imprisoning them on Corustloth. We have supporters in many places. I am the muscle of the League."

"So it would seem," replied Tam. "Are you the brains of the operation, too?"

"Not at all, my handsome blo'." Farthing stopped at the door at the end of the hallway and paused. "Sense anything out of the ordinary?"

Tam looked at the door and felt a very strange sensation of familiarity, but couldn't quite figure out why. "I guess I will soon know, won't I?"

"Open the door, then."

Tam opened it to see Mother Siren sitting in the middle of the darkened room.

"Come in, young Tam," she said softly. "We have news of Brogan and need your help. It's a good thing there are people out there who can keep track of you when I cannot. Farthing caught you just in time to prevent your untimely demise."

Farthing smiled and closed the door behind him, sealing the three of them in the dark room.

"Blessed Mother, I have had your cargo delivered from your recent rendezvous on Zemitis to your private compound on Alorion. We are now en route to return you to the Convent, as we feel this is safest." Farthing kissed Mother's hand and bowed. "At your blessed service always, Mother."

"Farthing, you are a marvel. Thank you for offering to deliver me back to the Convent. But I feel that having the *Starfinder* too close to Alorion is not a wise move. I sense problems to come. I will return in the shuttle I left in when departing from Alorion. My pilot will serve me well."

"Of course, Mother. At your command. I'll get your shuttle in ship-shape before your departure."

"Thank you for rescuing this young fool and bringing him back to us." Mother nodded toward Tam. Farthing bowed deeply and flashed a wide, white smile. Then, she addressed Tam: "For taking the time to rescue you from your follies, I demand a favor of you."

[*Farthing will prepare you. I need you to infiltrate the Senate and steal the plans for the prisons on Corustloth. We shall rescue Brogan and the rest of the men being experimented upon. Farthing will go with you, as your guide and mentor.*]

[*Bless and thank you, Mother. I am at your service, and forever in your debt,*] Tam responded, as formally as he could, despite his shame for having needed rescue. He sighed and resolved to set it all right, bowing deeply to her. [*It would seem I have work to do.*]

[*A lot of it, young man.*]

[I am in your debt, Mother. I give my life to serve the Sirens' cause, even though I feel inadequate for the task.]

Mother ignored his self-pity and spoke to the captain instead: "Farthing, prepare him for the voyage. Inform the crew of your immediate departure for the Senate's governing city on Kashtiloth after you prepare my shuttle. I must return to the Convent as soon as possible. There is much to do."

"Aye! Of course, Mother." Farthing bowed and exited, pulling the embarrassed Tam along with him.

Mother smiled as she recalled Tam's response when he had entered the room, then sighed, thinking of how their plan might lead to disaster. That charming young man might die as the result of what she was asking. A lot was depending on him—a young, untrained Life-Liner, longing for his lover.

[Asset or liability?] she wondered.

The Sirens listening to the day's events via Mother's mind responded in chorus, all the way from the Convent: *[Asset, Mother! Our boy will be our salvation!]*

[We shall see,] she responded.

"The League will have a hard battle ahead," she murmured to herself.

Chapter 20

No Prey, No Pay!

Farthing entered the bridge with Tam in tow. "Commander O'Keefe, has the Mother's shuttle been prepped and fueled, and the pilot notified of departure?"

"Aye, Captain!" affirmed Commander O'Keefe. "All ready to go. I just took the Sister to the shuttle. She is preparing for Mother's arrival. Shall I accompany her?"

"Thank you, Jennifer, but I'd prefer to do the honors myself." He turned to Tam. "In fact, Mr. Amergan-Faolin, you will accompany me. Commander O'Keefe, I give you the bridge." Farthing turned to go, but stopped suddenly.

[Farthing! Alert your crew! A warship is about to come out of curved space!] Mother's mental warning leaped into Farthing's mind as well as Tam's.

"Commander! Prepare for combat! A warship is on its way!" Farthing turned back to his captain's chair.

"Aye, sir!" she said as she opened a ship-wide channel. "Attention, all hands! Battle stations!"

"Tam, take a seat beside me—and keep quiet until I scope out this situation."

Tam swallowed, nodded, and slipped into the chair beside him.

[I don't believe they know we're here!] Mother messaged. *[Prepare an ambush, Farthing. It is a Senate warship! I can sense it!]*

"Commander! Leave your station and bring Mother to the bridge! It's the safest place for her. In fact, bring her pilot here, too!" Farthing barked.

"Aye, aye, Captain. On my way!" Commander O'Keefe rose and hurried out the door just before a security guard closed it.

"First Hand Byrne! Status of weapons?"

"Armed and ready, Captain!" Byrne called out. "Sir! Look—portside! The warship is emerging from curved space! Shall I target their weapons, sir?"

"Aye! Take out as many as you can! Start with their lasers, then the railguns! Then the missile launchers. We'll have to be quick." He turned to Tam. "Are you ready to see how pirates do things?"

Tam nodded but said nothing.

"There it is!" Byrne shouted as everyone looked at the screen, which showed a Senate warship shimmering as it exited curved space. "Firing railguns!"

Trails of light streaked towards the ship, colliding with it within seconds. The ship had no time to prepare for the assault. Bits and pieces of its weaponry flew off at all angles, small explosions spreading outward.

"Firing lasers!" Byrne called.

Flashes illuminated the hull of the warship as several railguns were destroyed. Those not damaged now began firing at the *Starfinder*.

"They're targeting our lasers and railguns!" Byrne shouted. "Brace for impact!"

Tam involuntarily raised his arms in front of his face in self-defense. He felt and heard the impacts as the ship began to shake.

"Byrne! Fire lasers again—if we have any left!" Farthing yelled. "Target the main part of the ship!"

[Belay that, Captain!]

Farthing and Tam turned to see Mother, O'Keefe, and the Siren pilot entering the bridge.

"Byrne, hold!" he ordered.

[By all means, target their weapons—but not the ship!] Mother signaled as she took a seat beside Tam.

"Give me a damage report on the *Starfinder*!" yelled Farthing.

"One laser left, two railguns!" Byrne responded.

"Target the rest of their railguns and lasers with what we have left, Byrne!"

"Aye, aye!"

Lasers impacted the warship and railgun pellets followed. There were multiple flashes of light and small explosions.

"They've launched fighters!" O'Keefe shouted as she took her station. "Twenty-five of them!"

The fighters streaked out of the warship toward the *Starfinder*.

[Farthing, hold your fire!] Mother messaged. *[Let the Sirens take care of it! Open a channel to the Convent—immediately!]*

"Hold your fire!" Farthing bellowed. "O'Keefe, open communication to the Convent! Mother is preparing to help us! Open a channel to the warship!"

"Channel opened. Communication is two-way!" O'Keefe responded.

"This is Captain Farthing of the *Starfinder*. Please respond." He turned to Commander O'Keefe. "Are they receiving our signal?"

O'Keefe nodded.

"Mother, now!"

Mother and her pilot had already started, closing their eyes as they began to sing. The sound started softly, then gradually picked up as more voices joined the two of them via the communication link. The fighters began firing at the *Starfinder's* weaponry. As the railguns pellets raked the ship, they suddenly veered off, at full speed, in random directions. They began tumbling and turning, as though they were operated by drunken pilots. The volume of the singing increased to a level just short of being unbearable for the crew.

"The moment they opened their communication to my call, they were hit with the Siren song!" Farthing explained. "I bet they be dazed and confused. They should be gettin' the Siren song full force—"

Suddenly, the fighters seemed to gain control of their jets and began returning to their launch bays.

"What's happening? Why are they doing that?" Tam asked Farthing.

"The Sirens are sending them a message to return to their ship. Their minds have no choice but follow the instructions they've been given!" Farthing responded. "Mother, our weapons are damaged. We have no defenses at the moment. Orders?"

Mother, in her trance, was unable to respond verbally, but Farthing could see in her eyes that she was waiting for the appropriate question.

"Go on the offensive?" he asked.

She nodded.

"Damage them?"

Again, she nodded.

"Head on?"

Negative.

"Destroy engine exhausts and disable them?"

Another nod.

"Byrne, set a course around the warship, to its rear! O'Keefe, prepare the nipper! We're going to rip their back end off!"

"Aye, aye! Nipper engaged," she replied.

"The nipper?" Tam asked.

"The salvage claw we used to rescue you and the prisoners! We're going to bite off their tail so they can't get away!" Farthing laughed.

The Siren song continued as the warship sat useless. There was no movement other than the fighters returning to their bays.

The *Starfinder* swung around the disabled warship and approached from the rear, turning sideways. The nipper was now visible on the viewing screen, as the distance between them and the warship decreased. The two ends of the nipper slid out perpendicularly from the side of the *Starfinder* like a giant vice, ready to clamp down on the warship's exhaust cones.

This was, indeed, what happened: the *Starfinder* sidled up closer to the warship and the nipper's clamps began making contact with the exhaust ports. Vibrations from the nipper could be felt throughout the ship as it crushed the exhaust ports of the warship. The sounds of rending metal vibrated through the hull and into the air of the bridge. Small explosions of light shot out to mark where the ports were now crushed and damaged.

"Crush the other port exhausts?" O'Keefe asked.

"Not necessary! They're disabled!" Farthing cheered. "Mother would agree. We need to give them a chance of repair once we've left the region."

Mother nodded and the sound of the Siren singing tapered off, then went silent. The bridge became suddenly quiet. Everyone seemed to be taking a breath of relief. All that could be heard were the buzzes and beeps of the ship's equipment.

"Time to message our friends in the warship!" said Farthing. "Byrne, open a channel."

Byrne nodded. "Channel open."

"This is Captain Farthing of the *Starfinder*. Do not launch your fighters again or you will lose not only your exhaust ports, but also part of your engine. Prepare to be boarded, so that we may negotiate your surrender!"

The screen came alive with a man growling indignantly: "What is the meaning of this?! How dare you attack a Senate warship, pirate?! Farthing!! You are a notorious thief and murderer. Where in the blue moons of Alorion did that singing come from?"

"Captain, these are extraordinary times, and we do what we must. Prepare to be boarded. If there is any resistance, my crew has the order to crush your engines. Is that clear?" Farthing was stern in his response. "No action will be taken unless you fail to comply." *[I didn't want to answer his question about the singing,]* he projected. Mother nodded in agreement.

"You will need time to maneuver closer to our engines. Why shouldn't I defend myself?" He turned to speak to someone offscreen: "Prepare to launch fighters."

Farthing lied: "We still have two railguns and one laser trained on your ship! Disregard that order, and we will open fire!"

The captain glared, then issued the order to stand down. "I will confer with my crew. I wish a few moments to speak to them." The screen went blank.

"That was rude! Doesn't he know he's in need of negotiating skills? We don't even know his name!" O'Keefe jested.

"Give him the time he needs," Mother replied. "Let him save face in front of his crew."

"Aye, Mother! You are wise," said Farthing. "We still don't know why they're here, though. Do you suppose they were looking for us? Maybe more are on the way? The last thing I want to do is encounter another warship. We're too damaged."

"I don't sense any more in the vicinity," Mother responded, "but one never knows." She paused. "However, I do sense sodbent on that ship! Tam, can you sense anything?"

Tam brought his hand to his head. "You're right, Mother! Now you mention it, there are at least four onboard."

"Try reaching into their minds."

Tam closed his eyes and concentrated. He sensed the furiously confused captain and continued, past the other bridge crew. He peeked open an eye to report, "The captain's name is Devin H. Cunningham." He closed them again after seeing a smile from Farthing, and continued searching.

In his mind's eye, he searched the minds of the crew and discovered four men in close proximity of each other. Quickly scanning, Tam could tell that they were very fearful.

He opened his eyes and reported: "I found them. They are in close quarters, in the stern of the ship. I believe they're imprisoned. They fear for their lives. Mother, do you want me to make contact?"

"Farthing, do you wish to board the vessel and retrieve these four men?" she inquired.

"Aye! I do. Tam, you will go with me."

"Then, Tam, please inform these men you will be rescuing them."

Tam closed his eyes and sent out messages to each of them individually. They were surprised but hopeful. All four had been separated from their partners.

"Mother! The four men are Life-Liners! They've been separated from their partners and dragged aboard as prisoners."

Mother nodded. "We must rescue them and return them home. Farthing, please prepare to board the ship once we hear from Captain Cunningham."

"Aye, aye!" he responded. "Commander O'Keefe, would you mind prepping the shuttle while I wait for this Captain Cunningham to respond?"

"Aye, sir! I'm on my way," said O'Keefe as she got up.

"The warship is requesting a communication line, Captain. Shall I open one for you?"

Farthing nodded. "Captain Cunningham, what is your decision?"

The screen revealed Captain Cunningham's sour expression. "What is it you want?! You plan on plundering this ship, pirate?! Rape the women?! Steal our money reserves?!"

"Nothing of the sort, mate. Not all pirates are pillagers." He paused. "Mind you, I have been known to do so when someone has something they should not—like those four prisoners you have in the stern of your ship."

"The degens?! They are to be delivered to Kashtiloth for processing, then sent to prison!!" Captain Cunningham responded. "And how do you know my name?!"

"Pirate insight," Farthing quipped. "Here's what will happen: we will board your ship, take the four prisoners, and be on our way. My commander will be waiting here to ensure you follow my instructions. Savvy?"

"Savvy?" the captain asked right back, apparently confused.

"Do you understand me?"

Cunningham sighed. "Savvy."

"We will board momentarily. Prepare your hangar."

Captain Cunningham nodded and closed the communication line.

∞

The shuttle glided into the warship's hangar bay, landing near a service hatch. "Ready to pillage, rape, and maim?" Farthing joked to Tam, alarming him—until he read the pirate's face.

"You're a hard man to read, Farthing! I swear, you almost had me convinced you were serious!"

"I'm serious about those prisoners. Aye, that's certain!" Farthing snorted as he undid his restraints. "Ready to head out, then? I see our hosts are approaching our shuttle. They look welcoming, eh?"

"Hardly!!" exclaimed Tam. "Aren't you concerned they might just shoot us? Or take us hostage?"

Farthing stood and pointed to the comm button in his right ear. "This is open, two ways, to the Convent, via Mother. Let them try!" He paused. "Activate yours, too, Tam."

Tam nodded as he unbuckled, stood, and activated the comm in his ear. Farthing handed him a particle beam weapon and a harness.

"I hope we don't have to use these!" Tam said.

"Be ready for anything," said Farthing. "It's best that any communication between you and I be mental. And Tam... let me do the talking, for Goddesses' sake."

Tam winced and nodded. He put on the side harness and holstered the gun, watching Farthing do the same.

"Ready?"

Tam breathed out heavily and nodded. "Ready!"

Farthing hit the exit. The external hatch lifted up, accompanied by the sound of a slight hiss of air escaping, exposing them to the approaching party of soldiers. [Follow my lead, Tam!]

"Captain Cunningham," Farthing addressed him, "under the circumstances, I'm sure you aren't happy to see us. Nonetheless, it's our intent to remove those four prisoners we discussed."

"Farthing," Cunningham started, "you blasted pirate! If the circumstances were reversed—"

"Well, they're not!" interrupted Farthing. "Let's not waste time. I'd like those prisoners—now! And I want to see video of your crew being sent to quarters. Now!"

"What is stopping me from just taking you prisoner?" Cunningham asked. His men placed their hands on their guns.

[Probe his mind, Tam, and keep me apprised of what he is thinking!] projected Farthing. [Can you be discreet? Will he know?]

[No. He's not a mentalist. He's more worried about what'll happen to him and his crew when the Magistrate finds out about this!]

[How does it feel to be a pirate, Tam?!] responded Farthing. [You'll be a wanted man, for sure! Aye, this is the life I was meant to live!]

Aloud, Farthing said, "Captain, let's not be hasty. Bring the prisoners here and I will promise you safe passage."

Cunningham's face reddened. "You think me a coward?! I ought to cut you down where you stand—you, a criminal, associated with those witches!!" He glared at Tam. "You may think that you've won this—but we'll find your haven of witches—and your pirate's nest. You've just landed yourself in an all-out war against the Senate. As we speak, warships are being recalled and sent here. There'll be no place for you to hide!"

"That may be," Farthing taunted, leaning forward, "but let me remind you, I can disable your ship in an instant. Care to test me?"

The men were growing tense.

"Let's make this as easy as possible. Bring the prisoners to me, and show me your crew has retired to their quarters." He leaned back and relaxed his arms.

[What's he thinking now?] projected Farthing.

[He's considering that he may have to get the prisoners and bring them here,] replied Tam. *[He's also considering waylaying us as we depart. Be careful, Farthing!]*

"Captain Cunningham, bring the prisoners to us," Farthing commanded. "I have sent instructions for the *Starfinder* to further damage your engines if you choose to hinder our departure in any manner. Should I show you what the ship is capable of? It would be much easier for you to just comply. It's your choice."

He looked at Cunningham inquiringly. *[Now?]*

[He's relenting,] responded Tam. *[He's going to send for the prisoners. Be on guard, though; he's dangerously close to changing his mind. I could try to make him think otherwise if you like. I'm not that practiced, but I have had some success.]*

[Is that wise?] asked Farthing. *[Are you sure he wouldn't know? Might you startle him into doing something desperate?]* Then, aloud, he pressed Cunningham: "Well?"

"Fine. I'll have them delivered to you," the captain relented. He held up a holo-screen and showed where all the life signs were on the ship. Virtually all of them were in the crew quarters. A handful were on the bridge and near the prison bay. "As you requested. You can see we have followed your... request. Now, what assurance do we have that you won't destroy us, or further damage our ship? What can a pirate's honor mean?" he snorted.

"Well, that's all I'm offering, mate. Pirates' honor. Take it or leave it."

"Go get the prisoners," Cunningham ordered. "You two, stay here with the *Starfinder* crew and me." He turned to Farthing again. "I have to protect myself, too, do I not?"

"By all means, do as you must. In the meantime, we'll retire to our shuttle," replied Farthing. "We'll be watching!" He motioned to Tam as they returned to the shuttle. *[Keep him in your thoughts, Tam. I want to know everything he's thinking. If you're not sure, tell me anyway!]*

[Aye, aye, Captain!] Tam projected with a grin. *[This is too easy!]*

[Don't get ahead of yourself!] Farthing entered the shuttle and Tam followed. *[This could get dangerous very quickly. Keep your wits about you, little blo'! We're not done yet!]*

"Close the door?" Tam asked.

"Aye!" responded Farthing. "Don't need prying ears and eyes in here." Then, he spoke into the *Starfinder's* comm unit: "Commander O'Keefe! Status report!"

"Repairs are slow. We've just about got the last railgun functional again. It will take time, though. All other weapons are offline. Instructions?"

"Continue with repairs as best you can. Keep the nipper ready in case we need it. I'll contact you once we have the prisoners."

"Aye, sir! O'Keefe out!"

"Farthing, look! The prisoners have arrived," said Tam. "Shall we go get them?"

"Aye, my little man, but be alert—and keep your link to Cunningham open. I want to know what he's thinking." Farthing approached the shuttle door. "Ready?"

They exited and saw Cunningham, his two bodyguards and the four prisoners, each accompanied by an officer. The captives were being held by electronic whip-irons. Tam winced, recalling Brogan.

"As promised, Farthing!" announced Cunningham. "I offer you the prisoners."

[He's ready to turn them over, Farthing. He's not going to fight.]

Tam then projected to the four prisoners: *[Are you OK? Ready to get out of here?]* The men just stood there.

Alarmed, Tam turned his attention back to Farthing. *[There's something wrong with these men!]*

"Cunningham, what's wrong with these prisoners?" asked Farthing.

"They are known criminals. They are degens. This is how we protect ourselves from their mental attacks. They have been injected with inhibiting drugs, newly developed by Senate scientists. They are of no danger to us in this state. Take them, Farthing, and be done with it!"

[He's not hiding anything! We can take them, no worries!] Tam's head turned to see Farthing already moving so fast that he didn't have time to absorb what was happening.

Farthing collided with the captain, knocking everyone off balance. *[It's not Cunningham we should be worried about!]* projected Farthing. *[It's his backup!]*

Two particle beams were shot, not causing any harm, as the men stumbled. The man in the back of the group recovered, lifted his weapon, and trained it on Tam.

[Tam!]

Still in shock, Tam stared blankly ahead as the man raised his weapon. He swallowed and began to fall to his knees as the man shooting received a boot to his chest from Farthing, sending him flying into the crowd. The particle beam streamed past Tam's ear, missing him by a mere hair's width, searing his ear slightly. The shuttle took the brunt of the beam, a cloud of vapor escaping from a damaged coil. The man tumbled to the floor as Farthing knocked two more of them down. Another took a swing at Farthing, who nimbly stepped in, grabbed the man by the head, and swiftly broke his neck. The sound echoed into Tam's brain as the man hit the floor. In the time he took to fall, Farthing took out two of the remaining men still standing. He then grabbed Cunningham and held him in a chokehold.

"Move, and your Captain will pay the price!" he commanded the last man standing. "Aye! Hold fast."

The man lowered his weapon.

[Tam, get up and get his weapon. Now!]

Tam shook his head, clambered to his feet, and moved to the man with the lowered weapon. As he approached, the man raised it, dodged to the left, and attempted to grab Tam. Tam turned his head in fear as the man grabbed him by the shoulders and pulled him in front of himself for protection. In that moment, though, the man was shot, and his lifeless body tumbled to the floor as blood and brain matter hit Tam in the face.

"Cunningham, you worm! Call your men off. If anyone approaches this shuttle bay, you will die as fast as he did," Farthing pointed to the shot man lying on the floor. "Tam, grab Cunningham's comm unit—quickly!"

"I—I didn't authorize this," Cunningham spat. "I didn't know!"

"Order your crew into a total lockdown. Close off all entrances, or we take this ship out!"

He spoke into his own comm unit: "O'Keefe, did you get that? Train the railguns on the ship. Prepare to fire!"

"Ready on your order, Captain!" she responded through their earpieces.

Tam stood there, staring blankly, holding the man's comm unit.

[Tam! Move, little blo'! Wake up! Bring the unit to me!]

Tam shook his head again and moved forward, toward Farthing. He raised the comm unit and offered it to him, who proceeded to shake the captain violently. Cunningham spewed spit, raising his hand against Farthing's massive arm around his neck.

"Please! I'll do as you say!" he sputtered, struggling to breathe. "Please!"

"Lock down, or *Starfinder* will fire in the next minute!" Farthing ordered.

[Hold the comm in front of the captain, little blo'! Come on! You can do it!]

Tam raised the comm unit.

"Do it now!" commanded Farthing. "I want proof on that unit, or *Starfinder* fires! Forty-five seconds remaining, Cunningham! Savvy?"

"Savvy!" he sputtered. Farthing loosened his grip enough for his prisoner to order the commands. "Attention, all hands! This is Captain Cunningham. I order an immediate, ship-wide lockdown. Code Cunningham four-five-nine-two! Each department, respond immediately!"

The responses began pouring out of the unit as each department signaled lockdown.

"Is that all of them?" Farthing asked, tightening his hold.

The captain just stuttered.

Tam, finally coming to his senses, projected: *[That's all of them. Lockdown is complete!]*

"O'Keefe!" shouted Farthing.

"Other orders?" she responded.

"Hold for now. The shuttle has taken a bit of damage, but I believe it's still spaceworthy! Can you check its sensors?"

"On it."

"Captain, let's take a little trip to your bridge, shall we?" Farthing stepped toward the entrance, Cunningham in tow. "Move, now!"

"What about the prisoners?" Tam asked.

"I'd say it's safe to leave them here. In fact, you four, board the shuttle and wait for us there." He turned back to Tam. "Help them."

Tam nodded and led the prisoners to the shuttle, settling them inside. Then, he leaned back out of the doorway. "Farthing, what about their whip-irons?"

"Leave them on for now," he responded. "I'll get the code later."

Tam moved toward the door, where the pirate stood with his prisoner. Tam glanced back at the carnage, then turned to go with them.

[Tam, comm unit!]

Cunningham received another shake, then spoke into it: "Unlock shuttle bay two."

The door unlocked and opened.

The motley crew proceeded without incident to the bridge. As it was unlocked, the remaining crew was surprised to find their captain being held prisoner.

"Don't move if you know what's good for you!" blurted out Tam.

[Aye, Tam! You're a real pirate now,] Farthing quipped, *[eh, little blo'?]* He guffawed, pushing forward.

"Listen to my mate," he commanded the crew. "Stay where you be!"

He advanced to the middle of the room, where the captain's chair waited, empty. He pushed Cunningham into it and placed a large boot on the man's chest. He gasped. The crew flinched in unison.

"Halt! Dead men tell no tales! Move, and he's a goner!" *[Tam, comm unit! Bring it to the captain!]*

Tam obliged. The captain looked up despairingly.

"I want ship blueprints on this unit. Now!"

"I can't do that!" sputtered Cunningham. "That is betraying the Senate! I—"

Farthing raised his particle beam and pointed it at the closest crew member. "How many will I have to shoot before you agree to my demands?" he growled.

Tam's eyes widened in surprise. *[Farthing! You can't be serious!]*

[Trust me, little blo'!]

Cunningham reluctantly obliged and began transferring the data to the comm unit, which beeped when the task was completed. He handed it hesitatingly to Tam.

[Take it, Tam. Oh, and probe his mind for the location of some whip-irons. I have an idea!]

∞

The two of them then navigated the hallways alone. The ship remained on lockdown, the crew on the bridge held fast in whip-irons. No one was minding the ship. Farthing laughed heartily and turned to Tam. "Look, there's the weapons locker. Make yourself useful and collect a crate of their weapons to bring with us! May as well be true pirates!"

"Aye, aye, Captain!" Farthing winked his approval.

Shortly after, they entered the shuttle with two crates of weapons, the comm unit, and some bottles of fine Alorion wine they had found in a galley on the way back from the bridge.

"Aye, mates! 'Tis a good haul!" Farthing quipped to the four prisoners, who were now free of the whip-irons. They were resting in seats as Tam sat with them, trying to soothe their nerves.

Farthing spoke into the comm unit: "O'Keefe, we're on our way back. Any word on the railgun?"

"Functional!" she responded. "Along with one laser."

"Wonderful. Any movement from the ship, open fire!" he ordered.

[Farthing, you know what you must do!] Mother messaged.

[I know, blessed mother. It pains me. I may be a pirate, but I am not a mercenary. I do this for the League!]

The shuttle cleared the landing bay and headed along the stern of the warship. As they reached the *Starfinder*, Farthing messaged O'Keefe: "Fire the railgun and light up the laser."

"What?!" exclaimed Tam. "You're destroying them?! You can't!! Why?!" He was shocked. "Mother would never approve!"

"My dear Tam, she is the one who decided this."

[Mother, why?]

[My boy, there are things you do not yet understand. We cannot leave a trace on their ship. It would only serve to lead them back to us—and possibly to expose you to the Senate, which would spoil our plans. Be patient, Tam, and understand this is necessary—as is the loss of the lives on that ship.]

They exited the shuttle with the four prisoners as the screen in the shuttle bay showed the warship exploding into a million pieces. Tam held his hand over his mouth.

[We do this for your salvation, young man! Sometimes, there must be sacrifices. We can't have your cover blown.]

Tam, silent and dejected, trying to make sense of the situation, continued to the bridge. Things were getting too dangerous for his liking.

Chapter 21
The Order's Awakening

"Yes, Father, he's been rescued," replied Bennett, "along with over a hundred imprisoned men. The ship was ripped in half by members of a pirate band called the Lambda Infinity Omega League. The cargo hold, along with the prisoners, were taken back to Alorion by a Captain Farthing."

Bennett stirred uneasily in the chair in Father's chamber, swallowing and turning away from Father's gaze. He felt drained and depressed. He was not relishing the following hour's interview. Trying to decipher the images he had been witness to over the past two days took a lot of energy.

Bennett was jolted out of his daydreaming by Father's polite cough. "I beg your forgiveness, Father. The last few days have been difficult for me." He looked down at his feet.

"Bennett, please continue," said Father, almost whispering.

Bennett drew in a breath of relief and continued. "There, he recovered from his injuries and was taken to the Mother Siren. It would seem she's in charge of this League. She does more than just represent a convent of religious fanatics. They're in charge of creating Life-Lines!"

Father raised his eyebrow at the Life-Line part, but remained silent. Bennett, not knowing what to do, continued with his report: "She has ordered Tam on a mission to infiltrate the Senate government on Kashtiloth and find the plans for the prison on Corustloth. It would seem to me that her plan is not only to help Tam rescue Brogan, but to save all the prisoners. She made a frightening reference to them being experimented on. What that means is beyond me at the moment. I'm sorry, Father."

"Bennett, young man," Father responded. "You've worked so hard to get all of this information. You are getting a little caught up. Have you taken a rest period, or even eaten yet?"

Bennett shook his head and lowered his tired eyes. "I have not as of yet, Father. I'll go eat right now and try to sleep."

"The next time you're sent in, I'll make sure you are fed intravenously. You are careless with your physical body, despite being so attentive with your mental abilities." Father sighed. "Anything else you feel is important?"

Bennett thought for a moment and considered telling Father about the memory Tam had had of being stowed away on a sail glider with Brogan, how they had had sex and, being linked together, mutually experienced both of their orgasms at the same time. He decided to not mention that part. He reddened a bit, causing Father to raise an eyebrow again. Bennett wondered if Father had read his mind anyway.

"Really, Bennett, you are getting to wrapped up in this situation. Mutual orgasms *are* important to me—not the need to have one, I mean—mind you, I can imagine—even at my age..."

Bennett reddened even more and looked at the floor.

Father continued: "Bennett, you need to understand—you have a job to do, which is to garner enough information about this group of people to determine if they are a piece of the puzzle of our origins. No little incident should be disregarded. After your rest period, you will report *everything* you've experienced—and I want the holorecords in my hands as soon as you've finished."

"I'm sorry, Father. I'll endeavor to be more accurate. It's just hard to read sometimes—like the unification Tam went through... I accessed his memories, but couldn't see or experience most of it... just the beginning and the moments afterward. For some reason, it went blank for the most part."

"What?" Father was startled. "You didn't mention that before. This is exactly what I'm talking about. I'm going to change your schedule. Eat and rest for two hours, then fill out the full report for me. I expect everything before my next sleep period, young man."

Bennett's pride had taken another beating. He had forgotten to tell all the details. Some of them hadn't seemed important. Others were hard to describe, like the forging of Tam and Brogan's Life-Line. He had probed Tam about the Sirens, but the mental picture was almost indiscernible—shadows instead of the vivid images of everything else that occurred in his mind.

"Father, I will try harder to be more accurate in my reports. I'll get to them right away." He stood to go and began walking to the door, but sensed Father looking at him, so he stopped.

"Bennett, I know this is a difficult task for you." Father's eyes softened a little. "I must try to be more empathetic to what you're going through. Please, take as much time as you need to get the rest and nourishment you require."

Bennett just about fell over, but held his ground, still facing away from Father. A tear sprang from the corner of his eye. "Thank you, Father. I shall do my utmost."

"Good, young man. Now, leave immediately, and get some rest—or I'll have you stunned and thrown on my chamber couch—and watch you myself!"

Sometimes the things that Father said made Bennett stop and wonder. But he turned to Father anyway, smiled, bowed, and left silently.

Father went back to his holomap of the galaxy, which was beginning to feel a lot smaller than it ought to be. The puzzle pieces were coming to him piecemeal, but he would have the secret soon. He sensed it. Young Bennett had no clue that he was the only current "lead" bringing the Order any closer to finding their origins. *Mustn't let him know that though,* thought Father to himself. The last thing he needed was an overly cocky junior mentalist.

Father shook his head, turning his attention back to trying to make the connection with Brogan. After countless tries, he was still without success. Fires of damnation! What did that young Bennett have that he didn't? Pondering this, he sent a mental command to his console: *[Transmit the full historical background and the medical and private records of Mr. Bennett Davis. Override privacy option—Father's priority one.]*

There on the table in Father's chamber sat Bennett's personal file, along with his holoreport on Tam and his experience. All he had to do was wave a finger and call them up from his personal console. He was hesitant, though. They had arrived over two hours ago and still sat blinking on the holoconsole, rotating patiently, awaiting his response.

He cast his mind out through the complex to Bennett's chamber, finding him sound asleep. The young man was exhausted, in a virtually dreamless state. Despite his slight envy, Father felt a warm sense of compassion for Bennett. If what he suspected was true, his decision might be fairly straightforward.

Well, may as well scan the files. *[Personal file for Bennett—open and await recall commands.]*

The console responded and opened the file, waiting for his commands.

[Begin reading biography.]

The console responded with a series of points on Bennett. He was born on the Order home world twenty-eight years ago. He had been in the Order training centre two years now, after being educated at home by his parents. His IQ was top-notch, and his mental abilities were far above those who had received equal training. Father wondered what Bennett would be like when he had completed his training.

He continued scanning, coming to the final point, which gave him pause. Bennett, currently single, leaned to the far end of the sexuality scale that indicated a total interest in other men and absolutely no interest in women.

Again, the idea of being a lover of men was at the forefront of this blasted puzzle. Was this the key?

Chapter 22
Tyranny, Trysts, and Tight Spots

Mother sat in her chamber aboard the *Starfinder* with Farthing and Tam. "It is clear to me that the ship was not ready for battle before this clash started. If you are to take on more warships, you will need Siren support."

"Dear Mother, you are right," Farthing responded. "We did not fare well against one warship! We may have to battle more than one at a time. What do you propose?"

"I believe the best course of action is to send the *Starfinder* to the asteroid cluster between Alorion and Kashtiloth. Commander O'Keefe can take the ship there and rendezvous with Siren shuttles carrying the retrofits. My pilot will go with them."

"Won't there be patrols?" inquired Tam.

"Warships tend to avoid the asteroid cluster because it's such a hazard to navigate. The Sirens have long used it as a hiding place for our technology. I trust your commander's ability to maneuver through it to get the necessary upgrades."

"You are wise, Mother," said Farthing. "I know I can entrust my ship to your sisters' expertise! How long do you think it'll take? What kind of retrofits are you considering?"

"My dear Farthing! You'll need more lasers and railguns than what you have. The addition of missile launchers, along with a few other little surprises, will help us in our cause. Those stolen plans will also be useful for our defense!" she added. "It should take a couple of Alorion weeks, more than enough time for you to get to Kashtiloth by shuttle—once you've dropped me off on Alorion, if you don't mind! My pilot will coordinate the refit and remain behind."

∞

Tam sat in the aft of the shuttle en route to Alorion, using holographic training guides on weapon use and hand-to-hand combat. He shook his head. *This is stupid stuff for a farmer to have to learn. I wasn't made for this.*

Despite Farthing's earlier plea to stay focused, Tam found himself drifting off. He began to cry, feeling that Brogan's body was convulsing across space. Tam's was doing the same, in sympathy. His mind began to cloud with desperation...

∞

"My little mate, if you truly wish to rescue Brogan, you need to be serious about preparing! I can't have you running into battle without at least some basic pirate training!" Captain Farthing exclaimed, shaking Tam awake at his console.

"I passed out," Tam responded slowly.

"Really? Looks more like lazing about!" Farthing laughed. "But you don't look well."

"I don't feel well," said Tam. "I was just thinking about when Brogan was arrested, when I received a jolt from him—the strongest since his capture. He must be in severe pain. It caused me to black out. Farthing, I'm sorry. I'm not much good at this."

"I understand your pain, my wee man. I have lost people in my life, too."

"Not a Life-Line, though."

"No, that's true. I may not be a Life-Liner, but I can connect with others through my mind. Until lately, I didn't even know I had more of the gift. The occasion never arose for me to engage my powers—until recently."

"Sometimes it feels like a curse rather than a gift," said Tam. "I miss Brogan so much that my body aches. I can't take it anymore." A tear slid down the side of his face.

Farthing responded by softly touching his shoulder. "We'll avenge this travesty, Tam! We'll rescue Brogan and destroy the prison! Let's wreak havoc on the Senate—let them know that the Lambda Infinity Omega League has teeth! All the more reason for you to steel your nerves and train as though your life depends on it—because it does. And so does Brogan's."

The soft hand on Tam's shoulder was gripping him tightly now, making him wince.

"I wish I could experience your anger, Farthing. It might motivate me."

"You can," said Farthing, "if you want."

"But I am a Life-Liner linked to Brogan!" Tam was taken aback. "Wouldn't that be akin to cheating?"

"Are you telling me that pleasure and pain from another would constitute cheating on your lover?" asked Farthing. "It's no different than having sex with a stranger for release. When was the last time you experienced sodbent, anyway?"

"On the sail glider all those months ago," he admitted. "Since then, I've not had the strength, let alone the time, to worry about sex." Tam felt bitter and hopeless.

"Mother knew this would happen. She's prepared to help strengthen you with a temporary link to me—if that be what you want."

Tam started to clue into what he was saying. "Is that even possible?"

"'Tis, for the Mother Siren!"

"What would Brogan think of it?" He would be cheating, surely! This couldn't be fair.

"Brogan linked with many men, including me," said Farthing. "He chose you for his Life-Line because he knew your connection went beyond communicating mentally and making love! You are his soulmate, Tam. Nothing but his death can take that away from you. All the more reason to give into this little tryst—to fuel you for what lies ahead! To rescue him."

"What would I need to do?" Tam asked.

"Lie down on the bunks over there, handsome man," said Farthing, "and I'll show you!"

Tam sensed Mother's mind close by, pushing him to take this small gift. He gave in and followed Farthing.

∞

Tam lay naked on the bunk. He was hesitant about the whole thing, but also felt excited to link with this large and mysterious man. *It can't be the sex that worries me. Brogan spoke of me having sex with other men if I so desired. But linking with another man in some sort of temporary Life-Line is another story.*

"Lie still and close your eyes. Mother will be here shortly to help us. Do you hear anything?"

"Nothing other than you breathing heavily," replied Tam. "You're a very big man, Farthing. How do you fare at sex with men that are almost half your size?"

"I am a gentle giant, I've been told, young Thamara-Afil." Farthing smiled. "'Tis all you need to know. You realize it's also in my interest to create a temporary Life-Line with you?"

"I can imagine," Tam responded. "I suppose you will gain greater access to the Senate's defenses."

"You are a brazen one," laughed Farthing, "aren't you? Has it occurred to you I may be motivated by something other than conquest?"

Tam stopped breathing, finally hearing something. Singing.

"The Sisters! I hear them singing their Siren song, Farthing! Where's it coming from?"

"From the Convent—channeled through Mother herself. She is in the shuttle cockpit at this moment. Have you ever wondered about her?"

"Yes," he admitted. "I've wondered why she never contacted me while I was a stowaway."

"The Mother and the Sirens are very powerful," said Farthing, "but only in the sense of giving power to others like yourself—and even me. Really, they are catalysts—not possessors of advanced mental powers. They can only access those open to receiving them. Are you open?" He turned his head. "Aye! Listen! The singing's getting louder! Mother approaches. I must prepare."

Farthing removed his clothing and lay on the bunk beside Tam. He grasped his smaller hands in his massive ones, pulling Tam close to his body, facing him. Farthing leaned over him and planted another big kiss on Tam's forehead.

"You seem to like doing that," said Tam. "Is it your idea of foreplay?"

Farthing laughed. "It can be, wee man. It brings me closer to your brain, and helps facilitate a link." He paused. "Mother is here!"

Tam heard the door open and moved to cover his naked body, but Farthing pulled his hand back. The singing increased in volume as she entered. Tam felt the familiar, warm vibration of the Siren song in his head and in his heart. Soon, his whole body was vibrating to the harmony. He gave in, losing what he perceived as consciousness.

He floated. Beside him was Farthing. He smiled. [*I can sense your thoughts, young Tam. We are linked, and will become a Life-Line triad! Do you feel something? Pay attention to what comes next!*]

Tam cried out in wonder and in pain. He felt Brogan's body in its entirety! He felt the injuries to his body: the old injury in his leg; the lacerations on his back from the whippings; his cracked, dry lips and crusty eyelids seeping puss from the open wounds above his brow.

[*My Brogan! What have they done to you? Can you answer me?*]

Farthing's mental image leaned over, holding Tam's head gently in his massive arms. For the first time since his capture, Brogan responded.

[Tam, I can hear you. I feel you! I haven't given up—I love you too much. Farthing, you old dirt-devil! You've helped my Tam contact me! Thank you!]

Farthing responded in his gentle manner and laughed out loud.

[You have an amazing partner, Brogan. Do you realize the lengths he's gone to in order to try to rescue you? Search his mind and see.]

All three men shared the visions of what Tam had done, all the way up to the point of the forging of their triad Life-Line.

[Mother!] responded Brogan. *[Goddesses, bless you and your Sirens! You have given me such a gift—to communicate with my love!]*

[Brogan, the Sirens need you alive,] projected Mother. *[Tam needs you alive. Farthing needs you alive. You are part of a much bigger plan. We will do everything in our power to help you escape. Do not give up hope!]*

[Mother! Tam! Farthing! I am so sorry for my foolishness! If only I could go back in time to evade this fate.]

Tam cried openly, tears streaming down his cheeks. *[Forget about it, Brogan! I miss your presence—including your impulsivity! I'll never take it for granted again.]*

Farthing's mental body leaned over Tam and kissed him on the lips. He projected to them all: *[I am your conduit. I give myself willingly, in the name of the Siren Mother and her Convent.]*

Tam felt three souls at that moment and realized the power of unity.

[We can overcome this if we gather strength from each other. I see it now, Mother! I understand what you want me to do. I am ready!]

Mother leaned over the bed, gently placing one hand on Farthing's head and the other on Tam's. *[I shall leave you before you awake. A Siren shuttle will be arriving shortly. You have the strength you need, if you rest. Goddesses' speed on your voyage, Farthing. Protect Tam and see that he does not stray from his path, as he is likely to do—we know his nature.]*

She laughed, and the men followed suit.

Tam nodded, closing his eyes as she left the room. *[I'll do my best, Mother.]*

He turned his thoughts to Brogan.

[We are coming to rescue you—hold on, my love. Don't give up hope. I'm ready to take on the whole Senate army to get to you!]

Farthing laughed. *[Young Tam, don't dispel the power of my link with you and with Brogan. It cannot be maintained for long periods. Brogan, I wish to make love to your Life-Line. Grant me this wish!]*

Brogan's last response was an affirmation: [*Take care of him. Make him feel again, so that he is full strength and full of optimism. Only then will he find the strength to do what he must. Tam, I believe in you. Farthing, I believe in you. Enjoy my lover's body. It is my hope I will sense his release, which will help me release my pain.*]

[*Brogan, I love you, and will be with you as soon as I can.*] Tam was adamant.

[*May we feel the closeness of our bodies soon, too! I sense you moving farther away in my mind, Tam. I'm afraid I will lose you. Keep sending me hope when you can. It's what has sustained me thus far. I love you, Tam. Farthing, he is your charge. Do not fail him!*]

Tam felt Brogan's mind slipping away. He cried out over the loss as Farthing cradled him against his chest.

"Young Tam, I will protect and honor you. Sleep, and we will play later, when you have gathered strength."

Farthing kissed Tam. He held him as he fell asleep, humming part of the Sirens' melody as he did. Tam was calm for the first time in a long while.

I have done my part, Farthing thought to himself. He lay there for a time before he, too, fell asleep.

Later, their lovemaking was, indeed, gentle. Farthing gave himself willingly to Tam and took Tam with the same kindness. Tam felt more at peace than he had since Brogan was captured. He understood the gift of release Mother and Farthing had given to him, and felt ready to leave.

He had to get to Kashtiloth and infiltrate the Senate directly—and gain the confidence of the leader himself.

∞

Bennett's report contained everything he experienced this time. Father knew from the boy's responses that he was being truthful, despite being embarrassed recounting the sex that had occurred.

Later, in his room, Father pondered what he had learned. He decided his next move: another triad link—Bennett, Tam, and Brogan. First, though, Bennett would have to link with Brogan, and familiarize himself with his mind.

If all this works, we are one step closer. I'll be remembered as the man who found our origins! Not bad for an old man like me.

He had to think of some way to speed the process of rescuing Brogan. He and Tam could not perish—his success, and the Order's, depended on it.

Father had begun mandating breaks for Bennett. This included a trip to the local matching booth to find him a compatible playmate for the night. He figured it was just what Bennett needed to feel a little more empathy for Tam. Bennett found a man in his thirties with blond hair and an engaging smile, who drew him into his arms, then his bedroom.

Father, alone in his room, pondered.

Who would have thought men who love other men would be the key to finding our origins? I wish for Bennett's ability. What caused this genetic restructuring of gay men's psyche, for this to occur? Who did this? And why? Are there any limitations to the links that they experience? Maybe, if we're lucky, they will take us all the way back to the beginning.

Part 4
Senate Infiltration

Chapter 23
Crossroads

Brogan awoke, as usual, to darkness. It would seem his captors were bent on destroying his will. They had taken away his light, along with everything else. It was only through pulling on Tam's that he was able to survive all.

What an idiot he had been. If only he had listened to Tam. Sensible to the last.

Now I know what I value most about our Life-Line: all the traits that I lack, I may draw from Tam. He makes me complete.

Brogan still had enough strength to cry. He sensed a shift in Tam's mood as he did, but could not clearly understand his emotional state from all the way at the other end of the system. It made him feel helpless to be virtually cut off from his other half. It was inhumane. The living cloth and the drugs inhibited him from receiving little of anything from Tam and Farthing. He wished it would put him to sleep.

There was the sound of a door opening down the hall from his prison cell. They were coming, again, to do more damage—to question him endlessly, until he passed out from fatigue or fainted from the pain. Despite this, he had not given up anything important about his lover. He wouldn't this time, either.

The door opened and a blinding light shone in his eyes.

"Time for your next questioning, you waste of a man! Grab his neck, Grayson!"

Grayson did so with his usual vehemence. Brogan was almost unable to breathe.

"My pleasure, Rothman. I'd strangle the degen to death myself had we not been ordered to keep him alive. These degens don't deserve to live. Filthy creatures! They disgust me." He gritted his teeth.

Brogan endured this, unable to respond. His will to fight had long been gone. As he began to feel his consciousness fading, he heard a voice in his head he had never heard before.

[Brogan, I am a friend. I will help you as much as I can from here, but I am far away. Father says my connection to you will help everyone.]

Brogan was startled. *[Who are you? What are you doing in my head?]*

[My name is Bennett. I'm here to help you.]

Brogan lost touch with reality and the lights faded. His eyes rolled upward in their sockets and his body went limp.

∞

Bennett choked back the involuntary response he felt to Brogan's torture. He reached up to his neck and massaged it gently, trying to lessen the feeling that he had just been choked himself.

Father would not be pleased. *He expects more than this from me,* thought Bennett to himself. *I've had so much more success linking with Tam. Maybe Brogan's body is too damaged.*

On cue, the intercom screen beeped, and Father's insignia appeared above it. He sighed and prepared for his own torture: Father's questioning. He had to remind himself to not think that way of Father. He meant well—it was not his fault he was so grim sometimes.

Bennett reached over, turned the light on, and sat up.

[Link communications,] Bennett projected to the unit. On cue, he was connected to Father's chambers.

"Bennett, I sense distress in you. What's happened? Were you successful?"

"Yes and no, Father. I made contact, but he was immediately silenced by his captors. They choked him unconscious."

"Barbarians!" Father exclaimed. "You'll need to try again as soon as possible. When will you be ready?"

"Give me a short respite, Father. I can start within the hour."

"Bennett, do you understand the implications of what we're trying to do?"

"Not completely, Father," he admitted. "But I know I've linked to Tam—and now to Brogan—for a reason: to learn as much as I can about them and their culture. We now know they are some of the most superior mentalists—rivaling many of us—without any formal training! Imagine what they could do if they *did* have the training!"

"Bennett," said Father, "you've just made my point. You, too, are that powerful. I cannot say more than that at this point, but you must make contact with Brogan again. Next, it's my hope you will forge a triad with the two of them. If it works, I'll know for sure what to do next."

"But Father!" Bennett protested. "That makes no sense to me. Why are you making me enter into lives that are so painful... yet full of love... and hope..." Bennett faltered and fell silent.

"I believe, my young Bennett, you've understood that what you're doing will further the Order's quest. Make no mistake, young man. You are doing something I cannot!"

"Father, you're mistaken! You're the most powerful mentalist in the Order— maybe the whole galaxy!"

"I'm honored by your belief in my powers, Bennett," Father sighed. "I've had to readjust my own beliefs in this matter. My studies and my experience focusing on these links over the years have given me the insight to move forward. But I now know I've met my limit, physically and mentally! I need your ability to move us into the next phase in my plans."

"And what are those, Father?" asked Bennett. "Will they be dangerous for me?"

"They might be, my son. However, I think that you'll agree that it's worth the risk. Let me tell you, in part, what I've discovered these past few weeks as you searched Tam's world. They are 'Life-Liners,' as they call themselves, because of their genetic makeup. They are men who love men, like yourself. They have genes that mark them as different, like you. You, like those two, are a genetically altered man."

"How?"

"I've not yet fathomed all there is to know, Bennett. Give me more time. All I know is that you should have the genetic disposition they have. Have you ever traveled by curved space?"

"No, Father. My family's known for space sickness. My father prevented any possibility of space travel for me. I've been planet-bound all my life."

"Then, prepare yourself for your first trip in curved space, young Bennett. It should prove interesting."

"You mean experience what they do when they exit from curved space?"

"Indeed," affirmed Father. "This is what I want to see. You leave within the hour. I am sending you to the neighboring system on a curved space shuttle. You will report to the Order's main hospital on Habbassin in three days. You will receive an intensive examination—a thorough physical, mental, and, finally, genetic marker examination. We'll scan your DNA for what makes you different. In fact, I'm making it a priority to have all gay mentalists scanned for these genes. And you'll keep me posted of any sickness you experience enroute. Understood?"

"Yes," agreed Bennett. He knew there was no argument to be had with Father.

He got up, gathered a few belongings in a cloth bag, closed the door to his room, and turned out the light. Then, he made his way to the space hanger of the Order's headquarters to wait to be shipped out.

What will be next for me?! A trip across the galaxy?! No! He wouldn't...

∞

"The reports have arrived, Magistrate." The page bowed, not daring to look the Magistrate directly in the eye. Instead, he stared at the man's bejeweled slippers, praying he wouldn't get on his bad side, which was rumored to come and go at whim.

"Excellent," replied the Magistrate. "Leave them on the table and get out."

The page bowed as low as he could and quietly exited. He didn't want to cause any trouble. He'd heard the rumors of what had happened to the last page.

The Magistrate leaned back on his couch and turned his eyes toward the report— a computerized tablet containing all information on the goings-on of the Corustloth prison. It would make for some exciting reading.

Torture does that to a man, he thought. *Stirs you deep down and makes you hard.*

"Now I can see what those imbeciles are doing in that prison," he said to himself. "Spending too much of my money. Really, they are. If I didn't need those prisoners alive, I'd have them executed and burned as fuel for the furnaces of the Senate palace."

The Magistrate willed himself to get off the couch and get the tablet. He should have gotten that gnat of a page to hand it to him. "I'll have to punish him for that later," he mused.

He pushed himself up slowly and, with effort, stood on his two feet. He waddled to the table and grabbed the tablet. He was out of breath.

"Blasted page! He will be whipped for this insolence!" He picked up the bell at the side of his couch and rang it loudly. "Where is that ignoramus now? I'll have his head if he's not here in the next thirty seconds."

The page, rolling his tunic in his trembling fingers and fumbling with his feet, entered the chamber. "Yes, sir? May I be of service to his Magistrate?"

"Yes, you may. Tell the headmaster of engineering to report to my chamber—and tell him to bring a snapper-whip with him."

"By your leave, Magistrate. I'll do so immediately."

"Hurry, too. I look forward to seeing you squirm under the guile of the headmaster, you lazy page!"

The poor sap knew there was no arguing. Not wishing to lose his life, he accepted what he would likely receive in the next hour. He bowed and exited, facing the Magistrate, so as not to offend him anymore than he already had.

The Magistrate sat on his couch, demurely reading the statistics of the prison:

573 prisoners currently alive

29 dead bodies of those who had not survived, frozen
for dissection

Over 100 missing, due to the recent hijacking of the Minorian-
class cruiser

4 lost, due to the mysterious destruction of the warship

"Those blasted pirates!" he exclaimed to himself. "They are a scourge! They're surely responsible for the destruction of the warship. I'd like to have them put to death in public ceremonies! Their heads would be removed so quickly, they'd face the horror of knowing they had been severed from their bodies. Ah, the joy of seeing their terror and pain! It would make my day to see them suffer. The Lambda Infinity Omega League, *bah*! I'd have them drawn and quartered—slowly—if I could catch them first! Maybe someone else should pay for this in the meantime."

The Magistrate continued scanning the files on the tablet, shifting his buttocks with a grunt:

Vivisection was scheduled to start next week.

"Blasted pirates! It would have started by now had the cruiser not been hijacked and the cargo stolen."

He picked up the bell and rang it as loud as he could.

The page came running. "Yes, your Magistrate? How may I be of service? I am honored to be your faithful servant."

"Indeed! Get me the headmaster of shipping lanes. Oh and also, tell the headmaster of hiring that I'll need an inventory of new pages. I'll be needing a new one soon."

"Very good, sir!" whimpered the page as he fled the chamber and ran down the corridor in absolute terror. As he left the Magistrate's communal house, he imagined the life he'd had before the Magistrate had taken control.

Oh, the irony of allowing this all to happen!

∞

Farthing insisted Tam continue his holographic training in curved space en route to Kashtiloth, much to his distaste. It would seem that strength drawn from a triad Life-Line was not enough. Learning hand-to-hand combat, both bare-knuckled and with the use of particle beam weapons, seemed to be of the utmost importance to Farthing. Tam was at a loss as to why until he reminded him of their recent battle with the warship.

"Farthing, must I do this blasted training? Do you really expect me to fight my way into the Magistrate's chambers? Or, better yet, shoot my way in?"

"Young man, training helps focus the mind—and keeps you occupied! You have less time to sit, wallowing in self-pity and worrying about Brogan. If you choose not to train, I will be forced to toss you out of an airlock!"

"Very funny!" said Tam sarcastically. "Mother would have your hide!"

"We could make you train hand-to-hand with another man.. how about me?"

Tam's eyes widened at the thought of fighting Farthing. "I wouldn't stand a chance!"

"Mate, you just don't get it." Farthing shook his head. "Size is not the determining factor in victory! Look at the Magistrate—he's a bullish, fat man who's nothing more than a bully, because he has military backup, thanks to his father's quest to take over the system. He holds a lot of power, but he's not big at all! Even someone as big as me can be defeated with the proper technique. No more holographic fight simulations for you, Master Thamara-Afil Amergan-Faolin. You'll train and fight with me."

He grinned one of his usual toothy grins and handed Tam a fighting baton.

Tam rolled his eyes. Being a hero was going to be a lot harder than he had thought...

Chapter 24
The Magistrate's Power: How It Came to Be

The Kashtiloth System had not always been a dictatorship. In fact, to the average human living on any of the worlds, save the Prison Planet, life had changed dramatically over the last few decades —just about everyone had to deal with the Senate.

The general public failed to notice that more and more technology was being withheld from them. The Senate said it was to allow life to revert to a simpler state, to be closer to the Gods; and few questioned them. Those who did disappeared. Life had gone from progressive to backward. The average person was now a farmer, worker, or pregnant with children. Only if you were in the Senate—or born into a family who was—did you have any sort of education.

The Senate had done a wonderful job at covering up the transition. The public saw that they were not hungry; there was enough food for everyone. There was a roof over everyone's head, and though their homes might not have been the most up to date, they all had running water and sewage systems for waste. A lucky few were employed in the menial jobs of gathering recycling materials left at the curb each evening in front of every home, which prevented scoundrels from scavenging in garbage heaps. Others sold wares in markets or worked for the Senate, securing the perimeter fences on Alorion or the internment camps on Zemitis.

Few remembered what life had been like before. Those who remembered the bloody military coup were either in the Senate themselves, languishing in prison, or dead. The Senate's power ran deep. Its veins traversed everywhere. Few were exempt from its all-knowing, all-seeing eyes. Those few who could escape them gathered off-world from Kashtiloth—usually on Alorion or one of its moons. To travel openly and declare opposition to the Senate on Kashtiloth itself would bring swift reprisal, and those caught would be put to death in a public spectacle, "to entertain the masses."

Oh, the Senate knew of the Lambda Infinity Omega League and its band of pirates. They knew, too, of Farthing, their leader. What the Senate could not do, though, was capture the traitor. Many a head had rolled since the Magistrate had taken it upon himself to assign someone the task of finding Farthing.

In fact, it happened with alarming frequency. So much so that credits were issued to any family directly linked to the Senate to encourage them to have a child. Some suspected it was just a ploy to have future playthings for the Magistrate, though they would not say so for fear of losing their life. Fear reigned in the families of the Senate—and that made the Magistrate very happy. He was in control.

The Magistrate's father, Alarius Kruger, had been the righteous victor in the bloody military coup that had taken place over twenty-five Kashtilothian years before. He was the one who had rallied the troops, inviting the uneducated into a life of military "pleasures and profit." Once he had succeeded in raising troops for the cause, he plotted his takeover with a few of his cronies and struck when the Kashtiloth System was celebrating the eve of summer. No one was working except the military, so it was really easy to just glide into the four major universities and take out the powerful Professors of the Learnèd, thereby cutting off power to the educated masses. Those with any education were soon delegated off-world. Some just disappeared.

Kruger consolidated his power and held public executions of any dissenters. Those left with any inclinations toward resistance soon learned to keep their heads low. What Kruger did not foresee was what his sadistic young son, Alarius Kruger II, would do.

For some reason, the younger Kruger lacked any morals. Members of the Senate consulted a few of the remaining medical experts. The possibility that Kruger was a psychopathic egomaniac was at the forefront of many people's minds. Kruger Sr. ignored this, dictating that Kruger II be groomed to replace him when he grew too old to rule effectively.

The older Kruger never saw it coming. One evening, lying in his bed with his mistress, he awoke to Kruger Jr. standing over them with a particle beam. He was forced to bear witness as the young Kruger burned his mistress from head to toe on a low setting as she screamed for mercy. Kruger Sr., unable to call for help in the middle of the night, received a beam to the left leg, amputating it cleanly, leaving a stump behind. His son warned him that if he were to make a move, the same would happen to the other appendages, including his manhood ("on an even lower setting," he sneered). The mistress's dead body was still smoking. The horrific smell of burned flesh and hair filled the air of the chamber, which Kruger Jr. inhaled deeply.

"Father, do you smell the sweet smell of my victory? I have done what you've told me to do. I am taking charge of the Senate. I shall be the rightful and righteous ruler. Thank you, Father, for loving me enough to give me this wonderful opportunity."

Kruger Sr. was too shocked to respond. He just blinked fearfully, clutching his stump.

"Now, Father, witness the execution of my plan."

Kruger Jr. went to the door of the chamber and pulled an unknown waif of a boy inside by the scruff of the neck. The youngster must have been no more than thirteen years old. He squealed with pain, making Kruger even more lustful. He smacked him across the head.

"Silence, child, or I'll remove your eyes from your sockets with my bare hands!"

Kruger Jr. handed the particle beam weapon to the child, who held it quizzically.

"It's virtually spent, child, so don't point it at me. This one, however, is at full charge." Kruger pulled out another particle beam gun and shot his father straight in the face, mutilating his head beyond recognition. Kruger laughed shrilly and crowed at the glorious sight of the gore. It made his body parts hard! It got him excited! "Now young thing, you will do one more thing for me."

Kruger shot the boy in the heart with his particle beam. The boy fell, his eyes open in terror, to the floor. Kruger placed the particle beam weapon in the boy's other free hand and left the scene of the crime, deeply inhaling, once again, the smell of his victory.

A chambermaid discovered the gory scene the next morning. Kruger Jr. was already long gone. He had "friends" testify that he had spent the night at his summer lodgings.

Coming home, Kruger was full of wrath and sadness for "the injustice" that had occurred to his father and mother. He swore that those who'd done it would be put to justice. To show his intent, he summoned several members of the family of the boy who had been found at the scene of the crime. He shot them in public for being traitors to the Senate. The reports said the boy had killed Kruger Sr. and his mother, then turned the weapon on himself. The boy was examined by the medical community and discovered to have the genetic markers of sodbent—he was a mentalist who linked with others. Thus began the hunt for all sodbent.

Calling an emergency session of the Senate, Kruger named himself successor. There was no opposition at all. Sodbents were now considered deviants to be hunted down and sent to Corustloth, to the newly completed prison. To the public, this meant they were as good as dead. No one knew of the atrocities committed on that world in the name of discovering the "wickedness of the sexual deviants and their powers of linking."

∞

Ten years later, Kruger had consolidated his power even more. There was less technology on the worlds in the system, and the general population had been dumbed down enough not to pose a threat. Sodbents were either rounded up and placed in prison or hidden in the hills. But Kruger slept easily, knowing he would find them all, sooner or later.

Then the Minorian-class spaceship full of prisoners had been hijacked.

This meant war. Kruger made plans to step up military training for new recruits. He intended to squeeze the life out of the resistance before he lost any more precious cargo to experiment on! Farthing would be hanged in the courtyard once he'd been caught.

"I think that I shall skin him myself and use the hide to cover my couches." As usual, he was not talking to anyone but himself, relishing in his glory.

∞

What Kruger didn't know was that his little world had been infiltrated—not by the League, but from the other side of the galaxy. Father had planted spies in the form of mentalists viewing the world's politics form various points of view. What Father saw frightened him immensely. Stepping up training of more mentalists was a high priority of his—hence the recruitment of Bennett and others like him.

Father would need to move on Kruger soon enough, in order to somehow save those men he needed to complete his search. Those men on the prison world would need to be rescued. So the seed of dissidence was planted in men like Farthing, who needed little goading into action. Father knew from his knowledge of him that he would be one to lead a rescue on the prison world. They had better hope to be fast enough, though.

And Bennett had better get me more information soon.

Chapter 25

Infiltration Begins, Histories Unfold, Truths Be Told

Tam had that narrow-eyed look that indicated he would be sick at any minute. Farthing had warned him earlier that an exit from curved space was coming. He had suggested that Tam take refuge in bed, where he could be monitored. The poor mentalist had instead decided to sit in a shuttle chair staring at the view screen, in the hopes it would prevent his space sickness. He had been doped up on anti-nausea medication and adrenaline blockers.

"Prepare for curve drive shut down. Batten down the hatches, mate!" Farthing looked over at Tam. "Are you ready?"

Tam nodded his head, but his eyes clearly said no. "Ready as I'll ever be!"

"Disengaging curve drive. Prepare for real space," Farthing announced. "Let me help you as best I can, my little blo'." Ordinary mentalists didn't feel what Tam experienced, but through his recent triad linking, he had gotten a good sense of it.

The shuttle exited from curved space. The view screen in front of them went from the rainbow-colored prism light of curved space to pinpoints of white stars in a matter of seconds. To anyone else, there would be no sensation. For advanced mentalists like Tam, it was devastating.

Tam's eyes grew wide with fear. Farthing saw and felt the young man's body trembling. *He needs my care until he's in Brogan's arms again—if that ever happens. By the Blue Sapphire Suns of Messier, I will succeed, even if it means giving my life for Tam's. The Magistrate must be stopped at all costs.*

Tam was now limp on the couch beside him. He'd gone unconscious from his struggle.

Farthing gently planted a kiss on his forehead and went to tend his ship, turning from time to time to make sure his precious cargo was still OK. *Love for another human being transforms the physical body.* Mother had once said that to him. Farthing could not help but love Tam as he loved Brogan.

Farthing's body ached. His head felt like it could split down the middle. For a moment, he sensed Brogan's mind, and felt warmth run through his veins, taking the pain away. *[Brogan, you old dog, you're always there when I need you! Focus on Tam—help him if you can.]*

The next hour passed. Dials were checked, distances were calculated, and a low orbit was set for Kashtiloth's moon, Opal Luna. Kashtiloth's security forces would be less likely to notice the presence of a rogue shuttle there, since the moon was uninhabited but for a few bots in a sensor lab on the near side. Another quick shuttle ride in a short burst of curved space would bring them to the edge of Kashtiloth's atmosphere without being noticed.

Tam stirred on the couch, stretched, and sat up. "Where am I?" Seeing Farthing, he remembered and lay back. "We've arrived, then?"

"Aye. We are now in orbit around Opal Luna. You'll have to take one more small curved space jump before you are on Kashtiloth, Tam. It's the only way to reach the atmosphere without being noticed."

"Understood," said Tam, though he wished he were somewhere else.

∞

"Mother's spies have been busy, young Tam!" Farthing waved his hands in the air. "You already have a cover. You'll never guess what you'll be doing! You're to be a page for the court of the Senate. One step closer to the Magistrate himself. How Mother does this is beyond me. Those idiots don't have a clue that she regularly accesses people inside the Senate."

"A page?! You're telling me I'm to be a servant?!" Tam was astounded. "You trained me for hand-to-hand and weapons use just so I could be a page to some rich slob?"

Farthing laughed. "Tam, you're getting ahead of yourself."

"How will I get there?"

"Easy! After a quick jump to the edge of the atmosphere, we'll drop the shuttle to the forested hills to the south of the capital, Central City. You'll have to walk a distance, though."

"How do you evade their sensors?" Tam asked.

"The Sirens will sing for us and create a screen of light that will bend around the shuttle, making it invisible to both the naked eye and the sensors of Central City. The Mother and the Sirens are a wonder, aren't they?"

"They must be magical to be able to do that," Tam marveled.

"To some, they may seem so! They're my saviors—that's for sure."

"How so, Farthing?" Tam shifted and sat up beside him.

Farthing breathed in. He began: "You've often commented on my size. As you can see, I am quite a bit larger than the average person. This is not a natural occurrence, but a genetic manipulation. I was created to lead a Senate army to victory many years ago. What the Senate did not understand was the sodbent nature hidden inside me. Up until recently, I didn't know if I carried any markers for being sodbent. Even without the gene manipulation, I think I'd have been a naturally occurring gay man, Tam!"

"You were genetically manipulated? How?"

"The Senate—and, specifically, the Magistrate—developed gene manipulation techniques years ago as part of their master plan for domination. I am one of their experiments."

"When did you come to know you were different?" Tam asked.

"I've always known I am different!" exclaimed Farthing. "My growth began early in my teen years and didn't slow until my early twenties. Mother did some research and discovered the Senate has a gene manipulation laboratory in Central City on Kashtiloth. It was there I received the genetic markers for what I've become today. It also explains why I don't feel spacesickness like you do. The genetic changes somehow inhibit the effects."

"Do you recall any of it?"

"Not really," he admitted. "Nothing other than being taken on frequent trips to the laboratory by Senate scientists for injections and small operations that didn't seem to amount to anything. One thing's for sure: my size makes me stand out amongst others. In the beginning, I didn't feel any different—but the growth was painful and intense in my teen years. I can still recall it."

"It must have been horrible." Tam winced.

"It was what drove me to hating the Senate so much!" agreed Farthing. "The pain made it clear I could not serve the Senate or Kruger Senior—and certainly not Kruger Junior. As soon as I was of age, I ran from the Senate school and made my escape on a flight to Alorion, where I met up with a roving band of pirates. They became my family. Later, I became the head of the Pirate Confederacy, because of my dedication to destroying anything to do with the Senate. I also discovered that the Siren Sisters had played a role in helping me escape. They saved me from my fate. Aye, that is why they are so important to me.

"The pirate band honored me with the right to be their leader. That was over four years ago now, and we've been fighting ever since. I've escaped many times and come very close to being captured by the Magistrate's cronies. He is a monster. We must do what we can to take him down when the time is right."

"Is that time... now?" Tam asked.

"No," said Farthing. "Not until Brogan and the others are rescued. Only then can we consider somehow getting rid of the Magistrate and his affiliates. We need their mental strength to overtake the Senate. Without them, we would fail."

Tam looked at Farthing with more understanding. Both had experienced gene manipulation, making them almost kin—though Tam's was ancient and Farthing's recent.

"Farthing, I never knew."

Farthing looked down at his hands and back at Tam. "It is what I carry, young man." He placed his big hand on Tam's shoulder.

Tam patted it tenderly. "You are a brave soul, Farthing. I love you deeply for what you've experienced—and for what you've sacrificed."

"Thank you, little blo'. There's something more that you need to know, though. Mother thought it best not to tell you until we were well into our voyage. Well, here we are, and I guess that there's no longer a reason to withhold what she suspects."

"What do you mean, what Mother suspects?"

"Have you ever wondered why the Magistrate made it his mission to find all the sodbent in the system?"

Tam's eyes widened as he realized he was about to learn something. He swallowed and felt a shiver run though his body. "Go on."

"The Magistrate has had access to records from the Ancients themselves."

"The Ancients?"

"The original humans who came to our galaxy thousands and thousands of years ago."

Tam's mind reeled. "We're not the only humans? There were others?"

"Yes," said Farthing. "In fact, there are humans in other parts of the galaxy and maybe also in the neighboring ones. Mother knows a lot, but not all. This is why she needs Life-Liners like you. You are part of a bigger scheme. Bigger than those of the Magistrate. Those men on Corustloth, in that prison, are the key to finding out the truth! It's up to us to find out before the Magistrate does. Mother says the lives of all those in the system depend on it."

"You're telling me, Farthing, that the key to the survival of the human race depends on the secrets in my genes?"

"And Brogan's—and those of all the men in that prison. Without them, Mother will never find the truth. Instead, the Magistrate will use this truth for his own gain. Even Mother won't venture to tell me what she thinks he might do with all this knowledge and power. I suspect that she is very afraid."

"Mother is never afraid!" Tam retorted.

"Aye," he said, "a wise person knows when to be afraid. Mother is the wisest of us all. There be dangerous times ahead for all of us—Mother knows this, and it saddens her to put her children at risk. She loves all her Life-Liners as though they were her own children. But risk yourself you must. She's foreseen a lot, and much of it may be pre-ordained. But if the Magistrate succeeds, much will be lost. So, Tam... are you ready?"

"Ready for what?"

"To get Brogan out of that prison and find the key to the mystery Mother is seeking!"

"Brogan!" exclaimed Tam. "Yes, by the Goddesses, I am so ready to get him."

"Then steel yourself, and prepare to take on the role of a page to the Magistrate. You have an interview coming up! We'd better get you ready."

Chapter 26

A Page's Day of Work is Not Always an Honest One

Tam sat silently in front of the Magistrate's secretary with his hands in his lap.

"Your resume is spotless, Thamara Amergan. You come highly recommended by aristocrats from Alorion. But how are you at following instructions?" The secretary leaned forward, chewing on his computer stylus. "We can't have pages blindly questioning the Magistrate, neither can we afford to keep replacing them for their insolence. It is of the utmost importance that you be passive. Agree to everything the Magistrate says—I'll have your head if you don't."

No doubt you are afraid for your own life, you poor sap! Tam thought, shifting his buttocks on the chair in front of the secretary's desk. The little, bookish-looking man gazed down over his glasses peculiarly at Tam, reminding him of those birds back on Alorion—*what were they called... budgies? This man twitters and squeaks just like the budgies in the bushes on the edge of the maize fields.*

Farthing, sensing this thought from afar, returned a notion back to him to do with staying on task.

The secretary was still droning on about compliance with the Magistrate. Tam knew his life depended on it. Hopefully, Farthing's distant assistance would prevent him from being rash.

"Well, I see no reason *not* to hire you as a page for the Magistrate," the little man said to Tam. "Just remember your place. You'll have to wear the appropriate uniform and be given the protocols of the Magistrate's daily routines before you meet him. Mustn't have a careless and unknowing page, doomed before he even starts.

Remember all this. The Magistrate himself will decide whether you are suitable. Above all, *keep quiet unless spoken to.*"

The little man turned from Tam and continued entering data into his pad, his stylus now half-chewed.

The poor guy really must get a job that isn't so hard on his nerves—or his hairline, Tam thought to himself. He stood quietly, bowed to the secretary, and said, "By your leave, sir, I shall endeavor to make the best page to the Magistrate."

The secretary snorted, not bothering to look up. "I've heard that one before." He pointed toward a door. "The changeroom is to your left. Get into your uniform immediately—you'll be meeting the Magistrate in a few short moments."

Tam stood up. As he approached the room, he wondered what the uniform would look like. He opened the door of the changeroom and entered. Looking down the rows of the same uniform design made en masse, he decided he would miss the clothing he was wearing, which he had recently purchased in Central City with the credits Farthing had given him. It would be a shame to change into one of those silly page outfits, with the tunic and the braided hat. Tunics, he had been told, were a deterrent from concealing weapons to hurt the Magistrate. It really was too bad Tam couldn't hide a particle beam weapon in a tunic.

[*Patience, Tam. Let's not be hasty or rash. You must gain the Magistrate's trust, not knock him off! We need information about the plans first. Killing him would place all of us in jeopardy—or at least delay our rescue trip.*] Farthing's words of wisdom rang in Tam's head.

[*Fine, I'll be a passive page and duck my head like a lowly slime slug, Farthing!*]

He looked down the rows of page uniforms, hats, and booties for his feet. He found his sizes easily enough, but cringed at the absolute disaster of an outfit.

[*I hope the League appreciates my sacrifice in wearing this uniform!*] Tam quipped to Farthing.

[*Do be quiet, Tam, and prepare yourself. You must ensure that your first meeting goes well. If not, we are out of luck—there's no plan B!*]

[*Of course, Farthing, I'll do as you ask.*]

Tam pulled off his new clothes and placed them in a storage locker. He wrote his name on the locker with a luminance pen he had found on the counter. [*Well, I've made my mark... I now have a locker in the Magistrate's palace. Quite the honor, eh, Farthing?*]

[*Don't get too cocky, Tam. You have a job to do.*]

[I got it! I'm ready.] Tam pulled on his narrow-rimmed braided hat, tunic, and blue booties, which looked and felt more like tissue paper than leather.

Tam opened the door of the changing room to find the little man's eyes full of disdain as he exited the change room.

"You look very much the part. Make sure that you also act the role!"

"Yes, sir. I'll follow your orders, sir." Tam could feel the bile rising in his stomach from the tiny little lies he had already told. What would it feel like at full strength? Best to not figure that one out. *It may prevent me from doing what I need to do here: be passive.*

The little man knocked on the adjacent door and awaited a response from the other side.

A bell rang. The door opened. The little man ducked his head as he entered, motioning for Tam to do the same. Tam's heart was almost in his mouth.

Chapter 27
A Page's Quest and a Pirate's Query

"Enter, Secretary Barrington." The Magistrate sat on his couch, pillows around him, propping him up. "Have you brought me a new candidate? The last few have been a blasted waste of my time."

"My Magistrate, my Lord, may I present Tam Amergan? After having looked through the final list of candidates, I have chosen him as having the most potential for your services."

"I'm sure you have my best interests at heart," the Magistrate said with subtle sarcasm.

Tam focused himself on the job at hand: gain the trust of a madman.

"Approach, young man. Let me have a look at the man Barrington says will be my next page."

Tam bowed deeply, swept his hands to his chest, and went down on one knee. "I am honored, my Lord Magistrate. I am here to serve." Tam's mind quickly probed for entry points in his mind. The jumbled, chaotic, sadistic ideas with which he was met shocked him.

The Magistrate remained silent. Barrington stood at the door, sweating profusely.

The Magistrate looked down at Tam and spoke: "You will serve as my page. Barrington, leave, now, and let us be."

Barrington bowed low and left without a sound, pushing his glasses up his nose, breathing out with relief.

Tam smiled and continued to press through the Magistrate's mind. It would take some time to find what he was looking for, but he'd find it. "I am honored, sir."

"Come, young man, and join me on my couch. I wish to learn more about you. We have much to do. I'll be needing much of your services."

∞

Farthing yawned and stretched. The flight into low orbit around Kashtiloth had been a tiring ordeal for him. Calculations needed to be exact, or the ship would exit curved space in the upper atmosphere, destroying the ship and everyone inside. Luckily, he had done what he had set out to accomplish, appearing just above the atmosphere of Kashtiloth, near the northern reaches of the planet's polar region. No satellites or bots were there to observe them.

He recalled the strain on Tam's face as they had exited the curved space jump above Opal Luna to a low orbit just above the atmosphere. His eyes were straining, clearly seeing objects that were not there. His mouth quivered, mouthing Brogan's name.

Farthing had grown furious lately. The injustice of it all was incredible. How could someone do such despicable things to other human beings? Why should someone like Tam—or Brogan, for that matter—suffer for the desires of a maniac?

Farthing's emotions started to well into a big ball of anger. He slammed his fist onto the console of the shuttle's food dispenser, causing remnants of his lunch to fly in all directions. The Senate had genetically altered him to be a soldier—he could feel that in every fibre of his being. Sometimes, it was all that he could do to keep himself from going on a rampage and doing harm to those seen as a threat to the League. But Mother's gentle reminders would arrive, like a whisper on the wind, his brow would loosen, and he would relax and smile.

Mother, however, was on Alorion at that moment, and her influence here was limited. She was no Life-Liner, like Brogan or Tam; she was their catalyst. It was her life's chore to bind them together and make them communicate as a whole. She was the glue that held it all together. It was no longer her task to merely soothe the shattered nerves of a soldier who craved revenge.

Being alone—separated from the rest of the crew—didn't help, either. The small shuttle was meant for only four or five occupants, but had served to transport only Tam and himself. The rest of the crew remained in silence somewhere in the asteroid cluster, waiting for Farthing's next command. What maddened Farthing the most was that he couldn't be seen in Central City. It wasn't every day that a man of his stature could be seen in Central City. He would be arrested immediately. Instead, he had to stay in the wilderness outside of the city and wait for news of Tam's success... or failure. It was exasperating.

He stood up, hit the release button to open the hatch, and pushed it open. The night air coming from the mountains to the north was refreshing, and it calmed him. He realized that sitting there for the past four days had been taxing on him.

There had to be something he could do. But what? Kashtiloth was a forested planet. It might have been the governing planet of the system, but it had many wild parts. Maybe a side journey would be in order. He could send a coded message to the *Starfinder* and let them know he would be making a little unplanned trip. The shuttle's automated response system would record any incoming messages from the ship and relay information to him. Besides, Farthing would be in constant contact with the shuttle, as long as he had his communicator pad and was part of his Life-Line triad.

Maybe a little digging in one of the universities would be in order. They were mostly abandoned after the Senate coup years ago, and most of the educated people had been rounded up and sent away to camps. In fact, there would probably be just a skeleton crew of Senate police at Central City University, on the outskirts of the city. It would be an easy feat for an experienced League pirate such as himself to enter without anyone knowing. Some spying would occupy his mind and his body. He pocketed a particle beam weapon and some recording units, and gathered rations into a satchel. He shouldered it as he exited out of the closing hatch of the shuttle, feeling a sense of freedom to be out and about. It was good to be doing something again.

Chapter 28
Gaining Trust, Finding Insight

Tam found it relatively easy to coax Kruger's mind into accepting him.

Since the Magistrate was a virtual hermit due to his obsessive fear of assassination, his defenses had been low, and it had been easy for Tam to do his work in secret. Tam even found he could manipulate him somewhat to do his bidding, as long as he didn't push too hard. Tam was starting to feel the whole situation was a little *too* easy...

The woods gave up the last of the night's mist to meet the dawn of Kashtiloth, and the air suddenly exploded with the sound of birdsong. Even someone as hardened as Farthing couldn't help but take pleasure in hearing the pleasant chirping and territorial songs.

Farthing had made his way to Central University under the cover of night, and had met no one on his journey. He was pleased his progress had been unhindered.

After a quick meal of rations for breakfast, Farthing made the last push to the entrance of the university. He chose to remain off the roads and used forest paths to approach the school. With the woods starting to thin, just as the sun was peeping over the eastern horizon, he realized he had reached his destination.

Arriving at the university walls, Farthing prepared himself to meet resistance. But he found none—not even a bot to greet him—as he approached the gate.

Tam sat and waited patiently for the Magistrate to finish going to the bathroom. It was Tam's job to wipe the very large backside of the Magistrate, as he could no longer reach far enough to wipe up after himself.

"Page, do be gentle—I have been feeling a little chapped lately."

"Yes Magistrate," Tam replied as he applied the tissue to the rolls of fat and dumped the soiled paper into the waste disposal unit. He gently massaged the rolls of fat, as the Magistrate had requested, and slowly pulled his under garments up as the man lifted his body into a vertical position with a grunt. Tam's arm went under the Magistrate's armpit immediately. He assisted him toward his couch.

"You are a gentle soul, Tam," praised the Magistrate. "I am growing very pleased with your performance."

"As always, Sire, it is my pleasure to be your assistant." Tam had become very good at hiding his loathing. Tam's love for Brogan was the one thing that prevented the hate from surfacing, giving him away and costing him his life.

They slowly lumbered to the couch as the Magistrate blabbered on about his latest work.

"More messages have arrived, Tam. We must have a look at them and assess our progress." He stopped, out of breath. "I feel my weight is getting to be too much. We may have to call the surgeons to help remove the excess. I shan't be taking the risk of exercising, even in the palace. There is too much that could wrong." He paused and considered. "Once my plans are in progress, all of this will change."

He continued trudging over to the couch, Tam propping him up, as he probed for ways to get the monster to let go more of his secrets.

"I'll be able to move freely and be free of any terrorist activities! The League will be destroyed, and my power solidified." He grinned and turned his fat face toward Tam, the rolls twisting as he smiled. "Would you like to know more, Tam?"

"If it is your Magistrate's desire." Tam knew he was pushing the man hard, but sensed that he could get what he needed right then. It was almost as though the man was swayed by Tam's scent. He sniffed his arm as he descended to his seat on his couch.

"Tam, I trust you like no other. You will be rewarded for your devotion to me." His eyes glistened a bit—almost like a tear might pop out of the corner of his eye. Where would this man be without having his mind manipulated? Probably going on yet another abusive rampage.

Tam sensed another crack in the Magistrate's armor and went for broke. "Magistrate, I exist to serve his lordship. I will do as you request." Tam's mind pushed a little more and felt the Magistrate's mind give. "Sire, it would please me to assist you in your plans. What can I do to make your success more accessible?"

Tam was really pushing now. Sweat started to pool in the armpits of his tunic. The Magistrate was oblivious.

Tam sent a message to Farthing, whose location he could not determine: *[Farthing, I may have done it.]* The response back was like a grunt of appreciation. *[I may get to the plans sooner than we thought.]*

"Tam, bring me some water. I am parched." Tam went to the dispenser and pushed the glass against the valve. The water was dispensed at the perfect temperature for his Magistrate's most sensitive lips. "Taste it for me first."

Tam lifted the glass to his lips and sipped from it.

The Magistrate smiled and continued: "No obvious ill effects. Give me my water."

Tam handed the glass to him.

"Sit, young man."

Tam sat gently at a distance from the man, in order to show respect. "Let me access my records, then we'll talk."

Tam handed him his console and waited.

"You may go, Tam. I am comfortable, thanks to you. Do help me raise my feet a little with a cushion before you excuse yourself, though."

Tam reached for a cushion, gently lifted his feet one at a time, and placed them on the cushion, massaging them slightly.

"You are a wonderful caregiver, Tam. I am so happy to have you serve me."

"Of course, Magistrate." Tam bowed deeply and again went to his knee. He knew he liked that little extra touch of respect.

By the time Tam had been pushing Kruger for several days, Captain Farthing had accessed Central University. Gaining entrance had been easy enough, despite his size. Farthing was a master at being secretive when needed. He was, after all, a trained solider.

There were no guards to be seen. Farthing found that strange. No bots, either. Why was no one guarding the university? The Senate would not want anyone to gain access to such a sensitive place, where there were so many secrets to be gained and used against the Magistrate. So why no welcoming committee? He passed by many a monitor that seemed dead. There was no response from anyone or anything. It didn't make sense!

Farthing gave up trying to figure out the puzzle and proceeded to the data bank in the library core of the university's computer. Pulling his data reader from his pack, he accessed the computer data bank without any resistance. Odd. There should be some sort of protection protocol to prevent unwanted entry into the university systems. The mystery was deepening.

∞

"Tam, I need you!" the Magistrate called. Tam got up from his seat in the waiting room and hurried to the Magistrate.

"Yes, sire. I am at your disposal!"

"I have a task for you, but I wish to share a little with you first." The Magistrate shifted his bulky weight on his sofa, turning to Tam, his face beaming with absolute joy. "My plans are coming to fruition! The prisoners on Corustloth are now designated as excess. We may do as we please."

"What is your plan, then, my Magistrate?" Tam ducked his head to show respect, secretly wincing, hoping his mental link hadn't pushed him too hard.

The Magistrate responded without hesitation: "Those men are slated for genetic manipulation and experimentation. My plan to discover the reason for psychic linking capabilities in homosexual men will soon commence. These links will be the key to my power over the system. With the control of these psychic links, I shall be able to govern the entire system with an iron fist." He shook his arm and waved his fist to the heavens, his triceps flapping back and forth. "No one will be able to withstand my might! I'll control everything and everyone. I'll know what every soul is thinking, doing, and planning. There'll be no more assassination attempts. I'll be the most powerful Magistrate ever to have lived!"

The Magistrate beamed as he gloated, not knowing he had just given up his secrets to the last person on Kashtiloth who he'd want to know his plans. Tam reveled in finding out the Magistrate's horrific plans, even if it scared the blue moons of Alorion out of him. The next task was to find the plans to the Corustloth prison. *No point pushing more,* Tam thought, and Farthing agreed with a mental nod from afar.

"Tam, I cannot do all this myself. I shall need your help. You've become invaluable to me. And I've located an excellent working partner for you—someone who has come to my attention recently, as a key to helping me unearth more information about the League!" He paused to catch his breath. "Call my secretary immediately! Tell him to send in my new assistant."

He waved Tam to do his bidding. Tam wondered what was coming next as he bowed and backed out in silence.

Tam contacted Secretary Barrington in the Magistrate's office at the other end of the palace. The holoconsole lit up and the secretary's bald head appeared.

"Yes! What do you want?" Barrington scowled.

"His Magistrate commands his new assistant to be sent to his quarters immediately!"

"Yes, of course. Inform his worthiness that he is on his way." He waved to someone out of Tam's view. He turned back to Tam. "You have been doing well with his Magistrate. Few have earned the honor of becoming so close with him in so little time. Conduct yourself accordingly. Remember, my life depends on you. Do not crush my hopes under Alorion Banderbeast hooves, as they say back home!"

"Yes, sir." The holoviewer went blank. "I'll trample you myself, you blathering idiot," Tam retorted at the empty screen. The stress was starting to get to him.

[Aye! Better be careful!] came a message from Farthing.

The bell sounded. He jumped immediately to the Magistrate's aide. The task was probably just another opportunity to wipe his fat buttocks again. He sighed, sent a message of goodwill to Brogan, and hoped for the best. He moved to the door.

As he entered the room, the Magistrate beamed. "Tam, your assistant is on his way. I think I hear him now."

There was the sound of shuffling on the other side of the door, then a gentle knock.

"Enter!" the Magistrate called. Tam sensed the man's mind and faltered.

No, it couldn't be!

The door opened. A man entered and approached the Magistrate, his head bowed. "At your service, my Lord Magistrate."

"Please, young man, tell us your full name—and by all means, introduce yourself to my page, Tam. You will be working with him closely."

"By your honor, Sire. My name is Artagan. Artagan Mangrouph-Charon, the first."

Tam swallowed hard, feeling faint. His plan had just gotten a little more complicated.

Part 5
Fates Entwined, Voyages Divined

Chapter 29

Curved Space for Bennett

The shuttle's engines changed pitch, indicating liftoff. Bennett felt the blood drain from his face. He had no idea what it would be like to be in space. He had been on local flights, within the atmosphere, but that was it.

The whine heightened and the ship slowly and elegantly lifted off the pad. Bennett's pulse raced. He closed his eyes for a moment. Brogan's plight flashed before his eyes. He was being tortured with drugs again. The scene shifted and Tam's attempts at winning over the Magistrate wavered before his eyes. Bennett shook his head and opened his eyes as the shuttle soared higher into the atmosphere. *I'll have to remember to tell Father about the flashes. It seems I can almost link at will with either of them right now.*

The shuttle soared higher and the view from the window softened from blue to jet black as they cleared the atmosphere. What he saw humbled him. The curve of the planet's beautiful shape lay behind him. The continents below were enveloped in soft clouds, still visible. Oh, the stars! They were so different from what he was used to seeing. He marveled at their clarity and, using his mental powers, could almost determine if they were mental blue or not.

Absolutely stunning! I've never experienced something so beautiful in all my life! I have indeed led a sheltered existence...

The speaker came alive with the captain's voice: "Mr. Davis, prepare for curved space. The nurses are arriving to monitor your physical and mental responses."

Bennett turned in his seat to see the two nurses approach through the open door, both smiling assuredly.

"Yes, Captain. I am ready."

"Are you prepared for the outcome? The doctors say you could be violently ill or have a seizure. Are you sure you want to do this?"

"Yes, I am." Bennett had to hold his ground and steel himself—for Tam and Brogan's sake.

The nurses took their seats beside his couch and monitored him silently.

"Curved space in ten seconds. Crew, prepare for entry."

The vision screen above gave Bennett a clear view of where the shuttle was headed. As he stared at the points of light, he noticed a shimmering wave of rainbow lights forming in front of and flowing toward the shuttle—or, rather, the shuttle toward it. Soon, the entire ship was enveloped in the rainbow. A wave of intense power flowed over Bennett.

"Curved space achieved. Heading on a flight path to the edge of the system. Exit in twenty minutes." The captain's voice sounded reassuring to Bennett. "Relax and enjoy your first curved space voyage, Mr. Davis. We'll check in with you just before exit. Captain out."

The shimmering tunnel of multi-colored light mesmerized Bennett. It seemed to him he was traveling down a tube of light that twisted and turned with gentle regularity and purpose. He felt so small in the grand scheme of things. There was so much more out there than what he had experienced in his short twenty-eight years.

When the twenty minutes were up, he was startled. The time had seemed to go more quickly. *It couldn't be twenty minutes already!* But somehow, it was.

"Crew, this is the captain speaking. Prepare for exit from curved space. Nurses, continue logging responses on Mr. Davis. Mr. Davis, are you ready?"

"Yes, I am," he replied, despite his trepidation. Bennett squirmed in his seat and stared blankly at the screen.

The exit came, and it was not pleasant. The shifts of light danced in his eyes drunkenly, whirling faster. One long flash, three short ones, and then a pause, before it repeated. His stomach churned. It was only a matter of time before he would become sick. But all the while, he was lost somewhere else.

"Father! What have you done to me? Why do you make me suffer so?" he cried out. Sweat beaded on his brow and the nurses stepped up their attendance of him. "Make the madness stop—please, I beg you. Tam! Brogan! Make it stop! *Help me!*"

From Bennett's point of view, he was drowning in a sea of viscous fluid, binding him downward to be drowned. The light around him flitted like the fireflies he had seen through Tam's eyes on Alorion. But they were different somehow—more menacing and dangerous. One flash, three short ones, a pause, then repeat. The nurses were incredulous. His mental powers were registering off the scale. There was no way to measure what he was doing with his brain!

What they couldn't know was the effect his reaction was having on the gay men in the system. One massive flash, three short ones, an ominous pause, and all the gay men lit up like blue Christmas lights on Father's holomap. It flashed brilliant blue as over two hundred points of light illuminated, linking to Bennett's location. Then, something new: the next system linked, then the next, until the Order's whole arm of the galaxy was linked to over forty thousand individuals. They all experienced what Bennett saw and felt.

Then, there was silence.

Bennett felt the forty thousand odd minds attached to his and, oddly enough, didn't feel afraid. He figured he would say something historic. So, he simply said, *[Hello!]*

He instantly received more than forty thousand responses back. Then it spread further.

The Sirens all stood and turned as the message came through. Mother received the message, sensing tidings of what was to come. Communication from individuals began flooding through Bennett on to the others. It was as though Bennett had become the conduit for all the minds in the galaxy.

Bennett somehow knew Tam had received the collective hello, as well as Brogan. Neither of them could yet respond, but they both wondered at the call.

Sensing a shift in the link, Bennett sent a final message: *[Father, we have contact!]*

Then, with a silence that seemed to collapse like a thunderclap, the link was severed and each of the genetically altered mentalists was left alone to question what had just happened. *One long flash, three short ones, and a pause...*

Some had received only echoes of the link, but it had been more than enough for Father. He had received the message because *Bennett had desired it*. Bennett was now the key to communication in the galaxy. Father knew then he had succeeded in phase one of his quest and wept openly for the first time in many years. He signaled for the shuttle to return home for debriefing after his physical examinations. Bennett had just become a hero.

Chapter 30
Thievery, Justified

Farthing stood silently as the reader continued to search for data relating to Corustloth and the prison blueprints. Pondering, he widened the search, keying in a request for all information about the League, Sirens, mentalists, and sodbents. The university computer responded with enough data to fill three holorecorders. It would be worth the wait to transfer the data. Then, he would have time to search offline, away from prying eyes, back in the shuttle.

Why were there no guards or bots? The question kept coming back to him as the recorder continued writing the data after having been placed into the slot.

It had been all too easy to gain access to the university's information. Farthing knew that most of the Professors of the Learnèd had been killed or exiled for what they had once held. Intelligence was now forbidden other than for the benefit of the Senate. Why on Alorion, then, would someone like Farthing be able to just walk into a university and take information? Where were the safeguards to keep out the prying, curious, or thievish? Farthing thought it ironic he would be considered a thief. What he had "stolen" used to be open information.

The second recorder signaled its capacity had been met. He pulled it out of the recorder and slid in the third. Looking at the readout, he realized he had another five minutes of wait time. Still feeling uneasy, he decided to pry a little further into the mystery of no security. Standing up, Farthing turned and looked down through the rows of data readers and books. There was no evidence of anyone having been there for some time.

He walked down the closest aisle to the window that looked out over the courtyard. The sun was higher in the sky now. He scanned the gardens below. They were void of people or technology. They were overgrown and long in need of care, but empty of any threat. This was beginning to irritate Farthing. He was used to fighting for what he needed.

Without an apparent threat, he returned to the recorder to find it almost finished. The screen flashed "indexing database for queries," then beeped to signal that the search parameters had been stored somewhere on one of the three holorecorders. He removed the third recorder, placed it in his satchel with the others, and made his way out of the library.

Pausing at the outside doorway he had entered earlier, he felt uneasy.

[Tam, I need your help right now. Can you tell me what you sense through my senses? I feel something is wrong, but cannot discover what.]

[There is no immediate threat I can figure, Farthing. I sense others nearby, but cannot ascertain where or how many. I would suggest going covert as quickly as possible. You may be in danger—I cannot say how I know! Wait—someone is watching you. Be careful!]

Farthing narrowed his eyes and slid quietly into the overgrown bushes and trees of the university gardens. He continued unhindered by anything other than the occasional impassable path caused by the thick undergrowth, blocking a large soul such as himself.

Farthing stopped only twice after that: once for a toilet break and then for food. As the sun began setting, he was close to the shuttle's hiding spot, still incredulous that nothing had stood in his way the entire trip.

Without warning, a buzzing in his head began to beat like a drum, with one long beat, three short ones, then a pause, repeating this sequence. A mental message followed: [Hello!] For several moments, he was dumbstruck, having visions of things alien to him. Other people's thoughts and sights, sounds and smells. Tam's response brought him back to present.

[Farthing, a message came to me—just a simple "Hello." I cannot say where it came from, but I was unable to move or think for myself for several minutes.]

[I felt a sensation of others' thoughts and feelings. Did you, too?]

[Yes. Including a very strong message from Brogan, saying he needed me.]

[Tam, I have reached the shuttle, with a wealth of information to read. I'll be returning to the Starfinder to ponder our next move once I process the information I've garnered.]

[I may be in danger of losing my cover. Someone recognizes me. I can't communicate further just now. Goddesses' luck, Farthing.]

Farthing reached the shuttle's hatch and keyed in his code for entry. As the hatch slid open, there was a gentle "whoosh" sound, followed by the sound of metal connecting with metal. He dove for cover and closed the hatch from inside, particle beam in hand, ready to fire if necessary.

Chapter 31
Twists of Fate

Artagan smirked. "Well, well, well! Interesting twist, don't you think, Tam?" Artagan sat down on the couch in the servants' quarters. "It looks like you've been busy, too!"

Tam swallowed uneasily, "What do you want, Artagan?"

"Nothing yet. I'd like to know more of what you've been up to since you became the Magistrate's page. How long has it been? A week or so?"

Tam nodded and kept quiet.

"I'll not expose you, Tam... since you are going to help me."

Artagan rose from his chair and paced around.

"It seems I have no choice."

Artagan raised an eyebrow and smirked. "I know you are digging deeply into the Magistrate's mind. I've been studying these techniques as a member of the Senate."

Tam wasted no time asking what was on his mind: "How did you survive the hijacking? That cargo hold was ripped off that Minorian spaceship by a massive force. Obviously you weren't blasted into space through a hole."

"No, I was very lucky. After I left you to your follies, I made my way back to the bridge. When the ship shuddered from the impact, I realized something way beyond my control was happening. I sought the nearest escape pod and jettisoned as soon as I could. Luckily, Senate patrols picked me up several days later—just when I ran out of coffee and sugar."

"Well, you were lucky to escape. I woke up with a concussion, surrounded by pirates." Tam rubbed his forehead where the injury had occurred. It still hurt sometimes.

"I warned you about going back there into that cargo hold with all of those degenerates! You ignored me." He paused. "Well, now it's in my best interest to find out what you've been up to since then."

"It would be easy to turn in a degenerate for a ransom, wouldn't it," Tam pondered, not looking directly into Artagan's eyes, "despite being just as much of one yourself?"

Artagan's eyes narrowed. "I am not one and the same as you, Tam. Oh, and no, that doesn't nearly amount to what I'll gain from all this. You've made my life so much more profitable with your spying and information-seeking. You've become a golden nugget to me. You are more valuable to me alive, continuing what you are doing—degen or not!"

"And what is it that you want from me, Artagan?"

"I simply want to be on the winning side. Either you will succeed and gather the information you need, or you will fail. I will wait for either. But why, you ask?"

"You know me well enough, I guess," Tam obliged. "Do you know what it is I seek?"

"Not yet, but you will tell me all, eventually. With your knowledge, then, I'll decide what to do. Either way, you will keep quiet. You wouldn't want to be turned in as a degenerate at this pivotal moment, would you?"

"Obviously not." Artagan, it seemed, was a slippery man—not at all the way he had seemed on the supply ship. *Heed what happens. Don't blow your cover.* "How would my failure service your needs?"

"Ah, that, my friend Tam is the best part about all of this." He smiled. "If you should fail, I can use what I know of you and your alliance. I've been monitoring your big friend. My sensor drones followed him around the university during his espionage, then sounded on his shuttle when he dove into it. That was just after that *[hello.]* I am still confounded as to where it came from. Any ideas, Tam?"

"Sorry, no." Tam told the truth. He looked at Artagan with new suspicion—how could he have received the message if he weren't sodbent, mind sifter or … a mentalist?!

"Once you've told me your plans, then I'll make my decision. And you will gain the Magistrate's trust in me. I will have the power to do as I choose."

Tam thought of sinking ships and rodents seeking escape.

"Do as I say, or I'll turn you into the Magistrate! You'll be put through a meat grinder if he finds out the truth!"

Tam was despondent. "Again, it seems I have no choice." *[At least I have my triad Life-Line intact, out of sight from this traitor. Farthing, do you hear me?]*

Farthing acknowledged with a simple *[yes!]*, nothing more.

∞

Farthing lay on the deck of the shuttle, breathlessly waiting to see what would happen next. The alarming sound of what had seemed like metal projectiles hitting the shuttle had stopped. There had been only two such sounds, but he remained concerned as to what they were.

With little to go on, Farthing decided lying on the deck plating would do little good. He rolled to his side from his prone position, bent his knees, and pushed himself slowly up onto them, weapon at ready. Nothing happened. He tried placing a foot on the floor and standing up. Still nothing. Obviously, whatever had made the sound was neither in the cabin nor sensitive to movement. If something or someone were bent on destroying him, it probably would have already happened.

Striding over to the computer console, he punched in commands to view the internal and external sensors. The computer screen lit up with camera feeds from inside and outside the shuttle, panning from side to side. Nothing out of the ordinary showed there. So what had those sounds been? What about heat sources using infrared? The computer continued scanning. It showed the shuttle's drive system, himself, and the food dispenser. That was it for larger heat sources. What about smaller ones? The computer narrowed the search and located forty-five various heat sources around the shuttle. As he scanned them, he recognized all but two as being within normal parameters. Two unknown sources were outside the ship on the hull. The visual cameras were useless; nothing could be seen. He would have to go out there for himself.

Lifting his particle weapon, he pressed the door release and waited for a moment. Still nothing. This was getting frustrating. He'd rather be fighting an army of men then skulking around after potential spies.

"Fine! Kill me if you must!" he shouted to the ether, and stepped through the hatch.

Nothing. No one.

"Blazed moons of Alorion!" he said to himself. With nothing to stop him, he glanced up at the shuttle's side to see if anything were visually out of the ordinary. Nothing could be seen. The sensors did, however, indicate that two heat sources were just above the hatch entrance. Cautiously, he reached over the hatch door and across the skin of the ship. Feeling like someone searching in the dark, he found one bump, then another. But they were invisible!

"By the Goddesses! What trickery is this?"

Invisibility of some sort, he supposed—beyond the capability of the League's technology, but not that of the Sirens. What about the Senate? If not, they'd be on their way as he stood there. A decision had to be made. He couldn't go back to the ship at this point—if it were the Senate rats that had sent the sensors, he would be giving away the ship's hiding place. Stay here? No way. Where to go, then, so that Tam would stay safe? Tam was of no help; he was busy tending to the Magistrate. Brogan was in pain, as usual, and didn't offer anything. It would be up to him and him alone.

Sliding his fingers over the two invisible mystery bumps, he made his decision. Back to Alorion he would go, to rendezvous with one of the priestesses and consult with Mother. He had enough fuel to make the trip by curved space. That would also give him enough time to pour over the database he had stolen.

"Off I go, then!" he said to himself, then stepped back inside the shuttle. *Let's just hope that those two mystery bumps don't do more than watch. The last thing I need is to be a traveling bomb...*

Forty minutes later, Farthing was jumping into curved space. As the ship flew into the rainbow tunnel, he felt uneasy. Tam was on his own. There was nothing he could do for him now. Consulting with Mother was the best decision. Mother was his comfort, Tam his worry.

He took the three data holorecorders and seated each of them in their own cradle on the shuttle's science console. "Computer, link the three holorecorders and begin download."

Now, what about the search index? What key codes should he enter to help find what he was not sure he was looking for? "Computer, index search, please."

"Index parameters, Captain Farthing?" The computer had a familiar, animated female voice.

"Let's start with the following. Log: Thamara-Afil Amergan-Faolin, Brogan-Afil Faolin-Amergan, Senate plans for Corustloth prison, Magistrate Kruger and, finally, Life-Line. No need for verbal index answers—visual readout is sufficient."

The computer began its search, blinking repeatedly as he waited. The list of references based on his search grew. "Computer, let's start with references to Brogan. Show me the list of parameters referring to him."

The list appeared and he scrolled slowly through them. They were timestamped, sorted by oldest to the newest. There was no risk of missing anything, as his parameters would remain in effect until all three holorecorders had been read. He continued to scan the growing references. He also scanned the results for his other searches, growing just as quickly. There was a lot of data to cross-reference. Maybe he had ought to find a common link.

"Computer, using all of my parameters, find references that refer to Magistrate Kruger and either Tam or Brogan."

"Reference list updating," replied the computer.

Looking at this new reference search, he noted the list was much smaller and easier to manage. What about references to Life-Lines?

"Computer, add another reference search. Narrow my current search by adding any references to Life-Lines."

The computer responded immediately with another list of references. He now had seven working tabs to search through as the computer continued to read the second card. This tab was void of anything except one reference to Brogan's parents, Life-Lines, and Kruger in combination.

Farthing's big hand came down onto the console with a bang. "Now we're getting somewhere!"

This opportunity to get information from the university was invaluable. The Pirate Confederacy's database would be greatly enhanced as a result. If there were only some way of getting the whole university database in one fell swoop—but he knew that would be next to impossible. Perhaps he could get Tam working on this from the inside. Once he found out what the Magistrate's plans were, he should be able to gain access to the Senate's entire database. There was one short entry available for his last query.

"My Goddesses!" he shouted. "I know what happened to Brogan's parents!"

Tam responded immediately with questions.

[It is not good news. my young man!] Farthing sent back. [I need to be sure before I reply. I will need to talk to Mother beforehand. Please be patient.]

Farthing felt Tam respond back with something of a sigh, then disappointed silence.

"Computer, how long until exit for the first curved space checkpoint pylon?"

"Twelve minutes to curved space exit at checkpoint one," the computer responded. That would leave only one exit before arriving. The distance between Kashtiloth and Alorion was not as great as the distance between Alorion and Corustloth, and did not need more than one checkpoint. He still found it amazing that Tam had managed to get through eight checkpoints of the total nine on the way to Corustloth. What would have happened if he had made it past the ninth, then to the prison? He shuddered at the thought of Tam's probable fate and considered what to do next. Farthing had another twenty-two Alorion hours to make a decision before he arrived in Mother's presence.

He pushed back the mobile chair and stood. With time on his hands and nothing to do, he felt very uneasy. A soldier should be fighting, not researching! He was no good at this. Pacing wasn't even an option, due to his large frame and the small size of the shuttle; one or two paces and he would hit his head on something. With a sigh, he went to his couch and requested access to data files. "Computer, verbal and keyboard input requested for search parameters. Place all requests on the large screen."

He pulled the sensor keyboard from the side drawer of the couch as the computer responded by bringing up the status of the searches on the main screen. A short while and the files would be in the computer database. Then, it would be up to him to sift through all the logs, records, and reports to find if there was anything else to discover about the fate of Brogan's parents. He rubbed his chin, stretched his arms, then paused. It occurred to him that Brogan's arrest would be of importance as a search parameter.

"Computer, cross-reference another search for me, please. Search the entire database for references to Brogan's arrest in Port Ali-Alorion."

"Request accepted," responded the computer. There were now eight tabs in his search. "Estimated time to reading of entire database: two Alorion minutes."

"Thank you, computer." He stopped and smiled at himself being so polite to a computer. "Computer, bring up the record on Brogan's parents."

A record came up, dated over ten years ago, from about the time of Kruger Jr.'s inauguration. He remembered the era only too well... Brogan's parents had been League spies when they met their fate in Kruger's cruel clutches. Little was known other than the fact they had disappeared quietly, leaving Brogan an orphan of the state.

Senate Report, Infantry Division
Date: The 20th year of our Lord, Kruger II, Day 14
To: Alarius Kruger II
From: Morcant Sechnaill

During the police raids of Kashtiloth, many members of the University of the Learnèd were arrested to be sent to internment camps on Zemitis this day of our Lord, Kruger II. For reference on names of members, please refer to file reference "Kruger, Internment of Professors," file number 89B.

Of important note, your Magistrate, is the internment of what
appears to be the ringleaders of a religious sect of some sort
based on Alorion. Despite lengthy questioning sessions, including
the latest physical pain techniques, one Drustan Faolin and one
Elisedd Faolin failed to locate or indicate the location of the sect's
main hiding place. Further questioning revealed they had information that led me to believe they were the top officials of this sect.

*My Goddesses! The Faolin couple allowed the Senate to think they were the leaders
of the Sirens! They protected the secrecy of the Siren Sisters, saving them from certain
death. Amazing and tragic.* He continued to read the document in amazement.

Several members of this sect and of the Faolin family were captured and questioned, but no additional information was derived.
There was reference to a son by the name of Brogan, but he was
nowhere to be found. He has not been located on Kashtiloth
to date.

*Brogan, you dog! You went incognito and disappeared into the life of Port Ali-
Alorion. What better a way for a man such as you to hide and satisfy your needs? A
smart move.*

With your Magistrate's permission, I would like to continue the
search for more members of this sect on Kashtiloth. I feel there is
no need to search any of the other three planets of our system for
members at this time.

I await your Magistrate's decision on this matter.
Respectfully,
Morcant Sechnaill

"Computer, can you find any other references to the Faolin family in other documents? I am curious about their fate and what other information might be impli-
cated in their demise."

"Affirmative, Captain Farthing. There is another file report by the same captain
of the infantry dated four days later. File input from holorecorders is now complete.

You have full database access. Would you like me to put all references the Faolin family up for you?"

"Yes." Farthing squirmed a bit in his seat, curious to know more about the fate of Brogan's family. The report appeared on the screen. Farthing read it with increasing amazement.

> Senate Report, Infantry Division
> Date: The 20th year of our Lord, Kruger II, Day 18
> To: Alarius Kruger II
> From: Morcant Sechnaill
>
> My Lord, thank you for permission to search for more members of this sect. Your wise decision has led to me finding more invaluable information.
>
> The Faolin couple were professors at the university. Their area of expertise was in the sciences—DNA research. Further investigation revealed that their interest lay in the study of genetic manipulation of sodbent by ancient human intervention (refer to file titled "Ancient Humans, Genetic Manipulation, Year of our Lord Alarius Kruger I, Day 1,956.")
>
> As you suspected, your father discovered there was genetic manipulation in our past. His continued studies led to the creation of a department of his own for gene manipulation in Central City, Kashtiloth.

So, Kruger, your father is my creator. His research allowed me to be manipulated into what I am today. I always felt I was a monster—this confirms this. I was indeed created to serve you. I spit on you! He continued to read the report, bile boiling in his stomach.

> As you have requested, sire, all information on sodbent has been cross-referenced and given the code name "Degenerate 1." At your inquiry about these men, we have begun to round them up on Kashtiloth and are commanding a search for these degenerates in all camps on Zemitis and the farming communities on Alorion.

Currently, we have located over 634 of these men, and have begun their internment in living cloth and shipped them to Corustloth for examination. We're not worried about whether they have mind reading capabilities or not—it is easier to just round the degenerates up and sort them out in the prison. Those without the mind reading ability are at your disposal for research. As per your Senate law request, "Degenerates 1A." You now have the permission to exploit any sodbent without worry. They have no status whatsoever. They are like cattle.

Respectfully,
Morcant Sechnaill

P.S. Female members are not included as they are not classified the same as sodbent. Should I include a search for them, too?

So that is how Corustloth became a degenerate prison! It was originally meant for murderers, child abusers, and the like. To be sodbent means, in the eyes of the Senate, we are no better than those who kill or abuse! Kruger never went after the female population because of his belief that none of them ever had the ability to mind read. Little does he know they do, indeed, exist in the system: the Siren Sisters of Alorion! Blessed Mother, your secrets are still safe from the prying eyes of the Magistrate.

"Computer, pull up the eighth search, please. Is there any information on Brogan's arrest in Port Ali-Alorion?"

"Yes, Captain Farthing, there is. On screen now. It was made four months ago, but never sent to anyone—just logged into the system for later indexing."

Senate Report, Investigation Department
Date: The 30th year of our Lord, Kruger II, Day 92
To: Alarius Kruger II
From: Artagan Mangrouph-Charon

My Lord, after many years, we have success! The man Faolin has been found. He was in the Main Terminal of the Space Port in Ali-Alorion, on the two hundredth floor. Scans demonstrated he had semen inside his rectum, indicating he was a degenerate. Upon later investigation, we discovered that he is the son of the Faolin family and has been interned on Corustloth.

Scans indicate the semen belonged to his traveling companion, one Thamara-Afil Amergan-Faolin. It would seem the affiliation is not one of farming, but of union—he must be his degenerate lover!

This Thamara is one that we should be searching for. He has not been seen for over two Alorion months. Only the guilty go into hiding, I say!

Signed,
Artagan Mangrouph-Charon

Why was this never sent to the Magistrate? This Artagan must know that death would come if the Magistrate found him out. Unless... Farthing's eyes narrowed. He was starting to suspect this Artagan was of more importance than he had thought. "Computer, can you bring up any information about this Artagan Mangrouph-Charon?"

"Searching, Captain Farthing. Over forty-eight references are available. Most of them are older than four Alorion months."

He must have gone undercover—or is up to something the Magistrate himself does not know. He leaned back into the couch and sent a message to Tam: *[Tam, it is Artagan Mangrouph-Charon who knew about the death of Brogan's parents.]*

The response from Tam was immediate and alarming.

[I'm sitting across from him right now. He was on the ship bound for Corustloth. He said he was the cook. He is obviously a lot more than that. He is also sodbent, but denies it to everyone! He is trying to blackmail me into telling him what I am doing here. He has plans to use me to get to the Magistrate. He'll not turn me in unless I fail at my task. Farthing, he is monitoring you as we speak. It was he who sent the drones attached to your ship. He knows where you are and what you are doing! You are in danger!]

[As you are, my young friend. The situation is grave for all of us. This Artagan could blow our cover, expose the Siren Sisters to the Magistrate, and sign Brogan's fate to die on Corustloth. We must seek counsel. But alas, I am not yet on Alorion. I will rendezvous in space with a member of the Sirens when I arrive. I do not dare land and expose the location of the Convent.]

[Goddesses save us! What should I do, Farthing?]

[Stall him somehow. Go along with him. Seduce him if you must! Just keep him from revealing any of us! Goddesses' speed to you, young man. May the blue moons of Alorion keep you safe!]

Chapter 32

The Challenging Life of a Level Ten Conduit

"Young man, you are a level ten conduit."

Bennett could not believe all that had happened to him since his arrival home. In fact, he had hardly slept since he landed. He had shaken so many hands and spoken to so many people; he couldn't recall any time being alone. Now, he was finally sitting in front of Father, having a conversation he never thought he would have—one between equals.

"A conduit? Level ten? What exactly is that?" Bennett asked weakly. He was still tired, overwhelmed, and not feeling at all like a hero, as some had named him.

"Our little experiment in space has revealed that you are a level ten conduit mentalist. You linked all the mentalists together in our arm of the galaxy. Once linked, the power of over forty thousand gay mentalists in our part of the galaxy was conducted through you, sending the message to all its other arms!" Father spoke with fervor, waving his hands. "This is what I saw before your conduit experience."

He waved his hand and brought up the holomap the galaxy. It showed the ever-familiar map of blue points Bennett had seen before.

"So far, in this complex alone, we've found ten different levels of conduits. Yours is the highest: one that communicates with other arms of the galaxy, using the power of all the other levels."

"I still don't understand, Father! I sent a message that bounced around the entire galaxy?"

"Yes, son! Watch the holomap as I show what happened when you made the link."

The map changed from regular blue dots to sparkling, laser-perfect points of light attached to each other.

"Do you see the largest one—the one that looks like a sapphire? That is you, Bennett! The ancient manipulation in your genes makes you special. All gay men carry this ancient genetic marker, hence the blue lights of varying brightness—but yours is the strongest."

"But not all mentalists are gay, Father. You are the most powerful mentalist I know, able to sense things everywhere in the galaxy. How could I be more powerful than that?"

"Bennett, this entire situation has been most humbling to me. I have, like my predecessors, spent the time working on the Order's quest to uncover where we came from. What I've come to understand is that all mentalists were genetically altered by the Ancients—and that includes me. Unlike you, though, I am a passive conduit. I may be powerful, but I am more of a *voyeur*, if you would—not a conduit like yourself. You are an *active* mentalist. You can link all of us together and *communicate* with the other arms of the galaxy. Let me show you what I've discovered since our experiment. I can now identify all the mentalists in our galaxy."

He waved his hand and additional yellow lights appeared.

"Notice the varying levels of light. These are the heterosexual mentalists. Do you see the largest diamond at the centre of our planet?"

Bennett nodded.

"That beautiful yellow diamond represents me, of course. I may be the most powerful mentalist, but I am passive. I can view, but cannot *change* situations. You have the potential to do that—and more!"

Bennett swallowed and got up. He wasn't at all prepared for this. "Level ten conduit, eh? What does this mean to me—to all of us? Why me? I'm not special— just a lowly trainee."

"Son, you are so much more than that!" Father replied. He got out of his chair and placed his hand on Bennett's shoulder. This was the first time that Father had actually physically *touched* him in all his life. "You are a precious resource I must now put in jeopardy. There is another task at hand."

"And what is that, Father?" Bennett replied, already knowing the answer.

"You must travel to Alorion and find Tam."

Bennett paused, his eyes wide. "Um... If you believe that's a wise idea. Might it be prudent for you to travel with me, Father? I know you would be a valuable guide."

Father shook his head. "No, Bennett."

Bennett lowered his eyes in disappointment.

"The others able to do what you do are to travel for me to the other arms of the galaxy. Please understand, young man—with our knowledge, the Order will attempt to find possible level ten conduits in the other arms of the galaxy and light up an entire network of mentalists. Your job is to help Tam rescue Brogan and make contact with this Mother Siren. She should be able to tell you who the level ten conduit is for their sector, the other large arm in our galaxy. I also suspect she is the key to the next level. There may be something unimaginably powerful in this galaxy—more than you and I put together, Bennett. Even with all our advanced scientific knowledge, there is no scientific reason as to why all of this is even possible! The galaxy is such a large and vast place! The implications of this situation even boggle my mind," Father paused and drew in a breath and let it go. "It's humbling to an arrogant old fool like myself, who has blindly pursued absolute power for so long, to discover that there is a limit on his abilities."

"Aren't you risking the loss of a level ten conduit by sending me to Alorion?"

"Yes, I am. In fact, I believe that only one can exist at a time in each arm of the galaxy. By leaving, you will either cancel the other out, or you yourself will be cancelled out."

"You mean I will permanently lose my power?" Bennett asked, worried. "Don't you need me here?"

"Only your ability as a level ten conduit. As a trained mentalist, you will be an invaluable tool to Tam and this League. Help them. Then return home. Once here, in our arm of the galaxy, your power should be restored. I suspect, however, that if you were stay away long enough, another level ten conduit would develop here— but we shall see. You may well be the only level ten conduit in the entire galaxy! We just don't know."

With that, to Bennett's absolute surprise, he hugged him fiercely.

"Just make sure you come home, young man. Now, get out of here before I change my mind."

Chapter 33

Allies Come in the Strangest Forms

The light of the last curved space exit loomed ahead. Farthing swallowed, preparing for the sensation with which he had become familiar since linking in the triad. He felt really bad for Tam and others who got sick like this. While he enjoyed the triad Mother had set up, he didn't enjoy this part—especially as a seasoned pirate. Big pirates weren't meant to throw up!

Farthing smiled, then sighed at his own silliness. He did love and care for Tam and Brogan. His purpose was to ensure they reunited, to live in peace. He would give his life to ensure it.

The shuttle dropped out of curved space and the nausea commenced. But his experience of it was secondhand—not direct, like Tam's or Brogan's. That little fact didn't seem to matter much, though. His stomach churned and his eyes felt ready to roll out of their sockets. The buzzing in his head came in one long spurt, three short ones, then a pause, over and over again...

Taking a massive swig from his bottle of Alorion blue gin seemed to help. In about five minutes, he felt more hungover than sick from curved space. Millennia had passed, but alcohol still prevailed as a cure-all!

As he rounded the sunward side of Alorion, he encountered the singing of the Sirens. A message streamed through to him, soothing his nerves and quelling his sickness. There was nothing like the Siren song to heal the sick or sorry heart.

The song told him to be at peace, as love would someday come to him as it had to Tam and Brogan. *Not that a mutant like me could be a Life-Liner,* he supposed to himself, wiping his eyes and looking at the main screen.

The computer responded with a notice: "Captain Farthing, a shuttle is approaching from the surface of Alorion on a vector that will meet with ours on the far side of the third moon, Sapphire."

It would seem Mother intended not to take chances and wanted the meeting in the most distant place possible, reducing the threat of the two sensors Artagan had attached to his shuttle.

"Time to first contact: twenty-five Alorion minutes."

"Thank you, Computer. I wonder who it will be?"

"I'm sorry, but I am not programmed to sense the occupants of other shuttles at this time," replied the computer. "Once linkup is available, I will inform you, Captain Farthing."

"That be alright, Computer."

He prepared for contact.

∞

The other shuttle was just a minute away. "Linkup requested from other vessel. Permission granted, Captain Farthing?"

"By all means, Computer. Link away!"

"Complete. Shuttle linkup indicates that it is one of our shuttles, Captain Farthing. Occupant: one priestess and a mechanical being of some sort. I cannot confirm at this time." Computer wasn't giving away many secrets. He still didn't know who the priestess was—not that it mattered which.

"Shuttle docking commencing in thirty seconds."

The jets firing on the outside of the shuttle vibrated gently through the cabin and the other shuttle arced into view as they came closer and closer to meeting over the far side of the Sapphire Moon.

Farthing was a fighter, not a poet, but did feel a sense of metaphor as the two shuttles connected in a lover's embrace of rubberized tubing, conduits, and rods, mating the two ships.

"Docking complete," reported Computer. "Enter when ready."

Farthing lifted himself off his captain's chair and lumbered to the hatchway he had dived through a couple days ago. He still wondered about the two invisible sensors attached to his hull and the danger they meant. "Computer, disconnect overrides and allow me to manually open the door. I'd like to do one or two things myself."

"Overridden. Door ready for opening."

"Are you going to do anything, big boy, or am I going to have to come after you?"

That voice! It wasn't coming from the computer this time, but the intercom between the shuttles.

"You have me at a disadvantage, Madame. I don't know you, but will be chivalrous and open the door, nonetheless."

"Oh, I just love a man with antiquated male inclinations toward dominance! Please do— open the door for me!"

He pushed the button and the hatch door slid away into the wall to reveal the docking tube extended from his ship to the other. The other shuttle door opened to reveal a priestess standing there in a shimmering, almost see-through dress.

"Priestess Anghelloise at your service, big boy," she announced, her hands on her hips.

Farthing laughed heartily. "I should have known it would be you, Anghelloise! It's been a while! How did your voice become that of my shuttle computer?"

"Long story, big man. With the Senate removing services for shuttles and technology being depleted, there leaves little help for repairing and adapting technologies. Let's just say that for a priestess, I make a fabulous tech—and I do it with style." She swished her blue gown in a circle and sauntered through the docking port. "We have lots to do, Farthing. Let's get serious."

Farthing, the fighter, found himself stuttering in the priestess's presence. "P–p–please have a seat, priestess."

She floated over in her dress and sat down lightly as he pushed a chair in beneath her.

"More chivalry. How darling!" She smiled. "So—status report, Farthing. Let me know what's happened since your muddled message from Kashtiloth."

"I've downloaded three holorecorders of information from the University of Central City. The data shows that what the Senate knows of the League is, thankfully, little. What is disturbing is who's been monitoring me: a man by the name of—"

"Artagan!"

Farthing was shocked. "Yes, how did you know?"

"Sing Siren songs as long as I have, and you hear things wafting through the music of space. We've known of his espionage for some time now. He works for the Investigation Department of the Senate. Has he given Tam's identity away to the Magistrate? Goddesses, let it not be so!"

"Not yet," he answered honestly. "He's blackmailing Tam to get information about his plans. Any idea on how he found out about him?"

"We let him have it."

"What?" Farthing was incredulous. "How could the Sirens do something so dangerous?!"

"Mother sees so much more than the rest of us," explained Anghelloise. "She's known for a while that he is one of her children, refusing to come to her and find his place. He is a sodbent who denies his right to love another man. He has the potential of a Life-Line, if he put his defense guards down long enough to see the honor in doing so. Instead, he denies himself. This is how he has become so twisted and, sadly, evil. He will come home to the Convent eventually. Mother will see to that."

Farthing was stunned. "There are two invisible sensors attached above the port-side hatch on the ship."

"I know. I've already sent someone out to see to them."

With that, there were a few bumping sounds of metal hitting metal, then scraping.

"Nick, have you found the sensors and removed them?"

A mechanical voice came over the communication system: "Found and removed as requested. Compute flight path for bot. Indicate whether sensor sweep and dissection is necessary."

"Yes, Nick. Take them to my shuttle and have them opened. We'll meet you there."

"Understood, Mistress."

"Is that a Senate bot that you have?" asked Farthing. "Where did you get it?"

Anghelloise winked. "Oh, that's Nick. He was the bot at the bottom of Tam and Brogan's field. He worked the fence there. It took me minutes to reprogram that Senate-made bot and turn him into a very happy and helpful Anghelloise-bot! He's got quite a personality now. Almost human!"

"So there's no danger of the Senate knowing where their bot is?"

Anghelloise shook her head.

"Won't he be missed? How is he functioning without his magnetic plates?"

"Oh, the questions of the uninitiated! Nick's cradle was destroyed by an accidental farming incident—farm fertilizers can make fabulous bombs, by the way, if you know how to mix them. I disabled him, brought him to my shuttle, reprogrammed him, and installed anti-gravity guides to eight parts of his sphere. Now, he can go anywhere he wants—or, I should say, anywhere *I* want him to."

"I still don't know how those sensors were made invisible."

"Elementary, Farthing. If you can bend light around an object, it can become invisible. It is Ancient technology."

"But virtually all the technology on the planet has been appropriated by the Senate. Where are you getting yours?"

"The Sirens have enjoyed thousands of years of peace, free from prying eyes, but our technology remains ours. I am trained in it, along with singing for Life-Lines. One might say I'm a true jack of all trades!" She rose in a shimmer of blue and said, "Come, let's see what Nick's found."

Farthing rose and motioned for her to go ahead. She giggled and led the way.

They walked through the docking port to her shuttle, where they found Nick, hovering over a worktable. His spherical body and human-like face flittered around the surface of his sphere. Smiling, pursing his lips when doing something intricate, he worked away on the two small sensors on the table, which were opened and disabled.

"Let me guess, Nick!" Anghelloise smiled. "They are sensor drones that monitor the destinations, communications, and flight patterns of the shuttle."

"Yes, Mistress, just so. Ready for your inspection."

"Thank you, darling Nick!" She turned to Farthing. "Did you know sensors can be bidirectional? If it can tell the receiver where *you* are, there should be nothing there to stop me from seeing where *he* is. We'll send a false signal back through the sensors, feeding him false locations—let's say the inner orbit of the second moon of Alorion, Oceania. Artagan will think the shuttle is there. What he won't know is that we have another signal piggybacked on this one, relaying his location to us!" She beamed. "Great idea, isn't it?"

"What will he think of the delay in sensor data? You've disabled it at the moment."

"There is a momentary lapse when the shuttle jumps to curved space. He probably thinks we're going into curved space at the moment. By the time we reprogram the sensors, the signal will resume and no one will be the wiser! He'll think that we're still in orbit around Oceania."

"We get to Kashtiloth with Nick, then what? We can't be storming the Senate palace."

"That's true," admitted Anghelloise. "Do remember, though, that Nick holds in his memory all of the genetic, and visual markers of Tam, Brogan, and anyone who's used the gate since his last mechanical upgrade. He'll have no problem locating them, should the need arise."

Farthing nodded. "I take it you and Nick are coming back to Kashtiloth with me, then?"

"Wouldn't dream of missing it! Mother sends her blessings, by the way." Her witty exterior suddenly became serious. "Farthing, do not worry. We will find Tam. We will rescue Brogan and destroy the Magistrate. Mother is very serious about the situation. I take it very seriously, too. Come on, big boy. Let's go get them." She laughed to ease his nerves.

Who would have known these two were his allies? Things would be interesting from here on out.

Chapter 34
Tam's Dilemma

Tam sat in the Senate kitchen, watching the cooks come and go as they prepared the Magistrate's lunch. The sounds of dishes being collected and the bustle of the cooks made the room active and lively. It was his job to watch them cook all meals, so that food would be considered safe.

I guess I should be honored that he trusts me enough to watch his food for poison. It is taking me away from him, though. I need to find those plans for the prison—and soon! I sense something about to happen. I need to be ready.

Tam watched the yellow-tunicked cooks bustling back and forth bringing meats, spices, and vegetables to the table for his authorization before they went into the meal. Sometimes, they'd honor him with a tip of their tall hats. The rest of the time, they ignored him. The smells could be quite glorious. Holding this position had done wonders for his appetite. He hadn't eaten like this since... well... ever!

And then there was Artagan. What to do about Artagan? He was a dangerous threat that could undermine everything he had worked so hard for—the Magistrate's trust, mainly, without which he could not push his mind to reveal the plans for the prison and thereby, crucially, could not rescue Brogan. Artagan had changed everything. Tam couldn't do anything without him questioning every move.

If there were some way to get Artagan to fall from his Magistrate's graces, he would be in the clear. However, Artagan had some other plan he seemed occupied with. So far, it hadn't conflicted with Tam's plans, but it made him uneasy.

Tam folded his hands on the tablecloth and twiddled his thumbs as the pots were being stirred vigorously. Kruger was getting beef stew with dumplings today, and an apple crisp with ice cream for dessert. Rather ordinary fare for such a grand man—but Kruger had simple tastes for certain things, like food and harming others.

Tam wished no harm to Artagan, but would not hesitate if he interfered with his getting the plans for the prison. But how to get him out of the Magistrate's presence long enough to complete his task, then make his escape to meet up with Farthing?

"Sir, the Magistrate's lunch is ready to be served," announced the head cook as he approached the table. "Would you like to sample it first?"

"That would be appropriate, thank you," Tam replied.

A bowl of stew was given to him. It was very hot, so he blew across the top of the spoon. The chef waited patiently.

"It is wonderful, chef. My compliments to you and your staff. The Magistrate will certainly enjoy his meal."

The head chef bowed, then turned away to issue orders for the waiters.

Tam got up, straightened his tunic, and looked around the gleaming steel tables and stoves of the kitchen. The whole place betrayed incredible wealth. It seemed tragic to Tam when he considered how the average family now lived on Kashtiloth. Some lived in even worse conditions than those—such as his family, who had been interned in the camps.

Three waiters filed in and sidled up to the serving tables.

"Are you ready, gentlemen? We can't keep the Magistrate waiting, can we?" Tam motioned for them to exit the kitchen.

They headed toward the Magistrate's chamber down the hallway, across the court-yard, into the next building, which housed the Senate sleeping chambers. All the while, Tam watched the procession, ensuring nothing was secretly added to the stew by any of the waiters. He had considered adding something himself. He'd gladly be rid of the Magistrate, but he could not be sure of Brogan's salvation—not to mention the welfare of the entire system—if he were to do so just yet.

As they entered the hall of the sleeping chambers, Tam looked at the grandeur of the paintings, the golden-gilded, ornate furniture, and the luxurious coverings of the rooms, windows, and hallways. One could feed an army of pirates for a month on the sale of just one room's furnishings! The injustice of the situation bit into Tam's stomach. He swallowed hard and forced himself to refocus on serving lunch.

The procession continued through three welcoming rooms, each more decadent, as they approached the Magistrate's sleeping chambers. Tam knew only the highest-ranking members of the Senate were allowed to see the last two. The place was locked up and guarded every minute of every day.

Tam seethed when he thought of the cost of the Magistrate's army and police, all hired to protect his interests. He knew the Senate members were just scared puppets of the Magistrate. They couldn't make a move without some general or captain of police informing on them. Kruger must have been spending a fortune in bribes to keep everyone in line!

As they approached, he considered the possibility of the whole system crashing and burning due to his actions. Would he be considered a hero, or an enemy of the state? He shook his head and brought himself back to the task of feeding the hideously obese Magistrate, then helping him with his toilet duties. *I live for these moments,* he thought to himself, smiling and grimacing at once.

"Look alive, gentlemen! Straighten your sashes! Hoist your dinnerware to the appropriate shoulder height, please, and do remember to lower your eyes when the Magistrate looks your way. Your life could depend on it."

The waiters were all experienced and knew this already. Tam realized that to do a proper job, he had to cover all possibilities and not make any mistakes— even having a waiter with a sash tied improperly.

"You, there, straighten that sash! I'll take your serving platter."

The waiter looked down and nodded quietly, handed the heavy platter to Tam, straightened his sash, and bowed. Nothing needed to be said. Tam had just saved his life. He could see the gratitude in his eyes.

Just then, the Magistrate's door opened and Artagan exited.

"Ah, Tam. I see lunch is ready. I am sure you've done your job well and that the food is safe and ready for his Majesty."

"Quite safe, but if you would like to make sure, by all means, test it yourself!"

Artagan gave Tam a dirty look and said nothing at first. Then: "The Magistrate will take his lunch now."

"May I remind you, Artagan, that there are protocols for the serving of food? Since you are new to his Magistrate's service, I will overlook the error. But do be careful! One could fall so quickly in his Majesty's eyes."

Tam's comments were like barbs. Again, Artagan said nothing, but glared back at him. He bowed and stood aside.

Tam addressed the group: "We know the routine. Enter one at a time. Stand in a line with your serving platters at shoulder height. Do not look at the Magistrate but at the floor. Allow me to instruct you in your serving and, above all, do not speak! You're an exception, of course, Artagan. You are welcome to say whatever you choose!"

Tam got nothing in reply but another stony glare.

The waiters were starting to struggle with their trays, so Tam hurried the process, lest someone drop something. "Let us proceed. Artagan, open the door, please."

He begrudgingly obliged.

The procession entered the room silently and waited for approval from Tam. Tam looked to the Magistrate's bed and saw him turning from his papers, strewn around him on the covers and the floor.

"Ah, Tam! Lunch is here. Wonderful! Beef stew, as promised. Do begin serving. Make a setting for three please. You and Artagan will be joining me today!"

Tam caught himself before his jaw dropped. Artagan was lucky to have his back turned at that moment, looking out the window at the courtyard.

"As you wish your Magistrate. It is our pleasure to serve." He turned to the servers. "Gentlemen, set your platters on the dining table and exit the room. It is a special day today. I shall serve the lunch myself."

The three waiters placed the platters on the table. They bowed deeply to the Magistrate, a little less deeply to Tam, and ignored Artagan as they left.

Kruger pushed himself up from his lying position and considered the platters. "Tam, my friend, you do your job so well. Artagan, I hope that you take notice. He is an inspiration to pages everywhere. You'll learn a lot from him!"

"Yes, sire. I shall learn a lot to better serve you," Artagan acknowledged, still not passing the opportunity to glare at Tam.

Tam moved to begin service. He set out three place settings, with the Magistrate at the head of the table. Silverware and fine china were a must. Napkins had to be straight, the silverware organized in the proper order, and the decorations on the plates facing the diner—lest the Magistrate become annoyed.

With the places set properly, Tam proceeded with the platters.

"Artagan, please take the tureen off the third platter and place it on the serving mat in front of my setting."

Artagan nodded and did so without speaking, though his eyes showed he would have loved to take a strip off Tam.

Having finalized the setting, Tam bowed deeply to Kruger.

"Your lunch is served, sire. Please let me assist you in rising and sitting at the table."

"Yes, of course! I am hungry. I do want to discuss with you as we eat." Kruger smacked his lips quite loudly in anticipation.

Tam rose off his knee and approached him. Kruger extended his arm, which Tam reached under, hoisting the massive man into a standing position.

"I am grateful for such a strong, strapping young man to tend to me. You are a marvel. Artagan, you will need to join the Senate gym and find a way to be in the same shape as soon as possible."

Artagan reddened a bit and bowed deeply. "Yes, sire. I shall begin immediately. Under Tam's instruction, of course."

Now it was Tam's turn to glare. That was the last thing Tam wanted to do—work out with his enemy in front of him.

"Of course. Tam, proceed immediately after lunch."

"Yes, sire. It is my pleasure to serve."

Kruger snorted and breathed with effort to walk the short distance to the table. As they approached, Artagan pulled out the Magistrate's chair in preparation. Tam moved Kruger into position. He swiftly plopped onto the seat and Tam gently moved into position.

"Artagan, please be seated. I shall serve you both."

Artagan sat. Tam lifted the lid off the stew and ladled it into a bowl for Kruger first, Artagan second, then for himself. Dumplings were ladled on the top and condiments were placed in front of each. Salt, pepper, and other spices were placed within reach of his Magistrate.

"Sire, the red wine is ready for service. Would you like it now, with your meal?"

Kruger was already spooning up copious amounts of stew and stuffing it into his mouth. He couldn't speak, so nodded, motioning with his spoon to proceed.

Tam poured the wine for the three and then sat down. It was finally his turn to eat. He reached for a spoon and gently sampled the meal, in order to not offend Kruger. It was almost pointless, as Kruger was so absorbed in his own feeding frenzy, he did not notice. As his bowl emptied, Tam rose to refill it. A grunt issued from Kruger as he started on his seconds.

"I would like to share something with you both," he said. Stew ran down the side of his chin, which Tam reached over and wiped off. "The prison inmates are now at my disposal. We begin experimenting today to determine the genetic makeup of these degenerates."

Tam almost dropped the napkin in shock. *Brogan! Goddesses help you! I will need to move quickly!*

Artagan silently gagged beside him, covering his mouth quickly with his napkin. He sent a smug smile in Tam's direction.

Tam barely heard Kruger as he spoke of his plans of torture, vivisection, and experimentation. He just sat silently, wondering if he had any hope at all.

Part 6
Voyagers

Chapter 35

Cocoon

The feeble ray coming from the small rectangular window cast a weak light that spread across the figure wrapped in cloth lying on the cot in the corner, surrounded by bare cement walls and a small door. Tubes of various sizes intruded upon the cocooned being. One tube extracted human feces, another, urine. Another inserted into the poor soul's mouth was used for injecting nourishment and water in amounts just enough to permit bare life. Wires were attached to the heart, lungs and brain area wrapped in wires and sensors. Over the entire area of the living cloth were small wires and tubes attached to needles, which would inject small amounts of sedative into the body of the hapless person.

The man could sense the pattern of the almost endless rhythmic injections occurring over the entire surface of his body: tap, tip, tip, tip, pause, then repeat in another part of the body. The sensations had long ago begun to cause him to go regularly insane. Now, they were just like dead pricks hitting his almost lifeless body.

The man, Brogan, was almost dead. The injections had recently increased, as had the brain monitoring, watching for the presence of a Life-Line link to some unknown man elsewhere in the system.

Small bits of information wafted into his half-lucid brain from Tam, though he himself was virtually incapable of sending any information out. When he felt any emotion, it was feeble, like his body. Hopelessness and darkness were all that was known to him. On occasion, the needles would pause to let his body gain its senses, and the sensors would whirr to life, trying to determine what his brain was doing and how it was communicating with someone so distant from his cell. These would be the times when the pain of emptiness and fear would press down as a heavy weight onto his chest, almost crushing the life out of him.

What the sensors did not notice was that small amounts of information were being passed back along at the same time as the injections... one long packet, three short, then a pause...This information was coming, unbeknownst to the beings on the other side of the sensors, from his Life-Line, Tam, to sustain him as best he could. Small snippets of memories and messages would waft into his near-consciousness. The living cloth would receive the tears that streamed from his eyes. A whimper or cry would sometimes emanate from his vocal cords, causing him to almost gag on the tube sticking down his throat. Moments of hope would bubble and pop inside his brain sometimes. He began to wonder what was real and what he hallucinated.

Then, the injections would start again, and the darkness would stretch over him, deadening his senses to near nothingness. No body movement, no flicker of the eyes. Everything would darken beyond even the dim light streaming into his cell.

Then, the injections would stop suddenly. His body would start to awake from the sedatives and telepathic inhibitors. His mind would slowly click on as a light clicked on, humming with a deafening sound. After ages of silence, it was tortuous.

The same two men as always, Grayson and Rothman, would enter in their turquoise gowns and white caps and slowly, carefully unzip the living cloth, gently removing the wrapping of wires. They would take care with all the sensors and needles. The equipment was worth a lot. Once all the sensors were removed, they would unceremoniously rip the tubes out of his mouth, his penis, and his anus. Body fluids would fly in all directions. His voice, long weakened and feeble, would cry out in a cracked gurgle that sounded more like a wounded canine whipped by its owners than a human being.

Often, Grayson would cackle with glee at his attempt to scream. Brogan would hear words like "degenerate trash" or "Alorion slime" as their voices thundered into his eardrums, unaccustomed to loud sounds. He would writhe and scream more.

Then, cold water would be thrown over him. His head, in a reflexive reaction, would lift up and return to crack hard on the table. He'd see lights dancing across his eyelids. His muscles would tighten and cramp without release after ages of not being used. He would shit himself.

Then, the brushes would descend, scrubbing him raw, with no care taken for any part of the body. Brogan would be able to see Grayson gritting his teeth and laughing as he carried out his duties. Often, Rothman would slap his penis with a brush, words like "degenerate" coming from his contorted mouth. His legs would be similarly abused, as would the souls of his feet. Not the heart or the head, though.

They were too valuable for the experiments. Scrape them, yes, but slap them, no. Nevertheless, Grayson and Rothman would revel in their job as usual.

His body would be turned over and the treatment would continue. More water would be poured, as though they were trying to wipe the tattoo clear off his back. Shit cleared away. Blood and puss washed away. Putrid smells lessened. Body turned over. A final douse of water would end the session, then the banshee sound of a dryer, which would whip the water into droplets and suck it from his body.

Several injections of muscle-stimulating drugs would follow, and his body would soon almost start to feel normal. The two men would leave, and all would again be silent. His mind would momentarily free up, his joy in his Life-Line would return, and sometimes, his cracked lips would form a slight smile as he thought of things long past.

Then, his voyage of torture would start again.

Chapter 36
Wormholes and Wandering Waifs

"To explain it in simple terms, you bend space and time, folding the points you wish to enter and exit. The computer calculates these points. You and the other mentalists create the wormhole by visualizing it. We use what I call negative energy to hold the wormhole open for a short time. It should be enough for you and your shuttle to make it through. It will have to be a one-way trip for now, though."

Bennett stared blankly at the technician and nodded, pretending he understood. "Time will be the same on both sides?"

"Approximately the same. Don't worry about losing thirty years of your life. This isn't faster than light."

The technician fidgeted with the display panel, running calculations while Bennett let his words sink in. "Why don't we just use curved space?" he finally asked.

"We don't have the knowledge to do so," explained the technician. "To keep it simple, curve drives are like traveling from point A to B on a moving walkway. You add your walking speed to that of the walkway. Your spaceship's speed is added to that of the energy flowing through curved space. It's like flowing downstream in a boat. We can only do this for relatively short distances—for traveling in our regions of space, not across the galaxy. That technology is beyond us or has been lost in time. The Chronicles indicate there was once technology that allowed for travel from galaxy to galaxy, but we've never found evidence of its existence. It was destroyed long ago. Now, the only way is through a manmade traversable wormhole."

Bennett didn't press any more. The only reason the technician would even talk to him was because he was the level ten conduit and thus a bit of a celebrity. Having Father's instructions to begin the process had helped, too. But it bothered Bennett that he would soon be flung across the galaxy into a dangerous sector, with nothing but his wits and his shuttle. The fact that he didn't understand the technology behind the wormhole wasn't reassuring, either. He was putting his life in the hands of technicians like this.

"When do you think I can leave? Have the tests been successful?" he asked cautiously.

The technician turned from his panel and looked him in the eye for the first time. "Tests have virtually all been successful. We've managed to send small probes to their corner of the galaxy. Confirmation can be seen here on the holomap. Want to look?"

Bennett nodded, approached, and waved his hand over the holomap's generator. The spiral form of Messier sprang to life. He rotated the galaxy to the side closest to Tam's world. "How do I find the probes?"

"Easy," replied the technician. "Think probe, Mr. Davis. Use your mind."

Bennett closed his eyes and thought, *[Probes.]* When he opened his eyes, every probe sent out showed up as a flashing blue light. "Mentalists can obviously sense them. Do they give off a certain frequency known to them?"

The technician nodded. "One long flash, three short ones, a pause, then repeat."

"I wonder if Tam's noticed them."

"Pardon me? Tam?"

"Sorry. That's my contact on the other side of the galaxy. I'm charged with finding him."

"Can you show me where he is right now?" asked the technician.

"Certainly." He closed his eyes and pictured Tam. "There he is!" said Bennett, pointing, as he reopened his eyes. "That blue point of light is Tam. He is in a dangerous place for a mentalist." He grimaced. "I've got to go there and get in touch with him without coming into contact with the Magistrate."

The technician turned back to his console. "You know, Father has instructed that certain equipment be included in your cargo hold. Here is the manifest. It includes instructions and manuals for all the equipment. The shuttle is quite advanced. Father has not spared any expense, giving you one of our best. Let me show you."

The technician got out of his seat in front of his console and strode to the airlock. Bennett tailed along behind.

The technician opened the airlock into the hangar. Bennett felt a slight change in pressure and smelled welding torches. As they walked down the stairway, the technician pointed out the golden, oval-shaped shuttle sitting closest to them.

"There she is—*Nimbus*. A fine ship! You might look up her name. Father thought it very appropriate for your trip. Something to do with 'dignified light'... The level ten conduit sails on a *Nimbus* because he is divine himself." The technician laughed, then mentally asked *Nimbus* to open her airlock, which she did. "Welcome to *Nimbus*, Mr. Davis. She will be your home away from home and, with all blessings, will bring you to your real home again, once we figure out the logistics of getting you there in one piece."

"Welcome, Bennett!" *Nimbus* chimed as he entered the hatch. Bennett thought the feminine voice very appropriate. "I will be your companion on the trip, exclusively programmed to work for you."

Bennett smiled and responded: "That's nice to know, *Nimbus*. Are you just about ready to fall through a wormhole to the other side of the galaxy with me?"

"Of course, Bennett. We will make a wonderful working pair, you and me. We can leave any time now."

"Good to hear. I'm eager to start the journey."

"Bennett," said the ship, "I am also programmed to notice the moods and motives of my passengers. I can tell with about 97 percent certainty that you are not yet ready to leave. But rest assured: I am at your service!"

Bennett blushed and the technician giggled a bit. "She's quite the charmer, isn't she?" he asked.

"Yes," he answered, "quite."

His thoughts were again on that nagging fear of falling through folded space and being ripped apart or crushed by gravity.

This Kruger person scared him, too—he was so anciently uncivilized and evil. It was hard to comprehend.

I am a mentalist, not a warrior.

The technician grunted. "I need to get back to my work, if that's alright. Thank you, *Nimbus*! Be ready to receive shipping-out orders in the next few hours."

"I shall await your orders eagerly!"

With that, they climbed out of the airlock. It closed behind them with a hiss.

"You know she can bend light rays around herself to make her invisible? She can jam just about any communication wave in that sector—and should be able to outrun most of their ships. You'll be in capable hands." He smiled. "Just make sure you keep your eyes on her and don't let her fall into the hands of the backward people of that system! You'll have me to answer to when you get back. *If* you get back..." He sniffed, then turned back to his console. Bennett bid him good evening and went on his way back to his temporary chamber at the spaceport.

When he arrived in his room, Father's symbol was rotating over his communication system. He waved his hand over the symbol and thought of him. The connection was instantaneous. Father appeared on the display with an eager smile on his usually sombre face.

"Bennett! You leave in the morning! All is ready." He was beaming. "Finally, we'll move this whole thing along. All you need to do is warn Tam that you'll be arriving."

"Father, I don't mean to be rude, but when I've linked with Tam's mind, I've never been able to really let him know I'm there. He's sensed me from time to time, but that's all. How do I know how to send the message only to him? How do I avoid linking up with everyone else?"

"Bennett! In due time!" commanded Father. "We shall do this together. I'll be arriving within the hour. I've been in transit for the past several hours. But I want to see you off on your voyage tomorrow, dear boy!"

"Yes, Father," Bennett replied.

"You are still troubled," remarked Father. "I can see it in your face and sense it in your soul. Rest assured that all will fall into place when I get there."

With that, his image faded, and Bennett was left alone in his room, as usual, waiting.

Chapter 37
The Floodgates Open

Anghelloise smiled. "That just about does it!" she announced. "The probes have been reprogrammed and are ready to send false data to Artagan. We should also be able to locate him and Tam almost immediately!"

"What do we do with the probes?" asked Farthing. "Do we just leave them there on the worktable or put them back on the outside of the ship where we found them?"

"Way ahead of you, darling!" she responded. "Nick, get ready to head outside and reposition the probes."

"Immediately, Mistress." Nick began to float toward the worktable.

"I can't see the probes," said Farthing. "Where are they?"

"They're currently bending light!" she replied primly.

"Oh—invisible, then."

"You're catching on, big boy!" she chided. "Here they are!" She held up her hands. They seemed as though they were holding something, but nothing was visible. "They bend light around themselves only—otherwise parts of my hands would be invisible, too! Elementary science, my dear Farthing."

Nick approached and gripped the invisible probes with his retracting arms.

"Remember to place them exactly where you found them, Nick!" she commanded. "There'll be precious little true information to be passed to Artagan. He shouldn't know what's going on under his supposedly watchful eyes."

Nick headed for the airlock, arms extended, holding the nothings in his mechanical hands. "At once, Mistress!" he chimed. The airlock hissed open, and he entered.

"When will they start transmitting?" Farthing asked.

"As soon as we pass to the other side of Sapphire," she responded. "Artagan will receive notice that the shuttle is in orbit around Oceania. That's where the forces will be sent to investigate. We should be able to sneak out from Sapphire's orbit, traverse the distance between Alorion and Kashtiloth, then head right to the Magistrate without even being noticed."

"I'll begin prepping for launch," he replied. "Let's hope we're not noticed." He didn't give away his worry that full Senate forces might be waiting when they arrived, and all their plans might be lost.

The airlock began to cycle as Nick returned.

"Probes replaced," he announced. "Exactly where they were before, Mistress!"

Anghelloise rose from her console and headed for the airlock to her ship. She patted Nick and motioned for him to go with her. "I'll return to my ship, and we should be on our way within five minutes!"

She sailed out of the shuttle in her usual shimmer of blue and closed the airlock door behind her.

The computer announced: "Airlock cycle complete. Detaching now."

"OK, boys, let the spectacle begin!" she sang. "We're going to be glorious! Follow me as closely as you can. I'm confident that we'll be OK, but, if confronted, I'd like to be able to use Siren song to shroud us, giving both shuttles enough time to safely reach Kashtiloth."

Farthing's shuttle engines began to rev up and, with a nod from Anghelloise sitting in her shuttle, watching on the communication screen, Farthing executed the flight plan he had set. The shuttles flew in formation, Anghelloise's in front and Farthing's behind it. They emerged from behind Sapphire into plain view of all— to either rescue or oblivion.

Light shimmered briefly around them, then they vanished, plunging through curved space toward Kashtiloth.

∞

It was Tam's turn to smile. This was the sixth time he had been drilling Artagan in the gym, getting him into better shape for his job as assistant to Tam. Artagan wasn't enjoying himself much. The sweat poured off his brow onto the bench press he was using. He exuded an odor that was bitter to the nose.

Tam could sense his thoughts without much effort. It was clear he hated the gym almost as much as he did Tam. *Don't worry, Artagan, hate can be a good motivator... Keep pushing.* "Keep your abdominals tight when you push upward. And stop arching your back. Do you want an injury that will make you feel like an old man?"

"I'm doing the best I can. What more do you want?!"

You can take your dumbbells and push them up your ass, that's what. Maybe it was a good thing that Artagan wasn't practiced enough to read Tam's mind!

Tam smiled as he turned away, beginning to giggle a bit. *I should be more serious about this. All of this is really stressing me out.*

He turned his thoughts to Brogan. *[More than all the blue light of Sapphire, I need you, Brogan. I want to feel your thoughts and feelings inside me. I will get to you somehow. Please know that!]*

Artagan finished his twelve chest presses and dropped the weight onto the rack above his head. "Hey, where's the help? Aren't you supposed to assist me with putting the weights back? Do you want me to break my neck? Pay more attention and stop sulking!"

By the Goddesses, if you sneer any harder, you will be permanently wrinkled, Artagan. I pity you. You are aging yourself with all your hate!

Artagan suddenly got up off the bench with a snort, frowning. "I'm doing this because the Magistrate wishes it. Tam, I'll get my turn soon enough. Watch yourself. You'll be sorry."

Tam's eyes widened in surprise. He suddenly had a sinking feeling that Artagan might know more than he let on. Putting up blocks to prevent Artagan sensing what he was thinking, Tam decided he had to find something to distract him so he could get access to the Magistrate's chambers without hindrance. *I'll not be tricked again!*

He could feel Artagan's stare boring into his back as he looked in the other direction.

He is a crafty man. I really do need to watch myself.

Tam turned to Artagan with a fake smile on his face. "Ready for some heat? The sauna's ready. Why don't we relax and allow our muscles to limber up? Come along—we've got plenty of time before we have to return to service."

"The first good thing you've suggested all day." Artagan groaned and walked toward Tam and the sauna.

I think I have a chance.

A feeling jolted Tam suddenly as he felt Brogan regain some of his consciousness. It must have been one of those times they woke him up. What he sensed was terrifying. Brogan was slowly dying, and Tam was beginning to feel it in his body. Then, Brogan was drugged again, and faded into just a glimmer in Tam's consciousness...

I have to move quickly, or we are both done for. I have to be a hero, but don't know if I have it in me. Brogan is my reason for being. Without him, I am nothing. My life ends as well, alone, in a darkness he and I alone can fathom. Goddesses! I must do something—now!

∞

"Bennett, you really need to relax," *Nimbus* chided. "All is well. We should be exiting in less than an hour. It really is a painless way to travel, folding space and popping out the other side. What would take hundreds of years takes a couple of hours."

Bennett sat with his hands gripping the chair in which he was seated, in front of a console of strange, blinking lights and panels he didn't understand. What bothered him was the fact that he was in between two points of reality and couldn't feel anything from either. To make things worse, it was black and lightless outside. There was nothing to see on the screen or through any of the small windows dotted around the hull. How could he even be sure they were moving?

"*Nimbus*, status please. Are we actually moving?"

"Indeed, we are, Bennett. Let me plot it on the screen." The frontal viewing screen came alive with a map of the folded space. "Here is where we entered the fold."

The blinking point was clear enough.

"Here is where we will exit."

Another blinking point was presented.

"Here is where we are at the moment." They were more than halfway there. "We should reach exit point in a mere forty minutes."

"Then I'd better get ready to execute Father's plan." He steeled himself. *I hope that Father's belief in me is warranted. I may exit to find myself an immediate target, and not even get the chance to link with Tam...* He gripped the seat harder, his knuckles turning white.

"Bennett, you really do need to relax," *Nimbus* chided again. "Here, breathe this in, deeply."

A little puff of air scented with something like flowers exuded from the panel, right into Bennett's face. *What have I got to lose?* Bennett breathed in and felt his anxiety strip away.

"What is this, *Nimbus*?"

"I'm just helping you calm down. You need a clear head when you get to the other side. This relaxant will not hinder that. All it does is soothe the adrenaline in your system, helping you focus on the task ahead."

"Fine by me," he replied. "Would you mind asking me first before you do something like that again, please? I am the captain of this vessel."

"This is true," she replied. "It is, however, my job to ensure your success. Nothing will prevent me in this—even if it's against your wishes, Bennett."

Great, he thought. *I'm heading through folded space and not even in control.* His little apartment suddenly seemed a more appealing than it ever had to him.

Chapter 38
Stratagem

Artagan placed his head against the wall and sighed. The heat was seeping into his body. Tam could sense he might nod off at any moment. His plan of turning the heat and humidity up to get Artagan to fall asleep seemed to be working. He stayed silent, listening to Artagan's breathing. His mind was starting to wander into nonsense.

He's falling asleep! Of all the things to start dreaming—naked men and... images of me pulling my clothes off...? If Tam didn't know better, he'd swear that Artagan was attracted to him. For a man who wasn't supposed to be attracted to men, he certainly had some very erotic dreams of men—especially himself!

He gently coaxed Artagan's mind to continue to drift. He felt a sense of excitement, then hit a sudden barrier. He allowed his mind to travel around the barrier and look at it from all angles. What was Artagan up to? How did he manage to place a mental block on his memories? He stopped with a start, pulling out quickly.

Artagan's left eye opened and looked at Tam calmly.

[Did you really think that I was so incapable, my dear Tam?] He closed his eyes again. *[You are a gullible one, aren't you? I played you so well; you had no idea I was preparing for the moment I had enough proof to show the Magistrate exactly who you are! Your life will be forfeit and I will be left to ply his stupid mind to my agenda. Oh, you want to know what that agenda is, do you? You're out of your league, my friend. I've been at this game longer than you know!]*

Tam faltered for the first time. He threw up his own barrier. *Two can play at this game!* Besides, it was still getting hotter.

"You think you are so careful, don't you?" Artagan mused. His eyes were still closed, his hands behind his head. "I knew the part about me being attracted to you would make you slip up!" He unfolded his arms and wiped sweat out of his eyes. "You're a fool!"

"You have no proof, Artagan! The Magistrate will not believe you. He's been manipulated to believe in me. What proof could you possibly have that could harm me?" Tam sat up, placed his palms on the bench, and leaned toward Artagan, peering at him through the rising steam.

"You think me a fool, Tam! I've come a long way since we first met on that spaceship. I've honed my mental skills and learned much from the archives at the Central City University—which your friend, Farthing, recently visited. The Professors of the Learnèd provided me with enough information to weasel you out of your hiding place and bring you here to the Magistrate. Your friend Farthing has enough information in his possession to do great harm to my plans. So, he must be eliminated."

Tam's eyes widened in horror. "Artagan, you must see that the Magistrate is a monster! He must be stopped. If you betray me, he may very well destroy us all!"

"Clearly we have different agendas," Artagan replied coolly. "Yours is to die. Mine is to take what I need and let the Magistrate destroy both your band of pirates and himself. You've been an enjoyable plaything. Now, we are finished playing." Artagan continued to sit with his arms crossed and his eyes closed. He was so sure of himself.

Tam stuttered. "M–maybe you're right. I didn't know what you were capable of doing. You've got me at the moment, Artagan." He shuffled his feet nervously. "What do you want?"

"I know exactly where your pirate captain is and where he will show up. Forces have already been sent to take him down as he comes to rescue you! He thinks he can play tricks, then boldly descend to the Magistrate's palace and rescue you without anyone knowing. Too bad, as he'll never arrive. I intend to make my move."

Tam began to panic. All their plans might be for nothing. All would be lost.

The Magistrate awoke from his slumber to hear a soft knocking at his bedchamber door.

"Begging his Magistrate's pardon, but may I have a word with you? I bring important news." It was Secretary Barrington, of all people.

He wondered why Tam or Artagan weren't here to tend him, then remembered his recent orders to have them train at the gym. *I've had to make sacrifices for those two. I have to look after my own affairs while they are gone. I find it very tiring. I may have to change my mind.*

"Enter, secretary, and give me your news."

The door slowly opened, and Barrington slid into view, bowing and waving his hat.

"Excuse me, sire, but news has arrived." The secretary paused and caught his breath as he looked at the Magistrate. Catching his eye, he bowed again and began sweating profusely, pushing his eyeglasses back up his nose. "My apologies for breaking tradition, your Magistrate, but I believe it is of the utmost importance to tell you that news has come from the military. The pirate, Farthing, has been found."

"Found?" The Magistrate repeated, his eyes widening with anticipation. "Where?"

"He is in orbit around Oceania. We could move in and destroy him!"

"I want Farthing alive so I can question him, then skin him alive! There will be no destroying until he's in my hands. Disable his ship and bring him to me!"

Secretary Barrington bowed. "Yes, your Magistrate. As you wish."

"Wait! To whose espionage do we owe this piece of fortunate news?"

The secretary paused and turned to the Magistrate, his eyes properly lowered this time. "To Page Artagan, your Magistrate. It was sent several hours ago after he left for his workout at the gym with Tam."

"How did that worm find out about Farthing's whereabouts?"

"I do not know, your Magistrate. I'll locate him and have him report to you immediately." He bowed and backed out of the room.

Kruger lay back down, fuming as he stared at the ceiling. The nerve of Artagan to send news while he was indisposed! And what was that blasted pirate up to? Surely, he wasn't stupid enough to be discovered so easily. There must be more to this story.

I have need of Tam—he could find me the truth!

Finally! Artagan was starting to waver! He was struggling to maintain consciousness. Tam watched the struggle, seeing him lose the battle. After waiting for several minutes to be sure, monitoring Artagan's breathing and movement, it was time.

He slowly got up and moved to the door. He would have about fifteen seconds to open it, close it, and bar it with the broomstick sitting nearby. Once trapped inside, Artagan would have to wait at least another forty minutes before any gym attendants were due to arrive. Later in the evening, few came by. He would then notice the emergency button and intercom had been disabled. Hopefully, he wouldn't have the capacity to project his thoughts to anyone other than Tam.

He made his move. He opened the door and stepped through just as Artagan sprung awake. His heart in his mouth, Tam pushed against it, Artagan screaming obscenities as he pounded on its other side. With his body pressed against the door, he reached for the broom and pushed it through the handle. He then piled several benches up against the door. Artagan glared out the little window in the door, projecting nasty thoughts to Tam, which he blocked out. He sent one final message to Artagan, hoping it got through:

[It is cooler on the floor!]

∞

The two shuttles continued to sail in a gentle arc to Kashtiloth after exiting curved space at the last checkpoint. The beauty of space was that there was no up or down. The planet was in front of them, growing larger by the minute. Both Farthing and Anghelloise remained silent, alone in their thoughts about what was ahead. The sounds of the shuttles were a constant background noise that rested just on the edge of their minds, only occasionally entering their thoughts. Even Nick seemed preoccupied, sitting on his charger as he juiced up for the next part of the adventure.

Farthing had been sporadically in touch with Tam since he'd received the message that Kruger was going to start experimenting on the prisoners. Some of Tam's messages were about going to the gym with the traitor, Artagan. Not much had seemed important, so Farthing didn't push to make any kind of contact, fearing he might jeopardize Tam's position. Brogan had been unusually silent and with his limited ability to connect, Farthing knew nothing of what was happening, other than the news from Tam that he might be dying.

His big frame twitched as he allowed himself to feel the sadness of knowing that two of his closest friends were in peril of losing their lives. The whole plan of rescue was hanging by a thread. He felt helpless, being unable to put his strength or military prowess to any good use. He could only depend on a Siren's ability to sing her way out of trouble. Farthing had the greatest respect for the Sirens, but what he knew best was fighting. It was in his genes. It was all he could do from slamming his big hand on the console and screaming into the ether of space.

Anghelloise, sitting in her shuttle, softly sang to herself, busying herself with diagrams and maps of the Magistrate's palace. Sensing Farthing's distress, she put down her work and contacted him on the other shuttle: "Hey, big boy, how're you doing? Need to talk?"

Farthing sighed. "Just worried about Tam and Brogan. Tam's been under a lot of stress with the Magistrate and Artagan. Brogan is clearly under extreme duress. I feel so helpless sitting in this blasted shuttle. I would feel a lot better sitting behind a weapons cannon shooting my way through enemy lines, instead of skulking through space in silence."

"I understand, my dear Farthing. Your genetic makeup is only one part of you, though. Tap into your love and compassion for both Tam and Brogan. It is paramount to you. Be patient. Your skills will be needed soon. I'd like your mind clear and resolute when we come to it."

"I'll do my best."

"Of course you will, dear." She sensed Farthing was a kind man, and his mental scars were evident in his persona.

Anghelloise always presented herself as sure, confident, and easygoing. But beneath her flowing blue dress and regal presentation, she was just like Farthing. She was worried for Tam and Brogan, too. She fretted over all the men stranded on the prison world, praying the Sirens would prevail. A lot could go wrong in the next few hours.

As she sat there feeling doubtful, she became conscious of Mother's thoughts, praising her for her valor and gently reassuring her that everyone was doing their best. Even the strongest caregivers, she seemed to say, needed a little caregiving from time to time.

Anghelloise smiled and went about her work, assured that everyone and everything was necessary.

[Thank you, Mother.]

She turned back to Farthing. "I sense a change in your mood. What's going on?"

"I just got a message from Tam. He is setting his plan in motion. He has trapped Artagan somehow, and is rushing to steal the plans for the prison. He will need transport out in a short while. It's imperative we arrive in time."

Their path to Kashtiloth was void of any obstacles. Not a ship to be seen! Anghelloise took a risk and listened in to the Senate messages bouncing around the home planet. If caught, they could be exposed, but what she heard confirmed was what she had suspected: most of the fleet was being sent to Oceania. Only a few strategic ships had been left in orbit around Kashtiloth, to protect the Magistrate's residence.

Their path seemed to be almost empty as they plunged toward the planet. Arrival would be in less than two hours at their speed. Who knew whether to increase their speed or slow down—what was the best call to be there at the right time to rescue Tam?

∞

Kruger sat and fretted. Where was everyone? He wanted Tam there now! He pressed the intercom button. "Barrington, how many ships are left in orbit at the moment?"

"Four, your Magistrate. The others have left for Oceania."

"Instruct two to descend to the landing pads behind the palace. I want armed guards and firepower at my disposal. Leave the other two in orbit to watch for any unauthorized flights to and from Central City."

"As you wish, your Magistrate." He sent messages out and two of the four ships in orbit began to plan for a trajectory for descent to the palace. They would be in place within the hour.

"And where is Tam and that blasted assistant of his?"

"I'll make inquiries right away, sir!"

Imbeciles, all of them! Kruger sat on his couch and began planning his requests for lunch. May as well set all in motion after having eaten. Much more sensible!

Chapter 39
Dragon's Den

The hallways were empty. There was no one present whatsoever. Tam left the gym through the halls, hurrying to the foyer of the palace. He knew he should check in with the Magistrate upon arrival, even though time was closing in to get the plans and make his escape. Artagan may be found sooner than he hoped, and he didn't want to try to explain how the man got trapped in a sauna for more than an hour. Artagan's wrath didn't scare him. It was the Magistrate getting news of his actions that was terrifying.

He kept moving forward, step by step, not out of courage but out of fear of what might happen to Brogan if he did nothing.

[Check in with the Magistrate,] came a message from Farthing. *[Find an excuse to get to the plans and make a copy. Take care of the Magistrate's needs, then slip out.]*

[Farthing! I'm so close and yet so far! I am going to need you soon. Can you help?]

With no response forthcoming, Tam pushed forward in the hope that Farthing would be there when he needed him. Might a plan B be necessary?

As he reached the door, Secretary Barrington stood up from his desk and called to him: "Amergan, I need to speak to you before you enter his Majesty's chambers. The last thing I need you to do is blunder in there and make mistakes that could cost us all!"

"Of course, Secretary. I'm listening." Tam stopped, the sweat dripping down onto his gym uniform.

"Where is Artagan? This affects him, too. The Magistrate asked for him as well."

"He has remained at the gym to finish his workout. I left to assist my master. Artagan will report when his shift starts. I've decided to come early to be of service. Would you like me to go get him from the royal gym?"

"No, leave him there for now. I can see you are trying to win points with his Magistrate," he smirked. "Go ahead, by all means—but listen to me before you blunder in there!"

"Yes, sir."

"The Magistrate has received news of the pirate band. One of their shuttles. It's orbiting around Oceania. The fleet's been sent to capture Farthing. There is word that he is in possession of information that is crucial to the Magistrate's plans."

"And where did this information come from?"

"Page Artagan," replied Barrington. "He seems to have informants somewhere. It's unknown for now. This is why the Magistrate requests Artagan's presence as soon as possible."

Tam began to shuffle his feet absentmindedly, trying to think of a way out of this situation. He couldn't have Artagan arrive without his immediate exposure.

"Please inform his Magistrate that I must change, then will immediately come to his aid." Tam smiled at Secretary Barrington, who frowned, then nodded his head.

"You had better get going. Can't have the Magistrate waiting too long—someone's head could roll…" He sat down, shuffled some of his papers, and continued to ignore Tam, who opened the door to the antechamber.

∞

Tam pulled off his workout clothes, wiped himself down quickly with a towel, then pulled on his page tunic, sash, and hat. *Got to be prepared to enter the dragon's den,* he thought to himself.

He swallowed, realizing this was his moment, when things had to happen—for the better or for total disaster. He summoned the courage to finally let down his barrier and sent a message:

[Farthing, I am about to attempt to get copies of the prison plans. I have no idea whether I'll succeed or fail. But this is not just for Brogan's sake, but for all of us—Mother, the Sisters, all those men in that prison—for all those people out there suffering from the Magistrate's hatred; for you, my dear pirate, and for me. I do this to chart a better course, hoping to make way for others to get through this hell.

Make your way to the prison planet, and save those men from their horrible fate. Give them back their lives. If I have to sacrifice myself, I will, but I'll try to take the Magistrate down with me. If I don't make it, and Brogan dies along with me, make sure we are buried on the hill of our farm, looking out at the sea. Either way, we need to be free of this tyranny. Enough is enough.]

Farthing's mind reached across the system from his unknown place and responded softly: *[My dear friend, you have grown strong and brave. Brogan would be proud of who you've become. Do not despair, for I know you will somehow come out of this alive. Mother believes in you. I believe in you. Brogan believes in you. We'll see you at our meeting place.]*

Tam adjusted his sash and tunic, breathed in deeply, and opened the door to the Magistrate's bedchambers.

"My dear boy, Tam. I'm glad you've arrived!"

Tam bowed. "I'm honored to serve."

"The time is right for me to strengthen my grip," said Kruger. "I'll unite the four planets and people will live as I have foreseen: as a glorious workforce, under my absolute rule, none of these filthy deviants running free. Would you like to hear the whole plan, my boy?"

"It would be my pleasure," Tam replied, gritting his teeth as he lowered his head.

"Come. Help me to my couch and I shall share it all with you."

Tam approached, and gently placed his arm under the sagging appendages that threatened to prevent him from breathing as he rendered aid. Tam was almost convinced the Magistrate had gained more weight in the time Artagan had been at the gym. He loathed the rolling fat and skin that rubbed against his own. He fought down the bile seething in his stomach.

"It is my duty to serve, sir. Please make yourself comfortable. Is there anything I can get you? Water, perhaps?"

The Magistrate wiggled himself into position and lifted his head to receive several pillows from Tam, who straightened his clothes, pulling the wrinkles out to make him more comfortable.

"I am fine, my boy. I am pleased with your performance. It has been exemplary. I wish to share my success with you, and honor you, by keeping you by my side as my servant when I become Supreme Magistrate of the entire system." He smacked his lips and wiggled his butt a little in joy. "Oh, and where on Kashtiloth is that page-in-training, Artagan? I have need to give him a piece of my mind. Bring him to me immediately!"

"Sire, he was in the palace gym about half an hour ago, after his workout with me. I left him there, as he wished to be alone to relax. Would you like me to go get him?" Tam was counting on a negative response.

"No, my boy! I wish to share my surprise with you. I'll deal with him later." He reached to the intercom. "Barrington, have an attendant go and retrieve Artagan. I wish to speak to him immediately." Barrington's affirmative response came back, and the Magistrate turned his attention back to Tam. "Go to my desk and bring me the plans. I wish to show you."

Tam bowed and did as he was bid. As his eyes scanned the table, he saw construction plans, military inventory lists, and a pile of cloth. With his heart in his mouth, he gathered them all and prepared to take them to Kruger.

Do not betray your nerves. Do not give him any indication of what you're about to do.

He walked to the couch and bowed.

"Please, sit here." The Magistrate patted the side of the couch and reached his flabby arms out, like a child reaching for his juice container. He lay them in his lap, wiggling his body in gleeful anticipation. The cloth draped across his groin. He lifted the blueprints for the prison on Corustloth. "As you can see, I've engineered whole new sections for scientific study in the prison hospital. The prisoner cells have been reduced in size, though we'll be taking in additional prisoners once I find that blasted Farthing and his band of pirates! I'll make him one of my experiments once I catch him today."

Tam scanned the plans, trying to make mental notes of everything, knowing he might have to rely on his memory alone. By the Goddesses' names, how could he copy them all without the Magistrate knowing? He'd imagined he might need to memorize one map—not five or six different documents. He needed time to consider his next move.

"Please, tell me more!" He pushed his mind to give up more. What was the cloth for?

The Magistrate paused, seemingly losing his train of thought. His hand dropped and the plans slid off his ample lap toward Tam. His eyes took on a dreamy look. Tam wondered if he had pushed him too hard. Had he just betrayed his mental abilities to the Magistrate?

Kruger turned slowly toward Tam. "Look at me, boy! I need you to see what I'm doing is *glorious!* Look into the eyes of the leader of the entire system! I honor you with this right!"

Tam slowly lifted his eyes from the floor to look into those of his opponent. What he saw horrified him: torture, vivisection, living brains being extracted without sedation, men in agony—and Kruger's eyes glittering with excitement!

"Oh, the fun I am going to have, my boy. This sample is the latest model." He held up the cloth, which by then Tam had figured to be the living cloth he'd seen used on the prisoners on the ship. "It can do so much more than earlier models. It will tell me so much—and even be able to record the mental messages of these degens. I'll be leaving for Corustloth soon to test it out. I plan on getting my hands very dirty. All for my pleasure—and power!"

Tam pushed the horror he felt into the pit of his stomach. "What do you plan to do, sire?" he whispered.

"I plan on using the mental capacities of these deviants to crush any resistance. Nothing will be out of my grasp! Millions of subjects to build my empire, and thousands of mental deviants to ensnare an entire system into being my playthings! *Glorious!*" Kruger was so excited that he was salivating. And his mind was so bent on violence and destruction that he'd turned himself on! He pulled aside the living cloth draped across his tunic, exposing his member.

He began touching himself as he went on to describe how he'd personally cut a man open to expose his innards and listen to his screams—how he'd expose his brain and pull it apart like a layer cake. His eyes glazed over as he envisioned the gore. He did not see the horror in Tam's.

Tam lowered his head and began to back away, deeply disturbed, when the Magistrate squealed. Tam surmised what had happened. He turned back, knelt by the Magistrate, and gently cleaned his loins and the sheets beside him.

"Tam, I am weary. I wish to nap, then start my departure. I'll need you at your best when I awake. Please, watch over your Magistrate as he sleeps. Be happy that you will be part of all of this! I want you by my side to witness my... glory..."

His mouth drooped and he dozed off.

Tam staggered to a chair to consider his next move. The plans were right there! Why not just take them and run? He knew he could not, though, lest the Magistrate awake. Kruger needed to think all was proceeding normally. He had no choice but to find a way to copy the plans—and quickly. He had no way of smuggling any technology in, though. What to do?

[Farthing! Help me! Brogan, are you there? Help me, someone! Please! How do I do this?] Farthing did not reply. Tam despaired. He looked at the Magistrate napping in amongst his plans and the living cloth. He might just have to kill the Magistrate on his couch and make off with the plans. He couldn't possibly, though—he'd never get away in time!

Suddenly, a message saved Tam from his despair.

[Tam, my love, use the living cloth!]

Tam started as he realized it was Brogan himself who had sent it.

[I can't go on much longer. The cloth!]

He had no time to respond, as Brogan's consciousness promptly went dark. Those short few seconds of contact heartened Tam, though, giving him some hope to go on. *Living cloth. My Goddesses! If the living cloth is meant to copy and imitate life, why wouldn't it be able to make copies of plans and lists?* Realizing he had something, he looked at the cloth, still in his hands. He could probably take half without the Magistrate noticing it was gone.

He gathered the plans from the couch and quickly placed them on the worktable. First, he laid the prison plans flat, placing the living cloth overtop and attaching the communication pad he carried. Creeping like it was truly alive, it moved over the plans, doing what it was supposed to. After a few moments of stillness, it signaled that it had completed its task. Tam lifted it gingerly and replaced the plans with the construction lists, then the military lists. Each was stored in the memory of the living cloth. Tam placed the unused portion, along with all the plans, back by the Magistrate's side.

Tam considered his last deed, then wrote a note to the Magistrate. He excused himself, explaining he was off to bring Artagan to his side as soon as possible.

With that done, Tam looked at the demon of man. Without bidding adieu, he opened the door and snuck away, leaving the Magistrate to himself.

Chapter 40
Betrayal

Artagan banged his hands against the windows of the sauna. He had been resting on the floor to reduce the heat building up in his body. Now, he stood by the door, frantically pounding in the hopes someone would hear him.

How could Tam trick him like this? *Damn him!* He had been sure he'd had Tam fooled, but instead it was *he* who was the fool.

He screamed louder.

After several moves to the floor and returns to the door to bang, Artagan was welcomed to a visit by one of the gym attendants doing his rounds.

"Get me out of here!!!"

The attendant looked shocked. He pulled the benches away and slid the broom-stick out of the handle, allowing Artagan to open the door.

"Are you OK, sir?"

"By the blue moons of Sapphire, of course not!"

Artagan, irate, pushed the bewildered attendant out of his way.

Didn't even say thank you, thought the attendant to himself, proceeding to the office to write up a summary of his rounds. *This little story should interest someone,* he thought, *assuming anyone ever reads the records.*

Artagan had nearly arrived at the Magistrate's private chambers. In his haste, he bumped into a woman coming down the marble stairs. She was dressed in a long, shimmering robe, with a veil across her face.

"Get out of my way, you silly thing!" Artagan bellowed. The woman just stood there, seemingly dumbfounded. "I've got to report to the Magistrate."

"My apologies, Page Artagan," she whispered as she stepped out of the way. "I recognize you from the Magistrate's office. I clean the locker room. Forgive my clumsiness."

Artagan brushed past her, his nose in the air. He shot her a final glance and retorted: "Lucky for me, I've no time to banter with staff." He turned and entered the office ahead.

"Where in Kashtiloth have you been, Artagan? I've looked all over for you!" Barrington demanded as he arrived at the antechamber of the Magistrate's private quarters. He pushed his glasses up on his nose. "I've been searching for you. In fact, Tam's gone to look for you—and I see he has not found you." Barrington eyed Artagan's clothing.

"I was locked in a sauna by that idiot! I've been trapped for over an hour, trying to get to the Magistrate! I want him found and to have the truth beaten out of him! He's a traitor—and a danger to the Magistrate!"

He moved toward the door, but Barrington barred the way.

"Not in those clothes, you aren't!"

"I'll change, you imbecile! Get out of my way, you infernal brat, or I'll strike you down!" He pushed Barrington aside, who stood there, shocked, as the door closed.

Artagan took off his clothing, wiped the perspiration off his body with a towel, applied some deodorizer to his armpits, and slipped his page uniform on. Checking in the mirror, he prepared himself, then glanced to the other side of the room, where there were lockers for the female staff. One was open, with clothing draping from it.

Slobs—all of them! That horrid cleaning lady he had bumped into was incompetent enough to leave clothes all over the place! *Can't even clean up after themselves. If I were running this place instead of Barrington, I'd have fixed that.*

With that thought, he steeled himself, straightening his tunic and sash as he knocked on the door and entered upon command from the Magistrate.

"Artagan! Where have you been? I've been waiting to ask you about your message for what seems like eternity!"

The Magistrate wasn't lounging on his chair in his usual slovenly way, but pacing in front of the curtained windows. Artagan was disgusted by the sight of his waddling, but swallowed his urge to cringe, and bowed deeply instead.

"Begging your pardon, my Magistrate, but I have more news to tell you. It involves Tam." He kept his eyes the floor, sweat beginning to bead on his forehead.

"Tam? He left over twenty minutes ago to look for you! What on Kashtiloth is going on?" Kruger snorted, moved toward his lounge chair, and eased his body onto the edge of it. "Don't just stand there—get over here and help me to my sofa! I want to know what's going on. I need to contact my militia. Where is that blasted secretary?" He banged on the intercom and yelled for Barrington.

"Sire," continued Artagan, "we need to stop Tam. I have reason to believe he is affiliated with a band of pirates that I've been tracking. You need to see my report, my Magistrate. I am sure you understand the importance of stopping this Farthing and Tam."

Secretary Barrington opened the door and bowed. "Sire, what is your will?"

"Get the communication screen operable and connect me with all fleet commanders and my military advisors. I want Farthing stopped and brought to me alive. I want everyone in motion! Now!!"

Barrington bowed and swiveled. "Immediately, my Magistrate." He busied himself with the communication console.

"Sire, we know where Farthing is! You can see it in my report. We need to send out a search party for Tam! Both he and Farthing must be stopped! We can't let him escape, and allow them to join forces!!!" Artagan was almost out of breath. He stood, his head bowed, waiting for the Magistrate's response for what seemed like eons.

"Page, I agree with you on one thing: Farthing must be found and brought to me. However, there is no *we* in this situation. Just *I*, the Magistrate. Remember your place, Artagan, and speak only when spoken to. I see nothing to indicate Tam has betrayed me. I do want him returned here, immediately, though—it is his job to support me, after all."

"Of course, your Magistrate," stuttered Artagan.

"Forgive me for interrupting, your Magistrate," Barrington intruded. "The fleet commanders have arrived in orbit around Oceania. There is no sign of a shuttle—or any ships, for that matter. It would seem, Page Artagan, that you've been misinformed!"

"What?!" Kruger roared. "What nonsense is this, Artagan?!"

"I assure you the information was correct," he stuttered in return. "Let me show you, if that is your wish, your Magistrate."

"Secretary, move over and let the page show us."

Artagan sat down beside Barrington, pulled out his communication pad, and interfaced it with the console. The data streamed onto the screen, showing Farthing located around Oceania.

"You are all fools!" bellowed Kruger. "Farthing has sent you false information! Barrington, contact the fleet commanders and tell them to find that pirate. Spread out over the entire system. Find him! Now!!"

Artagan rose and went to Kruger's side. Barrington bowed and got to work. Kruger stood up with Artagan's support, pushed him away, then flopped further onto his couch.

"You useless piece of garbage. What makes you think I won't have you killed for this mistake?"

"Please, your Magistrate! I can prove that Tam has betrayed you! Let me show you what I have." Artagan began pulling up video files from his holopad.

Kruger's eyes widened when he saw video of Tam interrogating Artagan on the Minorian-class ship. Seeing video of Tam with a man identified as Brogan, who was now incarcerated on Corustloth, allowed everything to fall into place for him. He had a spy in his midst. Someone who had betrayed him with his false portrayal as a devoted page.

What happened next shocked the other two men.

Kruger lay back on his couch and flailed his arms and legs, screaming and crying in hurt and in anger.

"No!! This cannot be!!!" The man he had trusted the most had lied. He flailed some more, screaming, spittle and tears flying in every direction. "Tam, I trusted you!! No!!! You are not a dear, faithful page!!!" Reports and maps flew in every direction as he continued his fit.

Suddenly, he stopped and wiped his chin. An abrupt calm came over him. "When I find you, I'll have you skinned alive and used as covers for my royal lamps," he sneered. He turned to the secretary. "Barrington, I want that man found immediately."

"Yes, your Magistrate—once I've finished contacting the fleet!" Barrington continued to bang on the console, dreading the threat of his sudden demise, at any moment, if he were to mess anything up.

Kruger continued to fume on his couch. "And you, page—get out of my sight. Return to your chambers and wait for my call. Deviate, and it will be your death! I want security to escort you, lest you betray me, too."

Chapter 41
Fight or Flight?

Anghelloise was messaging Farthing via the comm unit. "We have two warships ahead. They've just arrived. I'm not sure if I can maintain our current flight plan without being detected."

"Why not? You said we could remain invisible for most of the trip."

"But the energy needed to bend light around two shuttles simultaneously, traveling at this speed, is overtaxing my systems! We may need a backup plan."

"Aye. Then I should power up the defense systems and prepare to fight."

"Neither of our shuttles can stand up to those warships, my dear. We would last less than two minutes against them. The Sirens are not military."

"We may have no choice, Anghelloise. What about slowing down? Would that conserve enough energy?"

"Wonderful idea, Captain. It would help. We could delay arrival by as much as an hour if need be. Have you heard from Tam?"

"Nothing major. I got some sort of indication he was on the move, but that was all. It seems my link is either fading or is being blocked out for some reason." Farthing sighed. "Blast! I hate this! I want to go into a fight, not skulk under a cloak of invisibility."

"With all due respect, Captain, blazing guns would be our undoing. You are valuable cargo, and I can't allow you to fall into the Magistrate's hands. We must rescue Tam, or everything is for naught. My dear Farthing, please refrain from being yourself for just a while longer. I think I may have a plan—if you could give me a moment to think it through. In the meantime, I want you in a spacesuit and a helmet, ready to go. I need you to bring a backup of your computer system, including the information you stole from the university. I'm sending Nick to be your aide until I can figure this out."

"Understood." [*Mother, I trust in you, so I'll place my trust in Anghelloise, too.*]

Farthing got up and went in search of the spacesuits in the storage closet at the back of the shuttle. Three hung there in waiting. The largest, of course, was his. He pulled it off the hook, then reached for his helmet and boots. He stripped down to his undergarments, tossing his pirate's tunic and sash to the side. He pulled a thin insulating garment on. This, along with his underwear, would absorb sweat and provide protection from chafing from the suit. Being a soldier meant he was used to the whole process, which took him mere minutes. He did it automatically, like a drill. He placed his helmet on the floor near his console. He ran checks on the seals around his boots, leaving his gloves off until just before he had to put his helmet on. He checked the system automatic backups, removing them and then pulled the holorecorders from the computer reader, inserting them all into the waist pack of his suit. Then, Farthing sat and monitored the two shuttles' progress as they neared the planet and the two waiting warships.

A clanking noise on the hull of the ship pulled him out of his concentration. A signal over the comm indicated that Nick was outside.

"Ready to enter on your command, Captain," Nick chimed.

Looking on the camera from the airlock, Farthing could see the robot floating in front of the console, waiting patiently. He cycled oxygen into the airlock chamber to equalize the pressure.

After several beeps, the computer announced: "Captain, airlock pressurized."

"Open it, then, Computer."

The door opened and Nick sailed out into the shuttle.

"At your service, sir! Please prepare for vacuum conditions. I believe Mistress is about to carry out her plan. You will need to be in the airlock with me in less than five minutes."

"OK, Nick. Assist me with the rest of the pre-checks, then. Hand me my helmet."

"Yes, sir!" Nick floated to Farthing, reached his prehensile arms down to the helmet lying on the floor, and grasped it. Raising his arms as he floated upward, he moved toward Farthing and prepared to place it on his head.

"Hold it, Nick. I can do that myself." He took the helmet from the robot and placed it on his head, pushing the seals into place. "Now, check the seals as I put on my gloves."

Nick did as he was bid, then returned in front of the suited man to report that he had found everything in order.

"I've checked all the suit protocols, Nick. Everything is optimal. I can monitor the vitals on the helmet holoscreen or the one on my right gauntlet."

"Yes, sir. You are ready to go. You may enter the airlock and prepare to cycle outward."

Farthing knew he would be moving from shuttle to shuttle at high speed—something he'd never done before. "Nick! Are you coming with me?"

"Of course! It is my job to ensure you arrive when needed by the mistress!" Nick floated into the airlock and rotated his face toward Farthing. "Are you ready, then?"

Farthing moved his bulky body toward the airlock, bending his helmeted head as he entered. "Ready when you are, Nick." He paused, then consulted the suit's comm unit. "Anghelloise, how about filling me in on your plans? I'm dressed and inside the airlock. I would love to know what we're up to!"

"My dear, hold on. I'm a little busy at the moment. We are coming into range of the warships' weapons, and I want to be ready to execute my plan if we're detected. If not, you'll be able to take the suit off and sit back down, big boy. Stay at the ready. Back to you in a bit."

Farthing leaned against the wall of the airlock and sighed. *Sometime, I'd like to be in on the plans. I am a pirate captain, after all.* He tapped his foot absentmindedly and waited.

"Farthing! The decision's been made! Prepare to exit your ship. Instruct your computer to not release any information to anyone but yourself or me."

"You want the computer to self-delete if the ship is breached?" Farthing asked.

"Of course, my dear man. I think you know what we're about to do."

"Computer, by my voice imprint, I request you not release information to anyone but me or Siren Anghelloise. Authorization code: Farthing, bar one, short three, silence one."

"Understood, Captain Farthing. I will follow your instructions. All information will be deleted. Will you be coming back for me? I shall miss you if you don't."

"I don't know. But you've carried out your duties perfectly. Thank you, Computer." Farthing felt a wistful regret about possibly leaving his shuttle behind. The computer was not really sentient, but felt of a sudden as though he were losing a friend. "Regardless, Computer, I'll have a backup of you to restore later on. Maybe even in a better shuttle!"

"Thank you, my dear Farthing." Anghelloise's personality seemed to shine through Computer's programming. "I will guard your intel."

∞

Through the viewscreen, Anghelloise could see the planet as the ships sped toward an entry orbit. The two waiting warships hung just above the edge of its atmosphere. Watching her sensors, she knew that both shuttles would be quickly discovered if something were not done in the next few minutes. Her fingers flew over the console, sending instructions to various parts of the ships—both her and Farthing's. There would be a surprise waiting if the shuttle were to be seized.

"Farthing! Cycle your airlock and prepare to exit. Once outside, you'll see I've pulled the shuttle back beside you. Take your security line and program it to magnetically secure itself to mine. Just aim and shoot the security line booster and it should adhere to my airlock entry."

"Is that blasted thing strong enough to support me?" Farthing asked. "I don't want to be taking a long trip to the planet on my own!"

"My dear man! Siren technology is tested and true! It will more than support you both."

Farthing pushed the buttons for cycling the airlock. Warning alarms began to sound.

"Outer door about to open," Computer announced. "Captain Farthing, luck of the Goddesses to you."

The outer door opened to the vacuum of space. One half-expected to hear wind whistling by, but there was no atmosphere to transmit the sound. The silence was complete.

Farthing looked across to the other shuttle and felt a little disoriented by the streaks of light that outlined it. *How in the name of Alorion's Moons does Anghelloise see through that?* He reached for the security line and the booster, grabbed them, then turned to Nick.

"This had better work!"

The bot said nothing—just smiled and blinked.

It's funny—it takes the vacuum of space to shut the bot up!

Farthing lifted the booster, reached around, and attached one end of the line to the magnetic seal on the exterior of his shuttle, just beside the door. Aiming the booster toward the door of Anghelloise's shuttle, he released the trigger. Silently, it expelled gases as it sped toward its target.

As he watched, he realized the magnetic attraction of the door and the security line had begun. Despite being a bit off with his aim, the security line still managed to zero in on its target. With contact made, Farthing gave a sharp tug on the line to test it.

"Hold your position, Anghelloise! I am about to make the trek to your shuttle. Don't be giving me a joyride! I'd like to get there in one piece."

"Don't worry, Farthing, my dear. I want you here in one piece, too! Nick, follow along and provide assistance if needed."

"Yes, Mistress!" Nick chimed over the comm.

Farthing pulled himself through the door and, using hand over hand, made his way to the other shuttle. Nick followed along, using his mechanical hands in a similar fashion. An untrained person would have had a horrible sense of falling. Farthing steeled himself, and continued on as though it were the most natural thing in the world.

"Farthing! The warships are breaking formation. They've discovered us. I haven't heard anything on the comm from them as of yet, but it is clear they know we are here. Please hurry to my shuttle. Nick, let's get everyone on board as fast as possible!"

"Understood, Mistress! Captain Farthing, sir, please allow me to take over." Nick slid off the tether and jetted in front of him. "Hold onto me instead of the tether, sir! No time to argue."

Farthing reached for one of the handles that popped out of Nick's back with his available hand, released the tether, and brought his other hand to the other handle. "Anghelloise, this blasted bot had better know what he's doing! Letting go of that tether gives me a bad feeling."

Anghelloise ignored this. She just giggled and said: "Go, Nick!"

Nick jetted forward, allowing his metal hands to slide along the tether. They sped up and quickly neared the door of the second shuttle. As they neared it, he slowed his jets and clamped down onto the line, slowing them further. Now within reach, Nick swung himself into the airlock, taking Farthing with him. They hit the far wall with a thud. Nick spun off the rebound, reached the entry, and released the magnetic tether by reversing its polarity setting. As it began curling back to the other shuttle, he pushed the lever to close the door.

"Closing the door, Mistress!"

"Thank you, Nick! Farthing, are you OK? Let's get some air in there for you, then get you into the shuttle proper. We've got work ahead—and little time to do it!"

Farthing just grunted, feeling like extra baggage being hauled around.

The airlock cycled through and pressurized. The alarms shut off and the door opened. Farthing entered, beginning to pull off his helmet. Nick went immediately to help him.

"I've instructed your ship to prepare for a roll and pitch—to resemble a ship out of power. When the roll starts, I'll retract the shield from your shuttle, and it will appear as though it's malfunctioning. Then, I'll spring the little surprise!" Anghelloise turned back to her console. "Initiating shield separation from your shuttle. It will be now visible to the warships."

The shuttle seemed to shimmer as it disappeared from their view.

"Shuttle computer, initiate program!"

On the comm, they could hear what sounded like Farthing's voice: "Emergency beacon! My ship has been damaged and is unable to navigate. Assistance would be greatly appreciated!"

Anghelloise laughed, then began plotting a course to the Magistrate's palace via a lower orbit that would take them around the planet quickly a couple of times, then drop into the atmosphere on an angle that would take them swiftly to their destination.

"Let's just hope no one sees our entry burn. Even bending light can't prevent that..." She shrugged. "Next stop, the palace!"

Farthing plunked himself down on the seat. "Let's get on with it, then!"

∞

The two warships converged on the shuttle as it descended toward Kashtiloth, where it would burn upon entry into the atmosphere. They planned to seize it and its occupant, which their sensors indicated was a very large human. The voice that had requested help had also been consistent with Farthing's.

The commander of the two warships looked at his screen display and sighed. *Wouldn't it just be easier to let the pirate burn and be done with it?* It was not possible, however, as the Magistrate likely wanted the man for questioning and probably torture, if the rumors were true.

Four of his shuttles were zeroing in on the spinning ship as he sat there, pondering. Their job was to stop the spin, secure the shuttle, board it, and arrest Farthing. As the shuttle continued to descend, the ships sidled up to the vessel on four sides, maintaining the same speed. To stop its spin, magnetic thrusters were projected via boosters from each ship. Once attached, they began to slow the spin and even out the shuttle's flight path.

Achieving this, the lead shuttle began docking with the rogue. "Connection complete, Commander," announced its pilot. "Shall I board it and make the arrest?"

The commander considered this, then decided to signal what they were about to do.

"Farthing, this is Army Commander Reaghan Maguire. Stand down and prepare to be boarded."

"Commander Maguire, I wish to thank you for saving my ship, but I don't think I'll be staying for my capture," Farthing replied.

"Commander Maguire! Sensors indicate he's getting ready to jump to curved space!" First Hand Razfar announced from his station behind Maguire's.

Fine, thought Maguire. *We can play dirty if you wish, Farthing.* "Lead shuttle, disable his ship via the installed thrusters."

"Yes, sir! With pleasure!"

The thrusters fired, bringing the shuttle closer to the warships. "Disable his drive. The thrusters should have computer access to do so. That ship will not be taking off. Bring it into our holding bay instead. I'll see to Farthing's arrest myself."

"Shuttle disabled as requested, sir. Moving it to the holding bay now," the lead pilot replied.

Maguire excused himself from the bridge, leaving First Hand Razfar in charge, and went in search of Farthing's shuttle. "Instruct security to meet me at the shuttle with whip-irons big enough to hold that blasted pirate!"

"Yes, sir," replied Razfar.

Maguire was already on his way to the holding bay. He sighed, wondering why he had accepted this position with Maguire. He was known as one of the most cantankerous commanders in the military, and there had been very few times he'd even been recognized by Maguire for anything he'd done. He kept monitoring the shuttle and the lead captain's instructions being broadcast over the comm. Maybe, this time, he might be noticed.

When Maguire entered the holding bay several minutes later, he was joined by security. "Open that shuttle hatch immediately. Stun him if he so much as moves or speaks."

The security detail nodded, preparing to open the shuttle door.

Before they did, the door began to open on its own. The security detail drew their firearms and prepared the whip-irons for Farthing's capture. With at least twenty-five soldiers present, he wouldn't stand a chance trying to escape. Farthing would finally be in Maguire's grasp, and his success would be heralded by the Senate and ultimately praised by the Magistrate himself. A promotion would be likely. He was sure of it!

Farthing did not exit the shuttle door as predicted, though. Instead, there was total stillness.

"Send three men in to scout the shuttle out," Maguire commanded to the security chief.

"Yes, sir. You three, move in to board the shuttle."

The three soldiers slowly and carefully edged their way into the airlock, their weapons raised. What they found was an empty shuttle. The computer was still active, though.

Suddenly, it announced: "Executing Anghelloise plan A!"

With that, a low singing began to emit from the computer, growing louder—thousands of voices singing through every communication device on the entire warship. The singing grew louder still, wavering, seemingly creating a shimmer in the air.

All Maguire could think of was how much he needed to relax. He went back to his chamber, as did the others. Everyone was transfixed as they retired to their beds and couches. Razfar, still on the bridge, curled up on the floor in front of his station and went to sleep with a smile on his face.

The shuttle computer then sent instructions to both the warships' computers to execute a return to base. The disabled ships fired up and began to head home. Then, the computer began the sequence to erase itself, and Farthing's shuttle went completely dead. There would be nothing left to discover.

Anghelloise was singing to herself as they approached the palace. Nick was sitting in his recharging station. Farthing was reviewing files from the university, seeking to distract himself.

"Farthing, have your sensed anything from Tam?"

"Nothing."

"So, we have no way of knowing whether he's OK—or where he is at the moment?"

"No."

"Farthing, my dear, you have a way with words. I'm worried about him, too. I can see where Artagan is. The signal is returning from his comm link. He's still inside the palace."

"We have no way of knowing if Tam is with him," said Farthing. "What do we do next?"

"We land in the wooded area behind the palace, as we've planned. Arrival is in five minutes. Luckily, the shield has held. No one seems to have followed us after entry into the atmosphere. If he is there, we will have succeeded. If not... we search."

Chapter 42
Blurp!

Tam was dumbfounded as the man ran his hand down his naked back, reached his buttocks, and gave them a squeeze. *How in the blue moons did I get myself into this?*

"You're a beautiful wench if I ever saw one." The guard slurred as he tried to cop a kiss, which Tam accepted for believability's sake.

The man was drunk and wanted to play with Tam, thinking he was a woman. This wasn't part of the plan! How was he going to get to the rendezvous point? If he could just get the man off him for a couple minutes, he could put his strength into contacting Farthing, who had been harder and harder to reach lately. It would seem the Triad was just about severed.

There was a pounding inside his head. He went limp for a moment as the drunken guard haphazardly grabbed him and tried to pull his dress up in the front. Tam pulled his hand away and swung it around his back, hoping to distract him. The pounding in his head increased. Suddenly, he felt a flood of thoughts, emotions, and sensations pour into him—and, by the blue moons of Alorion, it was coming from Brogan! He seemed to be laughing!

[Brogan, what in blue blazes are you doing? You've been silent for so long, my love.]

[I've been conscious for several hours with no drugs! I'm free of the cloth, Tam! Perhaps they're preparing to let me go!]

[You're free? Are you still in prison?]

The guard's tongue slid into Tam's mouth, distracting him.

[Yes, I am in my cell, but they've left me alone for long enough that I have regained my senses. My love, I can feel you again! You're doing so well at entertaining that guard. How did you manage to get yourself into this situation in the first place?]

∞

When Tam had left the Magistrate's chambers, he had been unsure of where to hide until he felt the shuttle approaching. He'd hoped to contact Farthing—or be identified by sensors from the ship in time. When neither had happened, he'd had to improvise.

As he looked around the changing room, he saw the rows of lockers on the other side of the dressing room. It was reserved mostly for female workers, so he hadn't paid much attention. Now, focused on escape, he was suddenly very aware of it.

Gazing down the row, he decided to pick the first locker. He opened it. Nothing there. He reached for the second and found several frocks, but they were too small for his rather large and unwomanly frame. He'd need something from a taller woman...

Seven lockers later, he found what he was looking for—a dress made of shimmering blue material that fit his tall frame. It took him a while to figure out the contraption that went over the breasts, but he managed to get it attached. He stuffed surgical gloves and other rubber materials into the cups to give him a relatively realistic bust.

Luckily, he was not a novice at makeup; he used to help the young girls in the commune with theirs all the time. The only difference was having to apply it to himself. For his head, he decided on a wrapped turban with feathers and bows that made him look like a woman who enjoyed going out to the Blue Moon Café. A veil would hide his more masculine facial features, but promote his large and pouty lipstick-covered mouth. He chose a pair of clip-on earrings to dangle from his ears. For shoes, he picked comfortable sandals.

As he stood looking at himself in the mirror, despite the urgency of his situation, he found himself pausing to laugh at what he was about to do. All he needed were some lessons on how to walk like a woman. After some practice, he felt that he had some semblance of femininity and decided to proceed. By the Goddesses' love, he had better be able to pull this off.

For a moment, he stopped and berated himself. What about more jewelry—and maybe a bag like those he'd seen women carry in the markets of Port Ali-Alorion? A few minutes later, with jangling bracelets, several necklaces, and an attractive straw handbag to hold the living cloth, he was ready to go.

He went down the hallway to the entrance of the palace, past the doors that lead to the Magistrate's chambers. His heart skipped a beat when he saw Artagan coming up the stairs.

Tam attempted to step out of his way, but accidentally moved in the same direction Artagan was taking.

"Get out of my way, you silly thing!" Artagan bellowed. Tam just stood there, dumbfounded. "I've got to report to the Magistrate."

"My apologies, Page Artagan," Tam whispered as he stepped out of the way. "I recognize you from the Magistrate's office. I clean the locker room. Forgive my clumsiness."

∞

The guard reeked of alcohol as he swooped in for another kiss. Tam rolled his eyes and sighed. He needed to do something—and quickly—before he was discovered as a fraud.

Inspiration came out of desperation. Tam reached down to the guard's crotch and grabbed his member through his tunic.

"Oh, my man, you are exactly what I want tonight." He strengthened his grip, then led him outside the palace door. The guard, in his drunken state, seemed to enjoy being led about by his penis, and followed like a little lamb into the shadows, past the portcullis and around the palace walls that led into the foyer.

"My beautiful woman, I can't stand it any longer. I must have you here and now!" The guard slurred his words as he grabbed Tam by the shoulders and pushed him against the wall, pressing his body against Tam's.

Tam's reaction was knee-jerk—literally. His knee went up into the man's groin area with a smack. He spun the drunken man around so he was against the wall, and promptly smashed his head against it. Luckily for the guard, his drunkenness was almost complete, so he wasn't really aware of what had happened as he tumbled unconscious to the ground.

Tam made his escape from the side of the palace, avoided the warship landing pads, and headed around back through the gardens toward the woods, where he was supposed to make his rendezvous with Farthing and Anghelloise. Running as fast as he could in his delicate sandals, he realized Brogan was still howling with laughter. It really brightened your mood when your Life-Line seemed to be coming back to you. Could it really be that Brogan was safe? Might he really be set free?

[I'm coming for you as soon as I can, Brogan. Hold tight, and don't give up hope. I'll see you soon, my love. We'll make our escape and go home to our farm and our animals and our friends. I promise!]

[I know you will, Tam, my wonderful man. You give me so much hope when it seems there is so little to be found. I adore you, you silly man, dressing as a woman for me. Hilarious!]

Then, to Tam's dismay, he could feel Brogan's mood change.

Tam felt hands wrapping around his throat, swift kicks to his groin, and the sensation of being dragged across a floor to be dumped on a table. There was agony, which then faded out. Brogan had been injected with inhibiting drugs, no doubt.

Tam staggered, tumbling to the ground. He felt the tears well up in his eyes. He cried out to the sky. It was more than he could bear. He sent a simple message to Farthing, then: *[I am ready. Please, by the Goddesses' will, you pick me up and get me to my man. I need him back. I'll risk my Life-Line to do so. I will risk both our lives if it means he'll be free of this torture.]*

To Tam's surprise, there was a response from Farthing!

[We are on our way! We are almost there. Get to the rendezvous point immediately!]

Tam abandoned the sandals, stood, and ran as fast as he could into the forest.

∞

"Farthing! There's someone coming out of the woods."

"What in the blue moons are you talking about, Anghelloise?" He turned and saw a woman running into the glade. He was confused for a moment, before he realized what he was seeing. "Wait! Aye! It's Tam! He's pulled his veil off. We've done it! We've saved him!"

"It would seem we have, my dear," she smiled and let out a breath of relief.

Farthing smiled back. "It would seem you have competition in the beauty department, Anghelloise! He cuts quite the figure in that outfit!"

"Farthing, do be quiet as I land the shuttle."

He giggled a bit, then moved to the door bay to rescue his damsel-in-distress.

Chapter 43
Slipping Through the Lines

Artagan slipped out of his room, eyeing the corridor for guards. There were none. He placed two small orbs on the floor by the door, then continued down the hallway to access the stairs to the central hall of the palace. He approached the entranceway, where the door guards were waiting. They stood up immediately.

"Page, where exactly are you going? The Magistrate insists you stay in your room until you are called," the first guard commanded.

"That is none of your business. You had best get out of my way!"

"Really?" asked the second guard. "What makes you think you can do anything about it?" He reached for his weapon.

"I wouldn't do that if I were you. Drop your arms and stand still, both of you!" Artagan tried a mental command. *[Stand still! Do not prevent me from leaving. You will not stop me!]*

They both laughed, drew their weapons, and advanced on Artagan.

"You little fool! If you weren't wanted by the Magistrate, I'd be cutting you down right now!" the first guard sneered.

[Sit down and let me pass. It is my will that you do as I ask! Now!]

Nothing happened.

Fine! If commanding them won't work, then I'll try something else!

Artagan laughed and projected a command elsewhere: *[Activate! Follow my eyes! Begin!]*

There was a whizzing sound that flew past and the chests of the two guards suddenly exploded as the orbs made contact with them. There was no time for them to react. Their bodies tumbled back onto the floor, bleeding out. Their eyes were wide with surprise as the life gurgled out of them.

[Sensor drones can be useful in many ways! Glad I keep a couple in my room!] Artagan slipped out the door and ran for the cover of the woods behind the palace, avoiding the landing field that contained two warships. It would be necessary to get to the shuttle as quickly as possible—before the alarm went up.

As he ran, he giggled. He prided himself on his trickery. Too bad he hadn't had the chance to try that out on Tam! *Goodbye, Magistrate! I shall be seeing you soon enough—don't you worry about me!*

A short time later, he arrived at the small farm where his shuttle had been stored for a rather hefty price to keep the farmer quiet. He entered the stable and slapped the communications pad on the shuttle's door. It opened and he climbed in.

By the time anyone knew he was gone, he would be well on his way to Alorion.

∞

Artagan sat at the computer console in his berth on the Minorian-class supply ship, which was on its way to Corustloth. The supply ship was delivering supplies to the prison, and Artagan had bribed his way onto the passenger list.

Mentally pushing someone to do something he wanted took practice. His database confirmed that. The massive amount of information he had stored from his research before confronting Tam was becoming more and more useful. In fact, the access even gave him updates as to what was going on with the Magistrate. The data had been a goldmine for him. The Ancients' technology was on Corustloth.

Artagan wrung his hands in glee. *This is exactly what I need! Kruger could become my puppet if I succeed. Tam will be at my mercy. I'll crush that worthless, bottom-dredging worm!*

With access to technology like that, Artagan could proceed with his plans. *Imagine my ability to crush all I wish to destroy!* Tam and his allies. Kruger and his cronies. Hopefully, the system with them. Why would he care? He'd be happy living a solitary life, free of the likes of the idiots who populated it. *I need no one! I wish to be alone, free to explore Ancient technology.*

The database yielded interesting information. Certain minds, like Kruger's—due to the chaotic character of his insanity, could be easily manipulated.

That is why Tam so easily fooled the idiot! What is there from stopping me doing the same? Practice, my man! Practice! I have about four days to reach my potential!

∞

Captain Gallagher sighed and tossed his fork onto his plate as the table in the eating lounge erupted into a battle between two women seated at it. As he turned, he saw one toss her plate of food into the lap of the other, who, in turn, screamed and tossed her drink at her foe.

"You blazing ditch-digger! How dare you!" She threw the empty glass at the other woman, which missed her head by a hair's breadth.

"You deserve it, you dung beetle!" The other woman grabbed the first by the front of her uniform and pushed her backward.

"I'll kill you if you do that again!" The first woman pulled herself out of her fall and lunged at the other, and both fell to the floor. They were locked in battle, rolling around.

"Security!" Captain Gallagher called on his holopad. "We have another disturbance!"

He rose, deciding to wade in to try to separate them. He received an elbow to his crotch, making him bend over in pain as the women continued blindly. It was though they were possessed.

"Enough, you two, or I'll have you thrown into the brig for insubordination! Do you hear me?"

The women continued to pull hair, pummel each other, and scream obscenities. But eventually, security arrived, and they were separated. It took four men to pry them apart. It really was as though they were possessed. They continued to wail as they were pulled toward the door.

Without warning, they collapsed to the floor. The security guards gaped as they fell.

"Are you alright, Captain Gallagher?" asked one, seeing the captain clutching his crotch.

"I'm fine." Gallagher straightened up with a small grunt. "Put them in the brig until we can interview them."

He sat down in front of his meal and stared at it. This was the third incident in the last three days! Yesterday, a passenger had somehow gotten access codes to an airlock and tried to jettison himself into space. He was stopped by an ensign, who happened by when the alarm sounded. He was still in the brig, along with three others. Now this. That made six people going off without reason. The other three—one man and two women from the kitchen staff—were involved in what could only be described as a scene of sexual debauchery. They had been found covered in cooking oil, fornicating on the preparation table. All of them claimed not to remember having done anything. What on Alorion was going on?

Why were people starting to go crazy, then suddenly stop, and have no memory of anything?

His attention returned to the women being picked up and placed on stretchers from the infirmary. He pushed his meal away and stood up. To contact the company headquarters on the next drop from curved space later this afternoon seemed to be the logical next step.

Gallagher headed out into the hallway and made his way to the bridge. There were quite a few crew members and passengers coming and going, whom he weaved his way through. To his surprise, he felt a smack on his buttocks. He quickly turned to find no one claim responsibility, everyone continuing on their way. He grunted and pulled open the door to the bridge. *Safety here, at least,* he thought as he entered to see the first mate dancing arm-in-arm with another male in front of the viewscreen. He dropped into his chair and placed his head in his hands. He breathed for a few moments before preparing to break things up.

Artagan sat in his quarters and howled with laughter. This whole trip was becoming an absolute pleasure as he watched his abilities increase. Practice, indeed! He would be more than ready to take Kruger on when they reached Corustloth. One more step would be to make his presence known, so he could be arrested and delivered to Kruger as the warrants indicated. He was surprised that nobody had noticed him so far, though he did a great job at masking who he was. The last curved space exit was later today. That would be the most appropriate time to reveal himself. One more big headache and he would be there, ready to do what he had to.

He still reveled in the fact that he didn't have to suffer like Tam supposedly did. *I guess that is the difference between a degen like him and me!* It was all in the genes.

Chapter 44
Kruger's Master Plan

Kruger stood looking out the window. His mind wandered from event to event, never able to find anything he'd done to deserve Tam's betrayal. Artagan's videos proved it, though—along with the fact that Tam had a partner named Brogan imprisoned on Corustloth.

That led to another question: Why had Artagan withheld that information for so long? What was his agenda? He had known Tam was a traitor all along! How could Artagan be anything other than a traitor, too?

He slammed his fist into the table that sat beside the window. The curtain got caught on his hand and in his ire he turned away, pulling it from the window. He gritted his teeth and clenched his hands so hard that his nails bit into the skin of his palms.

The injustice of it all! I am the Magistrate! All that I've done for this system—all that I plan to do—and they are ungrateful. Can't they see that what I propose is best for all? How dare Tam betray me! He served me with perfection, yet left without any care or thought for me.

Tam, how could you do this to me?! Oh, I so miss having you take care of my meals and dressing me. I felt so at ease having you share my plans, my hopes, and my desires. After offering you all that, you turn on me and steal, lie, and cheat. You could have had a safe and happy life! It would have had meaning! Instead, you choose to be a traitor and pirate scum.

Kruger looked down at his bleeding palms and began to tremble.

"You will pay for your actions, Amergan! I will see you on a dissecting table! I will pull you apart to see what's inside—to find out why you abandoned me. I'll make you—and all the ungrateful—suffer for what you've done! You will be responsible for what's to come! This system is under siege now, and it is all your fault!" His hands flailed as he pulled the table down, slamming its contents to the floor with a crash. Anything that wasn't broken he stomped on and destroyed. "Those who stand in my way will feel my wrath! They will pay for opposing me!"

He strode over to the desk and slammed his hand on the intercom. "Barrington! Have that brat, Artagan, dragged to my chambers! I want him in chains, escorted by two guards!"

"As you wish, sire!"

Kruger looked at the plans and the living cloth, still sitting where they had been left after Tam had departed. He reached over the table to sweep the contents onto the floor, his teeth chattering as he approached.

Then he stopped. The living cloth—part of it was gone! That scum had taken half of the new model! That meant... the plans for the prison had been copied and stolen, too!

Well, well, my dear Tam! Your little theft may provide me with the ultimate revenge. You want the prison plans? Fine, take them, and make your way to Corustloth! That will be your undoing. Bring that pirate, Farthing, with you! Come, then, Tam. Come to me and see my delight in your demise—better yet, as a slave, like your partner! What glee! What wonderful revenge it would be to have the scoundrel surrender to his master plan. To denigrate him so much that he couldn't bear to live. *I will submit him to my will, as I shall with all those men!*

Kruger laughed to himself, picking up the plans and the cloth. "You've helped me again, Amergan! You've given me the opportunity to squeeze self-motivation out of your body and mind! I shall control you as I'll control all the others!" He lowered himself onto his couch and placed his hands in his lap. He was out of breath and sweating. He reached for a handkerchief and dabbed his forehead, furious that there was no one to help him.

Minutes later, the intercom signaled.

"Who is it?" he shouted from his couch. Thankfully, he didn't have to get up to respond. "What do you want?"

"Excuse me, your Magistrate, Barrington here. The fleet captains have responded and are awaiting your orders." He paused and coughed a bit. "There is... *er*, sire, the matter of Page Artagan. It seems he somehow killed his guards and escaped!"

"You fools! Is there no one I can trust?!" he bellowed. "If I had more time, I'd see to it that many a head would roll for this indiscretion. I have work to do, though, and that will have to wait. Barrington, inform Commander Maguire that I'll be boarding his warship at the end of the day. He himself will be escorting me to Corustloth. Let him know the honor of carrying me will weigh on how I treat his past indiscretions with the loss of Farthing!"

"Yes, sire! Is there anything else?"

"No! Get to work, and get that warship ready to receive me! Oh, and what is the status of the search for the witches? What did the visit to that convent on Alorion bring to light?"

"Ah, sire, it is just that: a convent of women who celebrate the old ways of the Goddesses. They are harmless, however misguided!" Barrington replied. "The search continues. Find Farthing and you will find the witches, too, no doubt!"

"Do not delay me with your idiotic banter! I will make the decision about the search."

"Yes, your Magistrate!" Barrington quipped.

"Have Maguire send a warship to Alorion and have the crew search the planet. If there's nothing there, proceed to Zemitis, then Kashtiloth—until someone finds them!"

"At once, sire! Maguire is ready to receive you. Shall I order you a shuttle?"

"Immediately!" replied Kruger. "Barrington, pack me enough supplies for the voyage. Ensure I am ready to leave early this evening to join him."

"At your wishes, sire! Barrington, out!"

Join me, Tam. Make my wishes reality! I am waiting!

Chapter 45
Next Level

Anghelloise pulled out the living cloth and spread it out over the table. "Tam, using this was genius! We'll have a working map of the prison within hours."

"Thank you, Anghelloise. I was desperate. It was Brogan who made the suggestion."

"Brogan has been in contact with you, then? That's wonderful!"

"He almost died, but seemed to recover later. But I've not felt his presence since then. I fear for him. We have to get him and the others out of there."

"We will, my dear," assured Anghelloise. "Maybe we should go and check on Farthing. He's setting us up for a rendezvous with the *Starfinder*. We should be able to meet with them in the asteroid cluster in two days. He's hoping we can make the first curved space checkpoint before the end of the week. If we do it right, we should make Corustloth in about three weeks."

"That's what worries me—a lot can happen in three weeks. Then there's the space madness for me and the other Life-Liners. It's not going to be pleasant."

"We'll get through it, my dear boy."

Nick appeared through the door separating the workroom from the cockpit. "Mistress, Captain Farthing requests you return to update him on your progress."

"Tell Farthing we'll be right there."

"Yes, Mistress." Nick turned and floated back through the doorway.

"Farthing misses us already! Let's not keep him waiting any longer. Tam, maybe you could change now? That dress really is ridiculous! Siren outfits are more refined, as you can see." She twirled around, her dress shimmering as it flowed around her.

"Good idea," Tam replied. *If I'm not mistaken, Anghelloise may be jealous of my outfit!*

"A uniform would be better traveling clothes, my dear!" she chided.

Oops. Tam wondered if she'd heard that thought. He headed to the lockers to get a change of clothing. Anghelloise smiled and turned back to her work.

Farthing was busy with the controls. He was preparing for a jump into curved space as Tam entered. "I see you've found a suitable uniform. Once we get underway, I'll want to hear the story of how you got into that disguise."

"Let's just say it worked, and leave it at that for now," Tam laughed. He placed his hand on his forehead in mock embarrassment.

"Suit yourself! However, when they tell the story of how we rescued the prisoners on Corustloth, they'll need details!" Farthing laughed, too, and turned back to his controls becoming more serious. "Bad news: the crew of the *Starfinder* has just informed me they are still five days from being able to leave. The upgrades are almost complete. I'm sorry, Tam, but we'll be delayed at least a week—maybe more—before we can set course for Corustloth."

Tam said nothing to show his disappointment. There was no point mentioning that the extra week or more could mean the death of many men, including himself and Brogan. Farthing knew it. So did Anghelloise. The other issue was the curved space jump to the asteroid cluster.

Joy, I'll be going crazy again, then doing it nine more times on the coming trip. It almost killed me the last time!

"Tam, I know you're worried about the trip, but we'll be here to guide you," said Farthing. "I know I'm no longer linked with you, but I don't need to be an empath to know what you are thinking." He placed a big hand on his shoulder and squeezed gently.

"I know, Farthing. I'm glad we're back together."

"And I'm here, too!" Anghelloise quipped as she entered the cockpit.

Tam turned and smiled at her. "Yes, it is good to have you here. Nick, too—though it's strange he's no longer a Senate bot guarding the fence at the bottom of our farm." He paused and sighed. "That seems so long ago. I miss the place—the animals, and Brogan, most of all. It's been hard not to give in to hopelessness. Having you all here makes it easier to deal with the pain. Thank you." A tear formed in his eye, and he turned away, embarrassed.

"We are here for you and Brogan," Anghelloise said softly. "It is our mission to save all the souls on that despicable prison planet—Brogan included. We need to stop the Magistrate from experimenting on those men. Mother insisted we'd get there in due time, so there is little need to fret over the four weeks ahead. I trust her in all she says. It will be so."

"I'm grateful she is there for us, too," replied Tam. "But I don't understand what role she'll play in all of this. How can she help a band of pirates try to take a prison planet?"

"Boy, Mother is a powerful entity," said Farthing. "Her abilities have not shown themselves to any of us yet. Rest assured, though, that we will arrive in time."

Farthing seemed so sure. Tam wished he felt the same.

∞

"I never thought to give the ship a name. I just kept the original name, *Starfinder*," explained Farthing to Tam. It was seven days later, and they were now on the Minorian-class spaceship Farthing called home. "I like the idea of christening it, though—especially after all the upgrades. It's like she's a new ship. The databanks came up with *Faramund*. It supposedly means 'journey' and 'protection' in an ancient language of our ancestors. I have no clue what language, and where from, but I like it."

The *Faramund* was on its fourth day in curved space. The ship was about eight days out of Corustloth. There were only four more curved space checkpoints left to drive Tam almost crazy. Each exit was harrowing. Tam found that having people there to look after him deadened the pain and the disorientation a bit. At least he wasn't hiding in a cargo bay this time!

With the next checkpoint exit a little more than a day away, Tam had time on his hands to rest and try to prepare. He did this by pouring over the plans Anghelloise had reproduced from the living cloth. He had enjoyed the christening of the ship, but had stayed alone since, not feeling very social. He'd been studying the plans for two days now, and felt quite confident about where everything was and how to circumvent security on their rescue mission.

Anghelloise had been talking about using some sort of gas to make everyone sleep or trying the trick that Farthing had used on the ship in which Tam had stowed away. Farthing had suggested a more direct and physical approach: land, enter, and kill anyone who got in their way. Tam was not sure about any of the ideas.

[What would you do, Brogan, in my place?]

He didn't expect a response. Brogan had been nonreactive for more than two days. He hadn't felt a thing. It was a strange feeling to lose the link in all their memories and experiences. Tam rested his head on the plans and groaned. He knew Brogan was still alive—but that was all.

[I am still no hero, my love. I wish I could find inspiration and hope by staring at these plans. Maybe Mother will send some sign to help us. That's the problem— there's no guide at the moment. Just a band of pirates, a Siren, a bot named Nick, and me, the stowaway. I will keep searching for you as long as I breathe, though. That's all I can muster for the moment.]

∞

"Exit to real space in ten minutes," Farthing announced over the comm. "Tam, ready yourself and make your way to sick bay."

Tam exited his chamber and did as requested. He knew the routine. Get on the bed. Lie down, receive tranquilizers. Doze off and feel the madness to some extent. There really was no escape. You had to feel something—if you didn't, you wouldn't be alive.

"Exiting curved space in five... four... three... two... one! Exiting now!"

Everything was quiet. Then, chaos hit. Tam sputtered, then inhaled deeply, his eyes widening. The sounds coming from his lungs no longer sounded like his own. The cries were alien and strange. Tam a felt a weight on his chest as he gasped for breath. The sick bay melted into a viscous liquid that flowed over and around him, threatening to drown him. He struggled to keep his head above the crest of liquid but was finally enveloped, causing him to gulp in the foreign substance. Somehow, he was still breathing.

He was pinned to an altar, ready to be sacrificed by Kruger. The monster loomed over him, brandishing a knife, cutting his flesh, inserting objects. Tam tried to scream, but spewed liquid. Living cloth was thrown over him, pulling the flesh back together to hide the incisions. A dastardly way to hide bombs! Bombs of the soul that destroyed everyone in their presence.

Tam's back arched, his arms stretching to their limit. His heart felt like it would pound out of his chest, tearing him apart. A shrill signal sounded in one long burst, three shorter ones, and a pause, before repeating again and again for what seemed an eternity. It repeated until it was but a whisper in his ear, like the wind whistling past as he ran down the farm field to Brogan. One long burst of wind, three short, then silence. Tam saw Brogan's hands extend out, reaching for Tam, his eyes pleading for help.

Light failed. Sensation fell away. Silence.

A voice in the distance said, "Real space maintained. Normalcy for Life-Lines should begin now."

Tam opened his eyes to the sick bay as it was before the exit. The madness was gone, but the images still continued to haunt his thoughts.

[Brogan, where are you? I need you. Don't give up. I'm coming.]

He slept.

Chapter 46

Waves

Sometimes, it seemed to Tam that each exit from curved space melded with the last. Time in normal space didn't seem to matter then. All Tam knew was madness. There were common threads between each: a high-pitched noise for one long burst, three short ones, and a pause. It repeated until Tam regained consciousness and sanity.

The other commonality was the mental images of explosions, surprise, and devastation. Brogan holding his arms out in desperation.

"Anghelloise, what does it all mean?"

Tam was sitting on his couch, having just come through the last exit only forty minutes ago. He was still recovering and drinking fluids, at the request of the on-duty doctor.

"I believe the Sirens could tell you, if we had access to Mother. She is indisposed, though, and I've not been able to get any information that indicates any change. Mother will act when Mother acts. She has her reasons. What does your heart tell you, Tam?"

"I miss the feeling of Brogan in my Life-Line. It's like I'm going through withdrawal, with no end in sight. I may never be whole again. I will die if he dies—even if we're somehow disconnected. Can life be worth living if that happens?"

"I'm sorry, my boy. I wish there was something I could do to help the two of you."

Anghelloise had made sure that Tam was sedated and in a relaxed mood when they exited curved space. Despite her efforts, he still had gone virtually insane.

I wonder what the explosions and the image of Brogan holding out his arms mean, mused Anghelloise. *Is there any way to be sure, short of consulting Mother? I feel I am missing something.*

"Tam, do you recall any time in the past when you experienced those images? Are they memories?"

Tam thought for a moment, then shook his head. "Our lives were relatively quiet until Brogan's capture. I struggle so hard to understand the waves of insanity that hit me. I feel like I am on a beach with waves crashing over me, battering me about. It reminds me of the time we were at the beach in Ali-Alorion, just after our joining. We were so happy... Now look at us."

"Tam, I know it is hard to not feel sorry for yourself, but I have to ask something of you. Do you remember the time well enough to recall all that took place at that beach?"

"Yes. It's ingrained in my memory. It was one of the first experiences we truly shared."

"Lie on your couch and close your eyes. I want you to recall the time and feel the happiness you felt again. I think it would do you some good."

"You're probably right. I could use some pleasant thoughts for a change." Tam lay down from his sitting position on the couch and closed his eyes. He meditated on the time at the beach, allowing himself to float away into his memories. He smiled to himself.

Anghelloise stayed with him for a moment until he was settled in. *It is wonderful to see him smile again after all he's been through. It must have been a truly memorable time. I'll return later to check in on him.*

Brogan stood on the rock outcrop that ran along the edge of the beach. He had his hands on his hips and his chest puffed out, a look of total confidence on his face. His movements began to take the form of a muscle man making poses to secure a mate. Brogan cut a great figure, though he was just playing around. He had such an air of raw sexuality.

[*Brogan, you have my attention—and my desire. You don't need to fluff and strut like a bubble bird looking for a mate, funny as it is.*]

Brogan's sly smile turned toward Tam, and his eyes bore into his. [*You are my man and I am yours. You are going to make love to me—but you already know that, don't you?*]

Brogan loosened the sash on his tunic and it fell away, revealing his naked body shimmering in the sunlight, his penis standing at attention.

[You want me, don't you...?]

[Yes, I want you. How about taking a break to go to the public bathing rooms to prepare? You have all the equipment to prep yourself in your satchel, do you not?]

Brogan nodded, pulled his tunic back on, and retrieved his satchel. He grinned as he turned to leave. Tam smiled and laughed to himself about the necessity of personal hygiene in their lovemaking. It was a natural part of their lives, but so many people out there didn't feel the same way. The common perception was that only degenerates used the anus for lovemaking. For Tam, it was a natural part of sexual expression. From time to time, Tam would reciprocate, allowing Brogan to enter him. He would get much pleasure from the receiving end, feeling Brogan's sensations as he made love to him at the same time. Both ways were pleasurable. It was still novel to Tam to experience sex from both sides.

With Brogan gone, Tam decided he would bathe in the ocean. He even thought about borrowing Brogan's equipment to clean himself up, too, as it might be the time to share in the pleasure both ways. It excited him. He felt his member stiffen.

The waves were now crashing quite heavily on the shore. Tam didn't think much of it, as he was a decent swimmer and could handle himself quite well in choppy water. Taking off his sandals and his tunic, he plunged into the waves at running speed, swam underwater for as long as he could hold his breath, then surfaced to breathe, allowing himself to adjust to the water temperature. It was warm and pleasant.

He was able to place his feet on the sandy bottom, but the waves kept making him bob up and down, fighting the currents. After fighting against it for some time, Tam realized that was not necessary.

Give in to the waves. Allow them to flow and ebb, following along with them. Enjoy the sensation of floating like a raft on the open ocean. Don't fight the current.

Tam turned and made his way ashore, swimming strongly for a bit, then allowing himself to back out with the waves, steadily making progress to the beach. When his feet again reached the sand, he gently leaned toward the shore and allowed himself to skim on the surface as the wave he rode crashed onto the beach. He stumbled slightly, but gained his footing, then walked the rest of the way to his sandals and tunic as Brogan approached from the public bathrooms.

[You're quite the handsome sight, Tam. Do you know how much I want you?] Brogan continued to approach. *[Aren't we lucky that the Sirens can screen people out of the beach area so we can be alone? There is no one in view to see us.]*

[I wouldn't have the nerve to do this if it weren't so,] Tam replied. *[I'd lose something else, along with my nerve, too. The danger of arrest still scares me.]*

[*Don't let that affect you. I want you ready to go.*] Brogan, now right in front of Tam, reached for him and pulled him close. They were just on the edge of the water line. Standing in the sand together, he sent an invitation: [*I want you to make love to me and be as rough as you want. I want you to make me your prisoner!*]

[*I'd like that, too.*] Tam placed his hand on Brogan's head and pulled his mouth to his. As their lips locked and Tam's tongue played over Brogan's, a sense of urgency came upon him. He grabbed Brogan's head with both of his hands and kissed him harder as Brogan moaned, opening his mouth wider to receive more.

[*I want to be opened up—to receive you any way you want. Take me, please,*] he projected as their tongues played and their lips met and parted. Their bodies began to grind against each other. Roleplaying was fun for them both. Feeling everything the other was experiencing made the event even more exciting.

Both had come to learn that sharing sensations could be overwhelming. Little accidents could happen before they were ready to let go. In their play, they learned to experience the double sensations, taking their time to lead up to the massive explosion they eventually shared.

A thought floated between them in the ether. Tam was distracted by an intruding thought about being separated and punished for their crimes. In the thought, both could feel each other's pain. He felt his member soften. He leaned back and paused for a moment. The thought sat there in between them, waiting, rotating, showing all sides to both of them.

[*Tam, stray thoughts are normal in a Life-Line. Don't be so concerned.*] Brogan released Tam's lips from his and looked into Tam's eyes.

[*It was the prisoner part that tripped me up. Do Life-Lines experience premonitions? I feel like something bad is going to happen.*]

[*I've been told we can sometimes see things to come. There is one thing to remember, Tam: we can't hold back from living in order to prevent something from happening.*]

[*The image is disturbing. You can see it, can't you?*]

Brogan nodded.

[*We can't know for sure about the future, but we can determine the present. Think about what you were imagining earlier while coming out of the water.*]

"Don't fight the waves," he said aloud.

Brogan nodded. [*Don't fight it now. Flow. Come back to me. Continue what we were both enjoying before the thought entered your head.*] Brogan reached for Tam and kissed him, pulling him closer. The rotating thought dissolved to nothing.

The feel of Brogan pressing against him jogged Tam back to the present.

Tam pulled Brogan closer and kissed him harder. The passion reignited within him. Still feeling a little exposed, Tam gently led Brogan to the tent by the shore they had set up earlier.

Brogan slipped his tunic off and let it fall to the ground. He smiled and turned to lean down to enter the tent, exposing his broad back, tattoo and firm cheeks. Tam grabbed him then, stopping him from entering the tent. Brogan moaned as Tam pulled him back.

[Are you my prisoner, to be used as I see fit?]

[I am ready.]

Tam reached for the ropes that had been stored inside the tent, and bound Brogan's hands so that they were positioned in the front, but could be raised if Tam so desired. Tam then pushed him onto the tent floor and closed the flap. He loosened his own tunic and let it fall to the floor, revealing his body at attention, ready.

Brogan looked up at Tam and sighed. *[I want to be free to touch and please you.]*

Tam shook his head and knelt beside his captive, bound and lying on his back, totally vulnerable. Tam moved his bound hands from in front to over his head and attached the rope to a peg he had embedded in the bottom of the tent earlier. With his hands bound, Brogan couldn't stop anything, Tam's hands and mouth played across his body—first gently, then more urgently. Every touch caused sensations to whirl and gyre through both their bodies, making them feel the same sensations. It increased incrementally—once felt, it was echoed and felt again by the other. The force of the sensations grew and grew, until both of them gasped, bringing them both to the edge of orgasm. Tam gently stopped, slowly massaging Brogan's chest, groin, and beautiful legs.

Looking up, Brogan saw Tam's green eyes glinting in the afternoon light streaming in from the front of the tent. Tam's own gaze was enveloped by the deep blue wells of Brogan's eyes, seeing him and himself infinitely, like a series of parallel mirrors. Love swelled in his heart, growing as Brogan added his own to the mix. Tam became overwhelmed as he lay on top Brogan, forcing his legs apart, pushing his groin closer, to meet his butt cheeks.

Brogan lifted his legs and felt Tam's member push against him. He closed his eyes and allowed the sensation to overwhelm him as he wrapped his legs around his body. There was a gentle release, then the feeling of lubricant being applied and a finger or two gently entering. They both moaned at the sensations spreading through their buttocks. Tam slathered lubricant onto his hard member, ready to do its work.

[*Take me, Tam. Please. I need you in me. Take me. I'm your prisoner.*]

[*Don't fight the current. Don't fight it.*] Tam's member slid up to its sheath, and they both gasped as the sensations multiplied. Tam began to slowly move in motion with Brogan. He leaned down and kissed him deeply, grabbing him around the head and mounting his full weight on top of him. Brogan wiggled and pushed against him, receiving his penis deeper and deeper as he squeezed his legs harder around Tam's torso. Finally, Tam reached up and loosened Brogan's ropes, releasing his arms, which immediately traveled upward to clasp Tam closer to him.

Their moans began to spiral in tandem as sensation after sensation increased, each wave passing through them, multiplying then returning, until both of their bodies felt like they were floating in a glowing light of emotion. The primal urges to unload into Brogan came upon Tam. Brogan's moans increased as he knew he was about to receive his lover's seed.

Pumping faster and harder, Tam reached the point of no return and virtually screamed into Brogan's parted mouth, adding to Brogan's own, until their moans flew around them in the ether. Their bodies felt like they, too, were floating. They both experienced Tam's orgasm simultaneously, pushing Brogan to release his own, building upon his. Sensations flowed back and forth between them until their bodies meshed together as if they had become one, floating on a wave of pleasure that ebbed and flowed like the waves outside.

[*Don't fight the current. Don't fight it.*]

∞

"Anghelloise, I know how to beat the madness of curved space exit!" Tam announced as he opened his eyes and sat up. "The next one will be different. I won't be left helpless in bed again."

"My dear boy, that is wonderful news! Can you tell me more?"

"Trust me, Anghelloise. I am truly ready to rescue my love from that prison. Nothing is going to stop me now except death itself."

"Well, let's see if we can avoid that unpleasantry, why don't we?"

Tam said nothing—just smiled grimly.

Part 7
Battles

Chapter 47
Back Door Planning

The *Faramund* had once been a transport ship like the other Minorian-class spaceships of the four worlds. When it was commandeered by the pirates, it became a rather infamous spacecraft to those in the know because of its modifications. No one knew where these changes had come from, let alone those who were involved in making them.

The warships surrounding Corustloth, there to guard the prison world and protect the Magistrate on his business, didn't know what to expect. True, it was known that the *Faramund* had been adapted to salvage parts of spaceship hulls and debris. The pirates seemed to take great joy in stealing old pieces and parts of derelicts scattered around the system. The warship commanders, who knew the ship as *Starfinder*, knew of its salvaging capabilities. It had ripped the cargo bay off one of their ships bound for the prison in a quadrant not very far from where they sat now—just before the last curved space checkpoint near Corustloth. There was also a rumor about the destruction of another warship.

Maguire sat in his command centre on the lead warship. He had been moody and distant since the unfortunate events leading to the escape of the shuttle supposedly containing Farthing. He was amazed he still held his title. He had been sure the Magistrate would have his head for the "Farthing failure," as it was now called.

Instead, he was given crash courses in what little was known about the mysterious band of women known as the Sirens. What was known was their ability to distract their opponents by latching onto transmissions and adding bizarre singing. If these Sirens were able to commandeer communications, little could be done to stop them.

Nonetheless, Maguire sat in his room, feeling secure that his arsenal of lasers, missiles, and pellet-based railguns would serve to destroy any ship that dared enter orbit around the prison. There was no real protection from their lasers. They could be fired from great distances, and pierce virtually any hull. The heat alone would be enough to cause any ship to boil in its own heat, killing everyone inside. Not even spacesuits would save them. No technology other than what the Senate reserved for their own ships was able to withstand them.

Maguire sat there, safe in the thought that Farthing's warship didn't stand a chance against eight Senate warships sitting in orbit around Corustloth. A cloud of projectiles would tear metal, plastics, and flesh alike to pieces. They held enough firepower to subdue many more ships. Let the Sirens sing! Let the pirate ship come! No one ship of the Senate fleet could stand up against the rest; the *Starfinder* would be no exception—modifications included. A salvage ship would be no match for his fleet.

∞

"Farthing, we've known for months that this would happen," assured Anghelloise. You've been party to the modifications made to the *Faramund*. This isn't new tech; it's existed for eons. The Senate has made a grave error in keeping its citizens defenseless by eradicating old technologies. The Siren's reserves extend far beyond those in the Universities of the Learnèd or in the data stolen by the Senate. We've kept records and examples for eons—almost as far back as the time humanity came to this galaxy!"

"I'm aware of the technology of the Sirens. My question is how many laser and projectile hits we can take before we boil or get shredded to bits? Even with this tech, we can't survive indefinitely. We need a way to get around the warships and make a landing. Better yet, we need to disable those ships like we did before. Can we depend on them to fall for parlor tricks again?" Farthing replied, pacing slightly.

"How about your shuttle?" Tam asked. "We can bend light around it to make it invisible. We could slip through their lines while the *Faramund* engages them."

Anghelloise nodded her head. "That's the plan. We've installed ionomer technology on the *Faramund*. This new second skin is self-healing. It's been adapted from those that we use to prevent ship collisions from space dust and meteors while in curved space. With this, we should be able to hold up against them long enough for the shuttle to get through, land, and collect as many prisoners as possible."

"And the lasers?" Farthing reminded her.

"The ionomer skin will help us to some extent," said Anghelloise, "but the time for a laser to penetrate something is so brief that the isomer will need time to adjust. The armor of the *Faramund* can serve for a time. The key is dissipating the heat generated by the laser. I believe we've worked it out. If we can bend light, we may be able to stave off laser fire for brief periods. It's not perfect, but will reduce the hits to an acceptable level."

"So how do we escape in the shuttle with all those prisoners?" Tam asked. "We may be able to get down there. The Sirens can help us take out the guards. But we still have to deal with the warships. Will the Sirens somehow help us to allow us to get through? How will the *Faramund* then depart without being destroyed?"

"I don't have an answer for that one, my dear. Only the Mother can say for sure if we can be saved. I believe we must try, though. It is better to save those men from experimentation and die later than to allow it to continue."

"Aye, I knew this could be a suicide mission," replied Farthing, standing still in his certainty. "We pirates are ready to do this! We must save those men! I just wish we could take out those warships and give the worlds a chance to fight back."

"One thing at a time, my dear," said Anghelloise. "Let's save the men first, then let the Goddesses help us on the other end."

Everyone bowed their heads in hope and faith. Dying to save others would be worth it. Stopping the experimentation would be worth it. Saving the whole system would have to wait.

Chapter 48
Engaging Enemies

The eight warships hung in a *W* formation over the planet's surface. To the *Faramund*'s crew, it looked like a web in which to catch a lonely fly.

They had just arrived in the system after dropping out of curved space. Tam had succeeded, somehow, in not going insane during the exit. He'd been given the regular round of medications, but managed to suppress the usual sickness symptoms. When questioned, he simply stated, "Don't fight the current—just let it happen. Flow with the waves." Though he left it at that, he assured the others he would help them when the time came. He had been mostly silent since then.

The crew of the *Faramund* now looked at the screen with trepidation. Knowing what was coming didn't help much. The scene was unnerving to them. It was one thing to follow Farthing into battle, but to have their captain hidden, depending on backup crews to defend the ship while the main crew started a rescue mission, was scary.

Farthing sat with Anghelloise in the cockpit of the Siren shuttle. Tam and Nick sat in passenger seats, waiting. Nick didn't have a care in the world, but Tam was sweating. Despite being happy with his newfound ability to overcome his insanity, he remained very worried about reaching Brogan in time.

"Ready for launch!" Farthing declared.

"Initiating light cloak," Anghelloise responded.

"Acting Captain O'Keefe, shuttle prepped and ready to launch," Farthing said over the comm as he flicked levers and pushed buttons. "Engaging light cloak. Open the shuttle doors."

"Goddesses' speed, Farthing!" Captain O'Keefe replied from the bridge of the *Faramund*. She turned to her crew and nodded to them. "Initiating Farthing Battle

Plan A. Keep sharp, everyone. We have eight warships to contend with. Let's hope the Sirens' technology will keep us alive long enough to rescue those souls."

Back in the hangar, the shuttle glistened, seeming to waver as it faded out of view from the crew working on it. It rested in the large airlock, prepped for launch.

"We will maintain radio silence for as long as we can. Remember to listen for our code so you'll know we're on our way back," Anghelloise responded.

"Will do. Goddesses be with you," she replied. "O'Keefe out."

She turned to look at her crewmates and sighed. Absentmindedly, she stroked her ponytail. Her round face was stressed, her brows arched. She felt the weight of command on her shoulders for the first time since her first command years ago. *There are too many variables,* she thought, but got to work anyway.

The shuttle, now invisible, lifted off the floor of the bay and exited. It arced away from the *Faramund* and began its descent around the eight warships—hopefully, unnoticed.

∞

Without warning, the lead warship fired a laser across the bow of the *Faramund*. As the warning alarms went off in the pirate ship, Captain O'Keefe responded with exactly the same shot to the lead ship. Wait for their next move, then counter move—that was the plan.

Just then, a message was sent from the lead warship: "Farthing! Stand down and prepare to surrender. You cannot hope to win a fight against eight of our ships! Be reasonable and I shall do the same. My name is Commander Maguire, in charge of the Senate Fleet. It is my task to take you into custody and have you stand trial for treason. Do so now, and the Senate will be lenient with your crew, despite their being pirates. We do not wish you any harm. Accept my offer or suffer the consequences!"

What a verbose man, O'Keefe thought. She turned to her crew. "OK, everyone! Let's get this going! Farthing's on his way. Let's make a stand. Disperse the minefield!"

On the sides of the *Faramund*, ports opened and guns protruded outward. They began firing—not in the direction of the warships, but the space in between. The tiny pellets reacted as though they were inert, forming a cloud between the fleet and the pirate ship. When the cloud arrived in the appropriate spot, the pellets were activated, slowing their velocity to zero. The cloud then rested in a shield-like formation.

"Let's see what Maguire thinks of this!"

Her answer came seconds later. The lead warship fired into the cloud with a laser blast, which was absorbed by it. It glowed as each individual pellet affected by the blast radiated the heat of the laser, dispersing it outward and away from the *Faramund*.

"Begin supplementing the cloud—fire round two!"

More pellets made their way to build a second barrier.

"Captain, missile ready to launch from the lead ship!" First Hand Byrne announced. "What do you suggest?"

"Nothing. The Sirens claim the cloud will handle it."

The missile launched, zeroing in on the cloud. The pellets that absorbed the impact glowed bright red as it exploded on contact. At least a third of the original cloud was destroyed. The second moved in to fill the hole.

"Firing third round with your permission, Captain," Byrne requested.

"Aye, fire away. We have enough rounds for about eight clouds. It should long enough for the shuttle to arrive at the surface. After that, we'll have to hope for the best."

Several missiles later, there was still no intrusion of firepower into the *Faramund*. Another layer of pellets was launched.

"Fighters launched from the warships—fifty of them!" Byrne barked. "Orders, Captain?"

"Hold!" she commanded. "The Sirens promised to protect us."

The remnants of rounds two and three activated and began to target the fighters. While the fighters attempted to ward off the cloud with lasers, the rest of it filled in to target the fighters, too. The pellets made contact at high speed, vaporizing themselves and the hulls of the fighters. Soon, all fifty were inert, floating uselessly.

"Casualties?" O'Keefe asked.

"About thirty so far. The others are still in their fighters. The warships can rescue them at any time," Byrne responded. "Shall we target them and take them out?"

"No," replied O'Keefe. "Farthing said to spare as many lives as possible. They may be on the wrong side today, but they are still our kin. Lives are valuable—machines are not."

"The warships are on the move!" shouted Byrne. "They're trying to flank us!"

"Widen the shield!" responded the captain. "Fire all remaining pellets. Let's hope we can slow them down to give Farthing more time! We'll attack them with the remaining pellets only if it becomes necessary."

There was no time to spare, though, as the fleet attacked anew with pellets of their own. They were launched from railguns from all eight of the ships. Now, a cloud of metal projectiles was honing in on the *Faramund*'s cloud of protective pellets.

"Last round of pellets launched, Captain. What now?"

"Hold and wait!" she replied, lips pursed.

The two pellet clouds merged, and the space between the vessels glowed red. Many pellets survived on both sides, but no one knew for sure which was which.

"Incoming projectiles!" yelled Byrne. Within seconds, they made contact with the hull of the *Faramund*, which shuddered from the impacts. The ionomers began doing their job, forming around the holes, beginning to repair them.

Another barrage of pellets was shot toward them. The cloud protecting the ship had been cut in half. O'Keefe stood there looking at the viewscreen, praying that the next volley could be curtailed. The last cloud of pellets formed the last wall and received the round at full force. The space between them again glowed red as they exploded. More pellets had gotten through. They made contact. The *Faramund* shuddered as it absorbed the projectiles again and the ionomers again protected the ship.

One, two, four, then five laser shots hit the *Faramund*. The ionomers began to give way. Heat began to rise inside the hull. A few more blasts would boil the crew alive.

"Your delaying tactics have only served to change the way in which you'll be destroyed," came Maguire's voice over the comm unit again. "Your crew is now dispensable. Farthing, you may be valuable, but we are not prepared to allow this to continue. You will be destroyed with your crew and your ship. You have ten Alorion minutes to surrender before we fire more missiles and lasers your way. You will be destroyed if we do."

With the channel closed, O'Keefe turned to her crew. "Gather around quickly, everyone. I want options and I want them fast!"

The crew left their stations and gathered around her chair.

"Send the remaining pellets to do as much damage to the warships as we can, so that we can escape!"

"Use our lasers to take out as much as we can."

"Fire all of our missiles at the same time. Fight to the end!"

"Allow the remaining pellets to protect us against them while we try to make our escape."

"Is surrender an option?" Byrne asked. "Could it serve as a delay tactic to give the team more time to rescue the others? Why not surrender, then fire a salvo at close range?"

O'Keefe held her hand up for silence. It was clear that she had made a decision.

"All hands to your stations. Now! Move! I'll explain as we go." Everyone moved to comply. They had six more minutes before they would be asked to surrender. "Let's do the pirate thing and give them the pirate response. On my mark! Prepare the *Faramund* for curved space! Fire all missiles! Target the warships with all four lasers! Send the projectiles to do as much damage as they can. Initiate light-bending ionomers on the hull! Mark!"

Everyone leaped into action, and a volley of lasers, missiles, and projectiles were launched on the waiting warships. Power drained from the ship as the ionomers shifted their purpose.

The warships, at this range, had no recourse. By the time they could respond, damage had already been done.

The *Faramund*'s lasers connected immediately, at the speed of light. The missiles arrived seconds later, and after a few seconds more, their barrage of pellets. They made contact with all eight warships—or so it seemed.

"Get ready to leave by curved space!" shouted O'Keefe.

"Two warships disabled!" Byrne declared. "Another seems to be in the process of exploding—" There was a flash of light as a warship exploded, expanding to take two more with it. Three ships destroyed, two disabled. "There are now three left."

As Byrne had predicted, the three surviving ships opened fire with lasers. The *Faramund* absorbed the heat of the lasers and exuded it back into space. The light-bending was working, for the moment. Another few hits might be enough to destroy them, though.

As commander and captain alike prepared for their next moves, they both found themselves suddenly distracted by something happening above them. A shimmering wave of light was materializing, expanding and spinning on its axis. Both of them paused, considering what was happening, neither having seen anything like it before. The light shimmered and grew until it occupied almost all the space that would be between the two of them were they on the same plane.

Suddenly, the light collapsed in on itself. There, in the space it left, sat a small ship.

Chapter 49
Contact

The ships hung motionless while Bennett considered the situation. "Tam's last known location," replied *Nimbus,* "is on Corustloth. He is no longer here but is down on the planet."

"So I guess we'll have to deal with these ships to get access to him." Bennett sized up the warships: three sitting off his port bow and one starboard. Two other inactive warships drifted further away from the active ones.

"They've been battling, based on the cloud of debris—the evidence of lasers and likely missile fire," *Nimbus* added. "The warship starboard registers as possessing unknown technology. The three others are standard warships from this sector. All this according to records of previous scans by probes sent here from our quadrant."

"The single ship to starboard is Tam's," Bennett supposed, "but he's no longer there."

"Correct," *Nimbus* concurred. "Contact all ships?"

"Let's wait to see who reaches out to us first."

On cue, the comm signaled a transmission from the starboard ship. "This is Captain O'Keefe of the *Faramund.* Please identify."

"*Nimbus,* open a channel."

"Channel open, Bennett," responded *Nimbus.*

"This is Bennett Davis of the shuttle *Nimbus.* I am searching for a man named Thamara-Afil Amergan-Faolin. Do you know him?"

There was silence. No response.

Bennett continued: "I've come from the other side of the galaxy to contact him, as he is in grave danger. I am here to lend assistance in his quest to find his lover, Brogan-Afil Faolin-Amergan. They are both of great importance to both your system and ours. We should meet, but I am concerned for you with those three warships so close. Could we lend you a hand with them, too, as an act of faith and trust? I respectfully request a meeting as soon as possible, Captain O'Keefe. Please respond."

Before she could, a message from the three warships signaled on the comm.

"Open the channel to the warships, Bennett?" *Nimbus* inquired.

"We need to get a better understanding of the enemy. Open them."

"This is Commander Maguire of the Senate. We've been monitoring your transmission with the traitors. Continue this, and we will be forced to open fire on you and the so called *Faramund*."

"We have no wish to engage in battle," Bennett responded. "I have my orders and I must carry them out—with or without your permission, Commander Maguire."

"And what is that mission?" Maguire asked.

"I'm not prepared to say at this moment," Bennett replied. "Close communications!"

"Done!" affirmed *Nimbus*. "It would seem lasers and missiles are now targeting us and the *Faramund*. Scans indicate we can survive quite a few blasts from their ships while sustaining minimal damage... Missiles are another matter, but they can be deterred. Orders?"

"Our main objective it to make contact with Tam, *Nimbus*," he replied. "However, I don't want to leave his allies outnumbered in a battle. Can we disable all four ships?"

"Why not leave the *Faramund* intact? I'd suggest they retreat while we go see about Tam and the others."

"You've got a point. Put me through to the *Faramund*."

"Channel open."

"Captain," said Bennett, "If I disable the warships, can I be assured you will retreat and regroup so that we can plan our next move?"

"This is not our plan," replied the O'Keefe. "I do not want to say more. Maguire is more than likely listening in on our conversation."

"*Nimbus*, can you secure a closed communication line between us and the *Faramund*?"

"Definitely. Secured channel now available."

Bennett's face appeared on their viewscreen. "Captain O'Keefe, let me be blunt: I'm much better prepared to descend to the planet than you are resting here in orbit facing three warships. What do I need to do to convince you I'm here to help?"

"Who are you anyway? Where are you from?"

"I'm from the other side of the galaxy, and am part of the Order," responded Bennett. "We exist to find where humanity came from and how. Our leader, Father, believes Tam is a vital link in helping us in this."

"A rather strange tale. Are you here to help free us from the Senate, too?"

"I can answer all in due time, Captain," he responded. "Right now, I must contact Tam—but cannot with those warships sitting out there. What would you suggest?"

"Destroy them—or distract them while we make a retreat. Better yet, disable them. We don't have enough firepower to do so ourselves. When you arrived, we had launched our last barrage of barrier pellets. We are set to ram them at my command. I'm loathe to kill all the people on those ships and ours, as they are our kin and serve out of fear of the Senate."

"Father would never condone killing people in this manner. Disabling them makes more sense. But I'd need plans and schematics in order to assess their capability."

"That would give you the opportunity to destroy us as well. We have the basic technology they have—but also some enhancements I'm unable to understand at the moment."

Bennett narrowed his eyes and thought a minute as he looked at Captain O'Keefe on his viewscreen. "If you're talking about the Siren enhancements, I know of that already. We've been aware of them for a while now. Do you know them directly?"

"Indirectly. But yes, we have contact with them. Why do you ask?"

"Well, we can't do anything until Tam and Brogan are rescued. That's my priority. But it would seem you are my priority, too, in granting me access to them. And I believe an alliance between the Sirens and the Order might be a chance to turn the tide against the Senate and free your people. It would also allow us to continue our search for our origins."

"What assurance do I have that you are not a scout for an invasion force?" she asked.

"Fair enough. I can understand caution. I will transmit as much information as I can about the Order and our technological capabilities in such a short time. Would that be acceptable? It would seem trust works both ways. I trust you wouldn't use that information against this ship?" He narrowed his eyes. "We need to act fast before those warships attack."

"Give us fifteen Alorion minutes. I'll contact you afterward."

"I'll await your message. Bennett out." He shut off the transmission and sat back in his chair, realizing then that he'd been sitting on the edge, with his shoulders and neck hunched up.

"Bennett, shall I give you another relaxant?" *Nimbus* asked.

"Absolutely not! I need to be awake and aware of what's going on. In the meantime, can you scan those ships to find a way to disable them without killing everyone onboard? And what kind of damage can their weapons have on you, *Nimbus*?"

"Scanning. I'll need several minutes to process the information." *Nimbus* paused for a moment, then continued, "Why did you tell Captain O'Keefe we need the plans when we have the ability to scan for ourselves?"

Bennett smiled wryly. "I'm not the best liar, but I felt it best not to let too much on too quickly. I'm sure the *Faramund* and its crew will come to accept us. I'm just making sure."

"I see. I am continuing scans of the warships. I would suggest that in the meantime, you relax and perhaps eat something."

Bennett sighed in agreement. A light dinner would take about fifteen minutes—just long enough to await a signal from the *Faramund*. Then he would try to contact Tam.

Chapter 50
Parallel

Maguire swiped his arm across his desk in anger, sending items flying everywhere. The Magistrate was going to have a fit when he found out three warships had been destroyed and two more disabled. What frustrated him most was Farthing's ship having foiled him—and the strange ship, supposedly from the other side of the galaxy, showing up in the midst of the battle.

A fast strike against both the ships might be what was needed. To take Farthing and put him in a brig. At this point, that is what would save the day. Maybe taking the alien ship would give him bonus points with the Magistrate. Disable both, capture their crews, then contact him. That would be the plan.

Maguire straightened his uniform and his disheveled hair. He took a deep breath, left his quarters, and returned to the bridge of his ship to find Razfar staring at the viewscreen. "Report to me. What is going on?"

"Sir, the two ships have been sitting idle. No incidents or transmissions between either ship. They seem to be sizing us and the other up to determine what to do next. What are we to do?" he winced, adding quickly: "—Commander, sir."

"Get the other captains on the comm for me."

"Yes, sir. Does that include the three from the destroyed warships? They escaped in pods and are now in our hangar bay."

"Yes, have them report here. Get the others on the comm. We need to begin our plan. I want everyone listening."

"Yes, sir. Do you want to know the casualty list from the destroyed warships, Commander? It just came in."

"No. We have more pressing things than dealing with dead personnel. Get the captains here and on the comm. Now."

"Of course, sir, right away, sir."

"Now my job begins." *My survival depends on getting these incompetents in line.*

∞

Captain O'Keefe sat with her crew in the boardroom of the *Faramund*. The screen was dually tuned to the warships and the alien ship. "Do we believe this Bennett person? What are we to do about the warships? I believe that, in Farthing's absence, we need to decide as a group. I realize as acting captain, I'll need to make the final decision, but I want to hear from everyone."

"Trust the stranger with the technology. Get him to disable the warships, then decide what to do," Second Hand Otto suggested.

"Make our escape and let the stranger deal with the warships," the chef said.

"Trust a chef to make a suggestion like that!" laughed Otto.

"I appreciate everyone's input in this matter. Chef, you may have a point," said Captain O'Keefe. "Other ideas?"

"Our goal is to maintain orbit as long as possible to help Farthing and his shuttle crew," First Hand Byrne offered. "We should negotiate with Captain Davis, trusting he is on our side. He can help us in our quest to help the others. I think he's good to his word."

"I agree," said O'Keefe. "Let's put it to a vote, then. All for trusting Captain Davis and trying to maintain orbit to help Farthing?"

All hands went up, and O'Keefe realized the decision had been made. "I think we need to move quickly. I sense Maguire is ready to make a move. I don't want to chance it. All hands to stations. I and the Goddesses thank you for doing your duty. We'll be rewarded, I am sure, when we see a shuttle returning with imprisoned men…"

The crew moved swiftly. Everyone was ready within minutes. O'Keefe left the room and entered the adjacent bridge. "Ready all hands! I am contacting Captain Davis."

∞

"Incoming message from the *Faramund*."

"Thank you, *Nimbus*. Onscreen, please!"

Captain O'Keefe's face appeared. "Captain Davis, we've reached a decision."

[261]

"Just Bennett is fine. What is it?"

"We've decided to put our trust in you. We need your help to disable those ships—long enough for Farthing to succeed and get back to us."

"As agreed, I am sending information about this ship, the Order, and myself. I trust it will be satisfactory in allowing you to make informed decisions."

"Thank you, Bennett. What do you need from us?"

"Schematics of your ship—and their warships, if you have them. It'll help me develop a plan to disable them in a way that will allow you time to make repairs. How much do you need?"

"At least three days. Would you also like plans for the prison? Tam was able to supply warship schematics, the prison maps, and much more. We now know more about the Magistrate and his plans than ever before. It frightens me. We need to act quickly to get those men out."

"Prison plans?" Bennett beamed. "Wonderful! I'll need those to reach Tam."

"You plan on going down there?!"

∞

"Launch all remaining fighters! Disable those two ships and you get bonus pay!" yelled Maguire.

"Yes, Commander. Fighters launched," replied Razfar. "Everyone is in agreement with you, sir." The other captains in their presence and those on the screen looked strained, upset—but were silent and compliant.

The three operating ships now spewed out the remaining fighters, forming squadrons that descended on the alien ship and the *Faramund*. There was no time for either to respond. Two squadrons of fighters approached the alien ship and opened fire on its tail with their pellets. The pellets exploded before impact. Another four began firing at the *Faramund*, raking the side of the ship as they passed, pellets exploding as they hit its side. There seemed to be little effect, so they took another formation and strafed the other side and its belly. The *Faramund* finally responded—some of its lights were flickering.

"We've got them!" Maguire yelled. "Take out their engines. Get ready to board and get that blasted pirate. He smiled and turned from the screen as he silently rejoiced in his victory. He didn't see what happened next.

"*Faramund* is prepping to launch missiles, sir! No damage to the alien ship!"

"What? They can still fire? I thought they were disabled!"

"It would seem not. The ship's starting to show signs of weakening, but it is holding up to a barrage that should have surely destroyed it!" replied Razfar.

"Launching!"

The pellets were sent out as a screen in front of the warships—extra in front of Maguire's ship, of course, to protect their leader. The missiles launched from the *Faramund* and began their quick flight toward the warships. The cloud of pellets intercepted the five missiles, which exploded on contact. The shockwave penetrated the cloud and rocked the lead warship.

"Alright, let's return the favor and fire a round at both ships!" he commanded.

"Eight firing now: two at the alien ship and six at the *Faramund*!" exclaimed Razfar. "Let's see them protect themselves! These are no pellets!"

The missiles exited their tubes and headed straight toward the two ships. Their disabling seemed imminent to him.

Even if I must destroy them, thought Maguire.

The missiles began their streak across the short expanse of space. Suddenly, eight bright lights streamed out of the alien ship. The missiles were attracted to them immediately! They honed in on them, connecting and exploding well short of their targets.

"What in the god's name...?" Maguire asked as the warship's power shut down to emergency. "Report! What is going on?"

"We've lost power to all systems of our ship except life support. The remaining fighters all have life support, but will need to be retrieved, replied Razfar. "Someone wants us disabled, but not dead!"

The crew witnessed Maguire's next fit of rage as he kicked the back of Razfar's chair. "Get that power on again. Get our crew out of their bunks to do their jobs, for Gods' sake!"

"Aye, sir," he replied. "Done. But we are open to attack! The *Faramund* can destroy us!"

"What's holding them back?" Maguire wondered out loud.

∞

"Captain O'Keefe, how are you holding up?" asked Bennett. "Do you have damage?"

"We have some from the pellet barrage, but nothing we cannot recover from, given time. How did you destroy those missiles? They would have caused widespread damage!"

"Luckily, I have something to deter them. And I shut down their systems, gaining access to their computer while they were firing their missiles. Quite easy, really! I even got access to the prison computers and silenced their communication systems, too. No one is reporting in or out."

"We could destroy them if we had any missiles left," she responded tentatively.

"I must insist you refrain from doing so," he responded. There are too many lives at stake. I don't want to have to shut down your systems, too. We are allies. Let's keep it that way."

"Agreed," O'Keefe replied, looking down for a moment.

"I've received the information that I requested from you. Thank you, Captain O'Keefe. I am prepping *Nimbus* for departure. I'd like to get underway. Those ships will need about four of your Alorion days to complete their repairs or contact the outside world for help. I'd like to be away from here when that happens. Departure in ten minutes. Bennett out."

O'Keefe turned again to her people. "Crew of the *Faramund*: everyone to their stations to make any necessary repairs. Group leaders report to me immediately of your section's status. We have four days before we have to fight or flee..."

Chapter 51

Facing Demons

Anghelloise placed her hands on her hips. "Really, Farthing. There is no need for chivalry. I can handle myself quite admirably. There's no point in having me stay in the shuttle to guard it. It's invisible. No one knows it's sitting in the parking bay next to prison shuttles."

"Fine. Let's just hope someone doesn't walk face first into it," he replied. "We've been lucky so far—Tam, it's left, not right here."

"OK. Sorry." Tam was still uncomfortable in his stolen uniform. The sash didn't seem right and the blast helmet didn't fit his head properly. "Let me take the holomap, then."

Farthing gave Tam the holomap and received his weapon in exchange. "Happy to oblige. I'm more comfortable with a weapon in my hand. I was born to do this."

"Yes, dear, you were. Just keep it in your pants for the time being—don't do anything rash," Anghelloise reminded him. "Let's try to get as far as we can in disguise. I told you that I am able to appear as a man to the uninitiated. Any guard passing will see me as such. Less distracting, isn't it? Oh, and you, Farthing, I've made you appear smaller. No picking the giant out of a crowd today!"

"I still see you as a woman," replied Tam, "but I trust what you say by the response we've had with the few that we've encountered."

"I'm confused about the small amount of people here. There should be more guards, more security," she remarked. "No one batted an eye when we landed in the shuttle bay!"

"That had to be the most uneventful trip I've ever taken," Farthing agreed. "I hope the *Faramund* has upheld the ruse that I am still on board. Tam, are we still going the right way? Do I have to take the weapon and the holomap?"

"I'm fine, Farthing," he replied. "We're going the right way."

"Careful, my friend. Haste to find Brogan might bring us to make a mistake," quipped Anghelloise. "Keep focus, my young friend."

Tam nodded and continued down the white corridor. It had periodic doors and minor passageways to the side. The lights shone a constant pale and sterile white. Their footsteps echoed slightly as they proceeded.

Just then, the comm system in their ears crackled a bit, and Nick came through with a message: "Mistress, using sensors and the computer interface, I've identified Brogan by his DNA structure, and located him. He's in an adjacent pod of prisons."

"Thank you, Nick," she replied. "OK, boys, we'll have to backtrack to the central section and try the next pod. I hope the Goddesses will keep the men in this one safe until we find a way to rescue them."

They turned and followed the corridor back.

"Nick, have you been able to find out how many prisoners there are?" asked Anghelloise. "Yes, Mistress. There are 553 prisoners."

Farthing groaned. "How in the Sirens' names are we going to get that many men out? We'd need the *Faramund* to either land or have a shuttle service for the next two days. There is no way we can do that without being found out."

"First thing's first!" she replied.

[Brogan, I am coming for you,] Tam sent to his silent partner. *[Hold on!]*

∞

"Young man, you are mine to do with as I please!" said the Magistrate to Brogan, barely conscious in his living cloth. "Oh, how I lust to cut you to pieces—to see how a sodbent bleeds!"

Kruger adjusted the drugs going into Brogan's system on the panel by the door allowing him direct view of his captive. He sat on his pillowed stool with armrests to support his weight. "You should find the next experience wonderfully painful! I've reduced the drugs that inhibit you from feeling what your partner does. Won't that be wonderful for you? To feel his feelings again? *Imagine what he's going to feel in return!*" He cackled. "My Gods, this is going to be wonderful—to see you writhe in agony and to know that horrid Tam is doing the same!"

Brogan's half-open eyes pleaded, but he couldn't reply. He had felt this five times before—and each had been excruciatingly painful. He'd already soiled his cloth and vomited.

"I'm going to allow you the joy of feeling as your arm is prepped to insert another cylinder. Very painful—for both of you!"

While monitoring Brogan's system via the panel, Kruger gloated, clasping his hands together. He rubbed his crotch to find his growing erection.

With the drugs receding to an acceptable level, Kruger began. "Don't bother trying to communicate thoughts to him. That's still blocked. Imagine him feeling you being sliced open!"

Kruger picked up the scalpel, waddled toward his captive and waved it in front of Brogan's face. "Are you ready, my boy, for more fun?"

Brogan's eyes widened as he tried desperately to shake his head.

Kruger lowered the scalpel and watched Brogan's reaction as he sliced into his right bicep, just above the elbow. He then inserted the cartridge into Brogan's arm, making him wince even more. Tears were running down his face, his teeth gnashing together in a silent scream. Blood poured from his mouth as he repeatedly bit his tongue. He lost consciousness, though his heart continued to beat frantically.

"Oh dear! He's fallen unconscious! I could wake him up to feel the sensations, but I should proceed. What a dastardly plan I have here!" He sensed semen running down the inside of his pants. *Gods, this is exhilarating!*

Kruger began the binding process to seal the wound. The blood lost would be replaced along with the addition of anti-rejection drugs. Even the scar of the cut would disappear! No one would be the wiser. The degen will be programmed to forget this incident. Besides, who would think to look for six little bombs placed in this precious little body?

You'll be as dead as this man, Farthing, when they go off! Two in the legs, two in the buttocks, and two in the arms! There's enough firepower to blow your ship out of the sky! I have all the information I need for my plans to unfold. Even with fewer degenerates than I have now, I have a few to do with as I wish. He licked his lips and rubbed his hands in anticipation. *Now, let's see what my little rat trap has caught. Maybe Tam, for my pleasure!*

The trio arrived at the central section and collected their thoughts. There was still minimal crew passing by, which they continued to find worrisome.

"We should arrive in Brogan's pod in a short while," announced Anghelloise. "Nick said he's located in room fourteen."

"I can't imagine what it's going to feel like to have Brogan near me again after so long. I—" Suddenly, Tam stumbled, wide-eyed, screaming at the top of his lungs. He staggered and fell against the wall, grasping at his right arm, fighting something invisible with his left.

"What in Goddesses' name?!" cried Farthing.

"He's feeling something," responded Anghelloise, panicked. "It must be Brogan!"

Tam continued to scream as he tumbled to the floor. "My arm! My arm!"

The sound of footsteps approaching could be heard as he crumpled to the floor, wailing.

∞

The troop of prison guards dragged the unconscious Tam down the corridor to the fourth pod. Farthing and Anghelloise followed. A crew of ten attentively surveyed the procession from behind. The door of a room opened and Tam was unceremoniously thrown inside. Anghelloise was pushed into another, and finally, Farthing, into the last one. Each door was locked. No one would be leaving.

The prison guards rested at attention as the warden arrived. "So, we have good news! How many captured?"

"Three men!" said the nearest guard.

"Was one a massive man with dark skin?"

"No, sir! Just three regular sized men, two dark and the other light skinned."

"Curious! Farthing must be on the ship, then! We cannot radio Maguire to confirm, though. The communication systems still aren't working. But I'll contact the Magistrate."

"Yes, sir."

The warden contacted the Magistrate on his comm. "I'm begging your pardon, Magistrate, but I have news for you."

"What is it?" came the response.

"We've captured three male spies—but not Farthing."

"Spies! How in the Gods' names did they get in here?! Detain them, and I will question them later. Have you been able to contact Maguire? I demand him to bring Farthing alive to me!"

"No contact yet, sir. I will keep you posted!" He started sweating profusely. *Let's hope we find Farthing before the Magistrate loses his patience. Gods help me if we don't.*

Chapter 52
My Path Laid Out to You

The moonlit landscape of the prison world loomed ahead of the shuttle on the viewscreen of the *Nimbus*. There was still no evidence of them being noticed.

Nimbus is performing exceptionally well. I'd rather not tell her that, though, since she'll brag the whole way back. I swear she's more human than I am.

"*Nimbus*, any luck locating Tam's shuttle?"

"Yes. It is resting beside several prison shuttles, but it's currently invisible to the sensors. It would seem the Sirens have the ability to jam signals and gain stealth. Very impressive."

"Agreed, *Nimbus*. How did the shuttle crew reach an airlock without being noticed? The docking bay is exposed to space and has no air. They must have gone by spacesuit."

"They probably tricked the prison computer into believing that they were prison employees. You will be doing the same when you enter." *Nimbus* paused for a moment. "Bennett, I am not comfortable with you going alone. Why did you not accept any *Faramund* crew members to accompany you?"

"As I said before, I want to limit access to you as much as possible for now. You're what might give me an upper hand. I appreciate your concern—but I'm the captain, OK?"

"Yes, Bennett," replied *Nimbus*.

Bennett grinned. *It's almost like she's jealous that I get to go, and she doesn't.*

"Entering docking bay, Captain Davis," she quipped. "I would suggest you start suiting up. I'll land as close to their shuttle as possible. I'm still jamming all signals."

"Starting the process, then. I'll contact Tam while in the suit, then make my way to him."

He began the process of getting into his spacesuit as he had been trained. He still felt awkward doing it. It was claustrophobic. *Mentalist training comes in handy at a time like this.*

"*Nimbus*, I'm suited and ready. I'm going to lie down on my launch couch and make contact. Please monitor everything closely. I need silence and calm in order to do this," he said. "And, no I don't need any calming mist, thank you."

"As you wish, Captain Davis," she responded demurely. "Being quiet now."

Bennett sighed and smiled. He sat on the edge of the couch and considered the situation. What a story he would have to tell Father in his next report! He lay down and closed his eyes. It was a little hard to concentrate, but silence came to his brain as he attempted to locate Tam.

As his mind searched, he encountered prison employees and paused for a moment, examining their memories in his mind, classifying them quickly as either extraneous or important. Most were of no importance at all. As he pushed further, he came across prison guards with minds busy with recently captured spies. He paused at the thoughts, sifting through them, before finding those of the warden. What he saw was three men being pushed into different rooms. His mind searched for the three prisoners.

One of them is Tam! The other two are cloaked and are not representing a true picture. He marveled. *Amazing! One of them, a woman, is projecting a mind screen around herself, Tam, and a very large man in another room. That must be Farthing! She's able to blank out perceptions of others and project something false. Fascinating. The prison guards have no idea who they have there! I need to get there before they find out the truth.*

He turned his mind toward Tam, entering his thought process. His mind was jumbled. There were thoughts and images of Brogan, home, death, and despair floating around. He quickly examined each memory, flipping it around at all angles then moving on. He paused a bit, pulled back, and tried to sense Brogan. There was nothing. That was alarming. He should have been shining brightly in Bennett's mind, as in Tam's. He must have been cloaked or drugged somehow. Tam had memories of things called "living cloth"—that must be it.

He collected all the memories together, binding them with a calming thought: [*Tam, I am a friend. I am here to help you. My name is Bennett. Do you sense me?*]

The memories held fast, and new ones popped up, so he wove another binding and pulled them all together.

[*Tam, I have contacted you before. You sensed me then.*]

A memory of the blue flowers nodding on the Order's world appeared.

[Yes, you remember. That was my memory from my world. That is me. Tam, I will do whatever I can to save you and Brogan. Can you tell me what you know of him?]

Memories appeared, rotating around. Bennett bound them together. There were the beginnings of calmness arriving to them. Tam was regaining his composure.

Then, he was able to communicate: *[Bennett, I am amazed at this wondrous event. Who are you? How did you come to be here? How can you save me? Save Brogan? Save Farthing and Anghelloise? Save the* Faramund*?]*

[Tam, stop pulsing your memories and allow yourself to relax. I will tell you all in due time. I need you to focus on the task at hand: to meet, join forces, and free your companions and then Brogan.] Bennett sensed a calm, seeing fewer memories needing to be bound together. Tam had reached a state of peace in order to properly link with him.

[This feels almost like a Life-Line! You have this capability! Amazing. Bennett, please help me find my Brogan! He is my Life-Line.]

[I will do my best. I offer you these ideas, thoughts, and memories. You will know me better.] Bennett released many of his thoughts and memories: that of his job, his work with Father, his scanning Tam's mind, and his contact with Brogan.

[Bennett, I am amazed at your Order's abilities. You give me hope. Please, come as quickly as you can. I sense the guards are about to question me.]

[Let me take care of that. I'll plant some seeds of distraction in their minds and send them off on a chase! That should give us more time.] Bennett sent a general message to all the staff in the vicinity of Tam. He projected an idea that prisoners were escaping from pod one—three pods over from where they were. Bennett sensed their reactions and smiled as he felt them moving away. All thought of guarding the prisoners was gone from their heads. But he noticed something else. *I only suggested the idea of prisoners in pod one. Where did the thought of forgetting the three new prisoners come from?*

[From me!] Tam responded. *[It seems I am your match!]*

[Well done, Tam. You beat me to my next thought. I will be there as soon as I can. Continue distracting those guards. I know where Brogan is, thanks to your memories. I'll seek out his thoughts and those of those around him. We make a good team! I'll be with you soon!]

[Goddesses! Thank you, Bennett. I only just met you, but already feel you are a friend.]

[I'm honored.] He blinked back a tear. It was time!

Part 8

Meeting of the Minds

Chapter 53
The Meek Shall Fight

Bennett eased off his couch. He found it incredible Tam was able to link minds so easily. He communicated with ease yet to be seen in an untrained mind.

"*Nimbus*, I am ready to depart. Please begin cycling the atmosphere out of the airlock. Spacesuit is at optimum—but you already know that, don't you?"

"Yes, Bennett. I have also verified the atmosphere on the moon base. You will have no problems breathing as it is virtually the same as the Order's world. Remember to keep the link open with me. There may be times I can help."

"Agreed!"

"Atmosphere will be depleted in one minute. Stand by," *Nimbus* continued.

The oxygen in the airlock whooshed out as Bennett considered what to do next. *Get to the docking port, get the door open, find Tam and the others. That's going to be tough. To think: I was on the other side of the galaxy a short while ago, doubting my abilities. I hope I can keep this momentum going—for everyone's sake.*

"Oxygen depleted. Pressure equal to outside. Opening pod door. Be careful, Bennett!"

"Thank you, *Nimbus*. Keep an eye and an ear out while I'm gone."

"I will, Captain!"

The pod door opened, and Bennett climbed out. It was amazing this was the very door through which this whole voyage had started. Now, he was on the other side of the galaxy, hoping to rescue two men and their friends for reasons still unknown to him.

[*Tam, can you help guide me? You've come this way before. Hopefully, with your help, I can access the prison and get to you sooner.*]

[*I'll do my best. The access port is ahead of you, to the left. You can't miss it. When you get there, send a message to the operator, and get him to open the door, mentally bending him into thinking you are prison staff. Anghelloise did that the last time with no problem.]*

[Good to know.] Bennett saw the door to his left. He sensed the operator who'd just arrived at his post. Bennett guessed he had gone on the wild chase he'd put in everyone's minds.

Get ready for another.

He focused on the man on the other side of the airlock, letting his mind sink into him. He fiddled past errant memories, locked onto the man's active memory, and sent a vision of a prison worker finishing his duties in the vacuum of the landing bay.

"Davis requesting entrance through airlock. I've finished my repairs."

"Understood, Davis. Hatch opening," replied the operator. The hatch door opened, and Bennett entered. "Beginning pressurization."

Bennett continued to search his mind. He found memories of the search for the prisoners, and also one of the three captives. He saw where they were being kept.

"Pressurization complete. Inner hatch opening."

The door opened. Bennett stepped through and unlatched his helmet, the sound of air escaping as he did.

"Thank you. I'm exhausted. Time to get some sleep," he remarked casually, placing his helmet against his hip as he spoke.

"Understood. I could use a break myself. Have a good sleep." The man waved to him and went back to his work.

Bennet turned to go down the corridor. *That was too easy. There seems to be no resistance to my mind impressing images onto these people.*

He exited the airlock area and accessed the changing rooms. He stopped to take off his spacesuit, leaving it in a locker for when he needed it. Looking through the clothing stores adjacent to the changeroom, he found a grey prison uniform that fit and put it on.

[Tam? I noticed you experienced a lot of sudden pain a while ago. Have you experienced any since then? Do you know where it came from?]

[I believe that Brogan was being tortured or operated on while conscious,] replied Tam. *[Someone overrode the drugs that remove my connection to him. I felt a knife slicing through my arm. It was horrible. I am still shaking from it, hours later. Bennett, we need to find him before they do something even more horrible.]*

[Do you know who's responsible?]

[The Magistrate commands this prison. He'd be the one ordering torture or experimentation on Brogan. I haven't the strength to probe any further. Maybe you could?]

[I can try. I'm heading to you now. I should be able to find the ones responsible.]

Bennett continued down the corridor, successfully dodging people as he went. A few instructions sent to their minds made them oblivious to what or who he really was. He reached his mind out, searching for Brogan, but did not find him. He sensed people in the general area where he was supposed to be, though, and latched on to their minds, one by one.

He found a man named Alan Grayson. *Jackpot!* He was an attendant to the pod in which Brogan was kept. He found memories in Grayson and his companion, Dennis Rothman, of torturing Brogan. There were also memories about another person... *They seem to be jumbled. They're both so afraid! There's adrenaline running through their systems, and they're huddled together, waiting.*

Bennett now knew the room and Brogan's current condition.

But he couldn't understand this third person! The man's mind was a jumble of images and flashes of violence! It could only be the one everyone feared: the Magistrate! He focused on the man's errant mind, sifting through it. He found images of knives slicing flesh, but could not get much further. His mind was a mess. *He's undoubtedly insane! It's bewildering!*

Bennett shuddered and sent a message to Tam: *[I know where Brogan is. He's alive, being operated on by a man who could only be the Magistrate. I'm so sorry, Tam. Now we have to deal with a madman. They can be the hardest to control because of the setup of their minds.]*

[Oh, by the Goddesses! Bennett, please! I did it before! We need to rescue him now!]

[I know, Tam. He may have been easy to manipulate, but understanding him is another thing. He seems to have memories of torture—and experimentation on other men, too. We need to get them all out before any more lives are lost. I can't be certain, but I saw memories in the attendants' minds containing body bags. Men have already died.]

Tam's mind began to falter, and Bennett started to feel him slipping away.

[Tam, I need to you to focus on me. Think of the blue flowers bobbing in the wind on my world. That is a tangible memory you can use to anchor yourself. I will need your help before long!]

Tam continued to falter, his ideas jumbled. Slowly, though, he calmed down. *[Bennett, I'm OK. I'm here. I can now sense where you are. You are close!]*

Bennett sped up his pace and passed through a white-walled junction that seemed to turn into five different directions. Sensing Tam, he turned into the fourth, and came to the doors where the three were being held. There were no guards—just two men in green uniforms. Bennett read them as Rothman and Grayson, the two attendants.

He sent his mind outward and found a mass of humanity on the other side of the fifth pod. It seemed as though they had been herded there, but he could not register more. There was something going on he could not even fathom through accessing others' minds. It was as though a shadow were settling over the compound.

Knowing their mental states, Bennett had little trouble sending the two men on a chase to the cafeteria to find bowls of soup and crackers for a well-deserved lunch. Off they went, without turning their heads towards Bennett as they left. He smiled and breathed a sigh of relief.

[Tam, I am here.]

[I know. I can feel you on the other side of the wall. Can you free us?]

Bennett checked the doors and found that they were all locked. Sensing Grayson's departure, he felt around in his mind, like fumbling for keys in a pocket, where he found the codes to release all three. Again—it was too easy.

With the codes inputted, Bennett opened the doors of the first room. Inside, he found the woman he perceived. The large man was in the second. In the last, he found Tam, who immediately embraced Bennett.

"You don't know how grateful we are for your help. Anghelloise, Farthing! This is Bennett. He is here to help us!" They were both were now beside him.

Bennett turned to Anghelloise and bowed deeply. "It is an honor to meet a mentalist of your stature, Anghelloise! Your cover is well made!"

"The pleasure is mine, young man!" she replied. "Let me present you Captain Farthing."

He was a massive man, looking down at him with a toothy grin. "Farthing, at your service! We are both curious about where you've come from."

"I think I'd better wait until later. We need to get to Brogan as soon as possible. The man known as Kruger is with him as we speak. It is hard to penetrate his mind, but I sense hatred."

Farthing scratched his head, pondering the smallish, unassuming man. Then, he turned to Anghelloise and smiled. "Are you ready to do this? I promised you we would together. We are all here. I want to see action."

"Of course you do, dear man. In you, Bennett, I recognize a Siren equivalent if there ever was one. I, too, have many questions—but I concur. Brogan and Kruger come first. Let's move!"

"I am honored. Please, lead the way."

The group began hurrying down the corridor to room fourteen.

[What a crew we are!] Tam thought. The whole group laughed.

"Let's go get Brogan!" Farthing said, slapping Tam on the back.

Chapter 54

All for the Sake of One Man

No one stopped to question them as they passed through eerily empty hallways. The group began to feel extremely uneasy as they proceeded. There should have been some kind of resistance!

"Hold on," said Anghelloise suddenly. "Something's not right! I feel it in my bones."

The others murmured agreement, sensing the same thing. "Bennett, you have a good sense of what everyone is thinking here," said Tam. "Can you tell what's behind this door?"

"We are all mentalists here. I am known as a level ten conduit. I can channel and link other mentalists' minds, but I need to jump to curved space, then exit, in order to do so. I did it once. Unfortunately, I can't right now. I can link with a mind or two, then proceed."

"You could link with Tam and Anghelloise," Farthing suggested. "They have the ability."

"Agreed, sir," replied Bennett, "but I sense you are quite capable, too. "Let's all try."

They all nodded their heads.

"Focus on my mind. Allow me to attempt to collect yours and focus them." Bennett, smiled, his eyes darting to the side. He was feeling unsure in his newfound role of leadership.

"Don't doubt yourself, Bennett," said Anghelloise. "I've only just met you, but sense you are an honorable and worthy man."

The group all focused on Bennett. One by one, he sensed their minds touching his. Soon, all four were connected. Bennett could sense them all.

[Focus on the other side of the wall.]

Their eyes and minds turned to the door, which seemingly stopped existing. They penetrated the room and saw Kruger standing over Brogan. Tam began to falter at the sight of his Life-Line. The others propped him up mentally. Farthing put his arm around him.

[Focus on Kruger! Enter his mind. Don't be gentle. We need to force our way in—sift through the madness to find his true plans!] Anghelloise thought to the group.

Through the fog of Kruger's mind, they saw the horror of his deeds—all the men he'd killed after torturing them. The experiments he had performed on their brains and their bodies. His glee in it all. They continued to sift past the horrible images to try to find his plans.

There it was: domination of the entire system! That was the goal. There was no more detail than that. He was somehow blocking them out! As the images faltered, he turned his mind toward them, giving them a wry look that chilled their hearts. He knew they were there—even behind the solid door!

The group stumbled backward in amazement.

"How did he know? He's not a mentalist!" Tam exclaimed. "He never demonstrated any capacity before. I was able to enter his mind without much effort. *Too little* effort, in fact." He was bewildered. "I think we've been tricked—especially me."

"Are you saying he wanted us here?" asked Farthing.

"I don't know," responded Tam. "This doesn't make sense."

The door opened and Kruger waddled out. He stood there, grinning at them.

"Tam, my boy, welcome to your new home. Oh, don't bother trying to get into my mind anymore. I've let you see all I wanted you to." He looked at the group and sneered. "You're all a band of thieves and pirates!" He looked at Bennett. "Except you. I don't know you."

Bennett said nothing, swallowing as Kruger surveyed him.

Farthing gritted his teeth and began to move forward.

"Don't make any moves, or you will be cut down where you stand," warned Kruger.

"I'll take my chances," he growled.

"So be it. Make him kneel!" He cackled and waved his hands.

"Who are you speaking to?" demanded Anghelloise. As she moved forward, Farthing suddenly grunted and was thrown to his knees.

"Make them all kneel!"

To their astonishment, they were all thrown to their knees.

"Now, my pretty little beings, witness my plan—then beg for mercy. I'm actually in the mood for it."

No one was able to move.

[*I wish I could contact you,* Nimbus,] projected Bennett hopelessly.

[*You already have, Bennett. I can hear your thoughts clearly.*]

[*I didn't know that you can read my mind!*]

[*Father wanted to keep that secret.*]

[Nimbus, *stand by. Continue to monitor.*]

Kruger continued to wax on about his plan, shaking his fists into the air: "Do you not feel the power of my men? They are all wrapped in their living cloth, drugged and ready to serve me. They give me the power to do all this. This is what your future will hold, Thamara-Afil Amergan-Faolin—for you and your Life-Line, Brogan-Afil Faolin-Amergan. Oh, don't look so astonished!" He laughed. "I know your true names—both of you. Soon, you will be wrapped in living cloth, and will join your Life-Line in my service. Delicious! All my playthings."

He waddled over to Anghelloise. "And to have a Siren here is a bonus. Exploring the world through your eyes will be very helpful indeed! I shall seek the Sirens out and destroy them! There is little they can do about it at this point!"

Anghelloise growled. She would commit murder if her calling didn't forbid it.

"Farthing! At last, I have you! You've been a bad little boy, escaping all those years ago. Maybe I should dispatch you now, to show your little group how serious I am about my plans!"

Farthing could only grunt in retaliation as Kruger grabbed him by the hair and pulled his head backward, exposing his neck.

"And you…" He looked at Bennett. "Just who *are* you? You seem very out of place."

Bennett said nothing in reply.

Kruger paused, let go of Farthing, shook his head, and turned to waddle back into the room. "I have work to do. I wish to know how Brogan's Life-Line is different from the others. What makes it so? Blast—why am I asking all of you? You won't help me… at least, not *yet.*" He turned his head and looked in the opposite direction as if to speak to someone.

Despite his mental bindings, Tam could feel a change. A grey fog seemed to descend. People were on the move. The prison guards were returning! And there was someone else. Someone familiar. He shivered.

[*Artagan! You horrid beast! What have you done?*] Tam didn't expect a response.

[*I shall have the last word in all of this, Tam. Prepare yourself for my revenge!*]

Tam winced as he and the rest of the group were flattened on the floor by an unseen force—controlled not by Kruger, but Artagan. Kruger turned and entered Brogan's room. The door slammed shut. It seemed Kruger was under Artagan's control.

Artagan added: *[Tam, you've become mine—all for the sake of one man.]*

Chapter 55
Tit for Tat

Two weeks prior to the *Faramund*'s arrival, the prison world went into an uproar. Life there had changed, putting the staff on edge.

All of the workers stood at attention, lining the hallways to welcome the Magistrate. Everyone had been briefed beforehand on the protocol. There would be no looking him directly in the eye. And above all, *bow as he walks by*.

Despite the briefing, tension remained high. It worried the warden. He was responsible for the staff. He had spent many minutes dabbing his forehead and face, wiping off the perspiration. With a deep breath in, he approached the opening airlock.

Out poured armed guard after guard, until what seemed like an entire regiment stood before him in an upside-down *U* shape, prepared for the Magistrate's royal entry. The warden stopped in front of the wall of guards and waited, dabbing his forehead quickly again.

"Attention!" commanded the leading guard. The entire troupe immediately stood at attention, their boots coming together in a slapping sound, their firearms clacking as they were presented across their chests. "Presenting his Royal Magistrate, Alarius Kruger, the second!"

Kruger exited the airlock with his head held high, sitting in the back seat of a tram driven by an attendant in a page uniform—with another by his side to attend to his needs. The tram stopped in the middle of the troupe.

"Greetings, my worthy subjects! I'm encouraged by the news that this facility has a high standard of performance! I'm here to increase that standard to its maximum. Under my supervision, you'll provide the entire system an invaluable service."

The warden bowed as low as he could. "It is a great honor, sire, to have you present to witness the work undertaken to further science for the Senate."

"Of course it is," replied Kruger. "Warden, I relieve you of all scientific duties. I will supervise the entire division of experimentation. Your newest duty will be giving me a daily update on security and communication with the rest of the system. Will that be a problem?" Kruger looked intently at the warden, who shook his head and stared at the floor.

"No Magistrate, it would be a pleasure," he responded as he bowed again.

"As expected. Now, if you would, take me to the scientific centre and have all department heads attend an informational session to bring me up to current. I'll expect them immediately after my luncheon, in an hour and a half."

The barrier of men began to move forward. The warden turned and quickly walked down the hallway to the central hub that led to the other sections of the prison. The procession entered the second corridor, proceeding to the scientific offices and the boardroom, then parted to allow the tram to enter, followed by the warden.

"Has my room been attended to? Will it be ready for my use after the briefing?"

"Yes, sire," assured the warden. "Would it please his Majesty to eat lunch shortly?"

"Make it thirty minutes. I need time to clean up after that trip on Maguire's warship! They are not the most luxurious transport, but necessary, given the times—and those blasted pirates somewhere in the system!" He turned to his attendant. "Help me up to prepare for my toilet. I expect the same quality that was set on Kashtiloth." *Damnation to you, Tam! I would love to hang you by your fingers and make you squeal—even if you did give me the best treatment as page that I've ever received. It's impossible to convince these idiots of what true, proper treatment should look like!* He was fuming.

The page bowed and assisted Kruger off the tram. The driver came to help. Thirty minutes were definitely needed to get Kruger settled onto his couch, ready for lunch.

The chef arrived with waiters holding the serving trays.

"Sire, we have baked fowl, a variety of Alorion vegetables, and a hearty gravy, with freshly baked bread. May I assure you the entire dinner was supervised directly by me and certified to be fit for your consumption!"

"As it should be!" responded Kruger.

∞

The department heads began to file in after the meal had been cleared up. Kruger lounged on his couch, sipping brandy, as the scientists bowed one by one, then took their seats. Lastly, the warden arrived.

Kruger coughed loudly and began: "I'd like a status report. How many prisoners do we have at the moment?"

The warden stood and spoke. "There are currently 567 prisoners alive, along with thirty-five bodies that have been frozen. Recently, six were deemed unsuitable and terminated, as per your orders. For some reason, they were not full mentalists, only degens. Despite having the genetic markers of one, three, one in their DNA, they were not full mentalists."

"That is unfortunate!" said Kruger. "Do you have any understanding as to why?"

The warden turned to the rest of the scientific team, and they all looked downward, unable to respond. Due to protocol, only the warden could speak.

"Not at the moment, sire. That will have to be the next point of study for the group."

"Then that will be our highest priority!" responded Kruger. "What about the Ancient technology you've been experimenting with? Can you get it to link to the men in living cloth?"

"Yes, sire, but we need a suitable mentalist to link to them. There are none available, as they're all wrapped in living cloth. It would not be prudent to let one loose, I think!"

"Blast!" sputtered Kruger. "There must be a way! Find me someone—or something! Now, get out of here. Send me your reports electronically. Oh, and warden? They are due no later than tomorrow morning. That should be enough time for you to settle into your duties!"

"Very good, Magistrate. I will have them to you then!" The warden turned to go, and the others rose silently and exited.

He would probably be up all night getting those reports together.

Kruger fumed until the room was cleared. Once he was a little more composed, he pushed the comm button and his page came running.

"Have one of the frozen corpses thawed out and delivered to the nearest examination room. I wish to do an experiment." *What a wonderful distraction this will be!* He smacked his lips.

∞

Kruger's solution to his mentalist problem was solved in a rather convenient manner several days later. It came in the form of a report from Commander Maguire, substantially raising his stature in Kruger's eyes after the recent events with the *Starfinder* shuttle.

Maguire had discovered Artagan Mangrouph-Charon on a supply ship that had arrived recently from Alorion. It seemed rather obvious Artagan had wanted to be found.

This did not matter to Kruger; all he wanted was to get that little worm in his grasp. He had ordered Artagan delivered to him directly, unharmed. And now, he stood in front of Kruger, his hands bound behind him, two guards on each side.

"You despicable little traitor! Where have you been skulking?!" demanded Kruger.

"Sire, I assure you that my disappearance had a valid purpose," responded Artagan.

"I'll be the judge of that. Explain. Your life depends on it!"

Artagan stopped and thought about what to say next. "Forgive me, your Magistrate, but I have been on a fact-finding mission." As he began saying this, he started to mentally push to get Kruger to release information—and to perhaps find a way to get on his good side. "Since that horrible day Tam betrayed you, I've been seeking information about how to best bring the scourge in, so you can deal with him."

"I find that hard to believe..." he started, relenting as Artagan's influence began to sway him. "However, I'm listening."

"Sire, I simply needed more time to find information that would service you." *[You have no need to worry,]* projected Artagan, *[you can send the guards away. I am here to help.]*

"Well, I don't seem to have a reason to worry about you," echoed Kruger. "Guards! Release this man and leave us. Please remain outside."

The men untied Artagan and departed. He smiled and continued to push.

∞

"As you can see, Artagan, the Ancient technology is connected to 566 men in their living cloth. There is one I cannot seem to connect to: Tam's degen partner, Brogan. It is still a mystery to me. What we need is someone who is a mentalist who can actually use the link. It's a paradox; I would need one of those degens to do this, but can't allow it, as it would be too dangerous."

"Are you aware there are people who are mentalists but not degens?" suggested Artagan.

"Do you have someone in mind?" asked Kruger.

"Sire, I am a mentalist, but can assure you I'm not a degen."

"You are a mentalist?! You're not a degen?!" Kruger repeated, incredulous.

[This is such a marvelous opportunity!]

"This is such a marvelous opportunity, Artagan!" said Kruger on cue.

[We should start testing me with the Ancient technology immediately!]

"We should start testing you with the Ancient technology immediately!" he continued.

"I would be honored, your Magistrate!" responded Artagan.

Kruger wrung his hands. "If this works, it will be a triumph!"

∞

"Artagan, the Ancient technology is ready. I need to you mentally link to it," instructed Kruger. "You should feel the 566 immediately."

"As you wish, sire."

Artagan closed his eyes for effect, and mentally projected into the artifact that sat in front of him. It consisted of a main, rectangular unit with many rods and projections sticking out of the sides. It was currently flashing multiple lights. As he projected toward it, it began to change its frequency. It now flashed one long flash, three short ones, and a pause, then repeated, over and over again.

[I am here. I am here to control this network, as is my right. Connect me now!]

Continuing its flashing sequence, it began vibrating, a high-pitched whine emitting from it as it signaled its willingness to link up. The whine lowered slightly as a cube popped out the side. It floated into Artagan's open hand, then opened, revealing what looked like a pill. The notion to swallow it popped into his head.

"It is sending me a message to eat this!" he told Kruger.

"Then do it!"

With a little trepidation, Artagan swallowed the pill and waited. Nothing.

"Well?"

"Nothing yet," he replied.

"Then we sit here until something happens," said Kruger.

Within a half hour, Artagan began to receive messages from the artifact. He found it a bit odd the way they just popped into his head, beyond his control. It was disarming. In fact, he felt rather ill. With a lurch, he fell to his knees and vomited on the floor. Kruger, sitting on his lounge chair, watched Artagan's eyes as they glassed over. He stared into nothingness, occasionally bringing his hands to his ears as though he were blocking them. Strangely, he began to hum, repeating over and over, until Kruger noticed the pattern of one long hum, three short, then a pause. This repeated at least eight times, at which point Artagan fell silent, his head hung and his hands placed on his bent knees.

He suddenly looked up.

"I have contact! I can now sense the men trapped in the living cloth! The artifact is working." He stood up and began pacing. "I can sense their minds. I can sense the power of them together. I can mold them and make them do as I please!" He was so excited that he broke protocol and looked Kruger directly in the eyes. "Watch this, sire!" He lifted his hand, and Kruger felt the lounge vibrate, shuffle a bit—then, he was off the floor!

"Put me down, you idiot!" shouted Kruger. "That is enough proof for me."

Artagan began laughing uncontrollably, wringing his hands and continuing to pace. "I feel I could do almost anything! What is your desire, sire?"

"Do not look me in the eye again without permission, or there will be consequences."

Artagan turned, lowering his eyes. "My apologies, your Magistrate. Please forgive me for having too much enthusiasm. It was quite overwhelming! I have control now, and will follow protocol, sire." He smiled, bowing as he projected: *[You will trust me with this. You will allow me to continue.]* He paused, then added, *[You will dismiss your guards, too!]*

"Artagan, you will be trusted with this experiment. In fact, I feel so confident, I'll dismiss my guards and send them back to Maguire's ship!" crowed Kruger. "Contact the science crew and begin testing your abilities immediately. And get someone in here to clean up the mess!"

"As you wish, sire!" replied Artagan. He now had 567 men under his control: 566 degen mentalists, and one pompous and insane Kruger.

Next up, it will be you, Tam, and your degen partner, Brogan, he thought as he flexed his mental might.

∞

Brogan lay on the table on his stomach, naked, too weak to move. He'd been cleaned by Grayson and Rothman with their usual cruel vigor. He groaned softly and tried to turn his head.

"I want him to receive a sedative, so he does not feel the full effects of the operation," the man's voice blared into his sensitive ears. A needle plunged roughly into his buttock. The intern to his right giggled as he winced. "I do want him to feel some of it, though!"

"Sire, should I prepare another sedative if this is too much for the degen to handle?"

"No! I want him to experience as much as he can tolerate. If he looks like he might faint, revive him!"

Brogan knew the sound of Rothman's voice. This was the first time he had heard the Magistrate speak, though. He was frightened beyond anything that he'd ever experienced. This was the monster that everyone spoke of.

The Magistrate continued: "How long before we can begin?"

"He should be ready momentarily, as his lower torso is nearly numb!" responded Rothman. "Shall I administer the coagulator?"

"By all means—we don't want him to bleed out! We want him alive to fulfill his task."

"Yes, sire." Rothman shoved the syringe with the coagulator into Brogan's other buttock.

"Young man, you are about to receive four little gifts that you will deliver to your friends! All you will remember is the pain!" He turned to Rothman. "Attach the artifact!"

Brogan felt a third needle, this time carefully inserted into a vein in his arm. He began to cry softly, trying to move away, but his body was too weak. He sensed nothing from Tam.

"It's online," replied Rothman as the machine began to vibrate, emitting its familiar pattern of sound waves.

"Go get Artagan, then!" He turned to Brogan, who began to convulse, then proceeded to vomit up what little was in his stomach. His head was now lying in it. Kruger smiled. "There, my boy! Feel it all! Experience it all! Show me what it does to you!"

Kruger began rubbing his crotch against the table in excitement, but stopped when the door opened and Artagan entered. Rothman and Grayson took their places on both sides of the table, ready to secure the prisoner so that he wouldn't thrash around too much. Artagan approached the artifact and smiled. [I am here. I will connect to the net. I wish to also connect to the person attached.]

The machine responded with additional vibrations as it emitted the one, three, one signal. Artagan was now immune to the nausea and insanity that emitted from it.

Artagan felt the net attach to the 566 men in the background. He paused as it considered Brogan. He snickered.

Brogan groaned, then began to whimper. His entire body and mind were going numb as inhibitors of his Life-Line connection were administered to him. The final vestiges of his and Tam's link were now gone. He was utterly alone.

But this only lasted a short few seconds, as he felt a new mental blast enter his brain, almost forcing him unconscious. His eyes fluttered and began to turn upward as his mind reeled. The mind was rough, pushing through his thoughts and his memories, brutally searching for something. It stopped to ponder his memories of Tam's contact after his imprisonment.

"I can now control his connection with Tam at will. He is totally under my control. No brain can handle the might of 566 other mentalists! He is at my mercy! I can erase parts of his memory as you requested! After the operation, I will have no problem erasing the memories of the surgery, too!"

"Glorious!" chanted Kruger. "Shall we proceed?" He held out his hand and received a scalpel from Rothman. Kruger gritted his teeth in anticipation.

Brogan screamed as the incisions were made, then darkness fell.

Chapter 56
The Gathering Storm

The four of them still lay on the floor, breathing heavily. The mental hold was gone. They were now free to get up—which they did, slowly.

"Now what do we do?" gasped Farthing. "How in the blazes can we defend ourselves?!"

"I'm thinking we need to regroup," said Bennett. "I suggest returning to the ships."

"Wouldn't that just lead the Magistrate or Artagan to us?" pointed out Anghelloise. "Don't you think it odd that no guards are approaching to arrest us?"

"Artagan is toying with us, no doubt," responded Tam angrily. "I can feel it!"

"How does this help Artagan? Why is he letting us go?" Farthing asked.

"It's a mystery," said Bennett. "I'm going to contact my ship to get some advice."

[Nimbus, *you've been monitoring the situation. What do you suggest?*]

[*I'm quite distressed by your predicament. I'd feel better if you were all to return.*]

[*We can't,* Nimbus. *We need another solution. We need to block out the force of the mental net Artagan has access to. We don't even know how he did it.*]

[*The Order does have a suit that scientists have been working on to help block out the space sickness for those mentalists who experience when they exit curved space. It hasn't been fully tested, but it might be your best bet.*]

[*The question is how to get it here without risking exposure.*]

"I may have a solution," he said to the others. "The Order has a suit that may allow one of us to block out the mentalist net. The problem is getting it here from my ship."

"I think I have a solution!" Anghelloise replied. "Nick, are you prepared to leave the ship and meet us?"

"Yes, Mistress," said Nick through the comm system embedded in her ear canal.

"Nick can," she announced. "We would need *Nimbus* to allow him on board to retrieve the suit. We can meet him at the airlock."

"Tam and I can probably block enough people to give Nick the time to move the equipment and arrive to meet us," said Bennett. "Hopefully that will be enough!"

"We'll need to block a lot more on our way there!" urged Tam. "I can sense many arriving from other parts of the base. We need to move—now!"

They began their voyage back to the airlock with a sense of urgency. They had quite a few people to distract as they approached. However, they all seemed susceptible to mind probing and were easily distracted. The one mind that worried Tam the most was silent.

[Where is Artagan? Why isn't he worried about what we're doing?] Tam wondered to the group.

[Tam, has it occurred to you that mentalist mind-probing can work in both directions? What would happen if we put our minds together to try and figure out what he's doing? I don't think he'd suspect us to be capable of such a thing. And he doesn't know Farthing or I are capable yet. I didn't feel his mind get past my mental blocks!]

[True, Bennett! He may have made a mistake in our favor!] Tam smiled, beginning to feel a little more hopeful as they arrived at the airlock. There was a group of guards to deal with.

[Maybe I should just take them out!] suggested Farthing. *[I haven't been much use yet. I could really let loose and have a great time at it!]*

"Captain, hold on," responded Bennett. "You'll get your chance soon enough. I fear there will be a time when we can no longer block people so easily, once Artagan discovers us!"

"You are all such doom and gloom!" Anghelloise stated. "Let me handle this!"

She cleared her throat and began to sing. It started slowly, in a low key, then picked up quickly. The sound was very entrancing, and everyone, including themselves, started to lose focus, drifting into a daydream state. She grabbed their arms one by one and made eye contact. *[Don't follow the rhythm. Focus on the guards or you'll be sucked in, too!]*

Her voice picked up rhythm and started to sound like it was taking on a harmony; what started with one voice became another and another. Soon, she sounded like a chorus. Tam shook his head and wiped a tear out of the corner of his eye. It was so beautiful. It was hard not to get pulled in! The chorus lifted and oscillated one time in a strong stream, then three slower ones, then a short pause, repeated again and again. One long, three short, one breath...

Bennett frowned. *[I can't help but think I've heard this before!]*

[Something in it is very familiar!] responded Tam. *[Look what it's doing to the guards!]*

They were milling about, wandering around, bumping into each other, unaware of what was going on around them, as though in a trance.

On the fifth time through, the chorus reached its loudest. It repeated itself once more, not so loudly, and then lulled three times. The guards tumbled where they stood and lay unconscious as the song began to fade away.

Tam stopped and looked down in wonderment. "Amazing, Anghelloise! The sirens can sing this far away from the Convent?"

"I can channel their singing, yes. I am their conduit. I sing my song, and they add their own, via the communications system and the shuttle."

Bennett's eyes lit up. "Conduit. You said 'conduit!' I am one, too! I have created contact with most of the galaxy."

"Did you happen to say just one word? Was it *[Hello?]*"

"Yes!"

"I received it!" Anghelloise echoed.

"So did I!" proclaimed Farthing.

"Now it's my turn to be amazed! So, Anghelloise, you are a conduit for the Sirens' singing. This is fascinating news!"

"Nick is here!" she announced suddenly. "OK, Nick! Enter the airlock."

They leaned forward and looked through the window to see the spherical Nick glide in.

"He always has that silly grin!" Farthing remarked. "Let's hope he has reasons to smile!"

The airlock pressurized, the door opened, and Nick floated out. "Greetings, everyone! I bring a suit and news from *Nimbus*. She tells me that the *Faramund* is close to being ready to go. Captain O'Keefe sends her blessings—and a message to hurry up!"

"What of the warships?" asked Bennett.

"They are continuing repairs, from what data *Nimbus* can gather from down here. They may be ready to fight by about the same time as the *Faramund* has readied herself."

"Then it's clear to me. I've got to send *Nimbus* up there to lend support to the *Faramund*. If we delay those warships, we could use the *Faramund* to shuttle the prisoners out of here!"

"Don't forget Artagan and Kruger," said Anghelloise. "We need to get past them, too."

"Very true," said Bennett. "Let me communicate with her. I'll instruct her to make contact with Captain O'Keefe and render service to the *Faramund*. There may be a few tricks we can try on those warships to slow them down even more."

"In the meantime, we need to examine this suit of yours. It will not fit Farthing or me. That leaves you or Tam to wear it," Anghelloise remarked.

"I've not been trained in battle techniques," said Bennett. "Tam?"

"Only what Farthing has taught me so far," responded Tam. "I'll do this for Brogan."

"Bless you, dear boy," said Anghelloise.

Farthing stood there, scratching his stubble. "You may find this hard to believe, but I think that I'd be more use up there to help the *Faramund* rather than down here. Something inside me says that I should go, even though I'd like to stay and do battle." He smiled grimly. "Let me go to *Nimbus*. You can let her know what my intentions are."

Bennett paused and turned to Anghelloise. "Your thoughts?"

"Let him go. He knows his ship and his opponents. I'm never one to stop a mentalist who has a premonition!" She turned to Farthing. "My dear man, please promise me one thing."

He nodded.

"Try to keep as many people alive as possible on both sides. They are our kin, even though they're on the wrong side."

"I'll do my best, Anghelloise. Thank you for believing in me. I still find it hard to believe that I'm a potential mentalist. Bennett, what do you think? Do you allow me to go?"

"Tam?" Bennett asked.

Tam nodded.

"Then it's agreed. Let's get the suit on Tam, then you make your way to *Nimbus*."

∞

"My boy, you look wonderful in that suit. A real warrior if you ask me!" Anghelloise examined it, then turned to Bennett. "Tam should be able to focus on tasks without being attacked by Artagan via the mentalists' net?"

"Certainly. The suit also allows protection from all sorts of dangers: fighting, shooting, *and* mind techniques, though we've been experimenting with it to help prevent the space sickness our mentalists feel when they drop out of curved space."

Tam nodded in agreement. He was amazed at the lightness of the suit. It was hard to understand how something this thin could protect him from assault. He moved his arms and saw images and signals appear in the face plate. "What do all these signs mean, Bennett?"

"On your left, you should be see a hologram of the energy level of the suit. It changes to red when running low. There's also a computer that will let you know of any changes."

"Got it. I'm at 100 percent at the moment. What's this on the right?"

"That's a 3D plan of people around you. When activated, you can identify everyone and their positions. This is especially helpful when your enemies are hidden. You can determine life signs based on the readings. Look at it directly and instruct the suit to begin scanning."

Tam did so. "Below me is another panel. What is its function?"

"That one indicates the force of an object connecting with the suit. If someone were to hit you with a metal bar, the meter would show its kinetic energy and potential impact on the suit."

"Next to that something else—it's blank at the moment."

"That one communicates between you and this shield, which you can use to deaden blows from your opponent. Look at that panel and tell it to activate." Bennett gave Tam the crest-shaped shield. "You could be shot with a projectile weapon, and would feel a just a bump against your skin. You might get a bruise in a fight like that, but it's better than being shot or sliced through with a sword."

"Nice to know, I guess!" Tam chided.

"You may have to use it to break through a line of prison guards, allowing us to follow. You should be able to break down the door to Brogan's cell and allow us to enter. There is very little I've seen in this base that could do much damage to you at this point."

"That's all I needed to hear!" laughed Farthing. "Nick, get ready to go. *Nimbus* awaits!"

Nick did a little happy spin and replied, "Yes, Captain."

Farthing paused and turned to Tam. "Remember what I taught you on the shuttle during your training. You may be wearing a suit, but you need to have some common sense when it comes to hand-to-hand combat. Don't do anything foolish, now!"

"I'll try not to. Thank you. Goddesses' speed to the *Faramund*. Let's hope the next time I see you, it is while we're evacuating the prisoners!"

Anghelloise turned to Farthing, grabbing his big arm. "You be careful, too, you big oaf! Come back in one piece please. The same for Nick, please—one piece!"

"I'll do my utmost!" He began to pull on his spacesuit, starting with the boots. Within ten minutes, he was ready to leave. "Nick, head for the airlock!"

"Aye, aye, Captain!" chirped Nick. He turned and entered, Farthing following behind.

Bennett closed the door and Anghelloise began cycling the airlock. Within five minutes, their group had gone from five to three. Tam couldn't help but wonder whether Farthing might have been of more service with them after all.

Chapter 57

He Who Fights...

They were now not far from the section that joined all the pods together. The guards were still out cold from the singing. That could change soon, though.

"Why can't we get the Sirens to knock them all out again?" inquired Tam.

"It doesn't work as well a second time, Tam. They were caught unaware. This time, many will be prepared. Remember that Artagan has access to all the mentalist prisoners' capabilities. He could block it."

"I still don't sense his mental presence," replied Tam, frowning. "What's he up to?"

As they headed down the hallway to towards Brogan's cell, his question was quickly answered.

[Don't bother proceeding to Brogan's cell. He's no longer there. Go to the recreational training centre next to the fifth pod. There, we will discuss the conditions of his release.] Artagan's message came through loud and clear for all three of them. They stopped and looked at each other.

"Now what?" asked Tam. "Do as he says?"

"I think that's the best plan," said Bennett. "We still have enough time to get into position and use the suit. We should use all our mental energy blocking out the fact we have it, though."

"Then forward we go!" answered Anghelloise. She smiled and moved onward. The others were surprised at her optimism at a time like this. The trio returned to the central entrances, turned into the area next to the fifth pod, and followed the signs to the recreational area. There were more and more people awake and moving around. They all seemed to know the trio was there, and were parting to allow them to pass. Someone had given them instructions.

Bennett checked Tam's suit one last time. "Turn on all the sensors and prepare yourself. You may need to use the suit to block Artagan out of your mind. However, make haste, as ours will not be protected. I suspect we can hold out for a time, but I don't know how long!"

"Turning all systems but the mental shield on. Computer, respond."

"Tam, I am ready and 100 percent at your command," it replied.

The trio continued down the hall to the recreational area. They pulled the door open to a large auditorium filled with people sitting and standing around the elevated perimeter. They shouted and cheered down at them as they entered. *[They must be the prison workers...]*

"What in the Goddesses' names is this about?" wondered Anghelloise aloud.

"Looks like we're the show!" remarked Tam. "Bennett?"

"I've no reference for this type of behavior. I truly do not know what to make of it!"

"Welcome, my friends! Enter the area and be recognized."

"Kruger!" exclaimed Tam angrily. "I'd recognize that voice anywhere!"

"There are three seats for you," called Kruger. "Take them." He rose slowly from his platform and leaned into the light. "Do it, or Brogan loses a limb."

Anghelloise grabbed both their arms and led the two men to their seats. "Let's oblige his little fantasy for the moment," she whispered.

They looked up at Kruger.

"My faithful workers, we will have a wonderful spectacle for you tonight. My dear traitor boy, Tam. Are you ready to play a game where, if you win, you get Brogan's life?" The crowd cheered loudly, goading him on. They wanted to see Tam play this so-called game.

Kruger addressed Anghelloise: "My dear lady, what an amazing trick you played earlier. It caught many off guard, myself included. We are now wise to your ways, though, you witch!"

Anghelloise sniffed, but didn't respond. A comeback might not help them at that moment.

"We also know of Farthing's departure. Sadly, I would have liked to make him part two of the show." He turned back to the audience. "My loyal subjects, for your informational pleasure, please turn to the front screen to see the prize!"

The screen flashed a scene that made Tam's heart leap into his throat. It was Brogan, tubes extruding from his body, the living cloth wrapped around him. Grayson and Rothman stood with scalpels on both sides of him. Their eyes gleamed with excitement—they were no doubt waiting for their cue. Tam swallowed hard and fought back tears. Brogan was splayed out like an experiment for all to see. He felt the ire build in his gut and started to stand up, but was stopped by Anghelloise's gentle touch.

[*Wait, my boy. Let him play his hand first. Then, we'll do what we can!*]

He sat back down, tears flowing down his cheeks inside the mask. [*I can't feel anything from Brogan!*]

Kruger seemed to read his thoughts: "Brogan is receiving a full dosage of drugs that inhibit all feelings being transferred to and from you." He smiled. "If you win, he'll be released."

Tam stood. "And what if I lose?"

The crowd went silent as Kruger waved his hand. "It might be better to not know."

Bennett stood beside Tam. Anghelloise rose, too.

[*Tam, we can't help you now. Are you willing to play this game?*] Anghelloise responded.

[*I am. I want my Brogan back.*] "Kruger, how will I know you'll fulfill your promise?"

"I forgive you for your betrayal. That should be enough. Trust what I say is true!"

The crowd cheered loudly.

Tam waved his arm. "It would help to know what the challenge is."

"Fine. Look and decide!"

There was a clanging noise as a door at the opposite end of the recreational area opened, and out walked a figure in some sort of suit that looked similar to his.

"I'll have to compete against Artagan?! What kind of treachery is this? You expect me to fight someone who has more than five hundred minds enslaved to his?!"

"I do, my boy. That number is 567—and includes your precious Brogan!" He laughed.

Tam turned to Bennett and Anghelloise for support. Their eyes showed worry. There was nothing they could do against that many mentalists.

"Computer, turn on the mental blocking ability of the suit," commanded Tam.

∞

Nimbus arced up toward the *Faramund* and the warships suspended in space. Farthing wondered what he'd find when he got there. "*Nimbus*, can you give me the status of the ships?"

"Sensors indicate the warships are still nonfunctioning. Life support systems are at maximum, so there is no danger of lives lost. The *Faramund* is faring much better. They are now mobile, but weapons are not yet back online."

"Are there any indications that the warships will have weapons capabilities soon?"

"There is a possibility. Computer links indicate weapons may come online in the next few hours. The pellet launchers could be used manually at this point, if they choose."

"That's bad!" lamented Farthing. "There must be something we can do."

"I can predict with about 94 percent accuracy the destruction of the pellets of the weapons directed at me. I can predict with about 85 percent the destruction of those meant for the *Faramund*."

"Those aren't bad odds, but we need to find a way to keep their weapons inactive until the prisoners escape! Even better would be to return to help—which we can't unless we do."

"I can't allow the ships to be destroyed. It is in contravention to my programming."

"Then what do you suggest? You need to protect Bennett, too. Wouldn't it make sense to return as soon as possible?"

"I do not deny that Bennett is my priority," replied *Nimbus*, "but he has also given me the order to help you where necessary. I do not wish to be in conflict with either order."

"Then help me disable those warships so we can bring the *Faramund* down to transport the prisoners out," insisted Farthing.

"I will agree to do so if you ask the *Faramund* to stand down. I do not wish to also disable your ship in order to prevent you from destroying the warships. What assurance can you give me that you will not attempt any sort of deception?"

"*Nimbus*, I may be a pirate and trained militant, but I'm a member of the Lambda Infinity Omega League, sworn to the Siren's Song. To disobey that oath would go against all I believe. I would not harm anyone except in defense of those I am sworn to protect. That means you."

"Bennett trusts you, so I do, too. I can access the warships' computers and shut down everything except life support systems for a second time. Please contact the *Faramund* and inform them. Remind them to not use weapons of any sort."

"Understood, *Nimbus*. Open a channel to the *Faramund*."

"Channel open."

"Captain O'Keefe, this is Captain Farthing, aboard the starship *Nimbus*. We are approaching you from your port side. Please acknowledge."

Captain O'Keefe's face appeared on the screen. "Farthing, I would like to believe it's you. Standard procedures dictate you send me the appropriate signal for proper identification."

"Jennifer, it is good to see you. Transmitting code. Please stand by. *Nimbus*, may I please have manual access to your communication systems?"

An entry pad slid out of the console before him.

"What kind of communication do you require?" asked *Nimbus*.

"Audio only. I need to transmit a series of sounds that the *Faramund* will recognize."

"Easy enough. Any particular frequency or type?"

"Nothing other than something audible to the human ear."

"Use the largest key. It will respond to your touch, sending a signal to the *Faramund*."

"Thank you, *Nimbus*. O'Keefe, ready to transmit." Farthing hit the key one time for several seconds, then three short times, and a pause for breath, then re-entered it twice.

"Signal received and recognized, Farthing. Nice to have you back."

"Thank you," replied Farthing, "but we are far from finished. Listen carefully: under no circumstances are you to fire on the warships."

"They are almost capable of firing on us!" exclaimed O'Keefe.

"Captain, as I said, we'll be disabling them shortly. They'll be defenseless, and I need your word you'll not harm them in any way, except in self-defense. Do you agree?"

Staring at the screen, she swallowed and paused. "Yes, Captain. Understood."

"Please stand by. If we're successful, I want you to prepare to land the ship and evacuate the prisoners. Any further communications will take place on this channel, following the code."

"Understood. Preparations will commence shortly. Goddesses' speed, Farthing!"

He turned from the blank screen and took a deep breath. "OK, *Nimbus*, do as you will."

∞

"Tam, you really are a fool! You are not the only one with access to Ancient technology. I, too, wear a suit equal to your own. I knew of your plans the moment you set foot in this prison!" sneered Artagan. "How can you even hope to defeat me?" He advanced two steps and stood arrogantly, hands on his hips.

"I will do what's right. Those men deserve to be released." Tam advanced, trying to stand as confidently as he could, hands on his own hips, copying Artagan.

"What is right?" Artagan snorted. "Because you have the power of the witches behind you? They cannot help you now. Kruger's laid these plans carefully! You are on your own! Even your two comrades here can't help!"

Kruger stirred, frowning at the blasphemy of Artagan using his name. When this was over, the man would be punished... if he could regain power over the imbecile. He looked down on Tam and Artagan and laughed. "Tam has no choice! He wants his Life-Line back!"

Bennett, behind Tam, whispered in his ear: "Kruger has no plans to let those men go."

Tam nodded his head knowingly. There was no way Kruger would do such a thing. There had to be another reason he was allowing this battle to take place.

Anghelloise seemed to sense this. "This is all utter nonsense! Kruger, you have no plans in releasing any of us. Why do you even bother with this?" She moved beside Tam.

Kruger reddened and nodded to Artagan, who smirked. With a whip of his hand, he sent Anghelloise flying against the adjacent wall. She gasped as the pain spread through her body, having no way to mentally control it. For the first time in her life, she actually felt helpless.

Bennett moved to help her, but was thrown against the wall, too. He crumpled, unconscious, to the floor as his head connected with the wall.

Artagan laughed as the crowd began to cheer wildly. They wanted more! Anghelloise was slammed against the wall again. She crumpled beside Bennett, unconscious.

"Do you not see the futility in this? Two of the most powerful mentalists in this region have been defeated with the wave of my hand! How can someone as puny and useless as you hope to defeat me?!" Artagan began to stride toward him. "Kneel and surrender, before I really show you what I'm capable of!"

Tam reviewed the screens he could see in his suit visor, showing everything at full strength. Hopefully there really would be little Artagan could do to reach him mentally. Bennett's technology could very well be superior to what he possessed. He made a quiet prayer to the Goddesses and then set his resolve.

"This is between you and me. Leave the others out of it." Tam advanced, as did Artagan. They came face to face in the centre of the room, then waited to see who'd take the first shot.

The crowd began to boo.

"Throw him senseless against the wall, too!"

"Throw him!"

"Throw him!"

The chant went up across the room. Kruger cackled and Artagan snorted. His hand came out to throw Tam. Nothing happened. He tried again. Still nothing.

Tam, seeing what was happening, smiled to himself. He lifted his hand to send Artagan flying. Again, nothing happened. Now it was Artagan's turn to smile.

"You really think you have any power over me, Tam?! I may not be able to use my mind, but I can use this suit!!" He lunged at Tam, slamming his fists into his midsection. Tam bounced backward, crashing to the floor, his shield flying off to the side.

Strange. I didn't feel that at all.

Tam looked at his visor screens as Artagan laughed, standing over him. Tam managed to stop his foot as he tried to slam it into his head. He grasped it, pushing it away. Artagan stumbled backward, thrown to the floor, and screamed with rage.

Tam quickly climbed to his feet and advanced on Artagan. He looked at his raging face, then shifted his eyes to his comrades. *I must protect them with all my resources. I don't know if I can harm Artagan or not, but he could definitely harm them!*

Artagan, who was stumbling to his feet, turned to see Tam's move. His moved his hand, and Bennett rose off the floor, still unconscious, looking like a corpse suspended by wires. Tam came to block his suspended body and tried to push back at Artagan with his mind. He didn't succeed in moving him, but it did cancel out Artagan's power to raise Bennett, who tumbled to the floor, cracking his head loudly.

With that, Tam screamed and charged at Artagan. They collided, arms and legs flailing, neither seeming to do much. Tam's plan to distract him from the others seemed to be working.

"Computer, is there any way I can blast a hole through the door—or maybe the wall?" Tam grunted as a blow from Artagan made him stagger backward.

"Yes, of course! You could use the shockwave gun to blast a hole in the door. Activate it here!"

Tam selected the shockwave gun from the screen in his visor using his eye as selection tool, turned to Artagan, and raised his left arm. The palm of his hand glowed as he aimed directly at him. The gun went off, sending Artagan flying into a bulkhead. Then, Tam raised his left arm toward the door. He blasted the door open, leaving a gaping hole. He shot again, this time at the bulkhead to the right of the blown-out door. A large chunk bounced outward, crashing to the floor.

"Shockwave weapon recharging," announced the computer. "Wait before you fire again!" The crowd was cheering. Artagan was getting back to his feet.

Tam charged and again grappled with him. He slammed him against the floor a second time. His arm came up in self-defense. and blocked Tam's arm to the side. An evil smile cracked on his face, and Tam realized something bad was about to happen. He stumbled to the side as Artagan raised his arm and his wristband started firing at him with a barrage of metal bullets, each making contact with his midsection. Tam was thrown backward, groaning as he felt the air in his lungs forced out. He gasped.

He checked the visor and saw there are no intrusions into his suit. It had protected him, for the most part, though it hurt like mad. He lay on the floor gasping for breath as Artagan advanced to stand over him again, this time, with legs on either side of his prone body.

"Move and I'll blast you again!" He pointed his palm at Tam.

Tam's hands went up in what seemed a protest, distracting him, as his right leg went up to connect with Artagan's groin. Now, Artagan was gasping for breath. He staggered, holding his groin and whimpering as he crumpled to the floor. It would seem his suit couldn't handle the endless collisions. There were weaknesses, after all!

Tam turned to his comrades. They were both conscious. Anghelloise was holding Bennett's head in her lap, trying to prevent further damage. He probably had a concussion of some sort. He turned the mental block off to get a quick message to her.

[Artagan can be hurt! Anghelloise, ready yourself! You'll know what to do!]

Turning the mental block back on, he turned his hand back toward Artagan, blasting him twice, causing him to slam against the bulkhead.

Artagan might actually be unconscious! Tam took the moment to mentally lift Anghelloise up. She started to rise, letting go of Bennett, who slumped slowly back to the ground. Tam lifted her, moved her through the door, and dropped her carefully to the ground. Turning to Bennett, he lifted him up, too, sending him through the hold into Anghelloise's arms. He was dazed and confused, but seemed OK.

[Stay there, you two, until I return!]

Anghelloise nodded, pulling strands of her hair out of her face, which looked bruised and red.

The crowd was cheering again. Tam turned to see Artagan stirring. He quickly reviewed his options. "Computer, particle beam working?"

"Ready to fire!"

Tam used his eye to select it, and raised his right hand toward Kruger. The particle beam instantly shot through the table behind which Kruger was sitting. It continued on through the rolls of fat on his left buttock. Kruger screamed like an animal caught in a trap. He had to distract Artagan for a few more minutes!

The crowd fell silent as Kruger continued to wail, then tumbled from his chair, flopping onto the floor with a wet smacking sound. Artagan raged and stumbled toward him, then changed his mind and staggered toward Tam, who had crossed to the hole in the bulkhead.

Tam lifted his left hand, sending the bulkhead slamming it into the door, covering the hole. It teetered dangerously on the brink of falling backward. He looked up as the shockwave recharged again, enough for just one shot.

Who should I shoot? Kruger? Artagan?

Chapter 58
Come What May!

Father paced back and forth in his room. His search for level ten conduits in the smaller arms of the galaxy had not yielded anything yet. More mentalists had been found, some very powerful, but none like Bennett so far. He had been following Bennett's mind while on his couch. He had witnessed the spectacle in the prison involving Tam and Artagan, but got cut off when he was knocked unconscious. He had not been able to reconnect. He hoped he was OK.

Father had been trying to use the woman, Anghelloise, as a contact point, but it didn't seem to work. Nothing in his training could help him access her mind. The man, Farthing, had been easier, but he was now off-planet in the *Nimbus,* trying to stop warships.

Nimbus would report from time to time to give him updates. The last had indicated she was disabling the warships. The other ship, the *Faramund,* might be able to land, but to what end? He would have no sense of what was going on until Bennett regained consciousness.

There was another ship prepped and ready to go, but there was no mentalist strong enough to handle the trip and be of use on the other side. Bennett had truly been the only one.

There was also the news coming in lately about the incredibly large and active black hole at the centre of the galaxy. There were mentalists close by, but the signal stopped there. There were indications that Bennett's communication attempt had made it everywhere but near it. Nothing to do with the mentalists seemed to go near it. No one in the Order could explain why. Everything else got pulled into it—why not mentalist energy, too?

Father continued to pace, frustrated that all his leads were going nowhere. Maybe he needed to be more proactive. He stopped his wandering and stood for a time, thinking. He made his decision. He had a plan—and a crazy one at that.

∞

Tam watched as medics attended Kruger, who was still wailing and threatening him. *Luckily, he's not up to hurting Brogan at the moment. Good thing they didn't know about me having a particle beam! Kruger was an easy target!*

Artagan stood on the other side of the room, just below Kruger, waiting. He turned every few moments to glare at him. The second wave would be coming soon—Tam was sure of it.

The crowd had grown silent, waiting to see what would happen to Kruger. They had enjoyed the flotsam that Tam had thrown against the door, blocking the exit that contained Bennett and Anghelloise. They waited in anticipation as Tam had time to consider his next move. What would be the best way to stop Artagan? *Destroy his suit. Kill him. Render him unconscious.* But Artagan was on the move again.

He strode across the room toward Tam with a murderous look in his eye. "You seem almost unable to be harmed in that suit of yours..."

He turned to the crowd. His right hand came up and a man from the first row rose off the balcony and was flung at Tam. The man screamed as his body connected with Tam's, blood splattering everywhere, his broken body clattering to the floor. Tam reeled at the sound of flesh being rendered and bones cracking apart. The man gurgled his last few breaths.

The fickle crowd was now screaming murder at Artagan. Before, they had cheered him. Now, they screamed like frightened children as they sprang toward the exits.

More of them were lifted from the crowd and flung at Tam, who stumbled. There were now three bodies lying on top of him, bleeding or dying. He retched in his suit, and the computer struggled to evacuate the vomit from his mask before he breathed in his own stomach acid. Another landed on him. He was on the ground with four bodies on top of him. Three more arrived, slamming into the others. Before long, there were more than twenty-five dead or dying bodies piled on top of him.

His face plate was covered in blood, blinding him. Only the sensors in his visor could help him. He continued to lay still, allowing the bodies to accumulate, unsure how to stop the madness. The weight was starting to grow oppressive.

Artagan was laughing hysterically. Bodies started arriving in parts: body first, head second—each with a horrified look on their face.

Kruger had been distracted from his injury. He was in a chair, cheering and gloating. His buttock was bandaged, and it was clear he was high on painkillers. He was loving the spectacle. But it was short-lived. The rest of the audience had cleared the room. There were no more bodies to throw at Tam. Kruger was disappointed.

"Kill him, Artagan. Render his body into as many pieces as you can. Pull him apart!"

Only the sounds of death came from the floor. Artagan strode across the room to the pile of bodies and began wading through them, tossing them aside as he dug for Tam. Finding him, he grabbed Tam by the back of his suit and flung him against the bulkhead, strode over to him, picked him up, then threw him across the room into the opposite wall. He did this again and again, smashing him against both walls. Finally, Artagan lifted him up by the neck and started banging him against the same wall, again and again.

"I may not be able to do this mentally," sneered Artagan, "but I can use the strength of the suit to kill you!"

Tam continued to panic, breathing heavily, jerking his appendages in every direction as he tried to orient himself. He could not. His suit was overloading. He heard a cracking sound, and the visor went dead. The dreaded pounding slowed as Artagan stopped to check his handiwork.

"Had enough, Tam?" he demanded. "I can now sense your thoughts. You're just a scared animal! Maybe I should put you out of your misery!"

He threw him to the floor.

Tam lay there, an echo flashing through his mind: *[Don't fight the current.]*

He blanked out his mind and let his body go limp as though he'd passed out. Artagan raised his right hand, dragged him across the floor, and lifted his slumping body into his original chair.

Artagan turned to Kruger standing on his platform. "It is done! I've defeated him. I want what you've promised me."

"My dear boy! You have certainly done amazing things today. You've entertained me to no end. There is still one thing left to do!"

"Oh?"

"Bring me the other two, and our deal is set."

"Fine."

He strode to the pile of rock and rendered metal and started to mentally lift the chunks away. As he reached the final bulkhead piece, it began to vibrate and glow. As he lifted his hand to throw it aside with his mind, it moved by itself. A sound came through so suddenly, he was stunned. Singing voices poured out. He clamped his hands to his helmet, trying to block it from his head. But the suit couldn't protect him.

Through the hole made in the door stood two silhouettes. They were both standing with their hands raised toward Artagan. The volume increased and Artagan began to vibrate, too. His suit tried to respond, then gave up.

Tam suddenly sprang from his slump in the chair and reached for Artagan, grasped his helmet, and pulled hard. The singing bent around him and continued to flow to Artagan.

Artagan shuddered as Tam ripped his helmet off to force his senses under direct effect of the song. Distracted, Artagan ignored Tam as he tried to fight the Siren song, his hands to his ears. He grimaced as he fell to his knees.

After a few false starts, the computer screen in Tam's visor buzzed and came back into life. *Bless the Goddesses and this suit!* he thought. He directed his hand and mind toward the medical bags lying around Kruger, lifted them off the floor, and delivered them to his feet. He quickly found what he was searching for.

Tam released his grip on Artagan and instructed the living cloth to do its job as it wrapped around him, injecting needles into him as he screamed in defiance, realizing he was trapped. His head flopped to one side as he lost consciousness and tumbled to the ground.

Tam stumbled a bit, pulling off his helmet. He began to peel off the suit. The singing began to change focus from Artagan to Kruger, who promptly flopped down into his chair, eyes wide. The singing continued for a short while longer, then slowly faded, leaving everyone with a ringing in their ears like the silence left after a loud noise.

Anghelloise and Bennett lowered their hands, then stepped through the hole in the door. They were a little disheveled, but had smiles on their faces.

"You're both OK!" shouted Tam. "How on Alorion did you succeed in contacting the Sirens?!"

He ran to them and embraced them both.

"Nice to see you in one piece, too!" chirped Anghelloise. "The Sirens were always there, just waiting for things to play out. It was a matter of time before Artagan slipped up."

"More good news! *Nimbus* was also able to make contact with the *Faramund*," added Bennett. "Farthing is on his way to evacuate the prisoners."

"Goddesses! That is wonderful news," smiled Tam. "Bennett, you were unconscious!"

"I was. Luckily, by the grace of all things in this galaxy, I was healed by the Sirens' singing. We make quite a team, I must say!"

The group turned and looked at Artagan, bound in his living cloth.

"We'd better get him in a cell," suggested Tam. "I don't think any of the workers will try to stop us now that these two have been defeated. What should we do with Kruger?"

"We should take him with us," responded Anghelloise. "Bennett, would you be willing to transport him to the *Faramund* for delivery to the Sirens?"

"I can do you one better," replied Bennett. "I'll deliver him myself, if you'll come, too!"

The group nodded in agreement.

"Please, let's get Kruger into living cloth and put both of them in a holding cell while we get Brogan," pleaded Tam.

"Of course, my boy!" said Anghelloise. "Let's get to work."

The crew delivered Artagan in his comatose state into a cell beside Brogan's old one. They then delivered Kruger to the same place, bound in living cloth, and comatose himself. They brought him on a flat trolley, as he was too heavy to lift.

Workers began to appear. They were amazed at the outcome after having fled the Artagan's wrath earlier.

Sorting out the hierarchy took some time. They finally found the warden and, upon the counsel of Anghelloise, he was put back in charge. Grayson and Rothman were charged with guarding the two prisoners.

"I would suggest the two of you do a good job of supervising those two," said Anghelloise. "Keeping them there will go a long way for you two if this comes to council or trial."

Grayson and Rothman quietly nodded their heads with disappointment, turned, went to the cell, and closed the door behind them.

"You don't suppose they'll do anything bad, do you?" inquired Tam.

"Not if they want a chance at their trial for crimes against the people," she replied. "Let's let Farthing deal with them when he arrives. He has the experience."

Everyone nodded and shivered as they considered what those two were capable of.

"I know where Brogan is!" announced Tam. "I plucked it from Kruger's mind before we wrapped him up. He's in a storage room behind the arena. I'm going to get him."

"Whoa, Tam. Hold on there," said Bennett. "I believe it would be prudent to travel as a group to find him. We will give you time to be alone with him once the base has been secured."

"Farthing should be here soon," added Anghelloise. "In the meantime, let's go get Brogan!"

Tam couldn't reply through his tears. He just nodded and took their hands as they went to find the room behind the bleachers.

∞

Kruger was still spasming in his living cloth. A moan issued from him. The two men jumped.

"He's conscious!" exclaimed Grayson.

"We'd better check him over."

The men moved to Kruger and pulled him onto his back. His head flopped toward them, and his eyes popped open.

"Get me out of here!" he moaned. It would seem that his weight had played to his favor, keeping him from totally falling comatose.

The men's eyes widened.

"Get me out and your reward will be beyond your imagination! I... know who you... two... are... Help me... and you will be... safe."

They looked at each other and then at Kruger. To them, it was an easy decision. Helping the Magistrate and winning his approval would be better than being free to return to a dreary existence with the other workers. They wanted a life like they had lived, with special benefits.

They began shutting down the living cloth connections. They removed it once it was inert. Kruger slowly regained his senses. He was soon demanding to be propped upright.

"Go to my shuttle and prepare it for launch. First, though, help me into a chair!"

"Yes, your Magistrate!" exclaimed Grayson. "Immediately, sire!"

The two men heaved his massive body from the table onto the chair beside the bed.

"In my office is a machine that I must take with me. Go get it—and also, prepare that fool for departure. Which one of you is a pilot?"

Rothman nodded. "I am, sire."

"After retrieving the machine, get to the shuttle—and take that idiot with you. Keep him sedated in the living cloth. I don't want him to wake up, under any circumstance!"

The two men moved to fulfill Kruger's orders. They prepped Artagan, moved him to a gurney, and pushed him out of the room.

"Sire, we will return shortly."

"Make it fast, or I'll change my mind. I want proof of your loyalty. Make this work, and you will have freedom to participate in experiments on the new prisoners I acquire!"

In less than an hour, the three men were on a cart traveling to the shuttle bay, Kruger hiding under blankets, looking like a hospital patient. The other two resembled hospital staff transporting him.

Artagan was already in the shuttle, unconscious, along with the Ancient artifact, which had been carefully secured. In another thirty minutes, they were leaving orbit for the awaiting warships.

Chapter 59
Crossroads

Tam strode to the door of Brogan's cell without hesitation. Tears were streaming down his face. He wasn't in the mood to talk or share his pain and anxiety with anyone. All he wanted was to open the door and be reunited with Brogan. After all the suffering—everyone's life being turned upside down—he wanted to find something like normalcy.

Anghelloise and Bennett placed their arms around him. There was no need for words.

[We *sense nothing on the other side of the door—except perhaps a faint sign of Brogan.*]

[*Neither do I. But he is there. I need to be with him!*]

"Then let's do this!" said Anghelloise out loud.

Tam pushed the handle, and the door slowly swung open into a dark room. Nothing was inside but the bed at the far side of the room, barely visible. Tam walked forward and the automatic lights began to illuminate the room.

There, on the far bed, was a body lying in living cloth. Brogan. As Tam looked more closely, he noticed the cloth was rising and falling, showing he was breathing. The dials and sensors attached were blinking and clicking. There was also the sound of a respirator and pumps that turned on to remove or replace liquids.

"Brogan!!" Tam moved quickly to the bed and looked into the face of his lover. "What have they done to you?!"

The sobs gave way to a flood as Tam broke down, leaning on the bed's edge, his hands trembling as he reached for Brogan's face. He slowly touched him, his hands sliding over his bandaged face to cup his head in his hands. He leaned down to kiss him.

[My love, I am here. You are safe. I have traveled so long and made so many mistakes. But, by the Goddesses' will, I am here to help you. Please come back!]

Anghelloise and Bennett strode silently to his side and placed their hands on his back.

"We can help you, Tam—and Brogan, too."

Tam was still unable to speak but forced a few thoughts out to them. *[Help bring my Brogan back to me, please! He has suffered too long. He deserves to be free!]*

"And so do you, young man!" said Anghelloise, tears running down her cheeks. "You have suffered just as long."

Bennett nodded in agreement. The man through whose eyes he had seen the world was very real to him now. He could not help but cry. "Tam, we will help him. Do you trust us?"

Tam nodded, still unable to speak.

"We need to revive him," said Anghelloise. She moved to the console and looked over the readings. "All of his vitals should be stored in memory blocks somewhere in the base. That should tell us what's happened to him since his internment."

She reached the video screen and selected vitals to be viewed.

"His heart is working, albeit slower than usual, due to the cloth. He is breathing through a respirator. Most of his internal organs seem to be fine, but his stomach is quite empty. He's been fed intravenously for such a long time."

She hoped for more good news. She swallowed and pulled up organ records.

"His kidneys are operating with some damage, but his liver is severely damaged. In spite of that his blood reading is fairly close to normal."

"Any damage to the rest of him?" asked Bennett.

"His arms and legs seem to have experienced some sort of trauma, as have his gluteal muscles. His sexual organs are inflamed with an infection, but nothing too severe. It can all be treated."

She frowned as she looked over the data.

"What is it?" asked Bennett gently.

"There are drugs in his system that have caused a block in your link," she said to Tam. "If I were to remove it from his system, you would begin to feel what he is feeling."

"Is that a wise idea?" asked Bennett.

"I believe only Tam can answer that. Tam, are you prepared to receive an onslaught of pain? It could overwhelm you. You may be injured, too. I advise caution."

Tam did not hesitate. "My Life-Line needs to be unhindered. I am ready to take anything on. I want to feel what he feels." He reached down to touch Brogan's face gently.

Anghelloise nodded, programming the changes into the living cloth. She squeezed Tam's arm. "Tam, take all the time you need. I don't think anyone will bother us now. The unit will notify me of anything important. We'll be only a thought away if you need us, and will stay out of your thoughts until you invite us back."

Tam nodded, and turned back to Brogan as she and Bennett left the room.

The lack of mental interaction deafened Tam. There was so much quiet, he couldn't imagine how much it would hurt to feel. "Brogan, we will be together again—I promise!"

Brogan's face began loosening, the grimace that was glued to his features turning to grief. Tears began to stream down his face, though he was still unable to move. Tam realized his tears were pouring down onto Brogan and mixing with his. He began to sob, cradling Brogan's head as a mixture of pain and confusion emanated from him.

[I want to share your pain, and my wellness with you—to give you strength and hope.]

Brogan's eyes opened, his mouth forming something that resembled a smile. Tam smiled back as he climbed onto the bed where Brogan lay. Tam cradled his body and cupped his chin so that they were looking into each other's eyes. The pain was becoming manageable.

[Brogan, think about being home again, on our farm, doing the things we loved to do. I'm not the best at this hero thing, but I've done everything I can to get to you. Now that it's almost over, I don't know what to say. All I can do is hold you and love you.]

Seeing the look in his eye, Tam knew what Brogan was feeling. It didn't take a Life-Line to know. [Brogan, your ability to share your Life-Line will return soon. Relax and let it happen. We will be together. I can't wait to feel your thoughts in mine. I want to be whole again.]

Brogan struggled to nod. He swallowed and mouthed the words, I love you.

"I love you too, Brogan."

Brogan smiled, closed his eyes, and slept. Peace reigned over the contours of worry on his face and, for the first time since his imprisonment, he slept without disturbance.

∞

"They'll be OK," said Bennett to Anghelloise in the hallway.

She nodded as she wiped away a tear. "It's going to be a long recovery. For both of them." She sighed. "I know it's not useful to wish that something didn't happen, but I do. They didn't deserve this. No one did."

"What do you think will happen to Kruger and Artagan?" inquired Bennett. "Who will take over the system's government?"

"That's a question for Mother Siren. I don't have a clue right now. What's important is to get all these men back to Alorion and treated for their physical and mental wounds." She sighed again. "Just getting them home and settled in will be a major chore."

"I'm here to help as much as I can. Speaking of which, Farthing should be reporting any moment now." Bennett stopped and pondered. [Nimbus, *are you there?*]

[*Yes, Bennett.*]

[*Status report, then.*]

[*Warships have been disabled. They are operating at maximum efficiency as far as life support systems are concerned. Weapons are offline. Propulsion, too. They will have approximately eight days of repairs. First ship to arrive from off-world will take five days.*]

[*And the* Faramund?]

[*She is on her way here with the entire crew ready to transport the prisoners off Corustloth to Alorion. The ship is about twenty minutes behind me. I should arrive in approximately fifteen, with Captain Farthing aboard.*]

[*Good to hear,* Nimbus. *How are you?*]

[*Operating at peak efficiency. I'm delighted you're concerned for me, Bennett.*]

[*Quite right,* Nimbus. *We will make quite the pair when we return to our homeworld.*]

Bennett turned to Anghelloise. "All is well. The *Faramund* and *Nimbus* will arrive within the hour. We need to get these men ready. Is there any way we can get the workers here to help?"

"I should think so. They're probably already planning how to get home. I doubt any would want to stay. I'll get busy and round them up. Will you watch Brogan and Tam for me?"

"I'd be honored."

Anghelloise smiled and hugged him. "We couldn't have done it without you."

"Nor you, Anghelloise."

She smiled and headed down the corridor. Bennett discreetly probed the room, to find the two men sleeping quietly in each other's arms. He smiled and sat down to wait.

∞

When *Nimbus* landed, Farthing was welcomed by Bennett.

"Mr. Farthing, I'm so glad to see you! We have Kruger and Artagan in custody. Tam is with Brogan now. Anghelloise is prepping the men to board the *Faramund* as soon as they arrive." Bennett smiled and got a whack on the back from Farthing.

"Good. And you didn't need my help!" He laughed.

"Oh, we could have used you so many times," replied Bennett.

"I have so many questions. This should be a great story, but I know it can wait. Aye, let's get ready for the *Faramund*. They will be here soon."

At that moment, Anghelloise received a signal in the command centre of the base from the *Faramund*. "This is Captain O'Keefe, requesting landing coordinates."

"*Faramund*, please use the second docking bay, and park beside the *Nimbus*. By the Goddesses, you're a welcome sight! We have quite a few passengers who will be happy to be aboard your ship as soon as possible. Well done, Captain O'Keefe! Let's get these men home!"

[One step closer to completing your plans, Mother.] Anghelloise smiled.

∞

At long last, everyone stood together in the landing bay area: Anghelloise, Farthing, Bennett, O'Keefe, and Tam, with Brogan in a wheelchair beside him. One could see in their eyes that their Life-Line was starting to reconnect. Color was coming back to Brogan's skin, his eyes returning to their clear blue.

The crew of the *Faramund* busied themselves getting the ship and the prisoners ready for boarding. Many men in living cloth had to be extracted and gradually awakened. Others, in comatose condition, were left in the cloth as they were loaded onto the ship.

"Captain O'Keefe, have you readied the brig for our two prisoners? We need them sedated and quiet in their cells," said Farthing.

"Ready when you are," she replied.

"Then let's get them loaded onto the ship immediately."

"Yes, Captain Farthing. I'll see to it myself." She turned and walked down the hallway to the area where Kruger and Artagan were held.

The others busied themselves with getting the prisoners moved from the base to the ship while Tam and Brogan retired to their room on the *Faramund* to rest.

Just then, Captain O'Keefe came running, almost out of breath. "I have bad news. Kruger and Artagan are nowhere to be found! Some of the workers claim they saw two men remove bodies earlier to the first shuttle bay."

Closer inspection of the bay found the Magistrate's shuttle gone, along with the two prisoners, Grayson and Rothman, the orderlies charged with his care.

"Blazing blue sapphires! What should we make of this?!" demanded Farthing.

"About the only thing we can do is get the men to Alorion as soon as possible and outrun Kruger, before he gets back to his seat at the Senate to wage war of the rest of the system!!" Anghelloise was alarmed. "How much longer before everyone is on board?!"

"Less than an hour," responded Captain O'Keefe.

"Then get aboard and ready the *Faramund* for departure," ordered Farthing.

"Aye, aye, Captain."

"Bennett, what are your plans?" inquired Farthing. "Are you coming with us?"

"I was sent here to ensure Tam and Brogan's safe arrival. My superior has indicated I need to go after Kruger and Artagan. *Nimbus* should be quite useful in tracking them down."

"My dear Bennett, you have truly been a wonder with all the help that you have given," responded Anghelloise. "Do you want me to go with you?"

Bennett smiled and looked down at the floor. "It would be an honor, but I believe your place is with the prisoners. I'm told their safety is paramount for both our worlds."

"Then, this is goodbye for now," said Anghelloise. She hugged Bennett.

Farthing slapped his back, then hugged the bewildered Bennett. "I'll miss you, too." He ran his hand down the side of Bennett's face and placed a very large kiss straight on his lips.

Bennett's eyes widened in astonishment, but he reciprocated.

"Here's hoping that I will return soon with good news, then!" he exclaimed, red-faced.

∞

Everyone was on board, and they were about to leave. Tam and Brogan were in their private room. Brogan was sitting by the window in his wheelchair, watching the launch sequences. Tam watched him from his seat on the couch.

"Brogan, our Life-Line is not yet completely healed. It's best you join me on the couch so that we can ready ourselves for curved space. We'll have many exits to deal with, and I want you right by my side."

"You're right. I need to lie down."

He moved slowly toward the couch. Tam got up to help him.

"I really want our Life-Line reconnected," said Tam. "You left earlier, and I had no idea where you were. I couldn't sense you at all."

He helped Brogan lie down on the couch before joining him. They snuggled up together.

"I'll not leave you again, Tam. I promise."

∞

The ship was now in orbit of Corustloth, readying for its first curved space jump.

Earlier, Tam had described his experiences with the exit of curved space. *Don't fight the current* had been regimented in prepping the mentalists for exit from curved space. Meditation practice was set up for all of them, so that the exits would not feel so extreme. They were taught to accept what was coming and thereby reduce the pain of what actually did, flowing with the waves of insanity as they left curved space. In combination with the use of sedatives, they could minimize the risk.

Everyone was settled into their rooms, the former prisoners prepped for the first exit, about three days later. All crew had been assigned to a group of them. Even Acting Captain O'Keefe was responsible for several men.

It was she who discovered something strange, which she reported immediately to Anghelloise. Nick, the bot, had been found tampered with. He was damaged so badly that no one was sure he could be repaired.

Anghelloise almost burst into tears when she saw him. "Who could have done this?!"

No one had an answer. The one piece of machinery capable of sensing anything out of the ordinary had been disabled. Speed would be of the utmost importance if the League was to succeed in delivering the prisoners before Kruger made his next play.

Chapter 60

Whose Revenge is it Anyway?

The *Faramund* made its final exit from curved space just outside the heavy traffic zones around Alorion. The view was different this time; the absence of warships was noticeable. Since Kruger's disappearance, the military had been absent. Instead, what the *Faramund* saw was the business of Alorion trade. Ships were coming and going with renewed confidence.

"*Starfinder*, this is Alorion ground control. Please acknowledge." Everyone breathed a little easier when the message came in. There might not be a battle after all.

"This is acting Captain O'Keefe of the *Faramund*, formerly known as the *Starfinder*. We are here to return the evacuees taken from Corustloth. Please allow us passage to Alorion."

"It is unusual for a rogue ship of pirates to announce their arrival, Captain O'Keefe!"

"Indeed!" she laughed. "But we are here on a mission of mercy, not of piracy. Do you grant us access?"

"You are cleared to dock. Ground control out."

"Wow! No searches, no seizing of ships or cargo. It seems Kruger's control over the system has been thankfully broken. Mother has been busy!" O'Keefe smiled and turned to the internal comm unit. "All hands, prepare for docking. Please report the status of your wards to your section leaders."

Reports began to come in from all over the ship. The men were waking up, all seemingly in better shape than before. The meditate-and-medicate setup, inspired by Tam's method of "not fighting the current," was working. Things were looking up for the crew. It shouldn't take much more to land in the port of Ali-Alorion and make contact with the Sirens.

Tam stirred in his chamber. Brogan, lying beside him, was still asleep.

He looks so haggard and thin. He's been through so much I've not shared in. I feel like I've been robbed—even it was to protect me from the horrors he experienced. He gently stroked Brogan's head and ran his hand down the side of his face. Tears welled in his eyes as he looked at his partner.

Brogan stirred in his sleep and started to murmur. Tam began to feel the link between them strengthen, and suddenly saw what Brogan was dreaming. The image was of Brogan, standing, his arms outstretched, in great pain. His body trembled as he screamed again and again. He arched his back, head flaying sideways—then, in an instant, he exploded in a rain of blood, bone, and flesh.

In reality, Brogan screamed aloud—as did Tam. He sat up, scrambling to escape, but encountered Tam slumping over him. They collapsed on the bed together, moaning in pain.

"What in the blue blazes of Alorion was that? It felt more than a dream!" Tam cried out. "Brogan, are you OK?"

Through his tears, he nodded and grabbed ahold of Tam. "Please don't let me go. I need you. Please help me." He was shaking uncontrollably.

[I'm here. I feel what you feel. We are in this together, my love.] Tam continued to hold Brogan, feeling the fear and the pain decrease in both of them. Their breathing was going back to normal. *[Brogan, I've seen parts of this dream before!]*

[You have? I remember parts of it, too.]

[I especially remember the pain you experienced in your arm.]

[I don't remember that.]

[I do. It felt like your arm was sliced open.]

[I have no clue where this is coming from, Tam. I don't recall that happening.]

Tam ran his hands down Brogan's arms, trying to make sense of the dreams. *[Could they be visions and not dreams? Is it possible to see something that has not yet happened?]*

There was a gentle tap at the door to their chambers. Tam sensed Anghelloise on the other side. He got up and opened it. She glided in.

"Are you both OK? I sensed a lot of anguish. Are either of you hurt?"

Tam returned to the couch and sat beside Brogan. "More bad dreams. We're both starting to wonder if they're visions of something that might happen."

"Curious. More explosions?" she asked.

Both men nodded.

"There are gaps in what we each see," explained Brogan. "Tam remembers his arm feeling like it was being sliced open."

"I remember that!" exclaimed Anghelloise. "Tam just about passed out, he was in so much pain. We were all so distressed. We didn't know what it was about."

"Maybe Mother can help us," suggested Tam. "There must be a way to find the truth."

"We can certainly ask her," she replied. "We should be landing in the Ali-Alorion spaceport within the hour. Then it's a short trip to the Convent!"

"At long last, we'll find an ending to this horror!" proclaimed Tam. "We can get back to our lives on our farm!"

"So long ago and so far away," mumbled Brogan. "I didn't think I'd ever see it again."

"Attention, everyone," O'Keefe's voice announced over the comm. "The *Faramund* is on its descent. Make yourselves comfortable and prepare for docking!"

"I'll be back after the docking, my dears!" chirped Anghelloise as she left.

[Tam, I feel something really bad is about to happen.]

[I know, Brog. I feel it, too.]

The *Faramund* arced downward through the atmosphere towards the spaceport.

Seeing the spaceport approach as the *Faramund* began docking felt like everything was coming full circle for Tam. This was where Brogan had been taken—where he had been left to stow himself away on the cargo ship.

So much had happened since those fateful days almost one whole Alorion year ago. So much sadness and loss had taken place. Many good people had perished.

[I know you feel very sad right now, Tam. But maybe now we can get back to what's important—our lives, our farm, and our friends.]

[What do you think Mother will say when she greets us?] asked Tam.

[We shall see.]

The *Faramund* made contact with the pylons attached to the top level of the spaceport.

"Attention, all sections: the *Faramund* has docked. Please be patient while the spaceport authority clears us," announced Farthing over the comm. "And Tam and Brogan Amergan-Faolin to the bridge, please. Anghelloise to the bridge, too."

[That's our cue, my love,] projected Tam to Brogan. *[We are one step closer to home.]*

∞

"I'm glad you're all here," Farthing said as everyone arrived. "The spaceport author-ity has given us clearance to disembark. The evacuees are to be cared for by the Sisters at the Convent. Mother Siren has indicated they'd be safest there."

"There is no resistance from the Senate?" Tam asked.

"None," replied Farthing. "They are glad to set up a new system for the people of our solar system—and rid the world of Kruger's horrors."

"And the Convent? Are we released to visit as ambassadors?"

"Whenever we wish!"

"Then, I suggest we go now," said Anghelloise. "Brogan, are you well enough to travel?"

Brogan nodded but said nothing. His mind was elsewhere.

"Alright, everyone," said Farthing. "Let's meet at the main airlock in about thirty minutes. We will coordinate the landing as a group. It will take quite a bit of work getting the former prisoners off the Faramund and down to the Convent."

Everyone headed back to their quarters to gather a few things. In their cabin, Brogan stood at the window without his wheelchair for the first time, staring toward the ground two hundred floors below. Tam approached him and touched his shoulder.

[It will be good to see Mother again. Maybe she can help us heal, both physically and mentally, from this tragedy.]

[I know. I need to do a few things before I leave. Could I meet you at the airlock?]

[Sure.]

[I'll be there soon, my love.]

Tam leaned over and kissed him on the lips. Brogan stayed distant, barely kissing back, before leaving the room.

Tam wondered if he'd ever see his old Brogan again. He was so out of character. There was no light in his soul—just darkness. Tam still could not feel all he felt. There were still holes in their Life-Line. He didn't even have a clue of what Brogan was doing right then. He hoped fervently that Mother could help.

Brogan continued down the hallway to the central meeting place and headed towards the chambers that held the former prisoners, a distant look in his eye. He surveyed those men still in living cloth, not yet revived, and sighed. There was still a lot of pain. He had been holding back, not allowing it to flow to Tam. As far as Tam was concerned, their Life-Line was repairing itself.

There was no indication as to what his brainwashed mind was preventing him from knowing.

∞

The group arrived by shuttle at the Convent amidst the singing of birds and a fresh breeze blowing off the bay. After weeks on the *Faramund*, it was very welcome.

"It's nice to have everyone here this time, Brogan included," said Anghelloise. "Now, if we could just contact Bennett."

Everyone nodded as they approached the door of the Convent.

Tam took a closer look at the door and the surrounding wood that made the door seem darker and thicker. There were more thorns on the walls than flowers—the opposite of what he remembered.

"It looks like the Sirens are preparing for war!" he exclaimed.

"Mother figures we need to be ready," replied Anghelloise, "though I can't say what for."

[Rest your minds and be at ease,] came a message from unknown origin. Everyone looked around to see that they'd all received it. *[Enter and be well. Peace will be here soon.]*

The thick brown door opened with its usual creak. The two guards stood there, smiling at them. Their white robes and red sashes, as usual, stood out against the thick incense smoke. The large group filed in, and the door creaked closed with a soft click.

It closes so quietly and lightly for such a heavy door, mused Tam. He was thrilled to be in the Convent once more.

They waited as more Sirens arrived to take in the former prisoners as a series of shuttles arrived. Once the intake was well underway, the guards led Farthing, Anghelloise, Brogan, and Tam down the halls past the ancient paintings and the mysterious singing. Tam felt the happiness he had the last time, though there seemed to be an underlining stress or anxiety that hadn't been apparent then. Time, it seemed, could affect even the most unchangeable things. He wished everything could be as it was before all this had happened.

The two Siren guards stopped at Mother's chamber door. The two seated priestesses rose in their flowing dresses and opened the door. The group walked into the blackened room just as Tam and Brogan had done what seemed like ages ago.

The guards closed the door and took up residence just inside, like two statues. Everyone stood in complete darkness. Brogan felt for Tam's hand and grasped it tightly.

[Easy, Brogan. No need to squeeze my hand into putty!]

Suddenly, he pushed Tam's hand away. Tam immediately lost his connection to him. He could be heard shuffling away from the group.

[Brogan, come back!] projected Tam.

[Anghelloise, Brogan is acting strangely. I can't feel his Life-Line!]

[I know, sweet man. Let me help.] She started to sing. There were no words—just a melody that made all present to stop in their tracks to listen. No one could hear or see Brogan. He had stopped somewhere in front of them. The singing must have done it. Anghelloise's voice was joined by others and started to cascade. The vibrations in the air became visible as light, frolicking about the room like firelight does around a campfire.

There, at the other end of the room, Mother Siren was looking out toward everyone. Brogan stood in front of her. As his arms came up, a scream issued from his mouth.

"By the Goddesses," cried Tam, "the dream is coming true! Brogan, no! Please! Don't!"

Chapter 61
The Apex

"*Nimbus*, are you sure the shuttle made its way to the warships?"

"Yes, Bennett. The trail ends in the shuttle bay of the lead ship."

The three remaining warships hung off the port bow. They were still in a state of disrepair. Lights and motion were detected as crews went about in tiny shuttles and spacesuits, making repairs and checking over systems.

"What would be the best way to recover Kruger and Artagan? I'm not a soldier. I should have brought Farthing with me."

"Fighting makes no sense," replied *Nimbus*. "You would lose, Bennett."

"I appreciate the honesty. So how do we get Kruger and Artagan off that ship? What do you propose we do? Fly right into their shuttle bay?"

"Yes, we should."

"You are acting so bizarre, *Nimbus*. It's like you know something I don't."

"Please pay attention to the viewscreen. Your answers will be found there." The ship turned away from the warships to empty space. "Be patient, Bennett!"

A shimmering wave of light began to materialize below them, expanding and spinning. It grew quite large, then collapsed on itself. As it collapsed, a ship appeared.

"It's a ship from home!!" exclaimed Bennett. "*Nimbus*, how long have you known?"

"Several days. I was told by Father not to distract you until it was important."

"So, this *is* important, then!" Bennett half-shouted. Suddenly, a very familiar thought pattern appeared to him.

[*My boy, you have done a remarkable job.*]

[*Father! You've come to meet me. Why?*]

[We need to get to those two men, Tam and Brogan, as soon as possible. They are the key to the Order's search! Please save your questions for later. I'll fill you in once we rendezvous.]

[Yes, Father.] Remembering his manners and Order protocol he also projected: *[Father, thank you for your belief in me. It is good to see you.]*

[Quite right, my boy.]

"*Nimbus*, please prepare for Father's arrival."

"Already underway, Bennett. The ships will be joined in mere minutes."

Bennett sat back onto his couch and laughed. This was all so overwhelming!

"Bennett, I notice an increase in your respiration and heart rate. Are you feeling OK?"

"I'm feeling as best as I could considering all that's happened."

"Would you like a little mist of sedative?"

"No!" Bennett exclaimed and then paused. "Sorry, *Nimbus*. I will be fine. Thank you for your concern."

"Of course, Bennett. Ships preparing for docking."

Father's ship pulled up portside of *Nimbus*. The ships shimmered as their sides merged.

"Docking complete. The ships are now joined. Father is coming now, as we speak."

Bennett took a deep breath, got off his couch, and went to meet him.

∞

Commander Maguire looked like he hadn't slept in a week. Everyone tried to avoid him, not looking directly at him as he passed or barked orders, save Razfar. He had no choice but to deal with the cantankerous man.

The ships continued to malfunction, despite all the repairs and checks the engineers had performed. Everyone was mystified as to why the warships sat there, useless. Razfar ran his fingers through his thick black hair, pondering what he was going to say to the commander when he made his next round—one he did almost with alarming frequency.

On cue, the commander entered the bridge. Razfar quickly stood.

"At blasted ease, Razfar. Keep working until you find out what's wrong. I take there is nothing new to report?"

"Nothing, sir." Razfar winced in anticipation of the biting remark that would come. But nothing did.

Maguire sat down in his captain's chair and sighed.

"Can I get you something, sir?" inquired Razfar carefully.

"Protocol be damned. Get me that bottle of Alorion whisky I keep in the meeting room. It's time we had a drink."

Razfar, with his back turned to the commander, almost sputtered saliva onto his station. This wasn't the commander he knew.

"Yes, sir. I'll get it immediately."

Returning with two glasses, Razfar poured one for the commander.

"Razfar, I want a real drink—double this, for Gods' sake!"

"Yes, sir."

"Pour one for yourself, too."

Razfar just about fainted when he heard that. The second glass almost tumbled out of his hand onto the floor.

"Thank you, sir. Very generous—and a little out of the ordinary, if I might respectfully add."

"Razfar, you are right. I've been nasty lately. You've performed admirably, and I wish to thank you for that. Are we any closer to finding out what's wrong?"

"Thank you, sir," he replied. "But to answer your question: no, there's still no news."

Maguire gulped a large swig of whisky. "Give me the bottle. This may be a long night."

"Yes, sir." Razfar rose and passed the bottle to the commander. "I can't seem to understand what's causing the malfunctions. The engineers have combed all three ships!"

"I know you're trying your best, Razfar. We all are."

"Thank you, sir."

"I've been doubly stressed since the Magistrate arrived. There was nothing I could do but put him in a room and tranquillize him. I may be put to death for that decision."

"I hope not, sir. We need a good commander like you."

"I've not been a very good one after that battle with the *Faramund* and that alien ship. Now there are these malfunctions. I feel like we're being manipulated by forces unknown to us."

"We've all performed to the best of our abilities, sir. We will keep trying."

"That's all I can ask for. You'd better get back to work. So should I." He rose and looked at the viewscreen. "Any progress on its use, Razfar?" He pointed at the screen.

"Nothing at the moment."

Maguire rose and walked toward the windows. Sometimes just looking with your own eyes could help. What he saw made him start with amazement.

"Razfar, there are two of those alien ships joined at the midsection approaching the shuttle bay. Get security down there, now!"

"Yes, sir, right away."

Maguire was already gone, running down the hallway to the exit. The bottle of whisky plunked to the floor and emptied itself onto the decking.

∞

"Father, it's so good to see you," said Bennett. "What brings you here?"

"We must rescue those two men, Tam and Brogan. They, along with you, are key to the Order finding what we've been seeking for eons. Let's get those men back to the Order's world."

"What about my mission to find Kruger and Artagan? The others are depending on me."

"Oh, of course. We can't have those two running around the galaxy with abilities like that. We must find them first."

Bennett took a seat on his couch. "*Nimbus*, continue into the shuttle bay of the lead warship. That's where we'll find Kruger."

"Understood, Bennett. Do you concur, Father?"

"Don't let me get in the way of your plan! Bennett's in charge here."

Bennett had to stop himself from falling off his couch. Father just smiled.

"Arrival in the warship's shuttle bay in five minutes," reported *Nimbus*.

They entered the shuttle bay several minutes later, landing beside Kruger's shuttle.

"I have Commander Maguire trying to contact you," announced *Nimbus*. "He's very animated, to put it mildly. Would you like to speak to him, Bennett?"

"Of course, *Nimbus*."

"Communications open."

"Captain Maguire, this is Bennett Davis. You must be wondering what we're doing here."

"That is an understatement!" he shouted. "What in the hell are you up to?! Are you responsible for all these malfunctions?! Step outside your ship and you will be shot on sight!!"

"You are rightly frustrated, commander. I'm here to parley a deal."

"Oh, really?!" Maguire slammed his hand on the console with a loud bang.

"I can help you with your repairs," said Bennett. "Maybe we could make a trade?"

"You caused this mess in the first place!" screamed Maguire. "I don't know you, but all our problems started when you appeared. Maybe you helped those damned pirates do it!"

"Actually, I refused to do so. Their acting captain wanted to destroy you. But I am obliged by my duty not to."

"Bennett—" started *Nimbus.*

"Quiet!" he snapped. "Maguire, here's the deal: give me Kruger and Artagan, and once we're off ship, I'll instruct my computer to relay all the repairs to your computer. It's that simple. I disabled your ships and can reverse that just as easily."

"What gives you the right?!" stuttered Maguire. He took a deep breath and paused. "Give me a few minutes to think it over. I'll message you shortly. Maguire out." His face faded.

"Well played," said Father.

"*Nimbus,* in future conversations with Maguire, please do not interrupt me," said Bennett. "I know you were the one who orchestrated the shutdowns, but that's irrelevant to him."

"Understood," replied *Nimbus.*

"You really think he'll be willing to give up the two men so easily?" inquired Father.

"No, not at all. I'll have to prove to him that we're serious."

The console beeped. "Maguire is ready to speak," announced *Nimbus.*

"Open the channel. Let's hear what he has to say."

"Davis, I've thought about your offer. No deal. Leave—or we will be forced to take your ship by force."

"I'm sorry to hear that, Commander Maguire," said Bennett. "Our quarrel is not with you. We wish you no harm. We'll help you once Kruger is in the hands of the authorities."

"Kruger is my superior! He'll have me court-marshaled for treason!"

"Take a listen to the communication coming from Alorion and the other planets on the far side of the system. They are celebrating that Kruger is no longer in power! He has no hold on you anymore," insisted Bennett.

"Bennett—" began *Nimbus.*

"I told you, not now!"

"Bennett!"

"What is it?" he started and then paused. "Cut communications!"

"Channel closed. I am sorry to bother you, but there are soldiers surrounding the ship. They have weapons. They may prove to have the ability to damage me. Instructions?"

Bennett looked at Father, who sat on his couch with his hands clasped together, watching him.

"Suggestions?"

None were forthcoming.

"*Nimbus*, shut down all their systems, including life support. I want all their lights out for five minutes. Then turn them back on. Maybe he'll change his mind then."

The vibrations of the ship began to grow.

"They've begun firing on my hull. No damage yet, but there is potential."

"Do they have spacesuits?"

"No."

"Shut off the power anyway. Is there any way you can defend yourself without killing them?"

"Yes. My priority is not to kill," replied *Nimbus*.

"I know," Bennett replied. "Do it. Please."

Bennett got up from his couch and walked to the view port. He saw the personnel firing on *Nimbus* with projectile weapons. No particle beams yet.

"Activating," announced *Nimbus*.

The lights all blinked out, including the emergency ones. The shuttle bay was in total darkness. The vibration of the shots stopped.

"That should show them," said Bennett. "What are they doing now?"

"They're fumbling around me," replied *Nimbus*. "They have handheld lights. Wait! They're leaving! Three minutes until power restored."

"Father, I feel horrible for doing this. I know that Tam and Brogan are so very important. It just seems wrong to have to do this, and I know this is the only way."

"Bennett, I do not see any other way, either. Let me tell you what I've learned. Perhaps it will give you hope. While you've been away, I've been busy with the task of finding any other level ten conduits such as yourself. It seems you are the only one." He smiled at Bennett.

Bennett smiled back, his eyes wide and questioning.

"What I've been puzzling over is why the messages stop close to the Messier black hole at the centre of our galaxy. There are mentalists who are relatively close to it, but all the messages stop there, never entering it."

"That's impossible! Everything eventually goes into a black hole—even mental energy!"

"My thoughts exactly. Something is preventing that from happening. There is no current comprehensible reason for it. Anything that powerful or advanced is beyond our understanding!"

"That means..." Bennett began.

"Yes!" exclaimed Father.

The console beeped. "Five minutes are up. Restoring all systems," reported *Nimbus*. "And Maguire is signaling!"

"Open the channel."

"What in the Gods' names are you doing?!" exclaimed Commander Maguire. "Are you planning on killing everyone on board with this blasted technology of yours? I've no choice but to trust you will keep your end of the bargain once I release the two men."

"I do not wish to harm you. I just want Kruger and Artagan. It is for everyone's benefit—even yours. You may not see that now, but will in time. Please have the two brought to my ship immediately. Make sure they are placed in living cloth and heavily sedated beforehand." Bennett paused to catch a thought from Maguire. "Oh, and please bring the artifact, too."

"For Gods' sake!" Maguire paused and stood still for a moment. "Fine—the two men and the machine. Maguire out."

"Think he'll try to trick us?" asked Bennett.

"I sense he won't," replied Father.

∞

Nimbus arced up away from Corustloth and the three warships, with the two captives heavily sedated and the Ancient artifact neatly stored in the storage compartment. The exchange had happened without incident, and Bennett had indicated he would make repairs to the ship as *Nimbus* departed.

"Begin the process, *Nimbus*. Bring all systems back online except weapons," he ordered.

"What about curved space capability?" asked *Nimbus*.

"Give that back to them. It will be more than two weeks before they arrive home. We can get there much quicker. Calculate the coordinates to fold space from here to Alorion," he requested.

"Calculations should take less than an hour and we should be underway in about two," reported *Nimbus*. "We could be in orbit of Alorion in less than five."

"What is the status of the *Faramund?*"

"They left over a day and a half ago, Captain Davis. My sensors indicate they currently past the first curved space pylon and are heading to Alorion."

"We will get there ahead of them," said Bennett. "What should we do until the *Faramund* arrives, Father?"

"We can rest out of sight and watch the proceedings without being discovered. When the *Faramund* arrives, we can rendezvous with them."

"Let's do it," said Bennett.

∞

The singing escalated, growing louder. Brogan stood frozen with the scream still on his lips, a frenzied look on his face. Tam was frozen, too, about four paces in front of Farthing.

"What in blue blazes of Alorion is going on?" yelled Farthing. "Why are they frozen?!"

"Mother can't respond right now," shouted Anghelloise over the singing. "The Sirens are holding Tam and Brogan in suspension. Brogan, it appears, has six bombs lodged in his arms, legs, and buttocks. If they go off, the entire Convent will be destroyed. Mother knew as soon as we entered the room that he was a danger."

"What can I do?!" shouted Farthing.

"You were once linked to Tam, weren't you?"

"Yes, to both of them! Technically, I still am, but haven't tried to make contact with either since." He pondered the situation. "Goddesses! I feel so useless!"

"My man, stop feeling sorry for yourself! Get yourself into Tam's mind!"

"I'll try!" he shouted back.

"Good! I just received a mental message that can't wait. I'll be back as soon as I can." With that, Anghelloise sailed out of the room, closing the door behind her.

Farthing made his attempt. *[Tam, I'm here. I want to try to help. Can you let me know if you're receiving any of this?]*

There was no response.

[Tam, I need you to hear me. Brogan is in mortal danger—and you are, too! Please, mate, link with me, and maybe I can help!]

Suddenly, a sound like white noise echoed through Farthing's mind. A signal of one long burst, three short ones, then a silent pause, repeating over and over. It was coming from Tam!

The pattern stopped after repeating eight times.

Farthing tried again: [*Tam, I need to communicate with you. You are suspended in time. Something is about to go horribly wrong. If this continues, the Convent will be destroyed by the bombs implanted in Brogan.*]

There was no response from Tam—just a sense of total fear and confusion.

[*I repeat, Tam: the entire Convent is in danger. We will do what we can. Hold on!*]

The pulses started again. Tam was sending them, perhaps out of desperation.

"If only we could make the bombs inert!" he shouted to no one in particular. The Sirens couldn't hear him because of the singing. Tam couldn't either. Farthing moved closer to Mother, who was sitting in the shadows outside the ring of light in the middle of the room. She was gripping the arms of her chair, clearly using every bit of energy she could in the singing.

Farthing suspected that Mother was the only reason Brogan had not exploded into a million fragments, taking everyone with him. Farthing swallowed hard and looked her in the eyes. They moved slightly toward him momentarily. She knew he was there!

[*Mother, I've made contact with Tam.*]

She nodded slightly.

[*He sent me a message that repeats: one long noise, three short ones, and a pause.*]

She nodded slightly.

[*Is that important?*]

She nodded more pronouncedly.

[*That's it!*] she projected. [*I need Anghelloise here!*]

Farthing could see the strain on her face. She couldn't hold on much longer. He swallowed hard, then opened his mouth, his voice joining the Sirens, hoping to strengthen them just a little bit. Mother managed a smile in return.

The door opened and Anghelloise returned with Bennett, Kruger, and Artagan in tow. Bennett was carrying a machine of some sort.

Farthing's eyes got bigger at the implausible situation. What on Alorion was going on?

Anghelloise tugged on Kruger's ropes, forcing him to approach Tam—clearly not what he wanted to do. He pulled a syringe came from his pocket and he plunged it into Tam's bicep. He emptied the entire contents into Tam's system.

Within minutes, Tam awoke, tumbling to the floor. Bennett rushed to help him to his feet.

The singing took on a higher pitch. Did it mean the song was almost over? Were the Sirens losing control over the suspension? Farthing could only guess as to what was going on. He continued to sing as hard as he could. Anghelloise joined in, lowering her voice to make it stronger. There was no doubt she had incredible Siren strength!

Bennett sensed Tam was no longer connected to Brogan due to the injection Kruger had given him. Tam stirred and opened his eyes. He started, his eyes panicked, before realizing he was conscious.

Bennett leaned down and spoke into his ear: "You need to get up and come outside the room with me for a few moments. It's too hard for you to link with me. Let me help you up."

He took his arm and helped him to his feet. They stumbled to the door and went through, closing it behind them. The singing was still loud, but they could hear each other much better.

"Tam, do you know what's happened?"

Tam nodded. "Brogan is going to die if the Sirens stop singing. He'll explode, taking the entire Convent with him. I'll die the same time he does." A tear slid down the side of his cheek. "I'm not crying for myself—I cry for him. I cry for all of you."

Bennett put his arm around Tam. "I understand. We have to try something to prevent him from exploding and save the Convent."

"To do that, both Brogan and I will have to die, won't we?"

"Yes," replied Bennett, letting go of Tam. The comment was lost in the sound of the singing. "I'm so sorry."

Tam nodded. "So if we die, the bombs might not go off?"

Bennett nodded, a tear sliding down his cheek. He looked into the eyes of the man he'd known so intimately through their connection from across the galaxy. It was like he had lived a big part of Tam's life. He felt like the decision would rip a large chunk out of him. Only Father knew Bennett had shared so much with him.

Father! He had suggested Father stay in *Nimbus* until the issue was sorted. He couldn't jeopardize the life of the leader of the Order to save Tam and Brogan. That had been his earlier call. Now, he wasn't so sure.

He turned his mind to contacting him.

[We need you, Father. Come at once. The Guardian Sirens will let you pass. I'll ensure that. You need to be at the Mother Siren's meeting room. Come as fast as you can!]

[Yes, Bennett. I'm on my way.]

Bennett turned to Tam to see Kruger putting another syringe into Tam's arm.

Within minutes, it was clear the connection had been reestablished. Tam was linked with Brogan again. Kruger administered a third syringe to Tam, and he tumbled to the floor. After a few seconds, Brogan fell, too, coming out of suspension. He was intact, but they both now lay on the floor, dying. The singing stopped and the room fell silent.

Without thinking, Farthing dragged Tam to Brogan's side. They lay side by side, each touching the other physically and mentally as the life began to fade out of them.

Farthing fell to his knees beside his two friends, his big hulk of a body shuddering and slouching forward in sadness, holding the hands of the two dying men.

Anghelloise yelled out suddenly: "Mother! Oh, dear Goddesses! Mother!" She rushed over to her slouching in her chair. Anghelloise took her hand and knelt beside her. "Mother, the Sirens have saved the Convent and all those inside except Tam and Brogan. Their sacrifice helped us."

Anghelloise turned to Kruger and glared.

"You demon! You've destroyed so many lives! Why?!"

"You inject me with truth serum, and I am forced to do things I do not want to, you witch. I wish for the destruction of all you degenerates, purifying this system and making a world for me to use for my pleasure. I helped save your cult of women and your friends because I was forced to!" Kruger spat at Anghelloise. "I am only telling the truth!"

With a loud scream, Farthing stood and rushed toward him. "It is your truth, not ours!! You should be put to death for what you've done to those prisoners, the people of this system, and the two dead men lying on the floor!!" His hands reached for Kruger's throat and clasped on tightly. Kruger gurgled and tried to wiggle out of his grasp.

"Stop, Mr. Farthing!" yelled Bennett. He approached Farthing and placed his hands on his, grasping Kruger. "Don't be like him, even though you've been programmed that way! I know you! You're strong enough to break the programming and find peace! Please!"

Bennett felt the tense muscles in Farthing's arms slowly loosen, letting go of Kruger's throat, who tumbled to floor, unconscious. The big man began to weep. He wept for his two dead friends on the floor. He wept for the Sirens' struggle. He wept for those lost because of Kruger.

Bennett sensed all this in Farthing and touched his downcast face. He began to cry, too.

"Farthing, you've also long suffered at the hands of Kruger," said Anghelloise, still holding Mother's hand. "Everyone! Take heart. We still have lots of work to do! Now's not the time to grieve, but to fight for all we deserve and have fought for so hard! Help is coming!"

The door opened and a long line of Sirens proceeded in, accompanied by a man in a brown robe. The man's eyes were wide as they explored the room. The Sirens surrounded Mother and Anghelloise.

"Father! You're here!" exclaimed Bennett. "Is there anything we can do?"

"How long have they been dead?" he asked.

"Less than two minutes," replied Anghelloise.

"Begin resuscitating the two men. Their brains may still be functioning though their bodies are not. We must keep them alive! Is there anyone who can do this?"

Farthing raised his hand. Artagan, filled with mental dampening medication and truth serum, did too. "Get oxygen into their systems immediately!"

Farthing moved to Tam, glaring at Artagan as he moved to Brogan's side.

"I'm watching you, leech," Farthing warned. Artagan, too drugged up, just proceeded as the serum made him do. They began artificial resuscitation.

"Bennett, my boy! Snap out of it! Where are the 566 men that were imprisoned on the prison world?"

"They have been settled into the Convent's lodging. Why?"

"They can help us," said Father. "We need to call upon them to link together to bring these two back! Their lives are important for more than all of you know! Move, boy! Assemble them here—and in the hallway if there's not enough room! I'll explain later."

"But that means, Artagan... the living cloth..." Bennett stuttered.

"Get going!"

Bennett nodded, wide-eyed, and ran from the room.

"Madame Anghelloise, how is Mother?"

"She is weak from the sustained singing. She is not yet coherent enough to communicate. She needs more time."

"How much time?" asked Father.

"We should give her time to recover before she can help."

"We need Artagan coherent enough to be able to link the men as he did before."

"To do that, we need to wake Kruger up again. He has the expertise with the drugs. Do you think that is wise, letting those two loose in here? Would Artagan turn on all of us? I don't want a battle between those men and the Sirens. It would destroy everything we've worked for."

"I believe I can help there," said Father. "I can instill fear of noncompliance in him when he recovers from the inhibitors. I've had to use it on some of my apprentices for their own protection. Poor Bennett has received a lot of it. Now look at him! I've underestimated him."

"Sadly, I've seen a similar relationship develop between Farthing and Tam," Anghelloise remarked. She looked at Farthing and Tam lying on the floor beside Brogan. Both Artagan and Farthing were continuing to massage their hearts, forcing oxygen into their lungs. "It's ironic that we must rely on the very men who tried to kill us to save Tam and Brogan."

Father nodded. "Let's wake up Kruger first, then treat Artagan."

"Agreed." Anghelloise let go of Mother's hand and rose, moving toward Kruger, lying on the floor, face up, jowls sagging with their weight. She shivered a bit as she saw the man who had tried to kill everyone in the room. There was spittle running down his fleshy face from the corner of his mouth. The satchel containing the syringes was by his side. *If only we had time to investigate the injections—then, we wouldn't have to use him. But we don't have any time to spare in saving Tam and Brogan!* She shook her head, nudging his leg. "Wake up!"

Nothing.

[Wake up, Kruger. This is an order!]

Kruger began to stir, a stern and annoyed look on his face as he awoke. "You dare speak to me that way, you demented witch?"

"I do!" replied Anghelloise. "You have no choice. Get up and administer the drug to Artagan to release him from the impediment medication."

"You'd have me use what I used to nearly destroy you? How desperate you must be!" Kruger giggled, then, for a few painfully slow and awkward moments, pushed himself to his feet.

"You'll do as you're told. You're not in control now," retorted Anghelloise.

"Really? Exactly what are you going to do?! Too bad that one didn't blow up as planned." He pointed at Brogan. "I'd hoped to be done with the whole lot of you by now." He snorted. "Why exactly do you want me to release Artagan? He'll be dangerous to you."

"We need Artagan to make contact with the men who were imprisoned by you. They may be able to assist in saving these men."

"They are important to the whole galaxy," agreed Father. "You've met my associate, Bennett Davis. I'm his leader. I am known as Father."

"Well, Father, if you really are that naive, by all means, let me release Artagan!" Kruger announced. He opened the satchel attached to his belt and removed another syringe.

Father's eyes sharpened and closed slightly. He was focusing on Kruger, trying to determine whether he was telling the truth or about to do something devious.

It seems he will do as he's been asked. But he thinks it will be to his benefit.

Kruger shuffled slowly over to Artagan, who was still trying to resuscitate Brogan. He prepped the syringe, then plunged it into his arm. Artagan squealed in pain, never stopping applying pressure to Brogan's chest, giving him breath intermittently, as he'd been trained.

Suddenly, he stopped.

"What's going on? Why am I doing this? This man means nothing to me!"

"You'll do as we ask, Artagan," warned Anghelloise. "Continue the resuscitation."

Father glared at Artagan and he faltered, before promptly calming down.

"As you wish." He continued as he was asked.

Bennett returned, and men started filing in through the door. Soon, there were more than fifty men in the room. The rest were in the surrounding hallways, some still in their living cloths.

"Father, the men are here and waiting. I understand you want Artagan to link to them, but won't they need to be sedated and connected to the living cloth?"

"No, they do not. You will be the conduit."

"How am I to do that? I'm not going to be able to exit curved space here and cause some sort of connection," lamented Bennett. "I don't know how!"

"My boy, I can guide you as I have before. You know I am a passive mentalist. I can point your mind in the right direction, and you, an active mentalist, will channel Artagan's thoughts through to the men. The mental energy of all the men may be enough to revive them."

"I am ready, Father." Bennett said. "Artagan, are you?"

"Yes. I am," he replied. *[I'll do my best, as I did before.]*

[I'm sure you will, Artagan. We're not going to let that happen, though,] returned Father.

Artagan felt for the connection to the artifact, making contact with it and then Bennett. A burst of energy seemed to pass through, then suddenly the men's minds were there for his bidding!

[Artagan, hold your course! Serve to wake those two men from their deathly sleep!]

Artagan shuddered as he paused, then sported an evil grin as he looked Father straight in the eye. After an intense few moments as he tried to battle with Father, he instead capitulated, suddenly feeling sheepish. He then allowed the energy to flow from him to Bennett, who transmitted to the men lying on the floor.

Suddenly, the two men shuddered, and their arms and legs flailed, but nothing more happened.

"It's not working!" exclaimed Anghelloise. "It doesn't seem to make a difference. We need more help!" *Mother, can you help? We need the Sirens! Please! Do you have the strength?*

Mother did not speak, but nodded her head slowly. The Sirens began to sing. As more joined in the song, the intensity increased. Soon, every Siren in the Convent was singing. As the song merged into one big stream, the song channeled through Anghelloise to Bennett, merging with the men's thoughts. Mother's hands started to quiver, and she gasped.

Anghelloise turned her thoughts from Artagan to Mother. She was amazed to see the Siren song channel from her to Bennett and join the voices and minds of all the men and women.

Tam and Brogan stopped flailing and began to vibrate like a string on an instrument that had been plucked. Both Farthing and Artagan got up and off the two men, stopping resuscitation. Their bodies continued to vibrate, then slowly lifted off the floor, head first, torso, then legs. They floated above the group of singers, their bodies beginning to glow.

Suddenly, Tam emitted a sputter, and his head raised into normal position. His eyes were open, staring wildly into the heavens. His head turned to Brogan, who also began to revive. His eyes opened and turned to Tam.

The song intensified, rising an octave. Both men were now fully awake and aware of each other. Everyone in the room was linked via Bennett, and felt the Life-Line rejoining of Tam and Brogan. It came together almost like a thunderclap, the sound echoing again and again, taking on a form: one long burst, three short ones, then a beat of rest. It repeated again and again. As the signal got stronger, Bennett felt the burst he had experienced while coming out of curved space the first time. He was linking to the rest of the galaxy! He felt the joining of millions of men and, as luck would have it, many women, too. It seemed many of them could have been Sirens, had they known.

The numbers doubled and tripled until every mentalist in the entire galaxy was focused on one point in space and time: Tam and Brogan. The circle of light expanded around them until the entire room was bathed in a blue light, all the way up to the now visible cathedral ceiling of Mother's chambers far above their heads. The light enveloped everyone in the room, seeping through the cracks and holes, around doors, and through walls until all the men in the hallways and all the Sirens in the Convent were bathed in it. The singing then stopped, and silence fell.

Father sent a message to Bennett: *[We've succeeded more than I could hope! Instruct Tam and Brogan to turn their thoughts to the black hole at the centre of our galaxy. The coordinates are zero, zero, zero: The exact centre of the galaxy. My boy, do as you were destined!]*

Tam and Brogan received the message and turned their minds to the centre of the galaxy. Soon, the blue light enveloping the room became focused on them. It then burst upward and outward in a spiral, continuing the signal: one long burst, three short ones, and one pause.

The message, not bound by the speed of light, arrived at the black hole minutes later, as the minds of the entire galaxy focused on it. The signal did its job.

Described in images a human can understand, a door, of sorts, had opened, and a new signal had exited and responded in return.

Chapter 62

Take the Back Door, Please!

Anghelloise felt Mother's grip on her hand loosen. She turned toward her. She was gone, lifeless in her chair. The chore of uniting everyone had been too much. Anghelloise began to sob.

Father, taking his eyes off Tam and Brogan, leaned over and put his hand on her shoulder. "She did what she was supposed to do. If the Sirens are anything like the Order, someone will replace her, receiving her energy and her wisdom. It is ordained that when I pass on, someone will take my memories, experiences, and abilities and strengthen their own. Each successor becomes more powerful. I suspect you are to be hers."

He nodded back toward Tam and Brogan. She looked up and saw the blue light swirling around the two men. Tam and Brogan turned their eyes simultaneously to Anghelloise to look deep into hers. She felt something akin to electricity pouring into her body. The light continued to swirl, then descended towards her.

She opened her mind as the energy poured in. She began seeing all that Mother and those before her had been. The energy came at her in one long wave, three short ones, then a pause. She understood then that it was her time to take on Mother's role. She accepted it gladly, smiling at Tam and Brogan, who returned her smile, then turned their minds back to the blue light.

It was suddenly clear to them that the new signal was different in nature as the one they had sent to the centre of the galaxy!

The two men, still suspended in midair, again sent the signal of one long wave, three short ones, and a pause. It bounced back in a different pattern: one long wave, two short waves, and then five even shorter ones. The signal was returning from somewhere, and had merged with their signal!

The last wave arrived, then all was silent. The glowing blue light started to fade, and the two men slowly descended to the floor of the chamber as silence fell on the Convent.

Tam and Brogan stumbled towards each other and held each other close. Their eyes were closed as they leaned on each other. The rest of the men were exhausted. They all sat down unceremoniously where they were and immediately fell asleep.

The only person left standing was Bennett. He continued to stand where he'd been when the whole situation began, staring forward. Having all that energy channeled through him suddenly disappear was a kind of trauma.

Father saw this and went to him.

"My boy, let me help you. Your mind has been through an incredible ordeal."

Bennett slowly exhaled. "Father, I feel like I've been battered and beaten. My heart feels like it's broken. I feel so little hope."

"I understand. I'm here. Let me take ease you out of being a conduit, back to being my apprentice. After all, young man, you still have training to do! I can't let you go now, even if you are a level ten conduit. Can't have an inexperienced trainee running around!"

"I appreciate your support." He then promptly sat down on the floor and proceeded to fall asleep with the rest.

Father sat in his chair, as did Anghelloise. Farthing approached and knelt in front of her.

"I be at your service, Mother." He bowed from his position on his knee.

"Thank you, Farthing, my dear man." She turned to Father. "Any idea what the rest of the galaxy received after that? How much do they know about what happened here?"

"Well, the secret's out. The whole galaxy knows there was a communication from somewhere else."

"Agreed! I'm curious to know what Tam and Brogan received and what they experienced. I hope they can tell us more when they're able." She looked over at the two men. They were propped up against each other, sound asleep.

Farthing approached the two men, slowly untangling them and laying them on the floor.

"My Goddesses! Brogan! All his injuries are gone! He's returned to his original form!" The others looked in wonder. "I'll get them to a bed in a moment," he said. "As for the others, I'll let them sleep where they are. Would you request the sisters to check on them?"

"Certainly! They've been through a lot," Anghelloise replied. "We all have! Now, let's get Kruger and Artagan back into their cloths."

∞

Tam awakened to the sound of birds chirping through an open window and the sight of sunlight streaming onto the bed in which they lay. Brogan was beside him, awakening at the same time. *As it should be.*

[Good morning or afternoon... my love, Brogan.]

[Good day to you, too, my love. I'm so happy to be here with you.] Brogan sat up slowly and winced. *[I'm still sore.]*

[I know, my love, I feel it as you do.]

"I really need to find out what time it is," said Brogan aloud. It seemed almost brazen to speak when thoughts sufficed. He sat up and pulled the blanket back. Since he was wearing what he'd come in with, it was clear to him that someone had placed them here in order to sleep off what had happened.

He got up, opened the door, and peeked out. "Hey! Sister, please forgive me, but what time is it?"

[Tam, we have been asleep for the better part of two days and two nights.]

[Incredible!] Tam responded. *[All that caused us to sleep this long. When should we convey the message that was sent to us? Should we get up now and let them know?]*

[Yes. They have a right to know.]

∞

Anghelloise sat on her chair in the summoning chamber with Father, Bennett, and Farthing. The two days spent waiting for Tam and Brogan had made everyone a little anxious.

The door opened. Tam and Brogan entered and were ushered to chairs by two Sirens.

"Nothing at the moment, Sisters," said Anghelloise, seeing them turn to her. "Thanks."

The Sisters left. The room was silent as everyone turned to Tam and Brogan, expectant.

"Let's review the events," said Anghelloise. "Can you tell us what you saw?"

Tam cleared his throat. Brogan looked at the floor and shuffled his feet.

"Well," Tam began, "first of all, we now seem to be able to clearly read just about everyone in the Convent. It's been a bit distressing, as we haven't quite figured out how to shut out everyone's thoughts. It can be quite overwhelming!"

"I believe I can help with that!" announced Father. "Bennett probably can, too. He's been trained by me to be able to sift thoughts—and filter out those that aren't needed."

"The Order has been developing these techniques for centuries," added Bennett. "I'd be honored to help you two."

"Mates, we are so relieved to see you both back to normal," said Farthing. "Brogan, you seem completely healed."

Brogan nodded. "I am! Even my injuries from before are gone. Blessed be the Sirens!"

"I don't believe it was just the Sirens," said Anghelloise. "It was the collective mind of the galaxy that accomplished that. We are so happy to see you in wonderful shape, but could we get on to discussing the message you received?"

"What Anghelloise is saying, my mates," said Farthing, "is that we've all been waiting since you went to sleep. We're curious about what you experienced. Come on, my little blo's, tell us!"

Tam nodded and smiled, then responded: "What we saw was difficult to understand. The best way I can describe it is that a door opened—and there was someone on the other side."

"A door?!" cried Bennett.

"It was like there was a hole in our field of vision," said Tam. "The signal coming out of it allowed us to sense a group of people on the other side."

"They told us simply: [*We are glad to make contact. Come to us. We are waiting for your arrival!*] Then the door closed," explained Brogan.

"This door," pondered Father, "must be a message portal coming from outside of our galaxy." He reached for a satchel and pulled out a device.

"This is a portable holomap of our galaxy. *Nimbus* has programmed it to include all the mentalists at the time the messages were sent to the black hole and, immediately after, the proceeding ones that came out of the door," Father added. He waved his hand over the device and the Messier Galaxy was projected in the centre of their circle. "This is the galaxy as seen from outside." He rotated it in various spins so that everyone could get a good look. "Bennett? Would you do the honors of showing our friends where the mentalists are?"

"Yes, Father!" replied Bennett. He confidently spun the holomap, easily commanding it. The map continued to spin slowly, then glowed blue. All of these blue points were the mentalists in the galaxy active at the time of the message. "That's me," he said, pointing to the area of Alorion, which was lit up with a very large blue point. Now, watch the moment I began to act as a conduit."

The map lit up, doubling, then tripling the points of blue light, continuing to multiply until there was an intense glow swirling between the inhabitants of the galaxy, all linked.

"When the signal issued via me as the conduit, everyone received it and projected it back to me, effectively joining us all like a massive mental circuit!"

The group was spellbound by what they saw.

"Amazing!" said Anghelloise. "Can you focus the map into the area of the Convent?"

"Yes," said Bennett, waving his hand, drawing the map in to focus on the Convent. "I'm stopping above it to show you an interesting phenomenon. The map showed a blue cloud of energy coursing around nearby." The cloud swirled, picking up speed. "Now, watch this."

The blue dot that represented Bennett in the Convent glowed, then a dual dot beside him formed. "That dual dot is Tam and Brogan." He smiled. "Do you see how the three of us are connected? The galaxy to me, via Artagan and then me to them! They are conduits well above my capability! I'd hazard to say level twenty or more. When they transmit, watch what happens."

As the connection between the three of them grew, the map began to automatically zoom outward to show the strength of the blue cloud swirling around the Convent. As its brightness increased, a spiral of blue light streaked off planet and angled towards the centre of the galaxy. The map quickly zoomed outward, decreasing in size as the light reached its centre. Then the map spun to the opposite side, and the center of the neighboring galaxy lit up.

"That is the Andromeda Galaxy—about fifty million light years away!" exclaimed Father. "I have records of it in the Order's history banks!!"

"Is that where the contact came from, Tam and Brogan?" Farthing asked.

Tam and Brogan shook their heads.

"Just wait," said Bennett. Suddenly, a galaxy near Andromeda also lit up. "That is called the Milky Way, about another 2.4 million light years further away than Andromeda. The Order also has some records on it. That is where the returning signal came from."

"Then it stands to reason that there are humans in those two galaxies!" exclaimed Anghelloise. "If both lit up, they're both are aware of our existence!"

"The question remains which is the origin of the human species," said Father. "Did they start in Andromeda and spread here and to the Milky way? Was it from the Milky Way to Andromeda to Messier? We do not know."

"What about our galaxy?" asked Farthing. "Did humans start here and migrate there?"

"No," replied Father. "The Order's records indicate that humans colonized Messier last."

"We must come from the Milky Way," said Brogan. "The message stated it was on the far side of the galaxy in one of the inner arms."

"How can we verify that?" asked Anghelloise.

"I've got the Order working on it," answered Father. "The answer may lie in the message that came back: one burst, then two short bursts, then five more short bursts. When the signals merged, it became a pause, one signal, then another single signal, then two, then three, then five. It would seem the pause at the end of our signal is actually the start. We have been mistakenly placing the pause at the END of the signal. With the sequence in order, I get the sense that there is something familiar about that combination. I may know...but I am not certain. I'll need to speak to the Order via *Nimbus*. I guess that Tam and Brogan will have to try and contact the others again in order to find out more, if that's even possible."

"We would need Kruger and Artagan again, which doesn't make me too happy," said Farthing. "How can we expect the whole galaxy to do all of that again? Do we have the right?"

"Things feel different for both of us," announced Tam. "We feel that something has changed. We were very close to death and were brought back. We'd..."

"... like to try," finished Brogan. "Allow the men to transmit to Farthing via the artifact to Bennett and then to the two of us. Let's leave Artagan out of it for now."

Farthing put his hand up. "Are you sure that I am the one to do this?" He looked worried.

Brogan put his hand on Farthing's wrist.

"Yes. You are more than capable, you big beast! You're programmed for it!" Brogan said as he laughed. "We can sense it!"

"Well, that's it, then!" said Anghelloise. "We shall try again. Well, big boy! You get the chance that you've been wanting!"

Farthing grinned his wide grin and just shrugged his shoulders.

∞

"I've just heard from the Order!" Father exclaimed. "*Nimbus* reported contact only moments ago. We have a couple of pieces to the puzzle, it would seem." Father stood in front of the group, sitting in the gardens at the Convent before beginning their next attempt. He shaded his eyes, sitting down in a chair beside Tam and Brogan.

"Based on your excitement, Father, the news must be interesting!" said Anghelloise.

"Forgive my brashness," he said. "Good morning, Mother Siren." He stood and bowed.

"So, what's the news, then?" Brogan asked.

Father reached for a cup of tea, sat down, and took a sip. "The signals have some sort of significance. The one long burst, three short, and a pause is a message opener that is consistent in this galaxy. However, it is backward. It should read a pause, one long burst, then three short ones."

"We've used it as a signal code in the Lambda Infinity Omega League since the inception of our resistance," said Farthing. "It was the Sirens who suggested it."

"In our records, the signal goes back as far as Siren history does," said Anghelloise.

"It would seem that it is in existence in many places, including my arm of the galaxy." Father added. "It's a signal we use to begin coded messages. And to think that we all had it in the wrong sequence: one pause, one long signal, and three short ones!"

Tam sat there scratching his head.

Brogan turned to him. "Tell them, Tam!"

"I've been seeing examples of that signal since I started looking for Brogan. I was just sitting here thinking about when I was stowed away on the ship going to Corustloth. The light by my foot blinked in that order! I never gave it much thought until you mentioned it!"

"Bennett, my boy, when you came out of curved space the first time, the holomap flashed in the same sequence!"

"Do I provoke that signal each time I act as conduit?!"

"Yes," replied Father. "What the Order has found in their research is nothing short of amazing. Every mentalist in our Order carries this signal in his genes."

The group grew silent as that thought settled in.

"I've done some testing on the men who were imprisoned. They also contain the coding in their genes—as do Tam, Brogan, and Captain Farthing!" Father added with excitement. "That just leaves one more thing." He paused to look at Anghelloise. "Do the Sirens carry it, too?"

"The signal has a religious connotation to us. While we do subscribe to technology, we have not had any reason to check for such coding. How would we?"

"It is a very simple blood test," said Father. "I could test you right now and *Nimbus* would have a response in minutes! With your permission..." He pulled out a syringe compact.

"Of course! I think it would be worthwhile!" She stood, moved to the chair next to Father, and offered her arm to him. He prepped her arm, then gently inserted the needle into it. He pulled a small amount of blood, then applied pressure to the entry point in with a piece of gauze.

"Thank you, Father."

"OK, I'm off. I'll return soon with the news!" Father stood and bowed to the group. Bennett suddenly thought of something.

"What about the general population? Could non-mentalists carry the gene?" Bennett stood up and hurried after him to ask.

"Tam and Brogan, you look like you're both about to say something," Anghelloise said. "If it's another question, maybe we should all get up and head to *Nimbus*!"

"We're wondering why sodbent have this ability. Shouldn't we find an answer to that?"

Despite being the Siren Mother, she giggled. "Come on, boys, let's go get answers!"

∞

Nimbus had never had this many passengers. Her three couches had been modified to become seats for six.

"This is amazing!" shouted Father. "The Sirens hold the genes as well."

"We are mentalists after all! It doesn't surprise me!" exclaimed Anghelloise. "And the general population?"

Father shook his head. "They neither carry the gene nor show any mentalist abilities. The only exception seems to be certain untrained women. Some, it would seem, have never been called into service, which is a shame. There must be many female mentalists in our galaxy."

"Your map did light up when you showed us the model during contact. It would seem even untrained mentalists can be conduits of some sort," remarked Anghelloise.

"What about us?" asked Tam. "What makes us different from the other mentalists? Why are we able to sense so much more, and able to create a Life-Line when others cannot?"

Father laughed. "This is what's so amazing and humbling for me! Tam, you and Brogan carry a second set of signals incorporated into your genes! You carry the one three and one signal in your DNA, but also carry the signal from the Milky Way: one, two, five! As far as I can see, all modified sodbents such as yourselves carry it. When Bennett is connected to a Life-Line, you become something incredible: a conduit with the galaxy's mental ability, able to communicate outside of it."

"One, two, five! That's the message that came back from the other galaxy!" exclaimed Brogan. "That must be a clue!"

"I also took the liberty of testing our prisoners," added Father. "Kruger has neither, but Artagan has both sets of signals."

"I always sensed he was sodbent," remarked Tam. "It's too bad he always fought that, seeing us only as degenerates."

"Artagan had too much fear to be his true self. He would have made a good ally," replied Bennett.

Father added, "There's one more interesting piece to this puzzle. I ran the signals through the Order's database. When the signals merged, we realized the pause at the end of our signal was actually the beginning of a set of signals! When merged, they produced zero, one, one, two, three, five. Those are the first six numbers of the Fibonacci Sequence! There may be a connection there!"

Chapter 63
Through the Looking Glass

The courtyard of the Convent was filled almost to capacity. The sound of everyone talking was like music to Anghelloise's ears. There hadn't been so many happy and enthusiastic people there in such a long time.

"Alright, everyone!" she called, "Quiet down, please. "I'd like to thank you all for meeting here today. As you know, we've had an amazing experience recently with the linking of our galaxy to the neighboring two. It is a feat that no one has seen, perhaps, in many thousands of generations, since our settlement in this galaxy." She paused and looked across the now quiet crowd. "We are so blessed to have the former prisoners here to help us the way that they were destined! Not as slaves to the Magistrate, but free participants in what might be one of the most important events this galaxy will ever see. We are going to try to make contact with our brothers and sisters in the other two galaxies again. This is something the Sirens have long awaited, and it seems our brothers in the Order are in agreement. The galaxy is united in contacting the people, who may very well be our relatives from the distant past! I celebrate all of you!" Anghelloise smiled, extending her arms outward to the assembly.

There were cheers and smiling faces. It was clear the men rescued from the prison were grateful for their freedom and ready to serve in what could well be their destiny. To add to the situation, the other 104 life-Lines rescued earlier were now present.

Anghelloise continued: "Some of you are still missing your Life-Lines, but as you can probably already sense, they are on their way to join us."

There was another large round of cheering.

"Now, we would like to try to make contact using several sources. First, we'd like you to try to link with Farthing via the artifact, then Bennett, our friend from the Order, and determine whether we can create an environment in which he can perform as a level ten conduit. It's our hope that you special men—Farthing, Bennett, and the newly powerful Tam and Brogan, along with the Sirens—might suffice in making the connection without the entire galaxy being involved. If it works, it'll be our chance to communicate with the Origin. If it doesn't, we may have other options. I'd now like to turn your attention to the Father of the Order, who will instruct you. Father?"

Father stood up and addressed the group: "Thank you, Mother Siren. The Convent is blessed to have a wonderful replacement despite the sad loss of Mother, who I would like to take the time to remember and salute for meeting her destiny, to help us communicate with our ancestors. I know she'd be proud of what we're about to do. Everyone, please bow your heads and join in focusing your inner sight on the memory of the former Mother Siren. Let us begin."

The entire crowd went quiet as the low hum of the Sirens' song started to echo across the courtyard. The singing began to flow and vibrate, taking on near physical form, enveloping the assembly. Each and every one of them felt it in their bodies. They were all driven to tears as the music lifted their souls, giving them immense hope, which they hadn't felt in a long time.

The song escalated and vibrated even stronger. The signal started to emerge: one pause, one long burst, and three short ones. It repeated, again and again.

For a second time, the men focused their minds, this time directing it toward Farthing, who linked to the artifact, then onto Bennett, whose eyes were closed, tears flowing down his cheeks. The signal reached its crescendo. It broke upon him like a thunderstorm.

Bennett felt the familiar surge and directed his thoughts to Tam and Brogan, who he could see in his mind's eye. They appeared as two blue entities on the back of his eyelids, like they were burned there for him to see. He could see their forms receive the energy of the signal. Their image in his mind glowed brightly, then exploded to engulf the assembly.

Everyone—Father, Farthing, Anghelloise, the Sirens and the men—could see Tam and Brogan in their minds' eyes!

At that moment, Tam and Brogan began to lift off the grass, floating as they had before. Unlike the others, their eyes were open. They gazed down and smiled. They were amazed at the power of the minds of these people, finally all here to do what they were destined to do: send a message to the galaxies beyond their own.

Tam and Brogan received the mental go-ahead from Bennett, and they focused their minds on to the coordinates at zero, zero, zero. It was working!

As the spiral of mental energy arrived at the black hole, the door again opened. The opposite signal of one long burst, two short bursts, then five short emanated from the doorway. The Others had made contact. The signals merged and followed the pattern that was seen before: zero, one, one, two, three, five. It repeated several times—and then something amazing happened.

New numbers were added. The signal burst loudly onto the group: zero, one, one, two, three, five, and then new numbers: eight, thirteen, twenty-one. It was indeed the Fibonacci sequence!

At this point, Tam and Brogan began the process of communicating as the entire assembly continued to transmit. No one but them would know what was being communicated until it was finished. They were the conduit to the other galaxies.

Father stood there, humbled and touched to find his search coming to an end. He felt comfortable in the moment, knowing that though he was a passive mentalist, he had played a key role in this whole process. His mind passed to his newfound friends—Anghelloise, Farthing, Tam, and Brogan—and then, finally, Bennett. The young man had surpassed his expectations! His pride in his young trainee was immense. His tears flowed freely.

Anghelloise felt the vibrations of the Sirens at an entirely different level; a Life-Line like link to all her sisters. The feeling was what one might call *ecstasy*, were it something concrete. It was the feeling of doing what she was supposed to: take over for Mother Siren and carry on the legacy. She felt wise beyond her years. She knew Mother was still there, existing as a line of energy that supported her. She let go of any trepidation about filling the role left in her wake.

Still, she was always the incorrigible Anghelloise! She couldn't resist a little, *[Go get 'em, boys!]* to Tam and Brogan—knowing Father, Farthing, Bennett, and the others would also hear.

Farthing stood with his eyes closed, feeling, for the first time, how it felt to belong. His abilities were now honed. The artifact no longer made him sick, as it had in the beginning. He saw he was a mentalist, and that no amount of genetic manipulation could keep him from fulfilling what he was supposed to do. He looked with his newfound ability, gazing with his mind's eye and upon Anghelloise. His inner sight softened as he felt a special bond with the woman, so brazen and so human. He sensed her understanding this. She smiled, as did he. The big brute of a man broke down blubbering.

He looked at Bennett, seeing something he'd never seen before, feeling emotions he experienced strongly. Finally, he turned his mind to Tam and Brogan. Those dear men.

[You are so special to me! You are my charges; I had to help to unite you. My goal has been reached. I am blessed to have witnessed your flowering.]

Their faces turned and smiled, with much love, in his mind's eye.

Bennett felt the energy coursing through his body. He felt each person as they looked at him, sensing what they sensed. In his state of being a conduit, he was experiencing the closest he'd ever experienced to a Life-Line. He sensed everyone's thoughts and, for the first time in his life, he felt he belonged somewhere, and that he was valued.

He scanned their faces in his mind's eye, seeing their smiles. Although he could not sense what Tam and Brogan were seeing, he could tell they were communicating with someone on the other side of a galaxy, millions of lightyears away. It like they were peering into a cauldron, and he could just see over the lip. He felt the flow of mental energy flowing from him to Tam and Brogan, and continued in his role.

Tam and Brogan floated together, their hands linked physically, their souls intertwined in their Life-Line. As a single, unified force, they looked through the door and sensed the people on the other side. Though they could not physically see them, they sensed what the others were like: standing in a row of eight, veiled as though bearing scarves across their faces, flowing robes draping down their sides. Although Tam and Brogan could not see their features, they sensed they were, indeed, human.

They spoke as one: [We are the Guardians of Knowledge. We protect the eternal memories of those who came before. All that is known of our ancestors is contained in our vessels. Come to us. We await your arrival.]

Tam and Brogan sent a message back: [We are humans of the Messier Galaxy. Give us your coordinates and we will search for a way to travel to you. We await your response.]

[We are the Guardians of Knowledge. We protect the eternal memories of those who came before us. All that is known of our ancestors is contained in our vessels. Come to us. We await your arrival.]

With that, the door closed. Tam and Brogan stopped receiving, and began floating slowly back to the ground. The light faded around Bennett, and then the crowd of men. The Siren singing faded into an echo, then stopped.

Chapter 64
New Beginnings

The entire Convent was empty, with everyone situated in the courtyard. All the Sirens stood in three circles around Anghelloise and the body of the former Mother Siren. Then the five men: Tam, Brogan, Bennett, Father, and Farthing. The rest of the men stood in another two circles. The crew of the *Faramund* formed two lines outside them. Behind them, Kruger and Artagan, bound and drugged, were sitting in chairs. The funeral procession had begun.

"We are here today to honor Mother Siren as we lay her to rest, so that she may find peace," said Anghelloise. "Here we stand to honor Mother Siren. Her name was Deoiridh Valencia-Sheehan before she became the Siren Mother. We honor her name and her service to the Sirens, especially by saving Thamara-Afil Amergan-Faolin and Brogan-Afil Faolin-Amergan by restoring their Life-Line, and linking the entire galaxy. In saving their lives, she gave hers. We owe her much gratitude. We commit the body of Deoiridh Valencia-Sheehan to the soil of her home planet of Alorion. All bless the Mother Siren."

Everyone repeated the prayer. The assembly went silent for many minutes as the casket was lowered into the ground. One by one, the Sirens placed soil on it, until the hole was filled.

"Bless you all," said Anghelloise. She bowed to the assembly. "It is my wish to fulfill her final wishes and continue contact with the other galaxies. Thank you, everyone. You may go."

The assembly began to filter out of the Convent gardens back inside as Anghelloise approached the others standing off to the side.

"Thank you all for coming."

They all nodded.

"Shall we discuss our plans, then?" Father asked. "Has everyone prepared, as discussed?"

Everyone nodded.

"Let's do this in my chamber, then," said Anghelloise.

The group walked together through the gardens toward the Convent.

"It is such a wonderful day," noted Brogan. "I wish we could have more time to rest and recover." Tam took his hand as they walked.

"I know everyone's been wondering about the inert bombs still inside Brogan," added Tam. "Father has given us council. Brogan should be free of them in a few days—without surgery!"

Farthing and Anghelloise looked surprised. "How's that?" asked Farthing.

"The Order has maintained a high level of technical expertise over the many millennia since we arrived in our galaxy. We have surgical nanites we can inject into his blood system that will travel to the foreign objects and break them down into minuscule pieces. Brogan's cells will dispose of them as they do with biological waste."

"A nanite?" Farthing asked as they approached the door of the Convent.

"A microscopic android. The bombs will be dissolved in Brogan's system within days of the treatment. The nanites will then break down and exit on their own."

"We are so grateful," said Tam. "We've been worrying ever since we found out."

"Alright, boys, let's take this discussion into my chambers," said Anghelloise.

When they reached her room, they proceeded to the sitting area and settled in. Anghelloise looked around at their faces.

"We are so fortunate to be here and in good health. It seems a shame that we may have to part ways soon. Is it really necessary?"

"Now that the Order has finally solved the problem of coming and going through folded space, I need to get back to continue our expansion and begin regular flights to and from your sector. Now that the entire galaxy is aware of everyone else, the Order needs to be there to help set up communications, establish trade, and organize the union of the mentalists for what may lie ahead. Then there's the issue of transporting Kruger and Artagan to the Order world."

He stopped and turned to Bennett.

"Are you sure, my boy, that you wish to go ahead with this plan the four of you have concocted? I'd feel more comfortable with you being our level ten conduit, helping with Kruger and Artagan's rehabilitation."

"I am, Father. Tam, Brogan, Farthing, and I want to proceed," Bennett said. "We wish that Anghelloise could come, too, but we know that's impossible as the new Mother Siren."

"I always had a taste for exploring," she said. "But duty comes first. Speaking of which—"

The door opened and the Guardian Sirens stood aside as a table was wheeled into the chamber. "I wish to do the fun part," she giggled. She got up out of her chair, strode to the table, and reached underneath the blanket. "It just needs a little prompting... and there you have it!"

Beeps and whirring emitted from under the blanket as Anghelloise pulled it back. Out popped Nick, his eyes blinking and his smile on the edge of a grimace. "Hello, Mistress! I'm here to serve!"

"That's wonderful, Nick! I'm glad to see you working properly again. Brogan did quite a number on you when he was in that horrid state."

"Indeed, Mistress. I am working to the best of my ability." Nick floated up off the table and did a small circle around the group, checking them out. "I am here to help!"

His eyes blinked and the pupils moved around as he scanned everyone in the room.

"Brogan and I are very happy to see you again, Nick!" said Tam.

"We are. I'm sorry for disabling you," said Brogan, looking down for a moment. "I was under duress. I didn't mean to harm you. Are you OK, Nick?"

"Doing as I am programmed, and happy to be here!" stated Nick.

"Nick, you will be going with Tam and Brogan. You are to serve them, Bennett, and Farthing, as you have me. They are going on a trip, and you will be joining them."

"Where are we going?" asked Nick.

"To the Milky Way," said Tam. "We are going in *Nimbus* to meet with the humans there. We made contact with them while you weren't functioning."

"Nick, I will complete your programming before you leave, and update you on all happenings. You'll also have access to *Nimbus* and her records," added Anghelloise.

"We may as well wait until the supply ship arrives from the Order's planet," said Father. "Fresh supplies, updated equipment, and information are crucial to this trip. I want these men kept as safe as possible. We are all depending on you, Nick."

"Yes. I understand," said Nick, spinning around a couple of times and winking.

"When do you expect the supply ship to arrive, Father?" asked Farthing.

"Within days. *Nimbus* will be updated, supplies added, and you can be underway."

So, it was settled. A voyage was to take place to a galaxy millions of lightyears away.

∞

Several days before they were to leave, Tam and Brogan sat in the Convent garden and relaxed. Farthing had been busy with getting supplies, Anghelloise was tending to Siren business, and Bennett had been mysterious about a "matter he had to attend to." He disappeared for two days, then suddenly returned in *Nimbus* as they were readying to go inside for lunch.

The ship settled down in the courtyard, and Bennett stepped out. He waved at Tam and Brogan. *[I have a little surprise for you! I can't tell you how relieved I've been to have been able to block this from you!!]*

[It's not like we haven't tried!] projected Brogan. *[Tam, as usual, couldn't get past it!]*

[Neither could you, Brogan!] chided Tam. *[You've blocked us both from knowing.]*

The thought rotated in the ether between the three men, shuddered, then started to disappear.

"Hey, stink bug! You still need to take a bath!"

Tam turned in surprise as Cassie stepped out of *Nimbus* and ran toward him, a big smile on her face. Tam got up and ran toward her.

"Cassie! Not in a blue thundering moment did I know you were here!!" exclaimed Tam. "Bennett, you sly man! You had us totally fooled!"

Bennett grinned and continued toward the two of them as Cassie thundered up and jumped into Tam's arms.

"Tam, I've missed you so much! Bennett came in his spaceship and visited me at Professor Hartman's. He told us we could come and see you. He's in *Nimbus*, too, by the way, and will be out in a few minutes."

"Professor Hartman?!"

"Yes, Bennett here tooked Professor with us!" She stopped and grinned, knowing Tam was about to correct her. "I know, 'it's took, not tooked!'" She laughed. "I'm just joking! Professor Hartman has me going to school, and I love it. I'm learning so much!"

"I'm glad you are OK, sweet pea. I've been so worried about you." He looked over at Brogan, who was looking quizzically at him.

[You going to introduce me, stink bug?] he projected with a grin on his face.

Tam nodded and set Cassie down.

"Cassie, I'd like you to meet someone very special to me." Tam motioned to Brogan. She turned to him and immediately cracked a smile.

[He's a stink bug, too, isn't he?] she projected with a grin.

Tam and Brogan's eyes widened in shock as the mental message came through.

"It would seem that professor's been teaching you a more than just facts!" laughed Tam.

"Your sister is also a mentalist-in-training!" proclaimed Bennett.

"Tam, I am so glad to see you well!" Professor Hartman said, exiting the ship. "That was an incredible trip, Mr. Davis. I never imagined traveling through folded space! The trip took twenty minutes! Amazing!"

Cassie went over to Brogan and jumped up into his arms. "You have really blue eyes! Bennett told me all about you, Brogan. I'm old enough to know what a Life-Line is. There's nothing to worry about. You're not degens, like my father called you!" She smiled and shyly touched his blonde hair. "Your hair feels different than mine! It's so soft and straight!

"I'm sorry, but your parents refused to come. They haven't quite yet understood the change that's happening in the system," explained Professor Hartman to Tam. "I'm sure they'll come around once this business with the Senate settles down."

"It'll have to wait until we get back!" replied Tam.

Cassie turned her head and let go of Brogan's hair.

Tam prepared himself for the drama that was about to happen. But before he could speak, he saw Cassie grinning again.

[I know you're going away, stink bug! Bennett told me, and I'm good with that. I know you'll come back, Tam. Brogan will make sure of it!] She crossed her arms and nodded.

[My, you've grown up, haven't you, sweet pea?] replied Tam. "This is going to take a little getting used to!" he said to the group.

"Bennett and Professor Hartman said maybe I should go to school here," said Cassie. "Is that OK, Tam? They said a really special teacher named Anghelloise would want me to enroll in her school. I heard she's a great teacher!"

"That she is!" exclaimed Brogan. He looked at Tam as the idea of letting Cassie stay at the Convent rotated in their minds.

Tam grinned and nodded.

Cassie squealed with delight. "I'll be even more special when you get back, Tam and Brogan! I'll make you both proud! Professor Hartman will stay in Ali-Alorion to help out!"

The professor nodded. "There wasn't much keeping me on Zemitis other than Cassie, so it made sense to make the change now that I can move around a lot more freely. I've even set up appointments to return to the university on Kashtiloth and revive the studies there—and later, here on Alorion!"

Tam took one of Cassie's hands and Brogan took the other.

"Shall we all have some lunch and make all the arrangements?" asked Tam, smiling.

They headed into the Convent.

Tam leaned over to Bennett as they walked through the garden. "Thank you for this! I couldn't have asked for a better parting gift."

"A pleasure, my friend," he replied as he put his hand on Tam's shoulder.

"When are you getting a Life-Line, Bennett?" asked Cassie.

Bennett laughed. "You never know!"

"The Goddesses do!" she quipped.

Tam smiled to hear her say it. He could leave knowing his sister was on a path to healing—that life would be getting better for her—and maybe even for their parents, when they came around.

∞

Nimbus sat in the middle of the courtyard. She now contained the galaxy's most updated technology, information, and supplies for a journey into the unknown.

Anghelloise stood with her new student, Cassie, in tow. She smiled and watched Tam and Brogan interact, marveling at the gift that they had. *I truly hope they find how and why this genetic manipulation took place!* The purpose of the Sirens would be even clearer knowing why sodbents were targeted for gene manipulation at this level, allowing them to link together. Why not men and women together? Why not woman to woman? And why were Tam and Brogan stronger than the others? Were there others as strong as them? So many questions...

She looked at Bennett and saw his dedication to his newfound duty being ambassador for the Messier Galaxy. He had a gleam in his eye, and it seemed to her that it was for more than just the voyage. He interacted with the other men easily and comfortably. The change in him had been immense since they had first met. Father's accounts of him having been a shy and awkward apprentice seemed even more absurd. *I wonder if he's figured out that Farthing might be a match for him? Maybe my services in forging another Life-Line will be needed soon.*

Bennett entered the ship and, moments later, exited with Farthing, who had the same gleam in his eye.

Farthing placed a big hand on Bennett's shoulder. He turned and looked up into the big man's eyes. Anghelloise smiled knowingly.

[Farthing, you old dog, you! I knew that there would be someone for you in the end!]

Farthing turned to her and winked as they walked to the Convent.

∞

The procession over the next week was a grand one. Many ships arrived to send off *Nimbus* and her sister ship, *Zephyrus*. Word had spread around the entire system that Kashtiloth, Alorion, and Zemitis were soon to become members of the Galactic Messier Community. Their lives would be changing for the better, and prosperity was clearly on the horizon with the promise of trade between the worlds. The people were free of tyranny.

In the Convent gardens, Anghelloise stood facing the spectacle above her. She could not see the grand procession with her physical eye, but could with her mind's eye.

[Safe travels, Father! We wish you Goddesses' speed and safety in reaching home.]

His resemblance appeared in her mind, and he nodded and bowed.

[OK, boys! I'm counting on you to return as soon as possible with good news from the Milky Way! Tam, stand true! Brogan, be well. Bennett, my new friend and ally, be confident in your abilities. Farthing, my dear man, protect them—oh, and give Nick a pat and tell him I'm proud of him!]

The group of men bowed and smiled to her in her mind's eye, and Nick spun around with a big grin on his face.

A flash of light signaled departure of the *Zephyrus*, then another as *Nimbus* also left for the Milky Way. Anghelloise stood a while longer, staring up into the sky, smiling. The galaxy had just gotten a whole lot smaller!

∞

Aboard *Nimbus*, the group of men settled in for their flight through folded space. *Nimbus* had estimated the trip could take several Alorion weeks.

[Brogan, my love, we have time to relax and be together. We are going to enjoy this, aren't we?]

Brogan nodded, and they curled up on their couch.

Farthing gently brushed his big hand against Bennett's cheek.

"How I wish we had some privacy!" he whispered. "Maybe I should ask *Nimbus* of the possibilities!"

"It's OK, we already checked," whispered Brogan, hearing him. "We can be put into induced sleep! Will that be satisfactory?" He and Tam giggled.

Bennett blushed and Farthing howled. "That it will be, mates!" he said, kissing Bennett.

Epilogue

The row of eight had stood fast in their dark cathedral for millennia. They had repeated their words over and over, whether someone was listening or not. The signal had projected continuously for one blast, two short blasts, then five shorter ones. They had not moved from their spots for nearly a million years. They just stood and repeated.

When they had received the new signal, their job was done, and they were free to fade out of existence. Silence reigned for the first time in thousands of centuries of Earth time. The silence didn't go unnoticed. The watchers knew the others were coming.